NOVELS OF THE SENTINEL WARS

RUNNING
SCARED

THE SENTINEL WARS

SHANNON K. BUTCHER

AN ONYX BOOK

ONYX
Published by New American Library, a division of
Penguin Group (USA) Inc., 375 Hudson Street,
New York, New York 10014, USA
Penguin Group (Canada), 90 Eglinton Avenue East, Suite 700, Toronto,
Ontario M4P 2Y3, Canada (a division of Pearson Penguin Canada Inc.)
Penguin Books Ltd., 80 Strand, London WC2R 0RL, England
Penguin Ireland, 25 St. Stephen's Green, Dublin 2,
Ireland (a division of Penguin Books Ltd.)
Penguin Group (Australia), 250 Camberwell Road, Camberwell, Victoria 3124,
Australia (a division of Pearson Australia Group Pty. Ltd.)
Penguin Books India Pvt. Ltd., 11 Community Center, Panchsheel Park,
New Delhi - 110 017, India
Penguin Group (NZ), 67 Apollo Drive, Rosedale, North Shore 0632,
New Zealand (a division of Pearson New Zealand Ltd.)
Penguin Books (South Africa) (Pty.) Ltd., 24 Sturdee Avenue,
Rosebank, Johannesburg 2196, South Africa

Penguin Books Ltd., Registered Offices:
80 Strand, London WC2R 0RL, England

First published by Onyx, an imprint of New American Library,
a division of Penguin Group (USA) Inc.

First Printing, May 2010
10 9 8 7 6 5 4 3 2

Copyright © Shannon K. Butcher, 2010
All rights reserved

 REGISTERED TRADEMARK—MARCA REGISTRADA

Printed in the United States of America

For Sherry Foley. No matter how tough things may be in your life, you always find a way to make the lives of those around you a brighter, happier place. You are a blessing.

ACKNOWLEDGMENTS

I want to thank my readers. You amaze me with your praise and words of encouragement. Whether I meet you at a convention or book signing, or hear from you through e-mail or on Twitter, I am continually awed by your kindness. It's your enthusiasm that keeps me motivated, especially on the days when writing is more work than joy. Without you I would not be able to do the job I love, so I must give credit where credit is due. Thank you.

Chapter 1

After a lifetime of successfully evading the hunters, Lexi Johns was no longer prey. She was bait.

Zach was here. She could feel him nearby, drawing closer with every beat of her heart, as if somehow he'd become a part of her. She wasn't ready for him to show up yet. She needed more time to prepare herself for what she had to do and what it might cost her.

The fine hair along her limbs lifted, and she felt a tingling run over her skin. She'd felt it before, the night Zach had marked her skin, and she knew what it meant. Zach was closing in.

Lexi wasn't sure she could do this—lie in wait for him to come to her—but she had no choice. The fate of the entire human race depended on her ability to fool him into thinking she needed his help—that she believed the lie he told, that he was one of the good guys. She knew better. Her mother had made sure of that.

As far as she was concerned, most people weren't worth the trouble she was bringing down on herself, but Helen Day was. And the Sentinels had her. Zach was her only way inside the compound where Helen was being held prisoner, her only way to help Helen escape.

Lexi's hands shook as she wiped down the worn wooden tables. The bar where she worked had just closed and was nearly empty. There was one man in back, cleaning the small kitchen. She could hear him singing in Spanish as he worked. Gus, the bar's owner, was at the cash register, figuring up tonight's sales. From the grin on his weathered face and the way her feet and back ached, she was pretty sure he'd made a killing.

The lump in her apron pocket from her tips wasn't as big as she'd hoped it would be. Not as many people paid with cash as they used to, and Gus liked to hold on to her money as long as he could, so she wouldn't see those tips until her paycheck. Not that she was going to be here long enough to collect it. She was sure Zach would find her before then.

The idea made her skin heat and her mouth go dry; it made her shake with fear and something else— something hot and illusive she couldn't name.

Too bad. It was time to suck it up. Helen needed her. Lexi had to free her friend, and then find a way to undo whatever brainwashing Helen had suffered. Thank God she had the Defenders of Humanity on her side. Those big ol' redneck boys seemed to know what they were do- ing, even if they were a bit . . . intense about it. If anyone could deprogram Helen, it would be the Defenders.

Lexi upended the chairs onto the table so she could sweep and mop. She'd just picked up the last chair when the skin on the back of her neck tingled with awareness. She looked over her shoulder to see who was watching. Gus's head was bent over a calculator. The mirror be- hind him reflected the dim room. She caught a glimpse of pale green eyes in the mirror and froze in panic for a split second, her heart pounding as it primed her limbs to flee. Then she realized it wasn't Zach. It was just the eyes of the leopard tattoo on her shoulder staring back at her from beneath the edge of her tank top.

Zach wasn't here yet. She still had time to get a grip.

Relief made her sag against the table. She was going to have to find a way to control herself before he showed up for real. And based on the tingling of her skin where his mark glowed beneath the tattoo, that wasn't going to be long. This time when he showed up, she wouldn't run.

Lexi had spent most of her life running, and she was sick of it. She wanted a real home with a real bed, not the backseat of her car and a rest-stop bathroom, or maybe a cheap motel room if she was lucky. If she couldn't have a real home, then the least she could do was make the Sentinels suffer as much as she had. After what they'd done to her mother, Helen and countless others, they deserved whatever they got. And then some.

Lexi turned to get the mop from the kitchen and caught sight of those leopard green eyes again, only this time, they weren't staring at her from a tattoo.

Zach was here. Watching her.

Lexi froze, unable to move, or even breathe.

She wasn't ready. She wasn't strong enough to face him yet. The urge to flee rose up in her, and she fought against the desperate panic, gritting her teeth and clenching her fists.

Zach made no move to attack her. Instead, he lounged in the doorway, one broad shoulder propped casually against the frame. He watched her with the uncanny stillness of a predator. His brown skin blended into the shadows falling over the paneled walls, making his light eyes stand out even more.

Lexi's heart kicked hard, though she wasn't sure if it was because he'd surprised her or because that was just what he did to her. Even in her dreams he had the ability to make her sweat with his hot stare.

He was bigger than she'd remembered, or maybe that faulty memory was just her mind's way of helping her face him down by making him less threatening. His straight black hair was different from the way it had been the last time she'd seen him—tied back like he was ready to go into battle.

Maybe he was. Lexi had no idea what to expect now. For all she knew, he was here to kill her despite his pretty words, and all the planning she had done with the Defenders would be for nothing.

I need you, honey. He'd said that only days ago. Said it in a way that made her resolve melt.

She had to stay calm and act casual. Move slowly. He was like a wild, predatory animal, and she was afraid that if she moved too fast, he'd pounce.

Lexi gave him a level stare, letting him know she'd seen him. Pretending that she wasn't afraid.

Zach smiled, showing off his bright white teeth. It wasn't a smile of greeting. It was a smile of conquest. Victory.

Lexi swallowed hard, trying to work some moisture back into her mouth. "Gus, I'm taking off early," she told her boss, keeping her eyes locked on Zach, watching for sudden movements.

"Like hell you are. Not until the floors are mopped."

"Sorry. Gotta go," she said. "Family emergency."

"You don't have any family."

"She does now," said Zach. His rich baritone voice sank into her skin, making her shiver.

"Who the hell are you?" asked Gus. "And how did you get in here? The doors are locked."

Zach didn't answer. Instead, he pushed off the wall with a powerful bunching of muscles and stalked toward her. Lexi held her ground through sheer force of will. She would not run. Not this time.

"Relax," Zach told her. "You're safe now." His green eyes held her still, mesmerizing her like she was some kind of prey—a timid little bunny rabbit frozen with fear. The image pissed her off enough to drive away some of that fear.

He was closer now. Too close. Lexi's breathing sped until her head spun, and she was sure she'd make herself pass out.

"You need some help, Alex?" asked Gus.

"Alex?" asked Zach, lifting a black brow in question.

Lexi tried to give him an indifferent shrug, but her spine felt stiff and rusty. "New town, new name."

"New look, too," he said, his eyes roaming over her body like the territory belonged to him. "I like it."

She'd had blond spiky hair when he'd met her. Since then, she'd dyed her hair back to its normal color—a plain, average brown. It was longer, too, falling over her nape, baby fine and completely limp after her long shift.

"You look . . . softer." He said it like it was a good thing, and Lexi suddenly wished she hadn't gotten rid of her spikes. At least she could have used them to put out his eye if he got too close.

Which he was doing right now.

"Alex?" questioned Gus again, this time with more force. He had a gun back there behind the bar and wasn't afraid to use it. Typical Texan.

"I'm fine," she told Gus, lying through her teeth. "He's just an old friend."

Zach's smile widened. "I just came by to catch up on old times."

He reached for her, and Lexi knew she couldn't flinch away. Gus would know something was up, and although Gus wasn't exactly the nicest guy on the face of the planet, he had given her a job when no one else would. She couldn't repay him with trouble. And Zach was definitely that. More than six feet and two hundred pounds of walking, talking trouble.

His wide hand wrapped around her wrist, and he

pulled her toward him. Lexi went, ensuring Gus's gun was kept safely tucked away. She let Zach wrap his arms around her. She wasn't sure what he was going to do. Strangle her? Grab her and haul ass out the door? Heaven knew he was big enough to fling her over his shoulder and run out of here before anyone could stop him.

But he didn't do any of that. All he did was engulf her in a hug.

Lexi's mind sputtered, trying to make sense out of his action. Her arms were limp at her sides. She couldn't even find the presence of mind to push him away. She tried to convince herself that it was because she didn't want Gus to get hurt, but part of her knew better. As much as she feared what Zach would do to her, as much as she hated him and his kind for ruining her life and the lives of countless others, there was still something about him that called to her—something that quieted the rioting corners of her soul. Maybe it was just his handsome face or his mouthwatering body. Or maybe he was already brainwashing her and she just didn't know it. That was how brainwashing worked, right?

His hands roamed over her back and down her bare arms. His skin was warm against hers, rough with calluses and utterly manly. She was pressed hard against him, subjected to every devastatingly muscular inch of his chest, abs and thighs. Her hands itched to reach out and see if he felt as good under her fingers as he did against her body, but she held back.

He was her enemy. Lexi couldn't forget that. Problem was, it was easy to forget right now. She couldn't remember the last time she'd been hugged, but she was sure it had been nothing like this.

His scent enveloped her, sliding inside her with every breath she took. She felt her body relaxing and knew this had to be some kind of trick the Sentinels used to subdue their prey. A chemical weapon. One that was working like a charm.

Against her better judgment, her cheek settled on his chest and she could hear the strong, steady beat of his heart. The shimmering necklace he wore pulsed with color, swirling in an almost hypnotic display. His arms were thick, hard bands holding her in place, locking her against him, but he wasn't hurting her, as she'd feared. In fact it was just the opposite. She could feel a subtle vibration running through his limbs, like he was being careful not to crush her.

Lexi pulled back, hoping to end the hug, but Zach didn't let go. His grip was desperate. Unbreakable.

He buried his nose in her hair and pulled in a deep breath. "You're okay," he whispered as if he'd been worried about her. "I didn't get here too late."

Those were not the words of a murdering madman, but Lexi knew better than to be tricked.

"Is Helen okay, too?" she asked.

Zach pulled back then, just enough to look down at her. "She's fine. Happy. Just like you'll be once I get you home."

Dear God, he was practically admitting he was going to brainwash her. She couldn't let that happen. Helen needed her.

"Tell me what happened," said Zach. "When the phone cut off last week, I was sure you were dead—sure I'd be too late."

Lexi prayed he couldn't see the guilty flush she could feel spreading over her face. That phone call last week had been one hundred percent theater, designed by the Defenders to get Zach to come running. She'd pretended to be in trouble, calling him for help. Her frightened voice, the pounding on her motel room door, the way she disconnected the call. It had all been a carefully devised lie to trick Zach into coming for her.

And it had worked like a charm.

He ran his hands along her arms as if checking for injury, or maybe trying to convince himself she was fine.

She didn't know what to make of it, and it left her reeling in confusion.

"Were you attacked? Did you get hurt?" he asked.

Lexi knew he'd have questions, and she had practiced her lie over and over, but with his hands running over her, so warm and caring, she could hardly remember the line. "No. I was in a cheap motel room. It was just some drunk guy looking for his cheating girlfriend. I shouldn't have called and bothered you, but I was scared."

Zach's eyes closed in relief for a brief moment, and she saw his mouth move as if offering a silent prayer of thanks.

"Excuse me," said Gus. "I hate to interrupt your little reunion, but this floor isn't going to mop itself."

"Sorry, sir," said Zach. "But Lexi's—Alex's—days of mopping are over. She's coming home with me."

Gus's eyes narrowed in suspicion. "That true?" he asked her. "You leaving with this guy?"

Best to just get it over with and get out of here before anyone else could get hurt. The longer she put off the inevitable, the worse it would be. "Yeah, Gus. I'm going with him."

"You've been running from something," said Gus. "Is he it?"

"No," she lied. "I'll be fine."

Zach still hadn't let go of her. His hand was splayed across her lower back, holding her close to his warmth. He looked down at her, and his leopard green eyes practically glowed with anticipation. "Time to go, honey."

Honey. He always called her that, like he cared about

her. Like he wasn't planning on brainwashing her and killing her for her blood.

Then again, Lexi figured turnabout was fair play. Her trunk was packed with explosives, thanks to the Defenders' plan. Once Zach took her back to the compound where he lived, and she got Helen out, she was going to detonate all that C-4 and kill every one of the Sentinels she could. Including Zach.

Chapter 2

Lexi was safe. Zach could hardly believe it, even though she stood right there in front of him, so beautiful it made his eyes sting. He'd nearly collapsed with relief when he'd cleared the bar's entrance and seen her safe and sound. The doorframe kept him from falling, and he stayed there for a full minute, just watching her move, soaking in the sight of her whole and safe. Whatever trouble she was in, whatever he'd heard over the phone last week hadn't hurt her.

He'd found her in time.

It took Zach another minute to steady his breathing and get enough control over his emotions to even think about approaching her. He couldn't screw this up. He couldn't scare her away. Not again.

When he was sure he wouldn't hurt her with his desperation to get her in his arms, he finally allowed himself to go to her. And now here she was, pressed up against him, right where she belonged.

He stroked her arms, trying to rub away the chill that roughened her skin. He wasn't sure whether the goose bumps were from cold or fear, but either way, he was going to take care of it for her. Whatever she wanted, whatever she needed, anything in his power to give would be hers.

She felt good under his hands. Maybe too good. His fingers closed around her slim arms and he had to remind himself to be careful. Go slowly. Don't scare her away again.

Zach had planned for this moment for weeks—every day since he'd met her on June 27, a day he'd always celebrate as the beginning of his salvation. He'd gone over their reunion again and again—a million different permutations filling up his brain until it was clogged with possibilities. In every single one, she'd stayed by his side because that was what he wanted.

Based on the way she held herself stiff in his arms, apparently reality wasn't going to be quite so easy.

He'd lost her once. She'd run away. The bloodmarker he'd left on her hadn't worked right and he couldn't find her. Even though it was supposed to be impossible, she'd managed to find a way to hide from him. It could happen again if he wasn't careful.

Zach planned on being really careful.

"I brought you something," he told her. He dug in his back pocket and pulled out a small velvet pouch. It took some doing to open the thing one-handed, but he wasn't about to let go of her with his other hand. If he had his choice, he'd never stop touching her again.

He pulled the delicate gold chain from the bag and dangled it in front of her. The bar's neon signs glinted off the links, giving it a tacky sparkle.

"What is that?" she asked.

"A present. For you." One that would make sure he didn't lose her again.

"I can't accept it," said Lexi. Her dark eyes were locked onto the thing like it was a poisonous snake.

"Sure you can. I had it made just for you. You don't want to hurt my feelings, do you?"

She lifted her chin and looked up at him. Those bittersweet chocolate eyes were full of questions and more than a little apprehension, but Zach would take care of that soon enough. All he needed was some time alone with her to explain and everything would be fine.

It had to be. Zach was nearly out of time.

"Please, Lexi. Just let me put it on you. If you don't like it, I'll get you something else."

She looked at the bracelet again, licked her lips and pulled in a fortifying breath. Her chest vibrated with silent fear.

She was afraid.

Zach fought the urge to fold her in his arms again and hold her until she got used to him and knew he'd never hurt her. Unfortunately, that wasn't the way these things worked. She needed time. She needed him to prove to her that not only would he not hurt her, but he'd kill anyone or anything that tried to.

If things worked out, he'd have a lifetime to show her what she meant to him. Several, actually.

Pain pounded at his body, and the need to stake his claim screamed at him to act, but he held on. He still had a few more days—long enough to do this right. He'd already lived with the pain for decades; he could live with it for a few more days. Lexi was worth it.

Slowly, she held out her arm. Her fingers trembled, but Zach pretended not to notice. She was a little woman—only about five feet tall—but her independent streak was anything but little. Lexi was a fighter, and he still had the scar to prove it.

Every time he saw the small puncture wound on his arm, it made him grin. Once he'd calmed her and showed her how to use his power, she was going to be unstoppable. A fierce warrior maiden. Lexi the Avenger. The stuff of legends.

Zach fastened the bracelet around her wrist, loving the feel of her silky skin brushing against his fingertips.

She had dainty bones, though he'd never dare say that to her face for fear of more scars.

He'd made the jeweler resize it twice so it would fit just right. And it did. It was loose enough to be comfortable, but didn't dangle so much it would get in the way. More important, it wasn't loose enough for her to slip it off over her hand.

He pretended to adjust it, straightening out the links while he pulled in tiny specks of power from the air around them. It hurt like hell to absorb any more energy, but he had no choice. He needed it to activate the magic Gilda had embedded in the bracelet—the magic that would make it impossible for Lexi to escape him again.

With a subtle click, he felt the sleeping power inside the gold links come alive, sending sparks cascading up his arm and down his spine.

So did Lexi.

Her dark eyes widened and she struggled against him, trying to pull away. "What did you do to me?" she demanded.

The barkeep looked up from his tallying. His weathered face darkened, and his body shifted. He was reaching for a weapon behind the bar.

"Time to go, honey," said Zach. He took her by the wrist and tugged her along behind him toward the door.

"You hold on there," said the barkeep. "She's not going anywhere with you unless it's what she wants."

"Stay out of this, Gus," said Lexi. "You'll only get hurt."

"I'll show him hurt." The man cradled a shotgun in his hands, looking comfortable enough with the thing that he probably slept with it at night. Not good. Birdshot hurt like hell, and buckshot could blow his arm off or worse. Zach couldn't let himself become incapacitated now. Especially not when it meant that his blood would be spilled, the scent drawing every Synestryn demon from miles around, leaving Lexi unprotected.

Not going to happen.

He shoved Lexi behind him and held up his hands. "Easy, now," he said. "I'm not going to hurt her."

"Alex, come over here," Gus ordered.

"It's fine," said Lexi. "Really. I'll be fine."

"We'll just call the sheriff and let him sort all this out," said Gus. "Make sure your beau here doesn't have any unpleasant history."

Involving human police was only going to make things messier. And he certainly didn't have time to sit in jail while the last leaf on his lifemark withered and died.

"We're in a bit of a hurry," said Zach.

Gus reached for the phone, never once taking his eyes off Zach. "Sorry to hear that."

"Don't, Gus," said Lexi. "Just let it go."

"He's a big man, Alex. I don't much care for the idea of you being alone with him."

"I'm not going to hurt her," said Zach through his teeth. "I'd die before I'd let something happen to her."

"I *want* to be alone with him." Lexi's emphatic statement made Zach's heart sing. He wasn't sure if she meant it or if she was putting on a show for Gus, but either way, it worked for him.

"You sure?" asked Gus.

Lexi gave Zach a hard shove, pushing him aside so she could step out in front of him. Zach kept his hands to himself, barely. And then he saw the tattoo of a leopard on her shoulder and was shocked to stillness. Jungle vines and stylized leaves started at the point where he'd placed his bloodmarker on her right biceps and wound up her arm and over her shoulder. The leopard was peering out of that foliage, staring right at him from underneath the strap of her tank top.

Zach had seen his reflection in the mirror often enough that he recognized his own eyes when he saw them.

It was odd seeing them in the skull of an animal—like he was some bizarre kind of Slayer. What was even odder was the fact that Lexi would permanently mark herself with any image that reminded her of him. Last time he'd seen her, she'd tried to kill him. He liked to think that the few conversations they'd had on the phone since then had convinced her to let go of her violent urges, but he sure didn't think he'd sweet-talked her enough for something like this.

"I'm sure, Gus," said Lexi. "Just let us go in peace. We won't bother you again."

Now she was talking. He wanted to kiss her for defusing the situation before it could escalate and complicate things further.

Hell, he just wanted to kiss her, period.

Unfortunately, that would have to wait until he got her out of here. At least until he got her to his truck.

"You got my cell number?" Gus asked Lexi.

"Yes."

"Use it. Call if you need me. I'll keep it on all night."

"Thanks, Gus. Sorry about the floor. Keep whatever you owe me."

Gus's eyes narrowed and he scowled at Zach. "You make it sound like you're not coming back."

Lexi looked up at Zach and there was a deep sadness darkening her eyes. He wanted to wipe it away, destroy it so it could never come back to haunt her again. Problem was, he was convinced that most of that sadness was somehow his fault.

"I'm not. Good-bye," said Lexi, then led Zach through the door out into the night.

The night air was warm and thick, and filled Zach's lungs with the scent of earth and asphalt. A pair of aging lights high overhead drew a cloud of bugs, and lit the cracked parking lot just enough to destroy his night vision and create deep pockets of shadow around the few remaining cars.

Lexi headed for her beat-up Honda and Zach was hot on her heels. He hadn't quite forgotten just how pretty her ass was, or the way it made his mouth water with the need to feel his hands cupping her cheeks while he kissed her senseless. As much as he hated it, he ripped his eyes away from the lovely sight and scanned the surrounding area for Synestryn. He wasn't about to let one of those snarlies take them by surprise and ruin his chances of fulfilling every one of his fantasies with Lexi.

And after so many weeks, he had a lot of those. Now all he needed to do was get her to go along with his plans.

"I'm not riding with you," she announced on her way to her car.

She didn't know that the bracelet she now wore prevented her from getting more than a few yards from him, but he didn't think it was diplomatic to bring it up just yet. If she tried to run, then she'd know. And if she tried to run, she deserved finding out the hard way.

"Why not?" he asked.

"I don't trust you."

Her words hurt, but he ignored the pain. He was good at that. "Why not?"

"You know why."

Zach grabbed her arm and gently pulled her to a stop. "No. I don't."

She stared up at him for a long moment. Anger tightened her mouth, making him want to kiss it away.

She poked a finger into his chest. Hard. "You put your

mark on me and chased me all over the country, making it nearly impossible for me to stay in one place long enough to find work. Do you have any idea how much gas costs? I had to pawn nearly everything I own just to keep my car moving so you wouldn't catch up with me."

The thought of her suffering like that made him sick. That hadn't been his intention. She ran; he followed her. How could he not follow her when he needed her so much?

"Why did you run?" It was a question he'd been dying to ask. Why was she so afraid of him? He'd never hurt her.

"Why did I run? Are you serious?"

Zach nodded.

"You kidnapped Helen. And Miss Mabel. I didn't want to be next."

"Kidnapped?" Well, Zach figured it probably had looked like that now that he thought about it. "Drake needed Helen. And we couldn't leave Miss Mabel behind to fend for herself once the Synestryn showed up."

"They showed up because of you," she said, poking him again.

At this rate, he was going to be bruised. "Well, yeah, but it's not like we can help that."

She rolled her eyes and shoved her hand into her apron pocket to retrieve her keys. "Whatever. Just tell me where we're going, and I'll follow you."

"That's not going to work."

"I'm sick and tired of running, Zach. It's over. You've won. I give up."

He reached for her, wanting to smooth away the pain he saw lining her face. The weariness. In the dimness of the bar, he hadn't been able to see just how tired she looked, but now he did. She had dark circles beneath her eyes, and they were red, like she hadn't slept for days.

Zach knew how that felt. He couldn't even remember

the last time he'd slept. He'd been too busy searching for Lexi ever since that terrifying phone call.

Before he could touch her, she flinched away and took a big step back, bumping into her car.

"Get whatever you want to bring with you, and I'll put it in my truck," he told her.

"No. I'm driving."

Zach didn't want to fight with her. They were a team now—or at least they would be once he got Lexi alone and explained everything to her. Surely she wouldn't deny him. He needed her too much to even consider the possibility.

"Your car looks like it's going to fall apart."

She lowered her head and stared at the cracked asphalt. "It's my home," she whispered.

Zach looked into the back window and saw a pillow and blankets. Tucked in the back window was a ratty teddy bear with one missing eye. Taped to the back of the passenger's seat were half a dozen photos of a woman Zach guessed was her mother. Lexi was in some of them, young and smiling. Her mother hadn't been smiling in any of the photos.

She meant it literally. She lived in her car.

Zach's heart broke. How long had she been living like this? And how much of that was his fault for not finding her sooner?

There was no place for her to move away from him now with the car at her back. He could have hugged her and given her comfort, but he worried it would only bruise her pride. So, he pretended that he didn't feel sorry for her and said, "Fine. You drive. I'll ride with you."

Her head shot up and she gave him a skeptical frown. "You will?"

Zach shrugged. "Sure. I don't mind. It won't kill me to leave my truck here overnight."

Chapter 3

Lexi's car wouldn't start. She used every trick she knew, and none of them worked. Twelve years and nearly two hundred thousand miles and this was the first time her faithful Honda had ever failed her when she really needed it.

Maybe the thing knew she was planning on blowing it up.

Lexi pounded her palm against the wheel and let out a frustrated growl.

"It's okay, honey," said Zach, his deep voice steady and soothing. He reached over from the passenger's seat and cupped her shoulder, stroking warm, gentle circles over her bare skin. "I'll get someone to tow it back home. I have a friend who knows how to fix damn near anything. He'll have her up and running again in no time. You'll see."

He was trying to make her feel better. Why was he being so nice when he was planning to kill her eventually? It didn't make any sense, and made Lexi want to scream.

"I'm not leaving my car," she stated.

"It'll be fine. Don't worry."

Lexi had too much C-4 in the trunk not to worry. She

repeated, more emphatically this time, "I'm not leaving my car."

"Well, it's not moving and I'm not about to let you sleep in it. It's not safe."

She snapped her head around and glared at him, thankful for a reason to be angry—to vent some of her frustration and fear out on him. "You don't get to tell me what to do. I'll sleep in my car if I damn well please, and there's nothing you can do to stop me."

Zach blew out a resigned sigh and nodded once. "I can see you're not going to make this easy, are you?"

Lexi just glared at him.

"Okay, fine. Have it your way. I can't exactly say I'm surprised." He got out of the car and strode toward a shiny black truck parked about fifty feet away.

When he was ten feet away, Lexi started to fidget. She felt restless and twitchy. She wanted to get out and go after him, though she had no idea why. Maybe it was her sense of duty bugging her—if she didn't go with him, he couldn't lead her to the Sentinel compound. She would never find Helen to rescue her.

By the time he was twenty feet away, she felt like her insides were covered in mosquito bites, and it was getting harder to breathe. She itched all over, but couldn't figure out where to scratch to make it stop. Her eyes kept going back to Zach and his long, powerful strides.

She needed to follow him. Get closer.

At thirty feet, Lexi gave up caring about why she needed to go to him and just went. She jumped out of the car and grabbed her suitcase from the floor of the backseat. Every step she took toward him made some of the itchy restlessness inside her ease.

She looked at the gold bracelet dangling on her wrist and scowled. He'd done it again. He'd marked her, only this time, there was no way she could cover it with a tattoo to mask its power, the way her mother had taught her to do.

Lexi tried to unclasp the thing, but it wouldn't budge—like it was welded shut. She tugged at it, but all she managed to do was scrape some of her skin away. Damn it!

Zach waited by his truck, holding the passenger's door open for her. He had known this would happen. She could see satisfaction glowing in his eyes.

"You did this to me, didn't you?" she demanded.

"You gave me no choice."

"You could have stopped chasing me."

His strong fingers pried the suitcase from her hand, and he set it in the bed of the truck. When he leaned past her, she caught the scent of his skin, warm from the night air. He smelled spicy and completely delicious. Her head spun and she resisted the urge to grab his massive shoulders to steady herself.

"No. I couldn't have," he said.

"Liar," she shot back.

It was a big mistake.

Zach whirled around and grabbed her by the waist. He lifted her up onto the high bench seat and he didn't let go. He held on to her, his big hands nearly spanning her waist. His fingers curled into her flesh, and his green eyes glowed with anger and something else she couldn't name. Something dark and desperate.

"I need you, Lexi. And I don't mean that in the sense of I need you so I won't be lonely or some shit like that. I need you to live. I need you to help me keep the rest of my people alive. I'm running out of time fast, and you're the only one who can save me from becoming a monster. I'm not taking any chances that you'll get away again, even if it means chaining you to me."

Wow. Okay. She hadn't been ready for that kind of

confession. Nor was she ready for the way it made her feel . . . important. Necessary. She had no family and few friends, and she'd always been sure that if she disappeared no one would really notice. Maybe she'd been wrong.

Then again, maybe this was the way the Sentinels got to their victims, telling them what they wanted to hear.

Lexi straightened her spine and stiffened her resolve to stay immune to his charms. She lifted her wrist and the gold links glinted under the security light. "You already have chained me."

His mouth lifted in a slight grin full of naked desire. "Not nearly as tightly as I want to. I'm trying to give you time to get used to the idea, but let me be perfectly clear. I plan on making you mine. I plan on tying you to me as close as a woman can be. I'm not playing games, and I'm not taking no for an answer."

"Slavery. Mom was right about you. You enslave humans and bind them to do your will."

He gave an amused grunt. "Hardly. You've been listening to too many bedtime stories."

"I know what you are, Zach. You can't fool me."

He slid his hands up along her spine and leaned in closer. He surrounded her with his heat and his strength, and for the first time in a long time, she felt safe. And totally confused.

His mouth was level with hers and she couldn't help but notice how soft it looked. The crazy part of her that had already been brainwashed wanted to kiss him. The sane part of her was screaming at her to run away before it was too late.

"Just what do you think I am, honey?" he asked.

"A killer." Who made her feel safe, even though she knew it was only a trick.

"That much is true," he admitted. "But I try to be selective about the things I kill."

"Are you saying you only kill the bad humans?"

"Never. I would never purposefully hurt a human, Lexi. At least not so long as I remain myself."

She wasn't sure what he meant by that, and she was too distracted by the feel of his warm fingers stroking her nape to figure it out. Every time he touched her, it felt better. If she wasn't careful, she'd lose herself. Forget her mission.

She had to get her car to the compound where he lived. She didn't dare risk taking the explosives out of her trunk for fear he'd figure out what they were and ruin their plans.

"Remain yourself? What, are you like Jekyll and Hyde or something?"

He stared at her mouth and licked his lips. She was sure he was thinking about kissing her. And God help her, now she was thinking about it, too.

"Something like that," he said. "It's time to go. It's not safe out here in the open. I feel like we're being watched."

The Defenders. She'd nearly forgotten about them. They were probably watching right now, making sure she did what she'd said she would. Making sure they didn't have to kill her, too. They'd warned her about what would happen if she turned on them—if she let the Sentinels brainwash her, too.

"Where are we going?" she asked.

"Somewhere safe. Where we can be alone."

Alone with Zach. Alone with his kissable mouth and sexy body. Alone with his casual strength and tempting lies.

Lexi was so screwed.

Jake Morrow watched Lexi ride away with the Sentinel, leaving her car and all the carefully prepared explosives behind. Dad was not going to be happy.

Jake tensed as he waited for his father's explosion of temper. After almost thirty years of watching, learning when to duck the blows, Jake knew it wouldn't be long in coming.

Hector Morrow surveyed the men gathered in the small house across the street from the bar where Lexi was working. His gray brows drew together, and Jake caught himself before he took an involuntary step back. Ever since his sister, Mindy, had been killed by the Sentinels, Dad had been a mean sonofabitch, but Jake was no longer a kid to be knocked around at his father's whim. He was a grown man and knew how to hit back. Harder.

The men shifted uncomfortably under Hector's hard scowl. Most of them were young and ambitious, the sons of men who had been members of the Defenders of Humanity for years.

"Which one of you was responsible for keeping her car running?" asked Hector in a drill sergeant's boom.

The men looked at one another, at a loss for what to say.

Jake stepped forward. "I changed her oil two days ago. If anything went wrong, it was my fault for not catching it."

Hector's skin darkened with his fury, and Jake straightened his body to its full height—two inches taller than the man who'd sired him. Two inches taller and a good fifty pounds of muscles heavier. Jake was pretty sure his father hadn't failed to notice.

"Our entire plan has gone to hell because you couldn't keep one lousy car running?"

Jake crossed his arms over his thick chest. "Lexi is smart. She'll find a way to contact us. We'll fix this."

"You really believe she's smart? Are you that much of a fool, son?"

"Apparently so. I guess we'll just have to give it some time and see who the fool is, won't we?"

Hector rubbed a hand over his crew cut. The iron gray hair was cut with such precision he could have calibrated a laser level off of it. "This was our one shot at locating the Sentinel's compound. If you've messed it up, there's going to be hell to pay."

Story of Jake's life. He was used to dealing with the consequences of his actions by now. "Lexi will find a way to contact us and let us know where they're taking her."

"You'd better pray to God that's true, son. Otherwise, I'm going to have to find another second-in-command. We've never been this close to getting payback for what those bastards did to your sister. I will not tolerate failure."

"I want revenge as much as you do. We're not going to fail." Jake was sure Lexi was going to pull this off. She hated the Sentinels as much as they did, though for different reasons than the ruined crops and poisoned land they left in their wake. The Sentinels had killed her mother just like they'd killed Mindy—sending their pets in to tear her to pieces.

The thought of his older sister's death still had the power to keep him up at night. He'd been only five, but he still remembered peeking through the slats in the bedroom closet door where she'd hidden him to keep him safe. She held the rifle she'd gotten for Christmas in her hands, keeping her aim steady. She'd waited to fire until the last second, knowing that the point-blank shot had the best chances of taking down the huge monster. But that .22 round had been no match against the giant, clawed beast that ripped her apart. If Hector hadn't come in with more firepower, Jake would have been next.

Jake knew his dad blamed him for his sister's death as much as he blamed the Sentinels for sending the creature that killed her. And he was right to do so. Jake was the one who'd stayed out in the yard playing after dark when he knew better. He was the reason that monster had found them.

"No, we're not going to fail," said Hector, "but you might. Don't think that I'll give you any slack just because you're my son."

A sharp band of grief tightened around Jake's heart, despite the fact that he knew it would do no good. "No, Dad. That thought never even crossed my mind."

Chapter 4

Joseph Rayd looked around his office at the men he trusted most. They weren't going to like what he had to tell them. Then again, that was pretty much the story of their lives these days.

As the only bonded Theronai around, Angus, Drake and Paul were the most steady men in the group. Their pain was gone, and he trusted them to think straight and to make sure he didn't take any unnecessary risks. All three of them had too much to lose to allow Joseph to do something stupid.

The others weren't so lucky. Nicholas Brand was holding up pretty well. He'd been through some nasty fights, to which the multiple thin scars crossing his face could attest. But even so, he seemed to be keeping himself together. Maybe it was the puzzle of all those techno gadgets he loved that helped him block out the pain.

Iain Terra was another story entirely. Joseph had no clue what went on behind those dark eyes, but he knew that every time Joseph had needed him, Iain was there, sword in hand. The man was more than lethal. He made killing look beautiful—like some kind of exotic art. Once his lifemark was barren, they were all in trouble. They needed him too much to lose him.

And then there was Tynan—a Sanguinar. Like all the

members of his race, he was beautifully made. Tall and lean, with icy eyes that Joseph was careful not to look into for too long. Just in case. Joseph didn't trust Tynan like he did the others in the room, but he trusted him to stay true to form. Tynan looked out for his own, and because of that—because they were all in danger—Joseph needed him on board.

"Is this going to take long?" asked Drake. "I need to get back to Helen."

"How is she?" asked Joseph.

"Exhausted. She and Gilda have been working at repairing the wall for almost a week now, and they're running out of steam."

"It's true," said Angus, Gilda's husband. "We're only halfway through the broken section and the progress gets slower every day. The women aren't regaining their strength fast enough to keep going like this."

"What about Andra?" asked Joseph, looking at Paul.

Paul shook his head. His hair looked like he'd been running his hands through it, making it a mess. "Andra's great if you want to blow shit up, but she's not so good at putting it back together. She's still so new to her power, and although she's been trying, all this repair job does is frustrate and exhaust her."

"Okay," said Joseph. "Take her off the wall. Put her on perimeter guard with the men. If something comes at us before the wall is back up, she can blow it up all she likes."

"Thanks. That'll help. Maybe she'll be able to spend more time with Nika that way."

Nika. Andra's younger sister. During an attack when she was a child, Nika's consciousness had been splintered and cast into the minds of dozens of sgath—creatures the Synestryn used to hunt their prey. None of the Sanguinar had ever seen anything like it before and didn't know how to heal her.

What they did know was that she was capable of saving the life of one of his men. They just hadn't figured out which one. Every free man here had gone to her bedside and looked for a sign she might be compatible with them. No one saw or felt a thing.

Joseph looked to Tynan, who was one of the most gifted healers they had. "How is Nika?"

"She still hasn't regained consciousness," said Tynan. "But she doesn't seem to be growing any weaker. If we find her Theronai, it's possible he would help her mind heal enough that she can wake."

If they found him. So far, they hadn't had any luck. He prayed one of the Theronai from outside these walls could save her. They needed her too much to let her slip away.

"We're looking," said Joseph. "I've sent out word that she's here to all the other men. It's only a matter of time before Theronai start showing up in droves."

"Tell them to hurry," said Tynan. "I don't know how much longer we can keep her body alive with her mind in its current state."

Joseph didn't like the idea of a bunch of strange men tromping through Nika's bedroom, but if that was what they had to do to save her, then they would. He still had men in the field who had not yet been able to return and see if Nika could save them. He wanted them to have first chance before he started bringing in Theronai from other countries. If none of them was compatible, then he'd send word overseas to the strongholds there.

"Grace has been helping us keep an eye on her, and she's doing a great job," said Paul.

"In the meantime," said Joseph, "on Tynan's advice, I'll give orders for all the Theronai to track down sgath and kill them. If parts of her mind are in the sgath, killing them may help free her."

"Madoc has been doing that for days now and it appears to be helping," said Tynan. "Time will tell."

Joseph wanted to ask more questions. He wanted to go to Nika to see if she could save him, but he didn't dare. He was the leader of the Theronai. His needs had to come last, after those of all his men. He promised himself that before he called the leaders overseas, he'd go to her.

"What about those wounded in the attack?" asked Joseph, hoping to distract himself with duty.

Tynan's eyes lit with an icy glow for a split second—so brief that Joseph wasn't even sure he'd seen it. "Cain is still unconscious. Logan, Alexander and I are doing all we can, but it's not looking hopeful. There are a few wounded humans, all of whom will recover."

But they'd lost two. Rosemary and Dylan had died protecting their son.

The weight of that loss hung heavy around Joseph's heart. Dabyr was supposed to be a place of safety and refuge. He'd promised all the humans they'd be safe here.

He'd been wrong, which made him wonder what else he'd been wrong about. How many other mistakes had he made? And how many of these mistakes were going to mean the suffering and death of those he was sworn to protect?

"If you need anything, let me know," said Joseph.

Tynan gave him a formal bow of his head. "Of course."

"Now, on to why I've brought you all here. It's not good news."

Drake rolled his eyes and scoffed, "When is it?"

Joseph hated speaking the words, but he had no choice. "We all believed that our walls were safe, that the Synestryn couldn't get in unless they came through the front gate. Obviously, we were wrong."

The men shifted uncomfortably. Except for Iain, who sat utterly still, his face expressionless.

Joseph knew they were all thinking the same thing. There was no way to keep the humans here safe if those walls didn't hold. There weren't enough of them left to stand guard and still fight the war. If the walls fell, they'd have to choose which vow to uphold—protect the humans, or kill the Synestryn and protect the gate.

"The good news is that the wall didn't fall because it was weak, or because the magic embedded in it had failed."

"Then why?" asked Drake.

A bitter taste flooded Joseph's mouth. "Someone inside Dabyr let them in. They sabotaged the protective stones and created an opening."

Thick, stifling silence filled the room. It had taken Joseph hours to digest the news Nicholas had given him. He figured he owed his men at least a few seconds.

"Who?" asked Iain, punctuating the question with the hissing ring of steel on steel as he drew his sword.

Joseph held up a staying hand. "Stand down, Iain. We don't know. Yet."

"How did you learn this?" asked Angus. The lines on his face deepened with fear. He had more to lose here than anyone—both a wife and a child. The only Theronai child left to them.

Joseph looked at Nicholas and gave him a slight nod.

Nicholas rose gracefully to his feet. "I went over the video surveillance of the attack. The breach happened at a point covered by two cameras. Both of them had been disabled."

"Are you sure it wasn't some sort of glitch?" asked Paul.

"Yes. I went back through the video to the point where the cameras stopped working. They were disabled one at a time. Whoever did it was visible on some of the hidden cameras, but they knew enough about our security to keep their face averted."

"Who is it?" asked Iain in a quiet voice.

"I can't tell. It's a man wearing a hooded sweatshirt. I got some footage of the back of his head."

"Show me," said Iain.

Nicholas flicked a nervous glance at Joseph. Iain's sword was still out, gleaming with lethal intent.

"Put the blade away, Iain," ordered Joseph.

"I'm going to kill him," said Iain. His voice was cold and steady, just like his dark gaze.

"No one is going to kill anyone until we are sure who this is and question them. Now put the sword away."

Iain sheathed his sword.

Nicholas opened his laptop computer and typed in a few keystrokes. He spun the thing around so the rest of the room could see the video footage. The image was clear, but there wasn't much to go on—just a few flashes of the back of a man's covered head. One shot of a gloved hand.

"Anyone recognize him?" asked Nicholas.

No one spoke.

"Are you sure it's someone who lives here?" asked Paul. "Could it have been an intruder?"

Nicholas shook his head. "It's possible, but I checked all the entries through the front gate for the ten days leading up to the attack and he doesn't fit any of the people who came in."

"He could be a human," said Iain.

"Maybe. It's hard to tell just what his build was like under the baggy sweatshirt, but he could have disguised himself—made himself look bigger so we'd think it was one of our own."

Tynan had been quiet through all of this, but Joseph saw the slight frown marring his brow.

"What do you think, Tynan?" asked Joseph.

"I can find out if any of the humans know about this. All I have to do is feed from them and search their memories."

"That might look suspicious," said Nicholas.

"Not now. Not when there are so many still wounded and in need of aid. Put out the call for blood, and that will help mask our true task."

"I don't want anyone else helping you with this. I don't want anyone outside of this room to know what's going on."

Tynan's mouth tightened. "Then I suggest you don't let any of the other Sanguinar heal you. If you're in need, you must call me, or the others will learn what you're trying to hide."

Joseph didn't like that one bit. Neither did any of his men, judging by their looks of disgust.

"We have no privacy with you leeches around," said Iain.

"But the dozens of cameras and electronic locks that track your comings and goings are agreeable?" asked Tynan.

"They don't screw with our heads," said Nicholas.

Tynan held up his hands. His fingers were long and elegant, like he was born to be an artist or surgeon. "All I mean is that a secret like this doesn't stay secret for long. Not in a place like this. We need to find out who this man is fast or he'll be gone before we can. Assuming he isn't already."

"Agreed," said Joseph. "Nicholas, I want you to compile everything you can on this guy."

"I'm already on it. I'm also working on a program that will try to identify him based on his appearance by comparing his movements on this video with current images the cameras pick up."

"You can do that?" asked Angus.

"Sure. It's not a hundred percent, but it will help weed

out people who couldn't possibly be our guy. I figure if we can get our list down to a couple dozen possibilities, it will make things a lot easier."

"Good," said Joseph. "In the meantime, I want you all to keep your eyes and ears open and your mouths shut. Angus, Paul and Drake, try to keep this from the women if you can. They have enough on their plates right now without having to worry about this, too."

The three bonded Theronai nodded their agreement.

"And when we do find him," said Iain in a cold, emotionless tone, "you all can have your fun with him and question him all you like, but when you're done with him, he's mine to kill."

Zach didn't take Lexi to the compound as she had hoped. Instead, he pulled up into the driveway of a modest farmhouse just north of the Texas-Oklahoma border, well off the beaten path.

"What are we doing here?" she asked, eyeing the house. It was dark inside, but the light on the front porch was burning bright in welcome. No way was it big enough to be the compound she and the Defenders were after. There were supposed to be dozens of these guys running around.

"This is one of our Gerai houses. We'll be safe here so we can get some rest," said Zach. "I don't know about you, but I'm beat."

She was tired, but only because she'd been working every shift available for the past week. She knew after her phone call to Zach, she wouldn't have much time, and she needed enough money to keep her and Helen safe once they were free. "I can take a turn driving. Just tell me where we're going."

Zach slanted her a suspicious look. "You just want my keys so you can run away again."

She held up her bracelet and waved it at him. "How can I run when I'm wearing this thing?"

"I don't know, but if anyone could find a way, it would be you. I wouldn't put it past you to gnaw your own hand off if that's what it took."

"You don't trust me, do you?"

"Hell, no. I've spent way too many weeks hunting you to make the same mistake twice. But on the off chance that you find a way, I want you to have this." He pulled his wallet out of his back pocket and handed her a thick stack of bills. Hundred-dollar bills.

Lexi looked at the money, staring at it. There had to be nearly two thousand dollars here. What the hell?

"If you are on your own again—if anything happens to me—I don't want you to have to take a job at a seedy place like that one. I bet the men there like to paw at your ass, and I just can't have that."

She didn't know what to say. She'd never had this much money at one time in her life.

"I can't take it," she finally managed to squeak out. She held the money out to him.

Zach took it, folded it in half and shoved it into the front pocket of her apron. "You might need it. I don't. Just consider it payment for all that gas I made you burn running away from me."

Before she could find an answer to that, he got out of the truck and grabbed her suitcase from the back. Lexi watched him shove the keys deep in his front pocket. She wanted to know where they were in case she did make it out of this mess. Not that it was likely. Unless there were some bolt cutters or maybe even wire snips in that house. Gold was soft enough that even a sturdy pair of scissors might get her somewhere.

And even if she did get free, what then? This was her opportunity to save Helen—to take out a bunch of dangerous maniacs before they could kidnap anyone else. She couldn't run away from that. She couldn't leave Helen to fend for herself.

Zach opened her door and offered her a hand down. He had nice hands. Strong, wide hands with just enough roughness to make her more sensitive skin tingle when he touched her.

When. Not if. She'd been with him all of three hours and she'd already lost it. At this rate, she'd be kissing his ass by dawn.

Which didn't sound like an entirely bad thing. If his ass was as nice under his jeans as it looked, she could really enjoy herself.

Lexi pulled in a deep breath, reaching for her resolve—her freaking sanity. She couldn't let him get to her, no matter how appealing the package. She couldn't let him hug her anymore. She couldn't let him touch her. She couldn't let him make her want things she knew weren't real.

Helen was real. The danger was real. The rest of it— the tingly sensations she got when he touched her—was just pretend. A trick of the mind.

She ignored his offered hand and jumped out of the truck, landing on his booted toe.

He didn't even flinch. Instead, he gave her a knowing smile. "Am I getting to you, honey? Maybe grating up against that independent streak of yours?"

"You don't know a thing about me. Don't pretend like you do."

He followed her to the door, felt behind the porch light and pulled out a small magnetic box holding a key. "I know plenty. Helen has told me all about you."

"Helen doesn't know me that well, either. I've only known her for a few months."

"You can't tell that by the way she talks. I swear she

acts like you grew up together." Zach opened the door and peered inside before letting Lexi enter. "She worries about you a lot, you know."

Lexi refused to let him see how much that bothered her. Helen was the one in trouble, and yet she worried about Lexi? There wasn't a more caring person on the face of this planet, and Lexi felt honored to have known Helen, even for as short a time as she had. With any luck at all, they'd have plenty of time to really get to know each other. "You should call her and tell her I'm coming. Better yet, let me use your phone and I'll tell her myself."

Zach stared at her for a long moment, making her want to squirm under his pale gaze. Finally, he unclipped his phone from his belt and handed it to her. "No funny stuff," he warned.

"Like what?"

"Like calling the police. I don't have time to deal with them, and I swear that if you make me, I'm going to turn you over my knee and spank you."

Lexi laughed. She couldn't help it. He was insane if he thought she'd let that happen. She'd kill him first. "You could try. But I promise you wouldn't try twice."

"A little thing like you hurt me? I don't think so."

"Shall we test that theory?" she challenged.

He grinned and winked. "Maybe later. After I've eaten. I have a feeling I'm going to need to keep my strength up with you, aren't I?"

"Definitely."

Zach left the room, flipping on lights as he made his way to the kitchen. Lexi waited until his head was in the fridge before she dialed Helen's number.

"Did you find her, Zach?" answered Helen. Her voice wavered with fatigue, making Lexi wonder just how much she'd been through. "Is she safe?"

"Hey ya, Helen. It's Lexi."

Helen's relieved exhale filled the line. "Thank God, you're okay. What happened?"

Zach wasn't paying any attention to her, but she guessed he was still listening to every word she said. She couldn't very well tell Helen that the terrified phone call she'd made last week was a trick—a way to get Zach to come for her.

And it had worked. Better than she'd hoped.

"I'll tell you later," said Lexi. "All you need to know now is that I'm coming to you."

"That's great! I've really missed you. So has Miss Mabel."

"She's there, too?"

"Yeah. The Sentinels couldn't clean away her memories enough to make it safe for her to live in her home, so they brought her here. They even managed to heal some of her arthritis so she doesn't even need a walker anymore. Pretty cool, huh?"

Lexi was speechless. They'd healed Miss Mabel? Why would they do that? She was too old to fight anything they wanted to do to her. They could have fed from her, taken all her blood and left her for dead in her home. No one would have ever known who had murdered her.

"Lexi? Are you still there?"

Lexi cleared her throat. "Yeah, I'm here."

"Are you okay?"

"Fine. Just . . . figuring some things out."

Helen lowered her voice. "Is Zach okay? He wasn't doing so well last time we talked to him."

Lexi glanced into the kitchen. He was slicing an apple. Watching her.

She turned around and moved away from the doorway, down the narrow hall. "He's fine."

"He must be right, then."

"About what?"

"He's your Drake."

"What?"

"It's a really long story, but I swear it has a great ending. Just listen to your instincts and you'll be fine. You both will."

"You're not making any sense, Helen." Then again, why would she? She'd been mind-fucked.

"Maybe not now, but give it some time. He's a good man. He deserves to be happy. They all do."

Happy? Clearly, the Helen Lexi had known was gone. She'd been completely turned around, brainwashed into believing whatever they told her. It took every bit of strength Lexi had not to let the tears stinging her eyes fall. She was too late. Even if she got Helen out of there, she wasn't sure she could save her.

The Defenders had warned her this might happen, but until now, Lexi hadn't wanted to believe it.

"If you have anything there you can't part with, pack it and be ready to go," said Lexi. Her voice broke, but she held the tears back. "Have Miss Mabel do the same." She had no idea how she'd get both of them free, but she had to try. She couldn't leave Miss Mabel behind.

"What? Why?" asked Helen.

"I can't talk now. I'll tell you everything when I get there." Assuming she managed to get Helen away from her captor long enough to talk privately.

"I don't know what you're thinking, but I'm not leaving Drake. I love him."

Lexi was ready for her resistance. She knew it wouldn't be easy to extract Helen from their clutches. "I won't make you," lied Lexi. "Don't worry."

"What are you up to?" asked Helen. "I know you're planning something. I can hear the gears in your head turning from here."

"I'm not planning anything." Another lie, but a necessary one. "Just forget I said anything."

"I know you don't trust these guys, but you'll see when you get here how wrong you were. They're not the monsters you think. I swear. I was wrong about my vision. About Drake. He'd never stand by and watch me die."

Of course that was what she'd say. They'd probably tricked Helen into believing her vision of her own death wasn't real. They'd made her believe it, just like they made her believe that Miss Mabel was alive and well when she was probably lying dead on the floor of her house in Kansas.

"I'm sure you're right," said Lexi, just to appease Helen. "I've got a lot to learn."

"Don't worry. Drake's a great teacher. I'm sure Zach will be, too."

Over Lexi's dead body.

She felt Zach's eyes sweep over her a moment before the heat of his body soaked into her skin. She hadn't heard him approach, but he was standing right behind her, almost touching her.

For how long? What had he heard?

"I gotta go, Helen. See you soon." Lexi hung up the phone and handed it back to him.

He was close. Too close. And he looked angry.

"Are you going to see her, Lexi?" he asked. "Or are you planning something else?"

"I suppose that's up to you."

"What's that supposed to mean?"

"It means that if you let me live long enough, then yes, I'm going to see Helen."

"*If* I let you live long enough?" Zach scrubbed a hand over his face in frustration. "How many times do I have to tell you that I'm not going to hurt you?"

He could say it until the sun winked out and she still wouldn't believe him. "What's left of my mother is buried in San Antonio. She's the only family I had. I'd like to be buried beside her if it's not too much trouble."

His face darkened, and she heard his back teeth grind together. "No one is going to be burying you anywhere. Not while I still draw breath."

"Yeah. That's what the Sentinels told my mother, too."

"Shit," whispered Zach. "You've really been through hell, haven't you?"

Lexi couldn't even bring herself to nod. He knew the truth. He'd probably been part of the torment her mother had been through—part of the reason Lexi had been dragged from one place to another for as long as she could remember.

The anger melted from his features and he cupped the side of her face in his hand. Concern wrinkled his dark forehead and shone bright in his pale eyes, making them glow. His thumb feathered lightly over her cheekbone, stroking her skin until it tingled.

This felt too good to be real. She tried to remember that, but still, it took every ounce of willpower she had not to lean into his touch. Not to lose herself in the comforting warmth of his caress.

He whispered, "I'm so sorry, honey. I know you've been through a lot. All I can say is that part of your life is over now. I'm not going to let anything hurt you ever again."

Lexi felt the strength of his resolve wash over her. His words were a promise given by a man with unnatural power. Her mother's journal said that meant he had to keep that promise.

Then again, maybe that was just one more lie they'd designed to make humans complacent and manageable.

"You don't know that," she told him. She'd meant to

put more heat into her words, but they'd come out as a breathless whisper.

He shifted his stance, closing the distance between them. The intoxicating heat of his body soaked through her clothes and into her skin. His spicy scent wrapped around her, making her head spin. Tingling sparks of energy spilled from his hand where it cradled her face. The urge to rub herself up against him to absorb more of that energy was driving her mad. She couldn't think straight when he was using these weapons against her. All she could think about was how to get closer to him.

Lexi licked her dry lips. Zach's eyes zeroed in on the small movement. His pupils dilated, swallowing up the pale green until only a thin rim of color remained. He looked hungry, like the predator he was, but Lexi couldn't bring herself to care.

Her fingers clenched around hard muscle, and until then, she hadn't realized she'd reached for him. She was holding his arms, gripping his biceps like a lifeline. He was vibrating with tension beneath her fingertips. She felt his muscles bunch and shift and then his arm was around her body, pulling her closer.

She didn't try to fight him. She didn't push him away. And she didn't know why.

His head lowered until his nose was only a scant inch from hers. Lexi's breathing sped, and her heart kicked hard. He was going to kiss her and she was going to let him. God help her, she *needed* him to kiss her. She didn't even care anymore that it was a trick. She wanted him too much to care.

His hand slid from her cheek to the back of her head. He tilted her head back so it was at a better angle. She could feel his big body shaking with need. Or maybe she was the one doing all the shaking. She couldn't be sure.

"You know I'm going to kiss you now, right?" he asked, his deep voice low in the quiet house.

Lexi couldn't speak. She gave a slight nod of her head. Not only did she know it, she craved it.

Zach closed the distance another minute fraction of an inch. Lexi closed her eyes and gave in. He was her enemy, but it hardly seemed to matter anymore. If she was doomed, she wanted to go out like this—kissing a man who made her blood race and her body melt.

"Well, you're wrong," he told her. "Just like you're wrong about all the rest."

With that, he let go of her and stepped away.

Lexi had to grab onto the wall to steady herself. Her head was reeling and her body was aching with the loss of his touch. She opened her eyes just in time to see him close a bedroom door behind him. She slid down the wall until she was sitting on the faded carpet, hugging her knees.

He didn't come back out. He didn't attack her. He didn't do anything. He just stayed locked behind that door.

Lexi waited in agony. She shivered with cold and confusion. Why hadn't he kissed her? She would have let him. Hell, she would have let him do a lot more than just kiss her.

And what did he mean about her being wrong about all the rest?

As the fog of lust faded from her mind, she realized that this was a good thing. She didn't want him to kiss her or do anything else. He was the enemy. She wanted to kill him.

Didn't she?

Lexi covered her face with her hands and let out a frustrated growl. He'd done this to her on purpose. He was using his evil magic to confuse her. To manipulate her.

This was what the Sentinels did. They tricked their prey into compliance. They used them and then they killed them. Her mother's journal had been clear about that.

Then why had he stopped? Zach had her where he wanted her. Why stop there?

Lexi pushed herself up onto her wobbly legs. She needed to think—to get away from him long enough to clear her head. She couldn't run away because she had to finish her mission and rescue Helen, but she could put enough space between her and Zach so her brain would start working again.

She turned to go find something to snip this bracelet off her wrist when she heard a deep groan of pain coming from behind Zach's door. It stopped as if cut short; then there was a thud like something heavy had landed on the floor. Maybe a two-hundred-plus-pound man?

What if he was hurt?

Lexi was reaching for the doorknob before she realized that this was probably another trick. Put her off balance, then make her come running to him.

It wasn't going to work. She wasn't going to fall for a con like that. Her mother had taught her well, and it was about time Lexi started listening.

She heard another groan filter through the door and had to cover her ears. Her feet felt heavy and her stomach twisted with nausea, but she managed to walk away from Zach without looking back.

Zach was dying.

His body heaved under another wave of pain so intense it blinded him. Sweat soaked his clothes and the clinging fabric grated against his skin until he was sure he was bleeding. He tried to crawl into the bathroom to wash the blood away so it couldn't draw the Synestryn to Lexi, but he was too weak. His limbs shook and even pulling in another breath left him exhausted.

He was such a fool. He should have never walked

away from her like that. He'd been so close to kissing her—so close to claiming her as his own—but something held him back.

She didn't trust him. He wanted to prove to her she could, and the only way he could think to do it was to show her his restraint.

Bad plan.

And now he was paying the price. He'd had his chance to taste her sweet mouth and walked away from it, and it was killing him. Literally.

Another pulverizing wave of pain slammed into him and forced the air from his lungs. Tears streamed down his face, cooling his hot skin. Every muscle in his body quivered under the force of resisting the agony of his swelling power. Huge fists of energy pounded on his insides, demanding that he go to Lexi and force her to let it out. Make the pain stop.

But it was too late for that. He couldn't go to her now. He couldn't even lift his head. All he could do was lie there and listen to the pitiful sounds of pain welling up from his throat.

He was pretty sure it would be the last thing he heard.

Chapter 5

Lexi stood on the front porch. It was as far as she could go without feeling that nagging itchiness the bracelet caused when she moved away from Zach.

She'd wanted to clear her head, but all she could think about was the noises she'd heard coming from his room.

He was in pain.

She told herself she didn't care. She told herself that he deserved it for all the lives he'd ruined.

Well, you're wrong. Just like you're wrong about all the rest.

What had he meant by that? What was she wrong about? Was it just another trick?

He could have kissed her. He could have used his bad mojo to enslave her right there in the hallway and she wouldn't have done a thing to stop him. But he hadn't.

Damn it. This was all too confusing. He'd turned her world upside down, making her question what she'd been taught all her life.

Well, there was one way to find out if he was playing her, and she was going to call his bluff.

Lexi marched back into the house, found a nice, sharp knife in the kitchen and flung Zach's door open.

The room was dark. She flipped on the light switch.

At first, she thought he wasn't even in here anymore because she didn't see him. Then she heard a sound coming from the far side of the bed—a low gurgling sound like he was choking.

Lexi hurried around the bed and found him lying on his side, curled into a tight ball. He was sweating and shaking, and his eyes were rolled up in his head like he was having some kind of seizure or something.

Panic slid through her limbs, taking over. She dropped the knife and knelt beside him. Her hands moved over his arms and up to his face. She had no idea what to do to help him, but she remembered hearing somewhere about people choking on their own tongue.

She moved his head so she could see into his mouth, but the instant her fingers touched his cheek, the gurgling noise stopped. He pulled in a deep, shuddering breath and his body stopped shaking.

Zach's eyes rolled around like they were loose in his skull, but apparently, he'd been able to see she was there.

"Lexi," he whispered, his voice rough and ragged like he'd been screaming for hours.

"I'm here," she said, at a total loss.

His hands fumbled blindly over her body until he found her bare arms; then he pulled her to him. Lexi didn't fight him. Whatever was happening to him, he seemed better now, and she didn't want to mess that up, as stupid as it seemed.

She let him arrange her body until she was lying on her side, facing away from him. He curled himself around her and held on tight. A few seconds later, she felt him tug on the back of her shirt until her lower back was bare; then he pulled the front of his shirt up. Lexi tried to straighten her clothes, but he blocked her attempts and pulled her back against him until bare skin met bare skin.

His skin was hot and damp, tight over his corded muscles, and a flood of energy sank into her spine, sapping her will to move. It felt too good to fight him. She was totally out of her element here and nothing in Mom's journal had said anything about feeling like this. It was like touching happiness. Blissful contentment.

Zach's chest vibrated with a satisfied growl and she knew then that he was feeling it, too. Whatever this thing between them was, it was good. Maybe it was just one more trick designed to enslave her, but she really didn't care. She was too sleepy to care.

She'd give him ten minutes. Then she'd move away. He'd be better by then and she would leave him and find her bearings. She'd read Mom's journal and remember why she was supposed to stay away from him—why she shouldn't let him touch her.

It was only ten minutes. She was sure that small amount of time wouldn't hurt her.

Nika watched Madoc through the trees. His powerful body was protected by a heavy leather jacket that did nothing to hide the bunch and swell of his muscles as he cut down the sgath that crossed his path.

In a small corner of the beast's mind that she now occupied, sadness and anger rose up at the death of its brothers. It wanted to lunge at Madoc and rip out his throat. It wanted to drink down his rich blood and feast on his flesh until there was nothing left but bones.

Nika gathered her will and forced the beast to remain still while she used it. She ignored its need to kill, and watched as Madoc sliced another sgath in two.

He moved so beautifully—a deadly, fluid grace that made her feel protected just knowing he was near. If only her human body hadn't been so weak, she would have gone to him and told him how much she needed him, asked him why he no longer came to touch her hand.

The mouth of the sgath she inhabited moved and she realized she was trying to speak to him. Of course, no human words could come out of her muzzle, and all she managed to do was let out a low growl.

Madoc's head swiveled her way. His sword was dripping with black blood, and he had to step over the furred bodies of the beasts he'd slain to come closer.

He moved cautiously, his eyes narrowing in the darkness of the forest. A snarl twisted his blunt features as he closed the distance between them. He was only feet away from her now, and a thrill ran through Nika's borrowed body.

She wanted him to touch her. To hold her.

She tried to tell him, but again, the words could not come out. How was she going to reach him?

"I see you, you furry fucker," said Madoc. "You're not getting away now."

He was going to kill her—or at least he was going to kill the body she now inhabited. As much as she hated feeling Madoc strike her down, she also knew it was safer for him if she stayed in the sgath's mind until he struck, holding the beast from attacking him.

Nika couldn't watch. She closed the sgath's eyes and froze it in place. The bite of the blade across her shoulder made her flinch and she heard herself let out an eerie howl of pain. Another hot slice of pain went through her chest and this time, she felt her heart sputter as blood spilled out of it, wetting her fur.

She opened her eyes, hoping Madoc would see some piece of her inside the sgath, but instead, she saw some huge, hulking beast high in the trees over his head. It had six eyes and they were all staring right at Madoc, glowing with hungry fire.

The sgath was nearly dead, and she leapt from its mind before it took her with it.

As she passed by Madoc, she tried to whisper in his ear that he was in danger, but made no sound. She tried to stroke his skin and warn him, but felt nothing. She was less than air and so light, she was already being sucked back into her wasted human body.

She couldn't help him here. She had to get back out into the night and find a way to tell him he was being hunted.

Nika's real eyes opened and she was in a room she vaguely recognized. Not the hospital, but Andra's new home.

The sweet woman who'd been caring for her body sat in the corner, knitting. She had a halo of dark curls, and sad brown eyes. Her fingers moved fast and sure, and stitch after stitch was left in their wake.

Grace. That was her name. Grace would help her.

"Madoc," said Nika. Her voice was thin and ragged, barely audible in the silent room.

Grace's head snapped up and her eyes locked on Nika's. They widened in surprise; then she rose from her chair and came to Nika's side, letting her knitting fall to the carpet.

"Shh," said Grace. "Don't try to speak yet. Let me get you some water first."

"No time. Madoc is in danger."

Grace poured water into a plastic cup and held a straw to Nika's lips. "Have a drink."

Nika drank just to get the woman to listen. "Call Madoc."

"I'm sorry, my lady. I don't know his number. Let me get your sister."

Andra had listened to her before. She would again.

Grace dialed a number. "Nika's awake. She wants to call Madoc."

Nika heard the faint buzz of Andra's voice through the plastic.

Grace looked at Nika. "What do you want her to tell him?"

"Look up in the trees. Above him."

Although she looked confused, Grace repeated what Nika had said to Andra, then, "Okay. I'll tell her." She hung up and sat on the edge of the bed. Her fingers stroked the back of Nika's hand—the first real contact she'd felt in a long time. "Andra's on her way. She's calling Madoc right now, and doesn't want you to worry."

How could Nika not worry? Madoc was out there alone. If anything happened to him . . .

"Have another sip of water," urged Grace.

Her lips felt dry and her body was almost too weak to swallow, but she did as she was told.

"How do you feel?" asked Grace.

"I need to go back out there with Madoc. He needs me." A frantic sense of doom settled over her, weighing her down. She couldn't lose him.

"I'm sure he's fine. He's a skilled warrior."

Grace didn't understand. No one did except Andra, and she only listened sometimes.

"I've got to go back to sleep—go find him."

"Please don't," said Grace. "Just stay awake until Andra gets here. Let her talk to you."

Nika's eyes were heavy. Being awake was hard. She felt so alone when she wasn't with him.

The door flew open and Andra stood there, breathing hard and pink from exertion. "Nika, baby," she breathed. "You're awake."

Andra crossed the room and Grace moved out of the way.

"Did you talk to Madoc?"

"Yes. He's fine."

"Did you tell him about the monster in the tree?"

"He'd already found it and killed it by the time I called him."

Relief poured through Nika like cool water, washing away her panic. She clutched Andra's hand. "Thank you."

Andra gave her a teary smile. "How are you feeling?"

"Tired. I want to be with him."

"Him?" asked Andra.

"Madoc."

"You need to stay here, baby. You're not strong enough to travel yet."

"I won't take my body," explained Nika.

Andra frowned at her and smoothed her hair back from her head. From the corner where Grace was hovering came, "Do you want me to call Tynan?"

"Yes. Tell him Nika's awake."

"I don't want Tynan. I want Madoc." No one listened to her and Nika started to wonder if her mouth in this body was working right.

She was slipping back into sleep, unable to stop it from sweeping her mind away. She wanted to stay awake so she could see him, but that was no longer possible. She was too weak to even go seeking out one of the sgath.

"Okay," soothed Andra. "I'll bring him here. Whatever you want."

"I want Madoc," said Nika as she drifted away from the world.

Chapter 6

Zach was dead. He knew he had to be, because he'd been alive for centuries and nothing he'd experienced had ever felt this good.

He cracked open his eyes and saw the top of Lexi's head. Her soft brown hair was a total mess, like he'd been rubbing his face over the fine strands for hours, tangling them with his beard stubble. Based on the bright light of day filtering in from beneath the curtains, that might have been the case.

His body was curved around hers, touching in as many places as possible. She was warm and pliant, and the feel of her sweet ass pressing against his hard dick was enough to make him believe in heaven. His arm was wrapped tightly around her, holding her in place, and his fingers had sneaked up under her shirt to curl over her ribs, right below her breast. The feel of naked Lexi skin under his hand was too good to be true. He had to be dead, or dreaming.

Slowly, the fog filling his head started to burn off enough for him to take in his surroundings. He wasn't dead. He was lying on the floor of the Gerai house with only the outdated carpet to cushion their bodies. It wasn't nearly soft enough for Lexi, but he wasn't quite sure yet how to fix it. His brain was still fuzzy and his blood simmered with a slow burn of sexual arousal.

They hadn't had sex. He knew it for a fact because there was no way he would have forgotten something like that. Besides, they were both still dressed and on the floor. Zach liked to think he was suave enough to at least have put her on a bed before taking her.

So, if he hadn't seduced her, how had he gotten her here?

The last thing he remembered was pain. Mountains of it crashing down on top of him, crushing the life from his body. He wasn't sure how he survived it, but he really didn't care. As long as she was here, in his arms, the pain was all worth it.

Lexi shifted in her sleep, reaching up like she was searching for a pillow. Zach moved his arm so it cushioned her cheek and she settled back to sleep.

She said she didn't trust him. The gleam of a large knife lying at her feet proved she'd meant it. So why was she here, lying next to him?

Zach didn't question his good fortune. She was here and that was enough.

He yawned, ready to settle down for another few hours of rest with the woman of his dreams. The expansion of his chest pressed him tighter to her back and she went stiff in his arms.

Shit. He'd woken her up.

"Sorry," he whispered over her hair. "I didn't mean to wake you. Go back to sleep, honey."

Apparently, Lexi had other plans. She pushed herself up and Zach let her go. It was too early for a wrestling match, and every muscle in his body still ached from whatever had happened to him last night.

She scrambled away from him until she was pressed against the wall. Instantly, his body tensed against a wave of pain. He sucked in a breath and tried to relax into it, let it wash over him. He knew how to deal with pain. He could do this.

In an effort to distract himself, he stared at Lexi. Her hair was a disaster and her eyes were puffy from sleep, but she was still the most beautiful thing he'd ever seen. He could wake up to a sight like that every day for eternity and still not have enough.

She rubbed her eyes and looked at him from head to toe. Her gaze paused, widened and backed up as she saw his erection, but there was nothing he could do about that. So she knew he wanted her. It wasn't exactly a big secret.

A frown creased her brow and she rubbed the spot under her breast where his hand had been while they slept. "What did you do to me?" she asked.

His muscles were locked up, hard and painful, and his dick was even worse, but he could deal with all of that. What he couldn't deal with was the look of fear Lexi wore.

"I didn't *do* anything," he said. "Your pants are still on, aren't they?"

She swallowed and her fingers moved to the waistband of her jeans, which were still securely buttoned. Hell, she still had on that short, pocketed apron from work. Some of the coins had spilled out onto the carpet while she slept, so Zach collected them and handed them to her.

Lexi didn't take them. She stared at his hand and stood, putting even more distance between them.

Great. Back to square one.

"Please don't, Lexi," he said. There was a hint of begging in his voice and he hated it. He'd never had to beg for anything in his life. "I could have done whatever horrible thing you think me capable of last night if I'd wanted to, but I didn't. Doesn't that prove to you I'm not going to hurt you?"

"It's a trick. Your skin is poisonous. Drugged. That's why it feels so good."

Zach was hung up on the making her feel good part for a second longer than he should have been. The idea he could do that to her made his blood heat. She'd inadvertently told him how to get to her, and he had every intention of exploiting the weakness.

Lexi was meant to be his, and now he knew how to convince her it was true, too.

He tried to hide his slow smile of victory, but based on the way her dark eyes widened, he was pretty sure he'd failed. "It's not poison, honey. It's chemistry. You and I are meant to be together and that feeling is nature's way of letting us know."

"Liar."

Zach ignored the insult and stood. She shifted her hips, signaling her intent to run, but he moved fast, blocking her in. She was trapped between the wall and his body and he wasn't letting her go.

He caged her in with one arm while he drew his finger lightly over her cheek. She was too soft to be real, and his eyes fell shut so he could soak in more of her. Little sparks of power arced between them, bleeding off a minute portion of the energy churning inside Zach. Some of the pain bled away with it. His finger slid lower until he traced a path over her throat, where his luceria would soon be.

Lexi let out a soft moan, though whether it was pleasure or fear he couldn't tell. He could hear her rapid breathing, and feel the brittle tension tightening her limbs. His hand spread out across her throat until he could feel the delicate ridges of her collarbone beneath his fingers.

More sparks wriggled into her body and she sucked in a fast breath.

Zach looked down at her. His dark skin stood out in

stark contrast against the paleness of hers. Even in dim light, Zach would be able to see his hands sliding over her body, pleasing her.

He could hardly wait.

Her head was tilted to the side, and her hands were tight fists. Her body vibrated in time with the faint current of power trickling into her from his palm.

He wanted to kiss her, but his instincts told him that restraint was the best way to get to his ultimate goal. Once she was his, he'd have forever to kiss her, to touch her.

"Still think I'm lying?" asked Zach.

Her eyes were the color of bittersweet chocolate and when she looked up at him, for just a moment, he thought he saw a flash of insecurity. "Please stop," she whispered. "I can't do this."

"Do what, honey?"

Lexi wrapped her fingers around his wrist. Her hands were small, but her fingers were graceful and strong. She tried to tug his hand away, but Zach didn't budge.

"I can't let you seduce me," she said.

"Why not? We're going to be good together. I'll make sure you don't regret it."

She closed her eyes and shook her head. "No."

Zach leaned over her and put his mouth near her ear. "Oh, yes. You and I were made for each other. The sooner you accept that, the more time I'll have to make you come. You want that, don't you?" He punctuated the question with a pulse of energy so powerful he could hear it crackle.

"Oh God." She bit her bottom lip between her teeth and he could feel her heart hammering faster beneath his hand.

"Stop fighting me. Let me show you how good it can be for us." He slid his tongue along the curve of her ear, making her shiver. "That's right," he coaxed. "Just let go."

"I . . . I have to pee."

It was an escape tactic and he knew it. He should have known she wasn't going to make any of this easy on him.

Zach sighed and grudgingly backed away. Lexi fled his arms, stumbling as she headed for the bathroom.

His dick ached with need, but it was going to just keep on aching.

He'd almost had her. He was sure of it. He'd felt her resolve crumbling. In fact, he was amazed that she'd been able to walk away. He sure as hell wasn't walking anywhere for a while. Not until he got himself under control.

The toilet flushed, the faucet turned on and off again and yet she still didn't come out.

Zach sighed. Apparently, their chase was not yet over. Part of him thrilled at the idea of chasing her, but the rest of him was just tired and hurting too much to want this to go on.

He rubbed his chest. The single leaf on his lifemark had withered more since yesterday. It was time for her to stop running.

He stood in front of the door and crossed his arms over his chest. There was no window in there. No way out but the one she went in.

She couldn't stay in there forever, and when she came out, he'd be waiting.

Lexi pressed the wet cloth over her face, hoping it would cool her fevered skin.

What the hell had she been thinking, letting him touch her like that? Was she insane?

Yes. Without question. She was totally certifiable.

She scrubbed viciously at her ear, trying to rub away the feel of his hot tongue gliding over her skin. Just the memory of it made her knees weak enough she had to lock them to stay upright. Whatever magic Zach was using on her was potent stuff. She wasn't sure how she was going to be able to resist him long enough to rescue Helen, but she had to find a way.

The Defenders had warned her this would be hard, but until now, she'd figured they just didn't know her very well. Because she was small, people saw her as weak and fragile. She was anything but.

Except where Zach was concerned.

Lexi growled in frustration, turned on the cold water and dunked her head under the faucet. The chill drove the breath from her lungs, but at least it helped clear her head of the fog Zach had filled it with.

She had to think. Come up with a plan. It wasn't like she had to resist him for a year or anything—just long enough to get them to the compound. The Defenders were sure it was somewhere in the Midwest, so she didn't have that far to go with Zach. Maybe a day's drive.

Just one day. She could keep his tongue off her ears— or her anywhere else—for that long.

"Need someone to wash your back, honey?" came Zach's deep voice through the door.

Even his voice made her body soften along with her resolve. She needed to gag him, or maybe plug her ears. And she definitely needed more clothes on. The less bare skin she had for him to touch, the better.

"Go away," she told him.

"Not gonna happen. Anything else I can get you?"

Some dry panties sounded nice, but she wasn't about to tell him that. "My suitcase."

"Sure thing, honey. Be right back."

He wasn't gone nearly long enough before she heard his hard knuckles tapping on the door. "Here you go."

"Just leave it outside the door."

Sultry amusement colored his voice. "Afraid the big, bad wolf is going to eat you all up?"

Only if she was really lucky. It had been way too long since she'd been with a man, and this thing Zach did to her was reminding her just how much she'd been missing. Even the insinuation of him kissing and licking her was enough to make her dizzy.

Lexi grabbed the sink to steady herself against the barrage of images he'd put in her head. She was sure that if he ever did get her naked, she'd feel like the luckiest woman alive, right up to the point where he killed her.

"Screw you," she said, but it came out sounding more like a feeble question than an insult.

"Anything you want. Just open the door and leave the rest to me."

"Not ever, Zach."

His voice dropped low so she had to strain to hear it. "It's just a matter of time now, honey. You can fight me all you like, but in the end, we both know how things will be."

Yeah, he and all his buddies were going to be little pulpy bits of flesh staining the landscape.

For some reason, that plan didn't sound nearly as good as it had just last night.

Chapter 7

Zach watched Lexi eat. Seeing her mouth move over the fork was the sexiest thing ever. Then again, there wasn't much about her that wasn't sexy. Her sweet, compact body and killer ass drove him crazy. The glimpses he kept getting of the tattoo at the base of her spine were going to end him up in the loony bin if he didn't get to see just how far down under her jeans it went. And the contrast between that spiky-haired, bad girl persona she'd used when he first met her, and the softer, more vulnerable side of her he was seeing now was the kind of thing that fueled a man's fantasies. She was every kind of woman he'd ever wanted, all rolled into one. Even that independent streak of hers turned him on.

Every single Theronai at Dabyr was going to want her. He couldn't take the chance that she would want one of them back. He had to stake his claim before he took her home—get her to wear his luceria so all the men would know she was off limits.

He slid another pancake onto her plate in the hopes she'd let him watch her eat a little longer.

Lexi wiped her mouth on a napkin and leaned back in her chair. "How long will it take us to get back to your home?" she asked.

Zach considered lying to her, making her think it was

farther away than it was so he'd have more time alone with her, but that wasn't how he wanted things to start out between them. Honesty was important to him. If he wanted it from her, it only seemed fair to be the one to offer it first. "About nine hours, but I'm not ready to leave yet."

"Why not?"

He took a sip of coffee to stall for time to think. He didn't want to mess this up. Lexi already had some wrong ideas about his world, and he wasn't sure just how well she was going to like what he had to say.

Finally, he came up with, "I don't want to share."

"Um. Okay. Share what?"

"You."

Lexi blinked fast a couple of times, but other than that, her face was stoic. "Please tell me that means something other than what I think it means."

"The other men at Dabyr—my home—are all going to want you."

Her fingers twisted the paper napkin until it shredded. "For what?"

She was afraid. He'd seen the look enough times to know that, despite that straight spine and high chin, she was shaking on the inside.

"We'd never hurt you, Lexi. None of the men would, no matter what you might think. We all want the same thing—to have you by our side for the long haul."

She grunted, but it sounded more relieved than disbelieving. "I hardly think so. And even if that was the case, I'm not looking for any . . . relationships right now."

"You may not be looking for one, but one found you."

"What's that supposed to mean?"

Zach reached for her hand, wanting to touch her, but she jerked away before he could. She folded her hands in her lap, pretending that she hadn't just rejected him.

Disappointment sliced through him, but he let her go. Now wasn't the time to push. Finesse would get him much farther. "I need you, Lexi. I've never hidden that fact from you. Even after you stabbed me."

"I figured that was temporary insanity," she said, "or that you were simply lying."

"Every word I've ever said to you has been the bare, honest truth. I need you, and I'm not going to share."

She lifted her coffee mug, and Zach saw the dark liquid vibrate under her shaking fingers. Great. Either he'd scared her more or pissed her off. He was guessing scared, since if he'd pissed her off, she probably would have dumped the hot coffee in his lap. "Okay. I'm going to start from the beginning. Stop me if I lose you."

Lexi nodded, but she didn't look at him. Definitely scared.

"I'm not sure how much you know about the Theronai."

"Not much. Just what my mom told me, and what she wrote in her journal."

That was something, at least. "We're one of the Sentinel races. Have you heard of the Sentinels?"

"Yes. Since before I could walk."

"Good, then I can skip the part where we're all out to save humanity and guard the gateway onto another world. Here's what you might not know. The Theronai pair up into teams of one man and one woman. The man can collect energy from the environment and store it, and the woman has the ability to channel that power, but can't store any of her own. Are you with me so far?"

"I think so."

He wasn't sure she meant it, but he pushed on, hoping to get through this as fast as possible. "We pair up, but when we do, it's a permanent kind of thing."

"Like marriage?"

"Sometimes, but not always. There have been rare

cases in our past when family members paired up, but for it to work, there has to be some kind of close bond. The longer a couple is together, the stronger they get."

"That's why Drake wanted Helen, right? Because she was one of these women?"

He nodded. "So are you."

Her dark eyes narrowed and a mutinous kind of anger tightened her mouth. "No, I'm not."

So, she didn't like the idea. Fantastic. That was going to make things so much more difficult, and he didn't have time for that. Even with the trickle of power she'd absorbed through their contact, Zach was still suffering. He had a tidal wave of pressure waiting to get out, and not long to make it happen.

He'd checked his leaf earlier and it was shriveled and brown, barely clinging to his tree.

"I can prove it," he told her.

Zach wrapped his fingers around her wrist. She felt so good under his touch that he almost forgot what he was doing. A swirling sea of blues and greens churned inside the band around his finger. "See the way the color in my ring changes when I touch you?"

Lexi licked her lips and nodded.

"There's more green and blue than any other color. Plus, you feel those little sparks of power arching between us, right?"

Again, she nodded, but she hadn't taken her eyes off the ring.

"Those are signs that you're like me. You're a Theronai."

"No. I'm not." There was more than just the heat of denial in her voice. There was something else—a kind of frantic desperation, like he'd told her she only had a week to live.

She couldn't accept who she was yet, but he understood that. Like Helen and Andra, she'd been raised as a human. Once he showed her his world, she would come to accept everything soon enough, just like the other women had.

Lexi tried to pull her hand away, but Zach tightened his hold. He needed this contact to remind him there was still hope. Still time.

He made his voice sound casual as he continued. "So, this connection that we have allows the power to flow between us. The longer and stronger that connection is, the more power can flow at one time."

"Won't you run out?" she asked.

"I can run low, sure, but there's more all around us, in the air, in the earth—everywhere. It soaks into me whether or not I want it to, which is why I need you. I've already absorbed more power than I can hold. It's killing me."

She was still staring at his ring and the hypnotic movement of colors within it. "And you think I can stop it?"

"You can siphon off enough to reduce the pressure. Enough to keep me alive. That's why I need you."

She was silent for a moment, and he gave her the time to absorb what he'd said. "And if I don't cooperate?" she asked.

"Then I die—or at least my soul does. I won't be one of the good guys anymore. I won't care about right or wrong, only about what I want."

Her voice was a thin whisper of sound. "I've never heard of this before."

"It's not something they teach in schools."

"Yeah, well, I never went to school. My education was a little more . . . practical than most. I learned all about the Sentinels and never once heard any of this."

It made him wonder just what she'd been taught and how much of it was complete bullshit. "I'm not lying to you, honey. I'm putting it all out in the open. I want you to know what I'm asking of you."

"Which is what, exactly?"

He put his finger under her chin and tipped her face up so she'd look at him. He wanted to know she saw he was serious. "I want you to wear my luceria. I want you to be my partner. Forever."

Her head shook slightly. Zach wasn't sure she knew she was even doing it. "I barely know you."

"I get that. I understand that this is scary for you. It's all new and strange, but it's not entirely a one-sided deal. You do get some fringe benefits."

"I don't care."

"That's because you don't know what you're missing. If you agree to do this, you'll have the ability to wield magic."

She jerked out of his grasp and moved her chair back so she was out of reach. She didn't even give him the courtesy of looking at him. "I don't want it. I don't want any part of your world."

Zach ignored the insult and continued. "You'll hardly age with the passage of centuries. We live a really long time, unless we're killed in battle."

"I don't want to fight."

Yeah, he wasn't always fond of that part, either, but it was necessary. At least he had a purpose.

He scoured his brain, hoping to find something she would want—something to convince her to save him. "You'll never be alone again. You'll have a family. A home."

On his last word, her eyes shot to his face as if searching for some kind of trick. "What makes you think I'd want to be part of your family?"

"You don't believe me." He could see it in her eyes, the way they narrowed with mistrust.

"I don't know what to believe."

"You don't have to decide right this second." He wanted her to—he wanted the grinding pain to go away—but he could wait until she was sure. "It's a big decision. Ask me anything you want and I'll tell you the honest truth."

"Is this what Helen did?"

"Yes."

"Is she safe?"

"Safer than she was before she was with Drake. Our jobs are dangerous, but we're careful with our women. You're rare and we take every precaution to keep you out of harm's way."

"So you coddle her?"

"No. Helen goes into battle against the Synestryn right alongside the men. We need her there, but we make sure that there are plenty of swords between her and the teeth and claws. That's all."

"And you think I'm like her?"

"I know you are."

"Let's assume I am. If I do this, you said it's permanent, right?"

"Kind of. It's meant to be permanent. You give me a vow, which was traditionally that a woman would fight by her man's side forever. But it doesn't have to be that long."

"If it's not?"

"Once the vow is fulfilled, the luceria falls off and you're back to where you were before."

"And so are you?"

He hated telling her this part, but he'd promised he'd give her the truth, so he would. "If we haven't bonded completely, yes."

"What if we have?"

"Then I'll be out of time."

"You'll die," she guessed, seeing through his euphemism.

"Yes."

"You want to give me the power to kill you?"

"No. The power to save me."

His hands were splayed flat on the table, where he'd been keeping them in sight so he wouldn't scare her anymore. He didn't want her to be afraid of him. He didn't want her to be afraid, period.

Her eyes went back to his ring, which, without her contact, had gone back to a slow swirl of shimmering iridescence.

"What if I say no?" she asked.

Shit. Here was the sticky part. He had to be careful to be honest without scaring her away with his intentions. Regardless of what happened between them, he wasn't letting her go. "If you refuse to help me, I'll take you back to Dabyr and see if there are any other men there who are compatible with you—men you could save. You can have your pick, of course, assuming there are others like me."

"What happens to you?"

"I have a few days left at best. Then I go into my final battle."

"You mean you would let yourself die?"

"Rather than become like the things I fight? Yes. But let me be clear, Lexi. It's not what I want. I want to live. With you."

"You don't even know me."

Zach shrugged. "We'll have years to get to know each other. I already like you. Given time, I'll come to love you."

"You don't know that. You can't predict who you love."

"Sure I can. I've seen it happen dozens of times over my lifetime. Don't you think there's a reason that not all female Theronai are compatible with all the males? I figure that the magic used to power the luceria is smart enough to know who will make good partners and who won't." Slowly, so she would really hear him, he said, "You and I were meant to be together."

He ached to touch her again, but she had stayed out of reach and he was doing his best to respect her choices right now. There would come a time when he would no longer be able to let them matter—when the lives of his family would take priority and he'd force her to go home with him—but they weren't there yet.

"I can't do this right now. I can't decide."

Disappointment nearly crushed him, making it hard to breathe. In all those fantasies of his, she'd always wanted him. She'd run into his arms and claimed her place beside him willingly. He'd never stopped to consider that she might not want him until now.

Zach wanted to push her, but it was a big decision for her. She had to make it with her eyes open. No tricks. No lies.

If Zach gave her the whole truth, and she still didn't want him, he'd find a way to deal with it. As long as she was safe at Dabyr, it would have to be enough to satisfy him.

"I'll give you all the time I can." Two days, maybe three. It wasn't long to convince a woman to spend the rest of her life with him, but he had to try.

"I'll think better in the car. We should get moving."

Toward Dabyr and all the other men there who would no doubt want her, too. He'd never once wished his brothers ill, and the fact that the thought even crossed his mind now proved to him just how little time he had left.

Lexi had practically memorized her mother's journals and there was not a single word in them that supported anything Zach had said.

The Sentinels want your blood. They use it to fuel their magic. They feed it to their pets.

And yet she'd spent the night with Zach, had been completely vulnerable, and he hadn't so much as spilled a drop. Maybe he was tricking her—lulling her into a false sense of security—but it didn't feel that way.

Of course, her instincts had always been off where Zach was concerned. Nothing new there. From the moment he'd touched her that night at Gertie's Diner, her world had been upended, and nothing made sense.

They'd been driving for hours and she still didn't know what to think of his proposal. Spend eternity with him. Never aging. Never alone.

She'd have a home. After all these years of running, she'd be able to stop. She'd have her own bed, maybe even be able to collect a few things beyond mere necessities. It seemed too good to be true, and that was what worried her most. Anything that was too good to be true probably was.

Lexi watched the landscape slide by the window as they drove north. They'd slept in late, and hadn't hit the road until well after noon. Now the sun was starting to set. Pretty soon, the monsters the Sentinels kept as pets would all come out to play.

At least she'd slept hard, was well rested and in better shape to face them than she had been in weeks. That was something to be glad about.

"Do you want anything to eat?" asked Zach. "We're getting close to Wichita and there's plenty to choose from."

"Sure. That's fine."

"Anything sound good?"

Someplace with lots of people and bright lights. "Whatever is fine."

Zach sighed. "I've completely freaked you out, haven't I?"

"Little bit." It was the understatement of the year.

He laughed and the sound rolled around in her ears, making her smile, right up until he said, "There's nothing sexier than a woman who can make me laugh. Just thought you should know."

"Let's get something straight right now," she told him. "Even if I decide to help you, and I'm pretty sure I won't, there will be no sexy stuff of any kind between us."

He flashed her a brief, amused look. "Why not?"

"Because I don't sleep with men I don't trust."

"You could learn to trust me if you let yourself."

When hell froze over, maybe. "Not likely."

His hand wrapped around hers, holding it against her thigh. A swarm of electric tingles slid into her, making her body buzz. Her head fell back against the headrest and she let the giddy feeling sweep over her.

"We'll just have to work on that," he said, but she could barely make sense of the words. "I've got a goal now, and I'm a very goal-oriented kind of man."

She just bet he was. She doubted there was much he'd let get in the way of what he wanted, and right now, that was her. A loud, crazy part of her was cheering over the news, so she told it to shut the hell up.

Lexi needed a distraction. Something, anything, to keep her from imagining just what kind of lover he'd be. Goal oriented, indeed. It was enough to make her squirm in her seat.

"What about my car? Getting it running and back in my hands will go a long way toward helping me trust you."

A slow smile warmed Zach's face. He was too handsome when he smiled. Too tempting. "It's already taken care of. I left your keys at the Gerai house, and as we speak, our men are likely repairing the engine. Once they're done, they'll drive it to Dabyr and you'll have your wheels back."

Unless they found the explosives hidden in her trunk.

They weren't obvious, and someone would actually have to search through her meager belongings to find the locked box filled with C-4. And then they'd have to break the lock to get in and see what was inside.

The good news was, if they did that, she'd know the Sentinels weren't as trusting and helpful as Zach led her to believe. She'd know for sure they weren't on her side, and she'd have no trouble blowing them all to hell if she got the chance.

At least that was what she kept telling herself.

Zach was giving her a funny look. "What? Isn't that what you wanted?"

"Yes."

"So why do you suddenly look sick?"

"I'm not sick. I'm hungry. I want steak," she blurted out, hoping to distract him.

"What?"

"I want steak." She hadn't had it in years, and thanks to him, she even had enough money to pay for a nice meal. Lexi staunchly refused to think of it as her last meal. She was going to get out of this mess alive and well with Helen and Miss Mabel in tow.

He laced his thick fingers through hers and said, "Then steak it is. I know just the place. It's a little out of the way, but more than worth the drive."

And once they got there, she was going to call Jake Morrow, her contact in the Defenders, and let him know she hadn't abandoned her mission.

Chapter 8

Joseph looked up from his desk to see Iain Terra filling his doorway. His black eyes sparkled under the bright office lighting, but his face was a blank, impassive mask. He waited in silence, even after Joseph had noticed him.

"Need something?" asked Joseph. His eyes burned, and he knew he wasn't going to sleep again tonight. There were too many things to be done and too many dreams to haunt him when he closed his eyes.

Everyone was counting on him to be some great leader. Didn't they all know he was just one single man? One no more capable of keeping his people alive than any other Theronai?

For what seemed like the millionth time, he cursed his position even as he accepted it. He would not fail. The lives of countless souls depended on him.

"I heard a rumor," said Iain. His deep voice was quiet, but carried easily across the office.

"Seems there are lots of those floating around these days."

"Not like this one."

Great. More problems. "Spit it out, Iain. I'm busy."

"Are there Synestryn with the faces of human children?"

No beating around the bush there. Too bad, too. Joseph wasn't ready to publicly acknowledge the spin that news had put on the war. He still wasn't entirely sure the Sentinels hadn't already lost and just didn't know it yet. Between that, the broken wall and slow repairs, the news that the European stronghold was crumbling from internal politics, and the constant, pounding pain in his head that made it hard to concentrate on the best of days, things were looking pretty bleak.

"Yeah. It's true," said Joseph, "but I'd really rather you not help spread the rumor any farther than it already has."

"Where?" asked Iain.

"Where what?"

"Where did they find these things?"

"There was only one," said Joseph.

"I'm going to make sure there are no more."

"I don't want you leaving. I need you here, at least until the wall is back up."

"If I wait, it will be too late," said Iain.

"Too late for what? Gilda and Angus already took care of the threat."

"You know as well as I do that the Synestryn won't stop with one. I'm going to find out how they are doing this and stop them."

Joseph rubbed his temples, breathing deeply as the pounding worsened. "Alone?"

"It's better that way. Most of the men here would balk when they saw what they had to destroy."

"And you won't?"

"No. I won't."

"So, you're just going to march into a nest and start killing things that look like our children?"

"They're not our children. I'll be able to remember that where someone like you wouldn't."

Maybe he was right. Joseph wasn't sure he could bring himself to do what was necessary, but Iain seemed to be. No one else had volunteered for the job.

"Fine. Check it out. Talk to Angus if you need more details. He was there." Joseph unrolled the map of known Synestryn nests and attacks.

Iain stepped up to the desk and watched where Joseph pointed. The dot identifying this incident was easy enough to spot. It was the only one on the map that was baby pink.

How fucking fitting that was.

Joseph looked away from the map. There were too many dots on it to count, and they were getting closer to Dabyr every night.

This had to stop. He had to do something—come up with some great plan—or nothing else he did was going to matter.

Five hundred thirty-seven people. That was how many were counting on him just here under his own roof. That didn't include the humans outside these walls who were preyed upon every night, or the other Sentinels scattered across the planet. It didn't include the who knew how many people there were in Athanasia right now who had no idea how close the Sentinels were to losing the war. The gateway into their world protected them, but only so long as he and his men stood guard and kept it safe. Once they were gone, there would be nothing left to stop the Synestryn from flooding that world, too—nothing left to stop them from slaughtering everyone there and heading on to the next planet.

No pressure.

Iain turned to leave without saying a word. Joseph felt compelled to say something, but he had no idea what. The man was going to do something Joseph knew he could never do himself. He was going to hunt down the greatest weapon the Synestryn had ever created—monsters with the faces of children. And then he was going to kill them.

"Be careful," was all Joseph could think to say.

Iain stopped at the doorway and turned around. "This isn't about careful and you know it."

"No. It's about having a strong stomach and remembering what's at stake."

"Don't worry. I'm your man."

Something about the way Iain said that bothered Joseph. It sounded empty. Hollow. Emotionless.

Maybe Iain was out of time, and this was his last heroic act. Joseph couldn't bring himself to ask. He didn't want to say good-bye to his longtime friend. "Are you saying you can do this and still sleep at the end of the day?"

"Who said I sleep?" said Iain; then he was gone. Joseph couldn't even hear his heavy footsteps echoing in the silent hallway.

Lexi had her doubts when they pulled into the gravel parking lot of the run-down restaurant. It was at the end of a long dirt road, miles from the highway, and completely out of the way, but the parking lot was full for the dinner rush, which had to mean something in this mostly deserted part of the world.

"I'm going to go use the ladies' room," Lexi told him.

He looked at her wrist to make sure the bracelet was still in place, chaining her to him. When he saw she hadn't found a way to remove it, he said, "I'll get us a table. Don't be long."

Lexi walked back to the doorway that led to the bathrooms and pay phone. There was plenty of change in her pocket from her tips last night, and she started plugging them into the phone. She dialed Jake Morrow's number, which she knew by heart, praying he'd be around so she didn't have to leave a message.

"Hello," he said, sounding mistrusting in that single word of greeting.

"It's Lexi. I don't have long."

"You okay?"

"Yeah. Fine. I just wanted to let you know to leave my car be. Zach is going to have it repaired and brought to me once I reach the compound."

"We've been watching it, and someone towed it to the mechanic's place earlier today. I talked to the owner and he said it had all been paid for up front—whatever needed to be done. He's supposed to call when it's fixed."

"Zach must have already got his men on it." Lexi leaned over, and peered out of the doorway, checking to make sure Zach wasn't headed this way. She saw no sign of him.

"Are you sure you're okay with this?" asked Jake.

He sounded worried, and she wanted to hug him for his concern. Of all the Defenders, he was the only one who seemed to be worried about what would happen to *her*. The others all saw her as some sort of tool to be used and disposed of as necessary.

"Absolutely. I'll try to call again when I can, but this was the first phone I've had access to that didn't belong to Zach. I didn't want him to be able to trace your number."

"If you get into trouble, don't worry about that, okay? Just call."

"I've got to go before he comes looking for me. Sit tight and I'll be in touch."

"Be careful, Lexi. Stay safe."

"Thanks, Jake. You, too." Lexi hung up and went to find their table.

As she neared, Zach smiled at her, like he was happy to see her. Like she was a friend.

Lexi's stomach twisted in shame. He had no idea
what she was planning. Of course, that was the point,
but somehow telling herself that didn't make her feel
any less like a lying bitch.

*They try to trick you. They use mind powers to suck
you in. Then they suck you dry and leave your corpse to
rot.*

Mom's words of warning. There were hundreds more
like them, too. Lexi had to remember that and steel
herself against any guilt she might feel. This was a job.
She was doing the right thing—saving countless human
lives. Whether or not she enjoyed the job was irrelevant.
Someone had to do it, and she was the best candidate.

So, she shoved away any residual guilt and pretended
that everything was fine. She wanted to be here, having
a nice meal with Zach. She wanted him to take her to his
home. She wanted to be friends.

Pretending was easier if she forgot why she was doing it, so that was what she did. Ninety minutes later, she
was stuffed full and more at ease with Zach than she
would have ever thought possible.

He hadn't grilled her about her decision to become
his partner, or talked about anything serious over dinner. Instead, he'd talked about small things, like how
he'd found this place so far off the beaten path one night
when his car had broken down, and how he and his buddies had a contest to find the best places to eat across
the country.

He claimed he was the reigning champion, and Lexi
had to agree.

But once they stepped out of the restaurant's door, his
charming, almost playful demeanor suddenly changed.
His pale eyes were bright and watchful and he casually
maneuvered Lexi so that he was between her and the
open farmland around them.

Zach walked close enough to her she could feel

the heat of his skin flowing between them, the tension cording his muscular body. He pulled in a deep breath through his nose, like he was smelling the air.

"Everything okay?" asked Lexi. Anxiety made her mouth go dry, and she was sure everything was most definitely not okay.

"No," said Zach as he grabbed her arm and rushed her toward the truck, practically carrying her to get her to hurry. They were parked at the far side of the lot. The dinner rush was over and all the cars that had filled the lot before were now gone, leaving the place nearly deserted. The cool night air suddenly felt chilly against her skin, and only the heat of Zach's strong fingers around her arm kept her from shivering.

"I think we might have visitors," said Zach in a tight voice.

"Visitors?"

"Synestryn."

She blurted out, "Your pets are here?" before she could stop herself.

Zach gave her a sharp frown. "They're not our pets, Lexi. I don't know where you heard that, but the Synestryn are anything but friendly, loyal dogs. They're our enemy, and will kill us if they find us. I can't risk you like that."

Couldn't risk her? What about *him*?

He unlocked the truck and pushed her up into the driver's seat. "Take the keys," he told her. "I need to keep my hands free to fight."

He grabbed her arm—the one wearing the gold chain bracelet—and closed his eyes for a brief second. A hot spark of power shot through her wrist and the bracelet fell free. He grabbed it and shoved it in his pocket.

Lexi gave him a questioning frown.

"I don't want you trapped by my side if things get ugly," he said.

Fear skittered around inside her belly, threatening to shove her meal up and out of its way. "Ugly?"

An eerie howl split the night, silencing the crickets chirping nearby. "There's a map in the glove compartment. On it is a dot in red ink northeast of Kansas City. That's Dabyr. Go there. Tell them who you are and they'll let you in. I'll catch up with you."

"You want me to leave you here?" she asked.

Sitting high in the truck, she had a good view of the cornfield. Tall stalks of corn parted as something big came closer. Several somethings.

"I can't leave these people here to fend for themselves. I've got to stay and fight."

"By yourself?"

He gave her a wink. "You're not ready to help me yet, though I wished like hell you were. Go now. There's no more time."

Zach shut her inside the truck and drew a sword that had been invisible only a moment ago. He walked away, toward the edge of the cornfield, his stride confident and steady.

Lexi's hand fumbled on the key, trying to separate the one she needed from the rest. It went into the ignition on the third try, and the truck started easily. Not at all like her ancient Honda.

Whatever was out there in the corn was getting closer fast—it was only fifty yards away now. Zach had moved to the edge of the tall stalks, putting himself between the people in the restaurant and whatever was headed his way. He lifted his blade to a ready stance, and stood there, waiting.

Lexi didn't want to leave him here alone. He said those things weren't his pets. The way he was acting proved he wasn't lying.

Another deep howl make Lexi jump. Thick, oily fear

closed around her throat until she could only pull in short, shallow breaths.

She needed to get out of here. Zach could take care of himself. He wouldn't have gone out there alone if he couldn't. Would he?

Her feet couldn't touch the pedals, so she slid the seat forward. The first Synestryn broke through the field, coming into sight.

It was a huge, hulking beast, as wide as it was tall. Long tusks erupted from its jaw, dripping with saliva. It had a thick snout and was covered in long barbs from top to bottom. Its spiny skin glistened wetly in the dim light, and all those barbs rattled as the thing laid eyes on Zach.

Lexi's body seized up in terror. She'd never seen anything like it before.

A loud hissing noise came from the thing, and Zach fell to the ground, flattening himself against the dry earth. Dozens of barbs shot out of the monster's skin and some of them embedded themselves in a nearby tree. Only a fraction of an inch of the long spike remained sticking out of the hard bark.

Lexi didn't want to think about what would have happened to Zach's body had they hit him. He was hard, but a hell of a lot softer than that tree.

Before she'd had time to even make sense of what she was seeing, Zach was back on his feet, sword in hand, closing in on the monster. His sword flashed as he attacked, but Lexi didn't watch. A movement farther out in the field demanded her attention.

There were three more things out there closing in fast. She didn't know if they were the same things that Zach was fighting or not, but she was pretty sure that it didn't really matter. Four against one were not the kind of odds a man survived.

She tried to convince herself it didn't matter if he survived. She didn't need him anymore. She had his truck, money, a map to Helen and her car on its way. She had everything she needed to get to Dabyr and blow it up. He'd even unchained her, freeing her to run away without getting sick.

Why had he done that? Because he didn't want her hurt? Or because he knew he was going to die?

Lexi didn't know. She didn't understand why he would free her when he'd been clear that he intended to imprison her for life.

What she did know was that until she separated the truth from the lies, she couldn't let Zach die.

She put the truck in gear and floored the accelerator. Gravel spun out from the wheels, but the truck got moving in a hurry. It careened toward the field, and she aimed it at the paths two of the monsters were making in the dry corn. They were the only two close enough together she could get them both at once.

A quick glance Zach's way told her he'd taken care of the first monster, leaving it in gory pieces on the ground. A second one sprang from the corn, shooting its barbs as it went. Zach's body arched as he dodged the spray, but his shoulder lurched backward as one of the spikes hit its mark.

Oh, crap. That couldn't be good.

Lexi pulled herself back to her driving just as the front bumper hit the first monster, followed closely by the second. The truck jumped into the air a couple of feet, and she heard a popping hiss come from at least two of the tires as the barbs punctured them.

A loud sound, like hail hitting the truck's roof, ricocheted from below. Three of those nasty spikes shot up through the floorboards only inches from her feet, flew past her, and lodged in the truck's headliner.

Lexi shrieked, and instinctively jerked away from the

attack. Without her foot on the gas, the truck slowed fast, sweeping a wide swath of cornstalks beneath it.

She checked the rearview mirror, looking for signs of movement from the two she'd crushed. They were lying in wet heaps, twitching, but not getting up.

She shoved the accelerator down, pulled hard on the wheel, and turned the truck around for another pass. Frantically, she scanned the area where she'd last seen Zach and saw nothing—not even movement in the corn or the tip of his blade reflecting above the stalks.

Panic took a tight hold of her, hollowed her out, like she was floating just above her body. It seemed like it took forever to get the truck headed the right way.

Was Zach hurt? Dead?

The thought left her cold and shaking.

She steeled herself against what she was going to do next just as the deflated wheels crunched over the monsters' bodies. If they got up now, she knew it was time to run.

Lexi pulled the truck to a stop, worried that Zach might be hidden in the corn. Lying broken and bleeding. If she hit him, she'd never be able to live with herself.

She left the truck running and jumped down from the cab. A wet, dripping sound came from beneath the truck, but she told herself that it was just condensation from the air conditioner, not squishy bits of monster guts.

Weaponless and desperate, Lexi pushed her way back to where she'd last seen Zach. The corpses of two monsters were lying there, slowly leaking thick, black blood into the soil.

Zach was nowhere to be found.

"Zach!" she yelled. She didn't even care if any of the people left in the steakhouse heard her. The Defenders and her mother had always told her they had to keep all this monster stuff hush-hush, but she didn't give a shit about that right now. She needed to find Zach.

She called his name again, but got no answer. Then she thought she heard something. A deep moan.

Lexi stopped in her tracks, letting the rustle of cornstalks settle around her.

There it was again. It was definitely a moan.

She moved toward it, chanting Zach's name, praying he was okay—better than he sounded.

He wasn't. His big body was sprawled on the ground, his sword lying a few feet away. Blood wet the shoulder of his T-shirt. She couldn't see the barb, and didn't know if it was embedded in him, or if it had gone all the way through. His dark skin was shining with sweat even as his body shook with chills.

"Zach," she breathed as she went to his side.

He opened his eyes and the pupils were tiny pinpoints of black. Not a good sign. "Go, Lexi. They can smell my blood. More will come."

"You're nuts if you think I'm leaving you here. We're leaving together."

She pulled on his good arm, trying to get him up onto his feet. Man, he was heavy, but she managed to get her shoulder under his and, with his help, she got him up. He was wobbly and she gritted her teeth against the strain of keeping him up. The man was packed with heavy slabs of muscle and probably weighed twice what she did.

If she didn't get him into the truck while he could still help, she never would.

"Sword," he said, sounding almost panicked.

"Leave it. You can get another."

"No!" He veered toward the thing and Lexi had no choice but to help him get there or let him fall. Apparently it was too important to leave behind.

She steadied him with one hand while she picked the weapon up, but had nowhere to put it. Frustrated, she shoved it under her arm and pinned it to her side, praying she didn't slice one of them open on the wicked blade.

Satisfied, Zach cooperated with her again and they headed for the truck.

"That's it," she panted under his weight, grateful she was no pansy. "We're almost there."

"Not going to last much longer," he told her. "Poison."

"The hell you're not. Just tell me what to do."

They made it to the truck and she propped him up against it while she fumbled to open the passenger door. She got it open; he went in headfirst, collapsing on the seat, but it was good enough.

Lexi tossed the sword on the floorboards at his feet, shut the door and ran around the truck. She was going to be driving on the rims, but that was just too bad. No way was she sticking around long enough to fix the tires and see what else showed up.

"Duct tape," whispered Zach.

She had no idea why he wanted it, but she didn't stop to ask stupid questions. "Where is it?"

"Box. Under the seat."

She found it and was already pulling up the end. "What do I do with it?"

"Tape my wound shut. Throw the shirt out as a diversion. The blood."

Right. They could smell it.

Lexi went to her knees on the seat and pulled hard on Zach's T-shirt. He hissed in pain, making her stomach turn, but she didn't slow down or try to be gentler. Now wasn't the time for gentle. Or slow.

The shirt came off, soaked with blood and sweat. She used it to wipe away the trickle of blood leaking out of the puckered wound. She couldn't see if the barb had gone through or not, but she needed to stop the bleeding, so she used a strip of tape to bandage him up, covering both the front and back of his shoulder. It was going to hurt like hell coming off, but they'd deal with that later. Assuming they lived long enough.

"Throw the shirt out the window. If they don't fall for it, throw me out."

Lexi squelched the surge of panic rising inside her. "Not going to happen."

He reached for the door handle, but Lexi hit the power lock button and it didn't open for him. He tried to operate the switch on his side, but his fingers were shaking so hard, he couldn't seem to make them work. He slumped back on the seat and his arm fell limp at his side.

Lexi put the truck in gear and headed for the road. Zach's shirt was in easy reach, ready for her to throw out, but she wasn't going to do it this close to the restaurant. She didn't want to draw more monsters here where all the nice, defenseless people were.

Both front tires were flat and she had trouble steering, but she managed to get them three miles down the road. The shirt went out the window and she kept on going.

Zach was making low, pained noises, but he hadn't said a word to her in several minutes. He was lying limply on the seat, sliding around whenever she took a turn. She reached over and pressed her hand against his forehead.

He was burning up.

A sick, helpless fear rose up inside her. This was just like when Mom had died. She'd found her too late. There was nothing she could do. Lexi had been a teenager, lost, alone and afraid.

She couldn't go through that again. This time, she had to do something to stop it.

Keeping one eye on the road, she felt over Zach's hot skin until she found his waistband and the cell phone clipped to it. She knew Helen's number by heart. She dialed it as she checked the gas gauge. Only a quarter of a tank left and they weren't making good time. The engine was screaming, but the missing tires were really slowing them down, making progress difficult, even with power steering.

It took Helen several rings to pick up. "Hello." She sounded winded and her voice was faint with fatigue.

"Helen. Zach's in trouble. He's been poisoned."

"Oh no."

"What do I do?"

There was a scratching sound on the line.

A man's voice came over the phone, strong and confident. Drake. "Lexi, are you safe?"

The question startled her. She hadn't expected to be talking to Drake, nor would she have thought that her safety would be the first thing on his mind.

"Yeah, but Zach's not."

"Tell me what happened."

Zach let out a deep moan and Lexi gripped the wheel harder. "It was some kind of porcupine thing. A spike went through Zach's shoulder."

"Only one?" asked Drake.

"I think so."

"Is he conscious?"

Lexi swallowed hard to ease the tightness in her throat. "Not really. He's sweating and shaking."

"Don't panic, okay? We're going to fix him up, but I need you to stop his bleeding."

"Already did. He had me duct tape over his wound."

"That'll work," said Drake. "Where are you?"

"Kansas. In his truck."

"What town?"

"I don't know. He took me to a steakhouse out in the middle of nowhere." She couldn't remember the name and started to panic all over again.

Drake must have sensed it in her voice. "It's okay, Lexi. I know the place, but you can't stay put. You have to keep moving."

"I am, but the front two wheels of his truck are out, and we're nearly out of gas."

She heard him utter a vile curse, but it was muffled, like he'd covered the mouthpiece, not wanting her to hear. "It'll be fine. Someone will be nearby who can help. Just stay off the main roads so you don't get pulled over by police, okay?"

"Yeah. I can do that." She hoped. "Can you figure out where the closest hospital is?"

"Human doctors can't help him, but give me two minutes and I'll find someone who can."

Before she could answer, Helen's voice came back on the line, full of mock cheerfulness. "Hey, Lexi. Drake went to find you help, but how about we catch up on old times while he's working on it."

It was hard keeping the phone to her ear while steering the truck, but Lexi needed the lifeline of her friend's voice to keep her steady. Too much was happening too fast. "How about you start by telling me why you sound so tired when I call. Don't they let you sleep?"

"I'm helping them rebuild a wall. It's exhausting, but necessary."

"I thought there were lots of burly men there. Let them do the heavy lifting."

"I'm not physically building it. I'm shoving a bunch of magic into it to make it stronger. Pretty cool, huh?"

Lexi wasn't sure *cool* was the word she'd use, but she didn't want to get into an argument over her opinion about it right now. "If you say so. Did you pack up your stuff like I asked?"

"No. Lexi, I—"

"If you can't talk, I understand. Just say something mundane and I'll get it."

"It's not that. I'm free to say whatever I like. I just think you might have gotten some wrong ideas about these people somewhere along the line."

"They're making you say that, aren't they?"

"No." Helen let out a weary sigh. "Listen, it will be easier to talk in person once you're here."

"Assuming I make it that far."

"You will," said Helen. "I see the leader of the Sentinels across the yard. He's already on his phone, likely calling in men from all around you to come help. They won't let you down."

The idea of a bunch of men like Zach closing in on her was more than a little daunting. She could barely keep her head about her with one big, sexy Sentinel. More than one was going to be too much to handle. "Don't. I don't want a bunch of people hunting me."

"They're not hunting you, Lexi. They're going to help."

Lexi remained unconvinced. At least if she knew help was on the way, she could leave Zach somewhere where his people would save him. She didn't have to stick around.

"Oh, hold on a sec," said Helen. "Drake's back."

He came back on the line, his deep voice filling her ear with calm confidence. "Ronan is going to meet you at a Gerai house near where you are. He's like a doctor. He can help Zach, okay?"

Lexi wasn't sure if she could trust anything Drake said, and she was even less sure she wanted this Ronan person near her. The good news was that if it was only one man, Lexi would have no trouble leaving while he was busy helping Zach. She'd find a way to swipe the man's keys and head to Dabyr by herself.

Lexi straightened her spine, and hoped she wasn't making a huge mistake. "Just tell me where to go."

Chapter 9

Grace barely managed to get the heavy tray through the door of the suite without spilling it. There was enough food here to feed at least three Theronai, but she only cared about getting one of them to eat.

Torr.

He'd stopped eating more than a week ago and no amount of logic or begging had worked to change his mind. She was done playing nice. There was no way she was going to watch him slowly starve just because he wanted to die.

Grace wasn't ready for that yet, and probably never would be.

Joseph Rayd, the leader of the Sentinels, was in there with him when she entered, speaking in low tones. Neither of the men noticed her entrance.

"No," said Joseph, his voice hard and unyielding. "It's too soon."

"It's my life. My choice. If I still had working legs, you'd respect my wishes." Torr's angry plea made Grace's stomach clench hard.

"I'm not sending you to the Slayers to be murdered. You still have enough leaves left to last you two or three years."

"Two or three useless years. I can't fight. I'm draining away precious resources we don't have to spare. Do you have any idea how much blood the Sanguinar have wasted on me?"

"It's not a waste, damn it. They'll find a cure to this thing. Just give it more time."

Torr was silent for a long moment. "I hurt too much, Joseph. You'd think that because I'm paralyzed that it wouldn't hurt anymore, but the pressure keeps building. I can't even exert myself enough to relieve it."

"What about meditation?" asked Joseph.

"I've tried. It no longer helps."

Grace heard the pain choking him from across the room and had to bite her lip to keep from rushing to him and offering whatever meager comfort she could.

"I'll send Tynan to you," said Joseph. "He can inject you with his blood and help ease the pain, if only for a while."

Torr shook his head slightly. "No. I can't go that way. I'm going to die sober so everyone knows I was in my right mind."

"You're not going to die at all. I order you to eat until we find a cure."

Torr pushed out a scathing laugh. "You're really reaching, man. Just let it go. I have."

Joseph placed a hand on Torr's shoulder, even though Torr couldn't feel it. "I won't give up on you. You need to know that."

Grace decided that it was time to make her presence known before she overheard something she shouldn't. "I'm not giving up on him either."

Joseph looked at her, and hurried over to help her with the door. To Torr, he said, "I see I'm not the only one with your best interests at heart." He gave her a gallant nod. "Good evening, Grace."

Grace averted her gaze, feeling the sudden urge to curtsy. Of course, had she done that, she would have dropped the tray full of food, so she settled for bowing her head. "Mr. Rayd."

"Joseph. You can call me Joseph like everyone else here."

No, she couldn't. The man had earned a place as the head of a powerful group of people. If anyone deserved her respect, it was him. "Thank you," she whispered, keeping her eyes down, tracking his hands.

She knew he'd never hit her, but some habits were harder to break than others. Learning to dodge fists was one of them.

Joseph held the door while she moved inside, easing away from him. "Since you're here, I'm going to go see to my work. Thank you for taking care of him."

"You're welcome," said Grace.

Joseph left, leaving Grace alone with Torr. "How are you tonight?" she asked him.

"Go away," came his gruff voice from the living room. His back was to her. He was staring out into the night, watching the slow progress of the broken wall being rebuilt in the distance.

"I brought you dinner," she told him, keeping her voice carefully neutral.

"Piss off."

Grace ignored his rudeness and grabbed a TV tray to set her load on.

He didn't even spare her a glance.

She stepped in front of his wheelchair and crossed her arms over her chest. His long body was strapped in, keeping him upright. He didn't look healthy at all. He was a little thinner, of course, but that wasn't what bothered her. It was the dark circles under his eyes and the dullness in his skin and hair that had her worried. They hadn't been there earlier this morning when she'd come by to check on him before work. He'd really given up on living.

His amber eyes slid over her body from head to toe and back. Everywhere his gaze touched heated more than a little. As much as she hated to admit it, she liked the way he stared at her like she was something he should dip in chocolate and lick clean.

Coming from another man, it might have intimidated her, but not Torr. He couldn't hurt her. He couldn't even move, and she felt completely safe with him.

"Lasagna, chicken alfredo or pepperoni pizza?" she asked him. He had a weakness for Italian food and Grace was not above using that weakness shamelessly.

He said nothing, but his eyes slid past her, dismissing her to look out his window again. Beard stubble shadowed his jaw and she made a note to give him a shave before she left tonight. The idea of having a reason to touch him was too appealing to resist.

An impatient sigh built up in her chest, but she refused to let it out and let him know he was getting to her. Patience and stubbornness were the key here and Grace was armed with plenty of both.

She pulled up a chair in front of him and took the lid off the first dish. Steam from the lasagna wafted up, filling the room with the scent of fresh roasted garlic. She put a bite on the fork, but rather than bringing it to his lips as she had countless times before, she ate it herself.

Torr blinked in surprise, but said nothing. She heard his stomach rumble beneath his loose sweats and it was all she could do not to cry.

He was letting himself die—the only man who'd ever made her feel safe. A rarity like him wouldn't come around more than once in a lifetime, and she wasn't going to let him go without a fight.

"Anything new on rebuilding the wall?" she asked to break the silence, then took another bite.

"No. They should have been done by now, though."

"There isn't enough manpower. Or womanpower, as

the case may be. They can only go as fast as Helen and Gilda are able."

Torr's mouth tightened, and his jaw clenched. She could practically feel him aching to go help his brothers, and wished there was something she could do to ease him. No matter how long or hard she thought about it, nothing came to her. She couldn't heal his spine, or make him walk again, and that was the only thing he wanted.

She took another bite, though swallowing it was hard. Her throat was tight, and she had to fight the tears that seemed to well up inside her whenever she saw Torr hurt.

He eyed the tray, then gave her a knowing look. "It's not going to work. I've made up my mind. Joseph won't give me an honorable death, so I'm choosing this one."

"You're giving up too soon," she told him. "It's only been a few weeks."

"If the Sanguinar were going to find a cure for me, they would have done so by now. All I'm doing is wasting valuable blood when it's needed elsewhere. I even offered to let Tynan bleed me dry, so at least I'd be of some use, but he refused."

"You're worth saving." This time, she couldn't stop the tears from stinging her eyes. She turned away so Torr wouldn't have to see her weakness.

"I've had enough, Grace."

Her name on his lips sent a shiver running through her. His voice was low and gentle, void of the scathing anger that she'd become so accustomed to.

"But what about the rest of us? We're not ready to give up on you."

"Will you ever be? It's easy to have hope when you're not the one locked inside this chair all day and night. You don't know what it's like."

"No, but I'd take your place if I could."

His voice hardened with anger. "I wouldn't allow that. No one deserves this fate. Especially not you."

Grace sniffed quietly and tried to be subtle about wiping her eyes on her sleeve. She had to hold it together. She was only making things harder on him and she didn't want that. He had enough to bear.

She went to him and knelt in front of his chair. "Please, Torr. Give it some more time."

He looked down at her, his gaze sliding over her face in an almost tactile way. "I've lived longer than you ever will. I've spent my life fighting evil and being useful. It's time to let go."

"But there may be a woman out there who can save you—one like Helen or Andra." Just the idea was enough to make Grace's stomach knot with jealousy, but she ignored that selfish reaction. She wanted him to get better, even if it meant he never looked at her again.

"If there is, I'll never find her. And even if I did, who's to say it would do any good? I was poisoned, Grace. My spinal cord practically melted where that slug thing attached itself. You don't just fix something like that."

"You don't know that. You're guessing."

His mouth flattened. "Why do you care so much?"

Grace had to look away. She couldn't let him see the truth in her face—how easily she'd fallen for him. How much she loved him. "You helped save my life."

"I don't see you hanging with Iain or Alexander, and they were both there that night, too."

"But they don't need me," she whispered.

"Neither do I, Grace." His words hit her like a fist and she barely heard the rest of what he said. "I'm beyond needing anyone. All I want now is to be left to die in peace."

She grabbed his hand and pressed it to her cheek. It was cold and limp and lifeless, but she held on to it, needing him to touch her, even if he couldn't feel it. "Just give it another few weeks. For me."

She watched him swallow, his throat moving as if suddenly dry. "You don't need to feel guilty. My injury wasn't your fault."

"It was at least in part. If you hadn't saved me and my brother, you never would have been in the position to be poisoned by that thing."

"I don't blame you."

"Of course not. You're a good, noble man. You're better than that."

"I'm not as noble as you think I am," he said.

She didn't believe it for a second. "You keep telling yourself that if you want, but you're not going to convince me."

"Damn it, Grace! I'm not some kind of hero."

She flinched at his harsh tone, but held her ground. "Yes, you are."

His cheeks darkened and his eyes lit with something she'd never seen before—something dangerous and hypnotic. "No, I'm not. And if I could move, you'd know that for a fact because I would have already had you in my bed."

Shock filled her lungs, making her dizzy. She grabbed his knees to steady herself and looked up at him, floundering for a hold on reality. "You mean . . ." She couldn't even finish the sentence. The idea that he'd want her was too ludicrous to even consider.

"Sex. I mean sex, Grace. I would have used your convenient case of hero worship to get between your legs. I would have fucked you and gone out to fight the next battle—find the next conquest—before you'd even had time to wake up and know I was gone."

She shook her head, making her curls sway around her face. "I don't believe you. You're just saying that to scare me away so I'll leave you alone."

"Wanna bet?" he asked. "I'm not a real man anymore, but I bet if we got creative, I could still make you come with just my mouth. That might be something worth sticking around for."

Oh God. Grace's insides vibrated and her skin felt like it was being zapped with an electric current. She had to get away—put some space between them.

She was halfway to the door when she realized what he'd done, and came to a dead stop. He'd been trying to scare her away. He'd meant to make her run and it had nearly worked.

Grace closed her eyes and prayed for strength. She didn't know if he'd meant any of what he'd said, or if it had all been a game, but she was going to call his bluff.

She locked the door and closed the bolt so no one could walk in, then crossed the room and pulled the curtains shut over the sliders.

"What are you doing?" asked Torr.

Her body was quaking inside, and a fine sweat had beaded up over her back, but she was going to do this. She couldn't let him die.

Her fingers went to the buttons on her shirt. "I'm going to give you what you want," she said, proud of how her voice was sure and steady.

"What the hell is that supposed to mean?"

The first button popped free and she saw his eyes lock on her hands. "It means I'm going to let you . . . do that to me." She couldn't even say it. She wasn't strong enough. "I'll take off one item of clothing for every bite of food you eat."

"What is this, some kind of joke?"

"No joke."

"Stop it, Grace."

Another button opened.

"Don't you want to play?" She had tried to sound seductive, but had no clue if she'd pulled it off. She'd never undressed for a man before.

"No." It was weaker and less emphatic than before.

Her hands stilled. "Does that mean you don't want to see me naked?" she asked.

His jaw bunched, but he didn't look away. Nor did he deny it.

Grace slid her fingers down to the next button. It popped free and she opened her shirt enough that he could see the edge of her bra. It wasn't fancy or lacy, but Torr didn't seem to mind. He seemed more interested in what it covered.

She stepped closer and leaned forward. Her breasts weren't huge, but they were big enough that she was used to men staring. She'd never liked it quite as much as she did right now, watching Torr's pupils widen and his cheeks darken with desire.

He was getting into this, and heaven help her, so was Grace. She felt a small thrill of power course through her, but even more than that, a sense of victory. She could see it in his face. She'd won.

"One bite and the rest of the shirt comes off," she coaxed.

"Fuck," growled Torr. "You can't do this to me."

"I can and I am." She forked up a bite of lasagna and put it to his lips. "Open wide."

He gave her one angry glare before his eyes were drawn back to the vee of her shirt. Then he opened his mouth and ate the food she'd offered.

Good to her word, Grace freed the rest of the buttons and slid the fabric from her shoulders.

She thought it would make her feel dirty, or like some kind of whore, but instead, all she felt was relief. She'd gotten him to eat and that was what really mattered.

Torr watched her move, his face a mixture of anger

and lust, and some desperate kind of hunger she'd never seen before.

He nodded to the tray of food and then his eyes fixed on hers. "More, Grace. I want more."

Grace was down to her bra and panties when Torr finally came to his senses. It wasn't easy, either, because she was built like his favorite wet dream. Her breasts were full and round, as were her hips, yet she still had a small waist that made him wish for his hands to work just long enough to feel her skin. All her soft curves reminded him of the women he'd lusted after in his youth, centuries ago, before magazines dictated how a woman was supposed to look. Her legs weren't miles long, but they were just the right length to wrap around his hips and hold on tight while he thrust inside her.

Not that he was ever going to be that lucky. She was almost naked, standing in front of him, and his dick couldn't be bothered to even notice, much less react. His mind was totally primed and ready to go, but his useless body just sat there, mocking him for his inability to act.

Angry regret hit him hard, and he wanted so much to let this fantasy play on—to let her finish what she'd started and make him feel like even a fraction of the man he'd once been.

But he couldn't do this to her. She was too sweet and kind. She didn't deserve to be turned into his whore.

And that was exactly what he was doing to her. He was forcing her to strip, paying her in meager bites of food. All because she didn't want him to die.

"Enough," he told her as she reached behind herself to unfasten her bra. "Stop."

Grace stilled in that awkward position. "I won't go back on my word, Torr."

"I know. I want you to stop."

A pretty blush slid over her skin, rising onto her cheeks. She tried to cover herself with her arms, as if she was suddenly ashamed of her beauty. "Why?"

"I can't let you do this out of some sense of duty," he told her. "It's not fair to you."

"Duty?"

"You feel like you owe me. You don't. Please, put your clothes back on. I'll eat."

Torr had never seen anyone dress as fast as she did. If he'd had any question about whether or not she was doing this because she wanted to, he knew now she wasn't. Not that he was surprised. Why the hell would anyone want to get naked with a cripple like him? Grace deserved a real man—one who could give her whatever she needed. One who could keep her safe from the Synestryn who wanted her blood.

She sat down between him and the tray of food. She was still blushing and she wouldn't meet his gaze. Not that he blamed her after humiliating her like that.

"What would you like next?" she asked in a wavering voice.

"Ice cream," he told her. He knew she didn't have any on that tray and he wanted to give her an excuse to leave. He guessed she wouldn't come back, either. She'd send someone else and he'd never see her again.

It was probably best that way. If she did come around again, he wouldn't be able to think about anything but how beautiful she was standing in front of him, nearly naked. He'd think about it, and she'd see him thinking about it, and be embarrassed all over again. All that was left for them was awkwardness and he didn't want that for her.

One way or another, he wasn't going to live much longer. Eventually, Joseph would see there was no hope and give him his death. The less attached to Torr Grace was when he died, the better it would be for her.

"Okay," she said. "I'll, uh, be right back."

"I'll be here," said Torr, knowing she had no intention of coming back ever again.

The man Drake sent to heal Zach was waiting for Lexi when she pulled up to the tiny house. Had Drake not been with her on the phone, giving her turn-by-turn directions, she never would have known anyone lived this far off the beaten path.

The house was run-down, tiny, maybe twenty feet along each wall and already brightly lit. Beside it was a black van, and on the cement steps leading into the house stood a tall, lean man. As Lexi turned, and the truck's headlights hit his face, she got a good look at him.

He was gorgeous—the kind of man that made women stop thinking and start stripping. His pale eyes seemed to throw off bits of icy blue light as the headlights hit them. His mink brown hair was swept back from his wide forehead in an artful wave, and his long black leather trench coat waved slowly in the summer breeze. He started toward the truck before she'd finished parking, and his movements were smooth, almost glidingly graceful.

Lexi killed the engine just as he opened Zach's door. "I'm Ronan," he announced as he pressed his pale hand against Zach's head and another against his bare chest. The large tree tattoo covering Zach from his left shoulder to somewhere well below his waistband seemed to sway as he breathed. The branches were bare from what Lexi could tell, and her mother's journal had warned her to be wary of men marked like this. They were dangerous predators—killers walking around in human suits.

"I'm Lexi," she told Ronan as she got out of the truck to help. As heavy as Zach was, Ronan was going to need her help now that he was totally out of it.

Ronan shifted Zach's body to the edge of the seat.

"Drake said the Synestryn that injured him had quills. Is that right?"

"Yeah."

"Do you know how many hit him?"

"Just one, I think. I don't know if it's still in there."

Ronan nodded. "Let's get him inside and check it out." Then he lifted Zach out of the truck like he weighed nothing.

Sickening fear rose up in Lexi's gut, making her suck in a breath. Ronan wasn't human.

These people were not her friends. They'd killed her mother. They'd kidnapped Helen. They wanted her blood.

Ronan arched a perfect brow at her. "Open the door for me?" he asked.

Lexi shook herself and nodded. She had to play along. Pretend to be nice, unsuspecting prey. Right up to the point she triggered the detonator.

Then again, maybe just getting Helen and Miss Mabel out would be enough. Lexi wasn't a killer or a soldier. She wanted no part of this war. All she wanted was to be left alone in peace.

Of course, to get that peace—to earn it for all of the humans out there who had no idea what was really going on—she had to kill those who hunted her. If she was ever going to be free to stop running, she had to make a stand. It shouldn't matter to her that her enemies were gorgeous men who pretended they wanted her to be safe. It was all just an act.

Wasn't it?

I just think you might have gotten some wrong ideas about these people somewhere along the line.

That was what Helen had said. She seemed sure that Lexi was the one who was wrong, and she'd been living with them for more than a month.

But what about Mom's journal? What about all those

lessons about how the Sentinels used humans for sport and food? Mom had seemed sure, too.

Lexi wished she could say the same.

"Are you squeamish?" asked Ronan. He had a rich, deep voice—cultured, like he'd been raised outside of the States, or in some fancy boarding school.

"Not particularly."

"Good. I'm going to need your help." He laid Zach down on the only bed in the house.

"Sure. Need me to get something out of your van? Medical stuff?" she asked. All she needed was his keys and she was out of here.

Ronan looked up at her, his gaze so intense, she felt like he'd taken hold of her face and wasn't letting go. "Do you think I'm a fool?" he asked.

"Because I'm offering to help?"

He stood, towering over her. Lexi was used to it, and refused to feel intimidated. As far as she was concerned, being shorter only meant it was easier to reach out and twist his balls, leaving him in a heap on the floor.

"I know who you are, Lexi Johns. Everyone does. Zach has been chasing you for weeks. I'm not going to let you flee and have him coming after me when he wakes."

Busted. Time for plan B. All she had to do was come up with it. "So he *will* wake up."

"It depends."

"On what?"

"On whether it was one or two quills that hit him."

That news left Lexi reeling. "Are you saying that's all the difference there is between him living and dying?"

"That, and my intervention."

"Then what the hell are you waiting for? Doctor him already."

"Not until I know you'll stay put while I do." He gave her a small smile—one that made him so pretty, she forgot to breathe. "Shall I bind you physically, or would you prefer to give me your vow to stay here?"

Lexi took an involuntary step back. The idea of him tying her up or locking her in a closet made her sick. "I'm not letting you touch me."

"Then give me your word you'll stay here until I'm gone, and not try to run."

"Sure," she lied, just to get him to back off. "I'll stay."

When she felt a sudden pressure fall upon her body, pinning her in place, she realized her mistake.

Never promise them anything. They can bind you to their will.

Her mother had warned her and she hadn't listened. Now it was too late.

Ronan's smile widened. "First time making a promise to one of your own kind?" he asked.

Lexi couldn't respond. She felt trapped and helpless. She wasn't like them. She was human.

"Don't worry," said Ronan. "It gets easier."

Lexi seriously doubted it.

"Fix him," she said through clenched teeth.

He gave her a little formal bow of his head. "Of course, my lady."

Chapter 10

Madoc wished he was anywhere else but standing beside Nika's bed. He had no business being here, but Andra had claimed Nika had asked for him.

She'd asked and he'd practically broken the land-speed record getting back to her side.

So much for his good intentions to keep his distance.

Madoc stood there, stiff and uneasy, unsure what to do now that he was here. He should never have come.

Nika barely made a lump in the bed. Her white hair had been washed and brushed until it shone, and it was fanned out around her head. She was thin, fragile, almost ethereal. Breakable. If he got too close, he was sure he'd accidentally hurt her.

Andra looked at him expectantly, like he had all the answers.

"What the fuck do you want me to do?" he asked

"I don't know. Just sit with her and hold her hand, I guess."

"I'm not touching her," he told Andra.

She ground her back teeth in frustration. "Fine. Then just sit your ass down until she wakes up again."

Oh, no. He wasn't going to be locked into babysitting duty. He had sgath to kill. He was up to seventy-two kills so far this week. If he had anything to say about it, he'd exterminate the fuckers from the face of the planet before year's end.

Maybe then Nika would be okay.

"I can only stay a few minutes," said Madoc.

Andra's jaw clenched and her mouth tightened like she didn't want to spit out the words. "Your safety was the first thing on her mind after being unconscious for more than a week. I'd think you could be a little more caring."

No, he couldn't. Caring was for men with souls. His was shriveled up. Only the frigid black ring he wore kept the last leaf on his lifemark from completing its fall. That leaf hung in stasis over his ribs, frozen midfall. His lifemark was bare. His soul was as good as dead. He didn't care about anything anymore but killing and fucking. And Nika wasn't good for either of those.

Still, he'd made an oath as one of the Band of the Barren—the secret, invitation-only group of Theronai that kept those with bare trees like him from being discovered and sent to their deaths. He'd promised to pretend he was still one of the good guys so none of them would be discovered. If one of the Band was outed, he knew every Theronai alive would be searched for signs of treachery. The fake leaves tattooed on his lifemark wouldn't fool anyone looking too closely. For now he had to play the part as he'd promised Iain he would. He had to act like he would have before his soul had died.

It was either that, or let them send him to the Slayers to be murdered along with all of the other brothers in the Band.

Not a fucking chance.

Madoc let out a long sigh, and eased himself onto the edge of the bed. Nika's body shifted toward the depression in the mattress.

He tensed, worried she'd bump into him and get bruised or something. But she didn't. She didn't even touch him, which was for the best. At least that was what he tried to tell himself.

Andra looked at her watch. "Joseph said that three more Theronai reported back here to come see Nika. They should be here soon."

"Fine. Let one of them play babysitter."

Andra's long body flopped into a chair and she covered her face with her hands. She looked tired, and Madoc had a split second of worry for her. Odd.

"I hope to God one of them is compatible with her. Tynan says it might save her, restore her sanity."

Madoc's stomach clenched against a punch of jealousy. He didn't want any other Theronai near her, as stupid as that was. He wanted to be the one to save her, which was utterly ridiculous. He'd been near her for long enough to know it wasn't going to happen.

In fact, based on the speed at which his ring was losing its color—its life—he was out of time for miracles of any kind. Even if a compatible woman walked through the door right now, it might not be soon enough. Once the colors were gone, he wouldn't be able to bond with anyone, compatible or not. He'd be broken, a wasted shell of what he was born to be.

"What? No empty words of hope?" asked Andra. Her eyes were shut, like she was too tired to bother keeping them open.

"Hope is for people who haven't pulled their heads out of their asses far enough to see reality," said Madoc.

"Ah. An optimist. Lovely." She let out a wide yawn.

Madoc snorted. "Go take a nap. I'll stay until the others get here."

A knock sounded on the main door of Paul and Andra's suite. "Looks like you're off the hook," said Andra. "They're here."

She left the room and was gone longer than he'd expected. Maybe she was interviewing them or something.

Eventually, she came back with a trail of three Theronai behind her. Each one had a smear of blood on his shirt from where he'd given Nika his oath to protect her.

She looked a little green, and more than a little uneasy as she stepped aside and let the men see Nika.

Madoc knew all of them, of course. He'd been fighting by their sides on and off for several centuries. That didn't mean he trusted them. Not around Nika. He was going to stay put until they left.

Or until one of their rings started reacting to her.

Just the idea was almost more than he could stomach. He clenched his fists and stood from the bed. He didn't want an up-close view of the show to come.

Nika let out a small whimper, so low he wasn't sure Andra had heard it. If so, she made no reaction.

Madoc frowned and held himself back from going to check on her. He could see the even rise and fall of her breathing from here. That was going to have to be good enough.

"Gentlemen," said Andra. "This is my sister, Nika."

The hopeful, reverent looks on their faces made Madoc want to pound his fists into something. How dare they look at her like that—like she was already theirs?

Neal stepped forward first. He still wore his leather jacket, likely fresh from the hunt. His dark hair was dusty, and there was a smear of dirt on his cheek. He hadn't even bothered to take a fucking shower before coming here.

Fucker.

He looked at her with eyes that glittered with intelligence. A laugh line at the corner of his mouth deepened as he smiled. He reached out toward Nika's bony, frail hand and it was all Madoc could do to stay on his side of the room.

He wanted to sweep Nika up in his arms and take her

away from all this. She was too weak to have these men pawing at her.

Neal watched his ring as he took her limp hand in his. Madoc watched, too.

Nothing happened. His ring's colors stayed fixed.

Nika whimpered and pulled her hand away.

Madoc let out a long sigh of relief and Andra's sharp gaze met his. "Problem?" she asked.

"No," growled Madoc, giving her his patented *fuck off* scowl.

"Anything?" she asked Neal.

The man's face fell, wiping out all signs of laugh lines from his face. "Nothing."

Andra nodded once, and motioned for the next man to step up. This one was Morgan Valens, womanizer extraordinaire. He didn't waste time, simply walked up and stroked his dark-skinned hand over Nika's cheek.

Madoc was going to have to kill the fucker for touching her so intimately. His hand was on his sword, ready to do just that when Morgan stepped back, almost stumbling away from her.

Nika's eyes popped open and stared at Morgan in horror. A high, pained sound rose up from her throat, and Madoc crossed the space to her side. Before he realized what he was doing, he was sitting on the bed and had pulled Nika practically into his lap.

She saw him and her clear blue eyes filled up with tears. "You came back," she said and buried her face against his neck.

Morgan shook his head, looking like he'd seen a ghost or something. "I don't know what that woman is, but she's not for me."

"How can you be sure?" asked Andra. "She had some kind of reaction to your touch."

"Not a good one. Believe me."

Andra put her hand on Nika's arm. "Nika, baby, are you okay?"

Nika's arms went up around Madoc's neck and she hung on tighter. When she didn't respond, Andra said to Madoc, "Check and make sure she's not hurt."

Like he was some doctor. Shit.

Madoc didn't know how to dislodge Nika without touching her, and if he touched her, he might hurt her, too.

As carefully as he could, he tugged her away from his neck and checked her face for damage. "Did that fucker hurt you?" he asked.

Nika's skin was red and a welt had risen where Morgan had touched her. She nodded her head, her eyes bright with tears. "Yes."

Madoc was going to have to kill him. There was simply no way around it.

Morgan's usual smile was nowhere to be found. "I'm so sorry I hurt you, Nika. Truly. I won't touch you again." He left the room like it was on fire and Madoc was glad to see him go.

Neal gave Nika one last longing look, and then left right behind Morgan.

Samuel Larsten stepped forward, his eyes fixed on Nika. Madoc had to squelch the urge to curl his body around Nika and hide her from his sight.

"Maybe I can help," said Samuel in a quiet, smooth voice. "I'd very much like to help you, Nika."

Her body quivered against Madoc's. He could feel her bones poking him wherever they touched. She was weak. Fragile. He wanted her to rest and heal.

Despite what Madoc wanted, Nika needed to find the man who was meant to protect her. For all he knew, that man was Samuel.

He reached out toward her. His left hand was covered in burn scars, making his ring almost glow clean and pristine in contrast.

Nika looked at his hand and sucked in a breath.

"Ugly, huh?" asked Samuel with a self-conscious smile. "Sorry about that."

"I don't want you to hurt me," she told him.

"I don't want that either. If you want, I can come back later," said Samuel.

Nika's throat moved as she swallowed nervously. Her fingers found Madoc's hand and she squeezed hard. The skin where Neal had touched her was red, too, and he thought he could see small blisters forming along her delicate skin.

Samuel looked past Nika to Madoc. "Your touch doesn't seem to hurt her. Are you sure she's not yours?"

Madoc said nothing. Instead, he held up his left hand, showing Samuel his faded ring.

Samuel's face blanched and he gave a short, curt nod. "I see."

He saw Madoc was out of time, and yet he didn't gloat or show even the smallest sign of relief. A spark of respect for the man lit up inside Madoc. If Nika was going to end up with anyone besides him, he wanted it to be a man like Samuel.

"Give him your hand, Nika," urged Madoc.

"No." She curled her legs under her and scooted farther onto his lap.

"He's not going to hurt you."

"The others did," said Nika.

Andra looked from Samuel to Nika with that same kind of hope he'd seen in the men. Madoc wasn't privy to everything Tynan had told Andra about Nika's condition, but it was clear she thought this was Nika's best shot, which meant it probably was.

Andra's voice was soft and quiet. "We need to find out if he can help you."

"I don't want his help," said Nika.

"But you need it, baby."

"I don't want to force you," said Samuel. "I'll come back a little later, okay?"

"No, no, no," said Nika. "Not later. Just do it."

Nika held out her hand and her body tightened as she cringed against the pain she thought was to come.

Samuel brushed the tip of his finger over her hand and Nika jerked back. His mouth turned down in a resigned grimace. As they watched Nika's skin darkened and turned a bright, angry red. This time the blisters came fast, bubbling along her skin as if she'd been burned.

He said to Nika, "Guess I'm not going to be able to help you. I'm truly sorry for the pain I've caused you, my lady."

Not as sorry as Madoc was. He knew this was just the beginning of her suffering. More men would come every day now that they knew she was here. They'd all want to touch her. Hurt her.

"This isn't going to work," Madoc told Andra.

Andra gave him a tight nod. "Apparently not. I'm going to go talk to Tynan. Can you stay here with her?"

"I've got things to do."

"More important things than making sure Nika doesn't try to wander off?"

"I thought you didn't trust me," said Madoc.

"I don't. But Nika does."

"I'm not letting you leave me again," said Nika. She sounded tired, worn out from her ordeal with the men. She didn't whine or beg, she simply said, "I need you."

Fuck. How could he say no to that?

"Fine," Madoc told Andra. "I'll stay, but only for a little while. Hurry the hell back here, or get Grace."

He felt Nika smile against his neck, the soft skin of

her cheek stroking his skin, his luceria. Andra shut the door, closing them alone in the room together.

Madoc tried not to panic. He wasn't going to hurt Nika. He was going to be very careful and make sure he didn't make any mistakes. All he had to do was sit here and let her hold on to him until she fell asleep.

It didn't take long. Her body relaxed and he eased her back under the covers where she belonged. Then, he moved the chair to the farthest corner of the room and sat his ass down.

He itched to go back to her, but he didn't dare. She was safer with him all the way over here. The farther he stayed away from Nika, the better it would be for both of them.

It took almost an hour for Ronan to finish whatever the hell it was he'd done to Zach. He'd sent Lexi to burn all the bloody tape and bandages, and when she came back, she realized that Ronan had been drinking Zach's blood.

An odd kind of fascinated disgust held her in place. She stood in the doorway, staring. Ronan lifted his mouth from Zach's wrist and there was no blood, but there was something different about Ronan now. His skin had a healthy flush to it and his face didn't seem quite so gaunt as before.

Ronan stripped his heavy trench coat from his body and rolled up his sleeve. He took a syringe out of his medical bag and slid the needle into his vein.

"Zach's the sick one here," said Lexi.

Ronan pulled the plunger out and the empty syringe filled with a pale yellow liquid. That glowed.

"Holy shit! What the hell are you?" she asked before she could think twice about it.

Ronan gave her an amused grin. "A Sanguinar."

Vampire. Mom's journal had dozens of pages going

into detail about how dangerous the Sanguinar were. They could hypnotize their prey with a single glance and drain their blood in mere seconds. They had long, sharp claws and fed on the pain of their victims.

And Lexi was trapped in this house with one of them.

Her heart kicked hard and she backed up, slamming her head into the doorframe.

"I suggest you get ahold of yourself, little girl," chided Ronan. "Zach doesn't have time for you to be afraid."

"I'm not afraid of you," she lied.

Ronan rolled his eyes. "Don't lie to me. I can hear your heart racing."

He could read her thoughts, too. Mom had said so.

Oh God. What if he knew what she was planning—that she was going to blow them up? What if he'd already read her mind? She was so dead.

"Get over here, Lexi. I need you to help me hold him down."

"Why?" she asked, hoping to stall for time to figure a way out of this mess.

"Because I'm getting set to inject him with the antidote to his poison and he's not going to like it. It hurts."

"It didn't hurt when it was inside of you."

Ronan crossed the small room in two steps. His eyes glowed with angry blue light, and his jaw was bunched with frustration. "Yes, it did. And it made me more than a little cranky, so I suggest you start cooperating."

He grabbed her arm and tugged her bodily back to the bed and pushed her down so she was sitting on Zach's legs.

"Try to keep him still," said Ronan; then he injected that glowing yellow stuff into Zach's arm.

The reaction was immediate. Zach thrashed and a scream of pain tore from his lips. Lexi's heart jumped into her throat and she bit her lip to keep from crying out in response to his pain.

Zach kicked, and she had to scramble to position herself so she wouldn't get hurt by his powerful body. Ronan had practically draped himself over Zach's torso and seemed to be holding him down with little effort. Lexi wasn't so lucky. She kept Zach from hurting either of them, but that was about it. Her ribs were going to be bruised from his struggles.

After what seemed like half a year, the violent reaction subsided and Zach settled back onto the bed. He was sweating and shaking and making pitiful, agonized sounds that made her stomach clench in sympathy.

"Can't you do something for him?" she asked.

Ronan fetched his coat from where it had fallen on the floor and pulled it on. "I've already done what I can. I'm not strong enough to ease his pain, too."

He was so flipping casual about it, Lexi wanted to scream. "There has to be something you can give him."

Ronan pinned her with a bright, hungry gaze. "There is one way. You could give me your blood. That would allow me the strength to ease his pain."

He wanted her blood. Just like her mother had told her. Fear closed in around her, thickening the air with its stench. She had to get away before it was too late.

Lexi backed up, stumbling over the leg of the bed. "Not a fucking chance, vampire boy. Stay back."

Ronan held up his hands, palms out. "As you wish. Let him suffer. I don't care."

"I thought you were his friend."

An amused, almost condescending smile played at the corner of his full mouth. "We Sanguinar have no friends. You would do well to remember that."

"Then why did you help him?"

"Because I need him to survive. Just as he needs you, young Theronai."

Lexi refused to believe she was one of them. It was just one of the tricks they used to ensnare unsuspecting humans. She was smarter than that. She knew the score. "You're wrong."

One second he was on the far side of the room; the next, he was right in front of her, holding her face in his chilly hands. His touch was gentle, but she felt his restrained strength vibrating through his arm. She feared that if she flinched, he'd break her neck.

His eyes flared with a burst of light, and Lexi felt herself falling. He was so pretty. She could stare at him forever.

"That's right," he whispered. "Just let go. I've got you."

She didn't want to do that. It was dangerous; she just couldn't remember why.

From somewhere far away, she heard Zach's low moan of pain.

"He needs you, child," said Ronan. "You need to go to him now. Soothe him. If he lives through the night, he'll recover fully. You should help him."

Yes. Zach needed her. "I don't know how."

"Your presence. Your touch. Bare skin on bare skin."

She could do that. Even more, she *wanted* to do that.

"You can touch him all you like. Anywhere you like," said Ronan.

Just the idea was enough to make her insides go liquid with need. Zach was laid out for her enjoyment. She could run her hands over him and no one would ever know.

"Perfect," purred Ronan. "Such a good girl."

His praise warmed her and made her feel giddy. Something wasn't exactly right here, but whatever it was, it couldn't be that important. Not as important as listening to Ronan and staring into his eyes. And certainly not as important as getting her hands on Zach.

"You'll stay here tonight and call me if his condition worsens, won't you?"

The urge to nod was strong, but she held back. She couldn't stay. She had to run. She didn't know why, but she knew it was important. "No. I have to go."

"Not tonight. It's safe here tonight."

Lexi wasn't sure, but surely Ronan wouldn't lie to her. "It's safe?"

His thumb stroked the side of her face and the light in his eyes glowed brighter for a moment. "Yes. And you'll be with Zach so you can touch him."

Safe and touching Zach. That sounded nice.

Ronan had to leave the house before he took Lexi's blood against her will. She smelled so sweet, so pure. He was sure that the power thrumming through her veins would be rich and intoxicating.

And he so desperately needed that strength. He was tired. Hungry. His insides were twisting against the emptiness no normal food could ease.

He needed blood. Lots of it. He needed a rich source so he could replace the power that healing Zach had depleted. A source like the woman inside that ragged little house—the one he had mesmerized so easily with his gaze.

She would have given him anything if he'd taken only a little more time with her. He could have had her blood as well as her body. She was such a pretty, almost pixie-like woman that the idea was more than a bit tempting.

Too bad Lexi wasn't human. If she had been, he would have fed from her without regard to her wishes. But whether or not she believed it, she was a Theronai. Protected. If he fed from her against her will, he'd be practically declaring war against her people.

That couldn't happen. The Sanguinar needed the blood of the Theronai too much to risk alienating them.

But not for much longer.

Project Lullaby was going well. It was only a matter of time before the Sanguinar would once again be free to do as they pleased—before they would once again be the strongest of all the Sentinels.

Ronan wasn't sure whether he should look forward to that day, or fear it.

Hunger twisted Connal's belly. He could smell his food nearby, smell the fear shimmering out from her where her captor hid her in the darkness.

The alley where Zillah had chosen to meet was a dirty stretch of pitted asphalt in downtown Kansas City that reeked of human garbage and greasy rain puddles. Most of the lights here had been shot out, leaving conveniently deep shadows. Not that Connal needed the light. Even as weak as he was, he could still see through the stifling darkness to where Zillah waited.

"Come closer," he hissed, his vocal cords vibrating like razor wire strung too tight.

"Not until you show her to me," said Connal. He was too hungry for Zillah's games, nearly wavering on his feet with his need for blood.

Zillah shoved the woman in front of him, taking no more care for her comfort than he would have for that of a used newspaper. She stumbled, but Zillah's iron grip held her on her feet.

She was young, perhaps two decades old. Her dirty hair hung limp around her gaunt face, stiff with tangles. He didn't know what color it would have been had she been clean, but now it was a dull, dirty brown, falling nearly to her hips. Her arms and neck were riddled with angry red marks where others had fed from her and not bothered to heal the wounds. A glazed, wild look filled her eyes, though she never quite met Connal's gaze.

How long had she been a prisoner of the Synestryn? Had she ever known freedom? Or had she been born into their hands?

Not that Connal cared. As long as her veins were full, nothing else mattered.

He moved forward, gliding over the rough ground, hoping she'd look at him for just a moment. That was all he'd need to ensnare her, trap her gaze.

"You've done well," said Zillah. "The wall surrounding Dabyr crumbled as you said it would."

"And yet Sibyl remains with us. You failed to keep her." After the chances Connal had taken, that failure scraped against his too-thin patience.

Zillah shrugged, and his movement shifted the frail woman. "There will be other opportunities. We're patient."

But Connal wasn't. He needed to feed. He needed to feel this woman's blood sliding down his throat, filling his belly, drenching him with its power. He wasn't going to make it to sunrise without her, and waiting for Zillah to give him the necessary permission was driving him mad with impatience.

"Her bodyguard is still unconscious."

"Perhaps you should be the one to tend him. Feed from him and finish what we started."

"I can't act so openly. You know that. If I'm discovered, they won't simply kill me. They'll strip my mind to pieces searching for your identity."

"I'm not ready for that to happen yet," said Zillah, as if he'd already considered allowing it to happen. "I have another task for you."

"No. Not until you've let me have her. I need to feed."

The woman stood listless inside Zillah's grasp. Even when Connal spoke of drinking her blood as so many others clearly had, she displayed no reaction.

Zillah tossed her toward Connal, and if he hadn't caught her, she would have simply crumpled to the street like so much garbage.

He held her by the shoulders, feeling the frail bones beneath his hands, smelling the stink of her unwashed body. She looked up at him then, and he could see now there was no life in her hazel eyes, only bleak acceptance. All that remained of whatever she had once been was a hollow shell of flesh.

Connal wanted to feel pity. He wanted to be the kind of man who would whisk her away and save her, but he wasn't. He was too desperate for that. Too hungry.

He laced his fingers in her matted hair, pulled her head back to bare her neck and bit deep.

Sweet, perfect power flowed over his tongue, making the hungry beast within him roar in triumph. Her pulse pounded in his ears, against his lips, a steady counterpoint to the frantic gulping sounds rising from his throat.

His food struggled weakly, but he held her still, taking his fill, knowing it would never be enough, even if he drained her dry.

"Enough," he heard Zillah hiss, too close for safety. "You'll hurt the child."

Child?

Connal's food was wrenched from his arms, spilling precious drops of blood down her neck as well as his chin. He scooped up the mess with his fingers and licked them clean.

Zillah slid his too-long finger over her open wound and her skin closed beneath his touch, stopping the flow.

Connal shook himself, trying to clear his head of the

blood haze fogging his thoughts. Power streaked through his body, burning him from the inside out.

Rage welled up inside his chest. He wanted to pound something to the ground, to grind it under his heel until nothing remained. The need for violence twisted within him until he was reaching toward the woman, toward Zillah.

"Stop," was all he said, and that single command, nearly a whisper of sound, froze Connal in place.

A slow, steady smile bared Zillah's sharp teeth. "I see our alterations worked. Lovely."

"What alterations? What have you done to me?" demanded Connal.

Zillah slid his hand over the woman's belly. His gray skin stretched over his fingers, giving the extra joint on each digit a deathly quality. "She carries my child. My weapon. You drank his blood and now you're mine."

"I was already doing what you wanted. You didn't need to resort to this."

"Didn't I? I could smell your sympathy for the woman a mile away. It was only a matter of time before you did something rash. Now, I no longer need to worry."

Connal tried to move, but his body refused to respond. It was as if he was a toy and only Zillah had the remote control. "There must be something you want. Just tell me and let me go."

"There is," said Zillah. "You're going to take a box back to Dabyr for me."

"What's in the box?"

Zillah smiled. "The Theronai's death. This lovely little creature will hunt and incapacitate their women, making them appear dead. You will declare them dead and bring their bodies to me."

"I'll be caught and killed."

"Then you're of no use to me and you may as well die."

Meaning Zillah would kill him. Or worse, stop feeding him.

Panic seized Connal, making his words come out rushed and breathless. "I'll find a way."

Zillah's smile widened, baring his sharp teeth. "For your sake, I hope so."

Chapter 11

Lexi shook herself, trying to get rid of the drugged feeling that fogged her brain. Ronan had done something to her. She was sure of it.

Anger flared bright in her gut, burning off the remaining fog that plagued her.

That bastard. She was going to kill him for fucking with her mind like that—or at least twist his nuts until he wished he was dead. Then she'd make him undo it. Whatever *it* was.

She rushed out to the living room and through the front door just in time to see him get behind the wheel of his van and drive away. She got as far as the bottom step before that same sickening, itchy feeling she'd gotten from the bracelet swarmed over her, making her skid to a halt. Her insides twisted and she clutched her stomach in an effort to figure out where to scratch. Nothing helped.

The need to go back inside overwhelmed her. With a frustrated shout, she turned around.

Defeated, Lexi shut the door and leaned her head against the inside of the cool wood.

She was no match for these men. She had no magical powers and hardly any knowledge of what they were capable of. That had been made crystal clear when Ronan had tricked her into promising to stay here.

Just until Ronan was gone, which he was now.

She could leave. At least she thought she could.

Lexi peered out the window, looking for any signs Ronan was still nearby. It was dark, but she saw no glow of headlights in the distance or plume of dust from his passage over the gravel roads.

He was gone. Could she go now, or did her vow still hold her captive?

Lexi opened the door and stepped outside, bracing herself for that awful feeling. It didn't come. She took another step and it still didn't come. She was halfway to the truck and feeling fine.

She could leave now and be free. The keys were in her pocket. The money Zach gave her was in her suitcase. She could make it last a long time—go into hiding where not even Zach would find her. She'd splurge on a new tattoo to cover the bloodmarker that had shifted farther down her back, and he'd never be able to find her. She would take the map revealing the location of the Sentinel compound back to the Defenders and let them deal with saving Helen. Heaven knew they were better equipped to handle something like that than she was.

But what about Zach?

She wasn't even sure he was going to live through the night, and even though she'd planned on being the one to kill him just yesterday, something had changed. She couldn't leave him here to die. Not if there was anything she could do about it.

So, what now? Was she going to patch him back up so that the Defenders could kill him? So *she* could?

Lexi rubbed her hands over her face in frustration. If Zach had been like Ronan, this whole mess would be a lot simpler. But he hadn't. He'd been kind.

He'd given her money so she could survive on the

run. He'd taken the bracelet off her wrist, releasing her so she could flee to safety without him. He'd gone out to face those monsters rather than let them attack the people in the restaurant.

Those were not the actions of an evil killer. They were the actions of a caring, protective man.

Maybe Zach was the one Sentinel worth saving. Lexi had to follow her instincts and take the risk that she was wrong. She'd never be able to live with herself if she didn't at least try to save him now so she could find out if he'd lied.

Of course, nothing in Mom's journal helped her when it came to dealing with monster poisoning.

Bare skin to bare skin.

It was probably some kind of trick Ronan was playing on her, taking advantage of her ignorance. But for what purpose? It wasn't like he stuck around to laugh at her when she fell for his trick.

Lexi went back into the house and stood beside Zach. His body was bathed in sweat; his chest was bare except for the large tree tattoo. Even from here, she could see the branches swaying in time with the wind outside. His muscles stood out in hard ridges, fighting the pain that poison or the antidote was causing him. The wound on his shoulder had closed up, but it was still an angry red pucker marring his smooth brown skin.

Even with the wound, his body was beautiful. Touching him would be no hardship.

He shifted on the bed and a deep sound of pain welled up from his lips. He was hurting and she had to make it stop.

Bare skin on bare skin.

Maybe it wasn't a joke, but some way of getting her to go along with whatever nefarious plan they had. If so, it was probably going to work. The idea of standing there while he suffered made her sick.

Lexi wet a cloth in the sink and went to Zach's side. She wasn't sure if she was wrong about him or not, but she was sure that she couldn't sit by and do nothing.

She sat on the edge of the bed and pressed the cloth to his face, wiping away the sweat. He sucked in a shocked breath and his eyes fluttered open.

A look of relief so intense she could feel it heat her skin crossed his face. He reached up with a trembling hand and touched her cheek. "You're safe," he whispered.

Lexi tried to give him a reassuring smile. "Perfectly safe. So will you be, once you get a little rest. Ronan patched you up."

His hand fell to his chest as if he were too exhausted to hold it up. "Tell me you didn't give him your blood."

"Nope. I'm keeping it all."

His eyes closed again and he let out a long breath. "Good. You're safe."

Just like that, he was back asleep again, leaving Lexi reeling. He hadn't asked if he was going to be okay. His sole concern had been for her.

That kind of selflessness was not like any version of evil she'd ever encountered. In fact, even good, decent people would have at least inquired about their condition. But not Zach.

Maybe Helen was right and Lexi had been wrong all these years. Or maybe his concern was some kind of act meant to confuse her.

Lexi didn't know what to think anymore. She was tired of being afraid. Tired of being confused and alone. One way or another, she was going to get to the bottom of all of this or die trying.

With a deep breath for courage, she lay down next to Zach and pressed her body alongside his. She hiked up the front of her shirt so her bare tummy touched his side, and draped her arm across his chest.

A weightless warmth sank into her skin, giving her a sense of utter contentment. Whatever it was about him that made her insides sing was still working, and she was glad for the momentary diversion from reality.

Her stomach was full, no one was chasing her and she had a gorgeous man in her arms. As far as she was concerned, that was as close to heaven on earth as it got.

Zach woke up to a need so intense he could hardly breathe. His skin felt too tight, and brittle, like it would rip apart if he dared to fill his lungs. His body was on fire, his blood pounding hot and hard through his limbs. His dick throbbed, aching to feel the slide of Lexi's body as he filled her. Only she could ease him, but she never did.

He'd been dreaming of her again. Hot, fevered dreams that left him shaking and sweating, on the verge of paradise, but never reaching it. He couldn't touch her in his dreams. She taunted him, swinging her hips and blowing him a kiss as she ran away. He couldn't catch her even though he knew she was running into danger.

He called her name, but no sound came from his lungs, only hot, desperate breaths of air that left his chest bellowing under the need for more oxygen.

Zach rubbed his eyes, trying to rid himself of the heavy sleepiness that plagued him. His elbow brushed against something soft draped over him.

Lexi.

She nestled beside him. He didn't need to open his eyes to know that. He could smell the sweet, fresh scent of her body and feel the soft cushion of her baby-fine hair on his chest. Her skin was cool against his, drawing away some of the heat scalding his insides.

His arms were weak, but he forced them to curl around her and hold her close. He couldn't let her leave him. Not ever.

She yawned and pushed herself away from his body,

robbing him of the cooling comfort of her skin. He tried to stop her, but he wasn't strong enough. The poison had left him helpless and hurting.

Lexi pressed her wrist against his forehead. "You're still hot. Let me get you some aspirin."

"Won't help."

"It can't hurt."

"Please, just come back down here," he told her through clenched teeth.

"Then at least let me get a cold cloth. It can't be healthy for you to be so hot."

She started to move off the bed, but Zach grabbed her wrist, stopping her. "No. Stay."

She frowned at him, then said, "I'll only be a second."

He couldn't let her go, not even for that long. He needed to feel her skin on his. All of it. Her touch was the only thing that could cool his blood.

Zach used a surge of strength to pull her onto the bed, then pinned her under him. The effort left him panting in exhaustion, but at least he had her where he wanted her, where he needed her.

"Let me up, Zach." Her tone was hard and cold.

He didn't listen. Instead, he shoved her shirt up over her breasts and pressed his bare chest against her body. Her bra irritated him, but he wasn't sure she'd let him take it off, too. In fact, the way she was wriggling under him, he wasn't sure she was going to stay put for long.

"You feel so good," he told her. "Your skin is so cool and soft."

He pressed his cheek to hers and couldn't resist the urge to slide his hands down her sides. He felt the subtle contours of her ribs, the narrow span of her waist, and finally, the gentle swell of her hips where they were bared by her low-rise jeans. Everywhere he touched, hot ribbons of power fled his body, sinking into hers. It felt so good, his head spun, and he started to shake.

Lexi went still beneath him and her voice was filled with apprehension. "What are you doing?"

"Just need to touch you," he whispered.

He buried his nose against her neck and filled his lungs with her scent. Sweet. Clean. His.

He had to taste her. Just a little.

The tip of Zach's tongue slid out, barely grazing her skin, but it was enough to go to his head. She tasted of salvation and woman and something else he couldn't name. Something powerful and elusive that belonged only to her.

Lexi shivered beneath him and her hands snaked around his waist and clutched at his back. "What the hell is happening?" she asked him in a soft, almost fearful tone.

Was he hurting her?

Zach pushed his head up so he could look at her face and make sure. He didn't think he'd survive moving away from her, and his arms were shaking like crazy, but if he was hurting her, he'd find a way to leave her alone.

He saw no sign of pain on her face. Her eyes were closed and her lips were parted. Her head was angled to the side, giving him better access to her neck. A deep flush painted her skin a rosy pink and he could see her pulse racing in her throat.

"What do you feel?" he asked.

"You're so warm. It's . . . sliding inside me and I can't make it stop."

"You're not supposed to try," he told her.

"But it feels too good. It's got to be some kind of trick."

"No trick. Just let go." He was hard and aching, his erection pressing painfully against the confines of his clothing. He wanted them both naked, stripped of all the barriers that separated them so he could take her properly and give her the kind of pleasure that would bind her to him forever. But he wasn't strong enough yet to keep her from running, and if he tried to strip her, his skittish Lexi would definitely bolt.

Every moment he spent touching her made him stronger, even as it drove him closer to losing control. If he could stay awake just a few minutes more, he'd have everything he wanted.

A wave of heat mingled with his power rose up inside of him and washed out over them both. Lexi sucked in a shuddering breath, pressing her breasts against his chest. The breath came out as a low moan of pleasure and Zach nearly came just hearing it.

"You're so good," he told her. "So soft." He stroked the side of her face, but his hands were clumsy and he feared he'd poke her in the eye. Instead, he settled for splaying his fingers through her baby-fine hair.

"I shouldn't let you do this," she said. "It's not right." Her voice wavered with uncertainty.

"I need you, Lexi." The words were all mangled. He was getting so sleepy, he could hardly support enough of his weight to keep from crushing her, so he rolled over so they were on their sides, facing each other, his arm clamped around her.

She licked her lips. "You need a doctor."

"I need your touch."

"Bare skin on bare skin," she whispered. "That's what Ronan said."

"To bleed off the heat," he realized.

"It's not working fast enough."

"It'll work," said Zach, even as he felt himself fading fast. He'd been poisoned before, and it took a while to recover. That was all. He refused to die and leave Lexi alone and unprotected.

He could hardly keep his eyes open anymore, even though he loved the sight of her so close to him. He could see a scattering of freckles over her cheeks and the way the skin between her eyebrows puckered whenever he said something she didn't want to hear.

"Are you sure?" she asked, finally looking into his eyes.

She was so beautiful he thought his heart would beat its way out of his chest. He'd never tire of looking at her, not if he was lucky enough to have her by his side for millennia.

"Yeah."

"How can you be sure?"

"Because I'm not dying until I get to kiss you."

Lexi watched Zach's eyes shut as he lost the battle against sleep. She thought it would help her relax to no longer have him looking at her like she was his salvation, but it didn't. Her body was tense, humming with some kind of weird energy she'd never felt before—like she was mainlining a Red Bull or something.

She smoothed his hair back from his face, enjoying the silky feel of it sliding through her fingers. He was such a handsome man, in a rough, dark way—nothing like pretty boy Ronan. Stubble shadowed his wide jaw, which was clenched in pain, even in his sleep. Her pale fingers glowed against his brown skin as she traced her fingertips over his cheek and across his lips.

Zach moaned, low in his throat, and the arm he had wrapped around her tightened. She probably should have pulled her shirt down, but the feel of his body on hers was too good to resist. Everywhere his skin touched hers, she felt his heat and power soaking into her. It was almost intoxicating.

Maybe he was drugging her, making her pliant to his plans. If so, she wasn't even sure she cared anymore. She'd never felt more alive. More *needed*.

It was a potent thing to be needed. She'd been alone for seven years now, roaming the countryside, with only herself to think about. Before that, it had been just her and Mom, and Lexi had been the needy one.

But the tables had turned and she was now important to someone else. Vital. She wasn't just rattling around the countryside, letting the years roll by while she kept hidden and alone.

In fact, lots of people needed her. Not only Zach, but all the Defenders were counting on her.

To kill.

Lexi's stomach gave a hard heave of nausea and she scrambled off the bed toward the bathroom. She made it to the toilet, but nothing came up. She just knelt there, on the cold tile, trying not to think about what she'd agreed to do.

It had seemed like such a good idea. A righteous quest to slay the dragon.

But now that dragon lay sleeping in a room only a few feet away, letting out low grunts of pain because she'd left him. He wasn't a terrible beast like she'd thought. He was a man—or at least close enough to one that she could no longer see quite so many differences.

Confusion and indecision had never been problems for her before. She needed to ground herself, to remember what was important and what she trusted. What was real.

Mom's journal. Lexi needed to reread it, regroup and resolve herself to the path she'd chosen—all while staying close enough to Zach to ease his fever, just in case he was what he seemed.

With any luck at all, she'd find some clue in those pages as to why Zach didn't seem like the monster she'd once believed he was. And if not . . .

If not, then Lexi was going to have to suck it up and grow a thicker skin. She couldn't let the Sentinels keep killing people and ruining their livelihoods, no matter how good one of them made her feel.

Chapter 12

Nika fought against the tug of the monsters, steeling her mind against the strength of their call. She didn't want to be with them tonight. She wanted to be with Madoc, in her real body, and revel in the fearlessness surrounding him.

When she was close to him, she wasn't afraid. She felt almost normal. Madoc strengthened her with his presence.

But he didn't want to be with her. He'd made that clear when he'd left her while she slept. He'd left and he hadn't come back.

The idea of sleeping alone frightened her. She needed him to keep the monsters from pulling her apart while she slept. Why didn't he understand that?

Andra came into Nika's room just as she finished pulling a big sweater over her head. The sweats she'd borrowed from Andra hung low on her bony hips and pooled around her ankles, but they helped keep her warm against the chilly air-conditioning inside Dabyr.

She was feeling stronger—hungry for the first time in what felt like years. She'd already had three meals since she'd woken, but was ready for another.

"It's time," said Andra. "The men are waiting for you."

Nika had only regained consciousness for a handful of hours, but since then, seven Theronai had come to see her. To touch her.

She tried not to be afraid, but without Madoc here, it wasn't easy to fight off the pain and panic of so many strangers pawing at her.

"I'm not going to let them touch me," she told her sister. "It hurts." The blisters from the last batch still hadn't healed.

Andra's mouth tightened. "I know it does, but it's the only way to be sure. They're good men, Nika. They don't mean to hurt you. In fact, one of them may be able to help you."

"I don't want their help." They weren't Madoc.

Andra looked down from her impressive height, giving Nika that look of desperate concern she'd come to know so well over the last eight years. "I know, but there's no other way."

"Please, don't make me do this." Panic started leaking into her stomach, driving away the hunger under its crushing weight. Nika couldn't stand the hands of the men on her. They all wanted something from her, and she felt their desperation sink into her more with every touch. She'd just reclaimed enough of her mind that she was starting to feel whole again, and then all these men came along, each one of them wanting to take a little piece of her away with them.

They left her with slivers of their need and pain, shoved them into her skin like needles, so deep she couldn't dig them out.

Andra sat down on the bed next to Nika and took her hand. Andra's fingers were long and strong and capable, unlike Nika's bony, weak fingers.

She wanted so much to be strong like Andra. To know what was real and what wasn't. To be able to stay inside her mind and not be flung across space into bloodthirsty monsters until she no longer knew who she was.

Andra stroked the back of her hand in a soothing circle. "I hate doing this to you, baby. I really do, but Tynan is convinced that the best thing for you is to find your Theronai. Once you do, he can help you heal."

"Madoc is helping," said Nika.

Andra's jaw tightened. "I know. He's been out killing off sgath right and left and that's great, but it's not enough."

"How do you know?"

Andra looked away, toward the door like she wished she could escape. Her eyes darkened until they were the same rich sapphire color as the luceria around her neck.

Nika's hand went to her own throat, which was bare and bony, and she felt a sense of loss.

"Madoc has checked and double-checked. You're not compatible," said Andra.

"How can he be sure?" she asked.

"Believe me, baby. It's what he wants, too. All of the men want you to be the one who can save them, but it just isn't meant to be."

Nika refused to believe her. "If Madoc isn't meant to be mine, then why am I drawn to him? Why is he the only person besides you who makes me feel safe?"

Andra stroked Nika's hair back from her face and a wavering sheen of tears glittered in her eyes. "It's a trick of your mind, baby. Like all the others."

"And the blisters? Are they a trick of my mind, too?"

"I don't know. Maybe. But I don't want you to worry. We'll find the one who can help you."

Nika wasn't so sure. She was broken. She might never find the man who could give her the gift of magic.

And if that man wasn't Madoc, she didn't even want to try.

"I'll be right there with you," said Andra. "There are only two men this time, so it won't take long."

"I don't want to," said Nika. She sounded like a willful child, but she didn't care. She was tired of doing things she didn't like. Tired of having no choices. Everyone told her what to do. She was almost twenty-one and more than old enough to make her own decisions.

"We can wait until tomorrow if you want. They won't like it, but they'll wait for you. I'll tell them you're not feeling well enough to see them."

"No," said Nika. If she wanted people to start treating her like an adult, she was going to have to act like one. Do the hard things. "Let's just get this over with."

And then, once the pain subsided, she'd slip out of her body and go find Madoc. He wouldn't know she was there, watching him hunt, so he couldn't run away. It wasn't as good as feeling his body, solid and strong against hers, but if it was the only way she could be with him, then she'd take what she could get.

Angus answered the tentative knock on his door, expecting Joseph to be the one standing there, looking for a report on the progress on the wall. Not that there was much to report. The women were exhausted and progress had slowed almost to a halt. At this rate, they were going to be out there in the dead of winter, building the damn thing back up.

But, instead of Joseph, Tynan stood there, his beautifully gaunt face pinched with hunger and fatigue.

It was nearly dawn and from the looks of it, this was no social call.

Great. Just what Angus needed to end his shitty day. More shit.

"Need something?" he asked Tynan, standing firm

in the doorway so the man knew he was not welcome inside.

"Is Gilda still awake?" Tynan asked.

"No. You'll have to talk to her tomorrow."

"I don't want to talk to her. I need to talk to you. Alone."

Angus hid his surprise. "Why?"

Tynan's throat bobbed as he swallowed. His slender hand reached for the doorway as if to steady himself. "Please. It's important."

Angus wasn't about to wake Gilda after the day she'd had, so he stepped out into the deserted hallway and quietly shut the door behind him. "Okay, talk."

"I think I might have done it," said Tynan. "I think I might have found a way to cure your people's infertility."

Hope flared bright inside Angus, but he clamped down hard on the emotion before it could wake Gilda. Not only did she need her sleep, but he knew without a doubt that she wouldn't share his happiness at this news.

"Are you sure?" he asked, hearing the way his voice wavered with a mixture of relief and excitement.

Tynan shook his dark head and his eyes shut as if the motion made him dizzy. "No, I'm not. I need to test my theory on someone."

"Me. You want to test it on me, don't you?"

"It seemed the logical choice. The other men are newly bonded and may have issues with a child so soon."

But he and Gilda had been together forever. Long enough that Angus knew how she'd feel about having more children. Their sons had all been slain in battle, and although Sibyl was safe, she wasn't normal. And Maura . . .

A knot of guilt and grief closed off Angus's throat, making his voice come out as barely more than a whisper. "I don't know. It's been so long."

"Gilda is still fertile."

"That's not the point. I mean, I'm not even sure she would agree to have more children."

"Certainly she sees the need to repopulate our ranks."

"You've never had a child. You don't understand what it's like to lose one. Or more." Even after all these years, Angus still carried around the gaping wound in his soul the deaths of his children had left behind. He could think about them now and remember the good times they'd shared, but it had taken decades to get to that point.

And after having nearly lost Sibyl less than a week ago, the fear that it could happen again was fresh and raw.

"Please, Angus. At least consider it. I'll go to Drake or Paul if I must, but we're not even sure where their women came from yet. My cure may not work for their unions."

"Then why not start on one for them? Seems like it makes more sense, considering how there are twice as many of them as there are of me."

"You don't understand. I've put decades of work into this cure. Changing it now would cost us precious time we may not have."

"Things aren't all that bleak," said Angus.

Tynan swayed and gripped the wall. Angus reached out to steady him, but Tynan shook his head. "My people have hidden how bad things are. There's not enough blood left. We're all dying. If we don't find the cure soon, it's only a matter of time before we're all gone and there's no one left to heal your wounds. Your people will die, too."

Angus felt the burden of so many lives pressing down on him. "Even if Gilda did agree to have another child, she certainly wouldn't agree to letting you bleed the babe."

"Not for years, but eventually, that child will grow up and allow us the blood we need."

"Not all children grow up," said Angus before he could stop himself.

Sibyl, his daughter, hadn't grown since she was eight. Not since the night her last brother—his last son—had died.

Angus pushed the memory aside before it could consume him. He needed to think with his brain, not his heart.

"I know this is a big decision for you, but there's little time left for you to make up your mind. I'm running out of time. I must sleep."

He meant sleep, as in going to sleep for years as was the way of his people. It was how they preserved blood when there wasn't enough to sustain everyone.

"How long do you have?"

"Days. Weeks at most."

Angus ran his hand over his face, feeling the deep lines the centuries had carved there. Worry and danger and laughter had weathered his skin and left their indelible mark. Seemed he was about due for another few wrinkles.

"Okay. Let me talk to Gilda. I'll come find you tomorrow with my decision."

"Make the right one, Angus. Please." Then Tynan turned and walked away, using the wall to keep him on his feet.

However much pain and sadness Angus had had in his life, at least he wasn't alone like Tynan. He had Gilda. He had love. He had hope.

Tynan had nothing to look forward to but the oblivion of sleep—a means to escape his hunger. Somewhere along the way, Angus had forgotten what it felt like to be as desperate as Tynan was. Or maybe he'd never been that desperate. His life had been hard, but it had also been filled with blessings.

It was time to step up and give back some of the good life had offered him.

One way or another, he needed to convince Gilda to give up her grief and move on. Maybe in doing so, she'd be able to heal and forgive herself for the things which she couldn't change.

Maybe Gilda would even remember how to smile again.

Zach woke up just before dawn. His body ached, but he was no longer plagued by the blazing heat of the poison.

He was going to live.

A surge of joy rolled through him, and he felt the need to run and find Lexi so he could celebrate with her. Only, he didn't have far to go. She was lying on the bed, asleep with her head pillowed on an open book and her pale hand splayed over his dark chest.

Zach grinned down at her, letting the sight of her beauty fill him up with a deep sense of satisfaction.

She hadn't left him. She'd stayed right by his side even though he'd taken the bracelet off her wrist, allowing her to leave.

He had no idea how much sleep she'd gotten last night, so he didn't want to wake her, but she didn't look comfortable, so he eased the book out from under her cheek and tucked a pillow in its place.

Lexi made cute, sleepy sounds, but didn't wake. He covered her up and went to find some coffee to help clear the rest of the sluggishness from his head that the poison had left behind.

They had a big day ahead of them. With any luck at all, today was the day Lexi would agree to wear his luceria. After all, she hadn't left him. That had to mean she cared about him, right? And if she cared, she wouldn't leave him alone to suffer. He knew she wouldn't.

Zach set the book down on the kitchen counter, marking her place by setting the napkin holder on the open pages. He rummaged around in the cabinets until he had a pot of coffee gurgling on the counter, then went to the bathroom, took a quick shower, dressed and came back just as the last few drops were making ripples over the dark surface of the coffee.

He poured a cup, added a ton of sugar and sat down to enjoy his jolt.

The book was still open to the page Lexi had been reading when she fell asleep. It was handwritten, in tight, almost minuscule handwriting, so small he'd thought it was type when he'd first glanced at it. When he looked closer, he saw certain words were underlined, or boxed in. Frantic scribbles filled the margins, with arrows pointing to different passages.

He wasn't generally one to snoop, but if this was Lexi's diary, he wasn't going to be able to resist. He'd be able to peek into her mind as soon as they bonded, so it wasn't really snooping, anyway. It was just getting a jump on what he was going to see soon.

Zach started reading the entry, which was near the beginning of the book. It was dated twenty-three years ago.

They almost found us today. I hid us in a trash bin and the stink of rotting garbage masked our scent. Your scent, Alexandra. That sweet baby smell of your head that seems to draw the monsters to us.

You were such a good baby, too. You didn't cry. You just held on to my finger in your chubby fist like you knew the monsters were scaring me. How can you know that? You're not even a year old yet.

You're special, Alexandra. Your daddy told me you would be the night we made you. He said I had to protect you. Hide you.

If anything happens to me, you need to know that the Sentinels are going to want you for your blood. You can't ever stop running. They'll find you and they'll trick you and then, when they've convinced you they're not the bad guys, they'll suck out all your blood for their magic.

You can't ever let that happen. You have to keep running.

Zach's body went numb. Lexi would have been too young to write twenty-three years ago. She would have just been a baby. This wasn't Lexi's diary.

This was her mother's diary. Alexandra was Lexi.

It was no wonder that Lexi didn't trust him, that she'd stabbed him and run away when he'd first met her. She had been taught that the Sentinels wanted to kill her—that they wanted her blood.

Which, he had to admit, was partially true. The Sanguinar would want her blood, not that he'd let them have any of it. And even if they did get it, they wouldn't want to kill her. She couldn't feed them if she was dead.

Zach flipped the page and kept reading. It was more of the same. Page after page described how evil the Sentinels were and how many times they'd tried to kill Lexi and her mother. The book went into detail about what the monsters looked like and how to avoid them. Zach recognized the descriptions as Synestryn, not Sentinels. Of course, Lexi didn't necessarily know the difference.

She thought the Synestryn that had attacked them last night had been his pets. She didn't know any better, which begged the question, what else had she been taught that was totally wrong?

Zach shut the book and rose from his chair. Anger pulsed through him that her mother would taint her with lies like these, but he held it in check. He had no way of knowing why her mother had done it, and more important, the woman had kept Lexi alive all these years, protecting her when he couldn't.

Lexi didn't need his anger. She needed him to straighten her out. As long as she had all these messed-up ideas in her head, she was going to be in danger, running from the only people who could keep her safe.

He turned, and she was standing in the kitchen doorway. Her eyes were puffy from sleep and her clothes were wrinkled beyond repair. The hair around her face was damp, like she'd just finished washing. She looked from him, to the book and back again and in that time, all the color drained from her face. Her dark eyes widened in fear and she sprinted toward the door leading outside.

Zach chased after her, unwilling to let her go. Whatever was going through that head of hers was wrong. It wasn't her fault, but he couldn't let her keep thinking those lies were true.

He caught her around the waist right as she jumped up into his truck. Her arms and legs flailed around, but Zach managed to keep her from hurting herself on the hard metal edges of the door. He got her away from the truck and sat them both down on the wet grass, holding her while she wore herself out.

"I'm not going to hurt you," he told her loud enough she could hear it over her enraged shouting.

"Let me go!"

Lexi clawed at his arms, but he held on. The sun had just broken free of the horizon and he had hours to patch up the cuts before the blood could draw any nasties.

Slowly, her fighting grew weaker and she sat in the circle of his arms, panting. Zach didn't dare let go. He didn't trust her not to try to run again.

"It's not true," he said, keeping his voice low and steady. He didn't want her to think he was angry at her, or give her any reason to believe he meant to harm her. "That was your mom's journal, wasn't it?"

"She knew all about you, but it didn't save her life." Lexi's body jerked with a silent sob and it broke Zach's heart.

"What happened?" he asked.

"She didn't take her own advice. She slowed down. Didn't run fast enough. Your pets caught her one night when I went to the store for groceries. I came back to the motel and all that was left was . . . pieces."

She shuddered against the memory, and Zach's arms tightened around her and he stroked her hair with his cheek. The comfort he offered was meager, but he didn't know what else to do. He knew better than to think he could fix this for her. Her mother was dead. No one could fix that.

"I grabbed her journal and my suitcase, and left. Thank God I had just gotten my driver's license and was old enough to drive."

How frightened she must have been. So young, all alone, on the run. If only she'd known the truth then, she could have come to live at Dabyr. He could have taken care of her and helped her move past her mother's murder. He could have taught her the truth slowly, while he still had time to be patient with her.

But she hadn't known the truth and she hadn't come to Dabyr. All she'd had to guide her was that journal full of lies.

Zach wanted to be angry at her mother for misleading Lexi, but he just couldn't. She might have been wrong, but at least she cared enough to do what she thought she had to to protect Lexi. And in a way, it had worked. Lexi was here in his arms, safe and sound, and she was damn well going to stay that way.

"I think we need to talk about the journal," he told her gently. "I read some of it, and there are a lot of things in there that are simply not true."

"Of course you'd say that," spat Lexi.

He ignored her venom. "Let's start with the part about how the Synestryn are our pets. That's flat-out wrong. They are our enemies. Monsters."

He could feel her listening. Her body went still and her head turned so she could hear him better. "Whatever it was that killed your mother, it wasn't one of the Sentinels, nor was it done by our orders. We don't hurt humans. We protect them."

"Easy to say."

"But not always easy to do, I know. We fail sometimes, like we did with your mother. I can't tell you how sorry I am about that, but I swear to you that if I'd known either of you existed, I would have done whatever it took to keep you safe."

"You would have kidnapped us, like you did Helen."

"Is that what you think?" How could she be so wrong? Who had fed her mother these lies? Certainly not the Synestryn. Only a few of their kind could even speak, and those that could were so monstrous that no sane person would have gotten close enough to have a conversation of any length.

So where had the lies come from?

"Helen is safe back at home. You'll see once we get there that she's happy."

"Only because you drug her, like you try to do me when you touch me. Your skin is some kind of weapon."

A slow smile pulled at Zach's mouth. "Do you feel drugged when I touch you?"

"Yes."

"Is it nice?"

"No," she said, but he could hear the lie in the way her voice quivered.

He liked knowing he could make her feel good with his touch. He liked it a lot. In fact, he had to stop himself from sliding his palms over her bare arms. As much as he wanted to, he had more important things to think about—like clearing up the lies between them.

"It's not a drug, Lexi. I've been trying to tell you that since I met you. We're meant to be together. All you have to do is put my luceria on and you'll see the truth. I won't hide anything from you."

"I won't let you collar me."

Zach's back teeth ground in frustration. He knew that if she just looked inside his mind, she'd see the truth, but he couldn't get her to trust him enough to do it. He had more than twenty years of lies to erase—lies that were tied to Lexi by bands of loyalty to her mother. That wasn't going to be something easy for her to give up. He was going to have to be patient, but he didn't know how much longer he was going to be able to hold out.

Since he'd been near her, since she'd been absorbing small streams of his power when they touched, he hadn't been hurting nearly so much. He wasn't sure if that was going to slow down the rate at which his leaf was dying or not, but he knew that once it was gone, he could easily turn into the monster she thought he was.

And then what would he do? Or, more important, what *wouldn't* he do?

"What is it going to take to prove to you that I'm not lying?" he asked.

Lexi's head fell back on his shoulder in defeat. "I don't know, Zach. I want to believe you, but isn't that the way the devil works? Tells you pretty lies you want to believe? I can't do that to Mom."

"Are you going to try to run away again?" He still had the bracelet in his pocket. He could use it to keep her nearby if he wanted.

He didn't. He wanted her to stay near him of her own free will.

Her head moved on his shoulder as she shook it.

"No," she said quietly. "I'm done running. This is going to end now, one way or another."

Zach hated the sound of defeat in her voice, but he believed she meant it. She wasn't running anymore. "Good. Because if you stick with me, there's only one way things will go. You'll see the truth, and you and I will make each other happy for the rest of our lives."

"Pretty lies," she murmured.

"No lies, Lexi. I'm going to take you home and prove it. Come on. The Gerai brought us a new car, and we're only about four hours away from the truth."

He hated taking her to Dabyr before he'd claimed her for his own lady. There might well be other Theronai at home who were also compatible with her, and he didn't want to let her slip away again. But what he wanted wasn't as important as it had been only twenty minutes ago. He had to protect Lexi from herself as well as the Synestryn, and if that meant she ended up with another man, he'd just have to suck it up. At least she'd be safe. That was what really mattered.

If she did choose another man, it wasn't like he'd have long to suffer, anyway.

Chapter 13

L exi made mental notes of the location of the Sentinels' stronghold, just in case she needed to give the
Defenders directions via phone. It was set way back in
a thickly wooded, isolated area in Missouri, well off the
main highways. A few houses and farms dotted the surrounding area, but the fortress itself was shielded from
view by heavy bands of forest.

The compound had a high stone wall running all the
way round it. Or at least she thought it probably did. She
couldn't see the whole wall for all the trees that obscured
it, as well as a monumental building and a few smaller
structures. The main building was made of a pinkish-
grayish stone that sparkled under the late-summer sunshine. Huge wings, like welcoming arms, spread out from
either side of the structure.

Even though it was a refuge for demons and killers, it
was still a beautiful place.

They went through an iron gate that opened for Zach
only after he swiped his ID and talked to someone on
the other end of a camera. The paved driveway was easily half a mile long, and led to a gigantic garage filled
with numbered parking slots.

Zach pulled into one, and for a second, Lexi thought
her faithful old Honda was beside them. Of course, her

faithful Honda was still in the shop back in Texas, but she gave a wistful sigh of longing for her beloved set of wheels. Her home.

"Looks like they beat us here," said Zach.

"Who?"

"Vance and Slade. Your car must not have needed too much work."

Lexi looked at the Honda again. Primer gray, lots of rust, even more dirt. Yep, that was her car, all right.

"It's mine!" she shouted, jumping down from the truck.

Lexi picked up the keys from the front seat and got behind the wheel. She cranked the engine, and it started with a smooth purr that hadn't been there for years. In fact, it had probably never run this well since she'd owned it.

"From the sound of it, Nicholas has been getting his hands dirty," said Zach. "That man has a way with moving parts."

They'd fixed her car. These people who were supposed to be her enemy had repaired her home and brought it to her. It wasn't worth much—in fact, they'd probably put more money into repairing it than she could have sold it for—but it was the one constant in her life and she loved it.

Her vision went watery and she had to blink back hot tears before they could fall. "Thank you," she told Zach without looking at him. She didn't want him to see how much this gift had affected her. How vulnerable she'd felt without a means to run as she'd been doing all her life.

Those days were over—she'd meant that when she'd told Zach she was done running—but knowing she could if things turned ugly made her feel so much safer. Like life was back to normal.

And then she remembered the explosives in the trunk and all those feelings of safety and normalcy vanished.

"I didn't fix it," said Zach. "How about we go inside and find Nicholas. You can thank him yourself."

Lexi nodded. She couldn't speak right now, not with the lump of dread lodged in her throat. All she had to do was connect a couple of wires and push a button to detonate the C-4. The Defenders had made her practice how to do it over and over until it took her less than thirty seconds for the whole process.

And that included opening the broken lock on her trunk, which was a chore on the best of days.

Zach's fingers settled on her shoulder. They felt warm and strong and comforting, which was ridiculous. He should not be comforting her when she had the means of destroying his home and family. It was just wrong.

"Ready?" he asked.

Lexi gave a tight nod. "Sure. Just let me grab my suitcase."

Zach beat her to it. He slung his heavy duffel bag over his shoulder, grabbed the handle of her suitcase, and offered her his free arm. The whole time, he wore a proud smile, like he wanted to show her off.

A sick sense of guilt clung to Lexi's insides. It was stupid. He was her enemy, so planning to blow this place up wasn't a betrayal. The real betrayal was the way her resolve to do the job she'd promised to do wavered.

The Defenders had taken care of her and her mom since she was a kid. Whenever things got bad, Mom would go running to them. Neither one of them liked sticking around. Hector Morrow, the leader of the Defenders, was a raging asshole, but he was better than the monsters that hunted them. They'd stay long enough to get back on their feet and Mom would take off running again.

Lexi hadn't had much to do with them since she'd grown up. It was only after Zach had begun hunting her that she'd gotten desperate enough to seek them out. They'd taken her in and welcomed her back as if she'd never been gone, like she was one of their own. They'd gotten her the job with Gus and made sure she had a paycheck and a place to sleep every night. It was more than she'd had in a long time, and the fact that she was even thinking about not doing as she'd promised them was the worst kind of treachery.

They'd warned her about how easy she could be swayed. Her mother had warned her of the Sentinels' powers of brainwashing. She knew these risks, and yet she still questioned her objective.

Lexi took Zach's offered arm, reveling in the comforting warmth that flowed between them. Two days ago, she would have just as soon stabbed him as touch him, and now she couldn't seem to get enough of him.

It was all too confusing. She hated this uncertainty, the weakness inside her that made her question what was right and wrong. Even knowing this confusion was part of the Sentinels' strategy, she still couldn't shake it off.

She was weak. That was the real problem here. She'd never thought of herself that way until now. She'd always believed she'd be immune to their charms, but now she knew the truth. This wasn't something she could shrug off. No wonder Helen had been tricked so easily. She hadn't even had the benefit of a mother who knew the score.

Lexi had, and yet she was falling right into their trap.

"We'll put this stuff in my suite. Then I'll take you to see Helen while I go check in and find Nicholas," said Zach.

Lexi nodded, wishing she was a stronger person. How was she going to save Helen when she was being sucked down herself?

"Are you okay?" asked Zach.

She looked up at him, plastering a smile on her face. His eyes glowed with concern, his dark brow wrinkled.

"Fine," she told him. "Just a little overwhelmed."

"This place will do that to you. I guess I'm just used to it."

They passed through a hallway that led into a ginormous open area. The ceilings here were glass and so high up you could fly a kite inside. There were green plants and small trees growing everywhere, making the room feel almost like it was part of the outdoors.

Dozens of people sat at tables, eating lunch, chatting like they were spending the day at the mall. There were women and children here, too. Lexi hadn't expected to see kids.

She stopped in her tracks and took everything in.

"Who are all these people?" she asked.

"Humans, mostly. People we've saved from the Synestryn but who can't go back home."

They didn't have the look of prisoners. They seemed . . . happy. Kids lounged on couches at the far side of the room, watching TV or playing video games. A group of women was playing cards at one of the larger tables. Through the glass doorway on her left, she could see a bunch of people outside, working out on all kinds of exercise equipment.

No one wore chains or prison uniforms. No one looked sick or like they were starving. In fact, the smells coming from the dining area were making her stomach growl in anticipation.

Which left only one conclusion.

"You keep humans as pets?" she asked, appalled at the idea.

Zach let out a bark of laughter. "You're kidding, right? What is it with you and this obsession with pets?

If we want pets, we get cats and dogs like everyone else, though most of us are gone too much to have them."

"Then, why are there people here?"

"Because we couldn't clean away enough of their memories for them to go back out in the world safely. Several of them have little pieces of the Synestryn in their heads, and it draws the demons like a beacon. If we didn't give them a safe place to live, they'd be hunted down for food."

Lexi's mind whirled, trying to add this new piece of information into those she already knew. Try as she might, it simply didn't fit, which meant that either he was lying, or something else she thought was true was a lie.

She had to figure it out soon. She couldn't stay frozen in indecision like this forever. She had to either go through with her plan, or get back out there and make sure the Defenders knew how wrong they were about all of this.

"I need to see Helen," said Lexi. Maybe talking to her would help straighten things out.

Zach gave her a funny look, half curious, half suspicious. "Sure, honey. Anything you want."

He set down the bags, and dialed a number on his cell. "Helen, Lexi's here and wants to see you. Where are you? Okay, we'll be right there." He hung up and said, "She's in her suite. I'll take you there."

They wandered through several long hallways until they came to a door that looked like all the others. Lexi memorized the room number, hoping she would remember how to get here.

Helen opened the door before Zach had finished knocking. She wasn't caged or starved or hurt. She looked . . . fine. Lexi stood there confused, trying to add this new piece of information to the puzzle.

Helen didn't wait for Lexi to catch up. Instead, she

rushed out of the door, past Zach and grabbed Lexi for a hard hug.

Lexi hugged her back. After a month of worry, she'd finally found Helen—the best friend she'd ever had. It was a sad comment on her life that a woman she had served dinner to a couple nights a week back at Gertie's Diner for a total of three months was closer to her than anyone else since her mother, but there it was. Plain and simple. She'd missed Helen so much, and now they were together again.

It wasn't until Lexi felt the cool streaks on her face that she realized she'd been crying. She pulled away and swiped at the tears with the back of her hands. Helen did the same, though she gave Lexi a watery smile.

"I'm so glad you're here," said Helen. "We've been so worried about you."

"Worried about me? You're the one who got whisked off by a group of scary men."

Zach cleared his throat. "I'm going to leave you two alone to catch up. Helen knows my number if you need me. Otherwise, I'll find you later."

Helen grabbed Zach around the neck and pulled him down for a hug of his own. She smooched his dark cheek and said, "Thank you for bringing her home safely. I owe you."

"Then stop kissing me before Drake sees and cuts off something of mine I like."

Helen laughed, patted Zach's chest and took Lexi's arm. "I don't want to see you for at least two hours—got that?"

"Yes, my lady," said Zach, his voice warmed by his grin. He touched the side of Lexi's face, barely grazing her skin. Happy tingles slid down her throat and settled low in her stomach. "After you're done talking to Helen, after you've figured things out, then you and I are going to have some things of our own to discuss."

Lexi wasn't sure if it was a promise or a threat, but she found herself looking forward to being alone with Zach again. Which made her crazy.

"We haven't eaten, so I'll have some lunch sent up for you both," he told them,

"Breakfast for me, please," said Helen. "It was a late night."

"The wall?"

Helen nodded. "Yeah. Unfortunately."

"Right," said Zach. "Breakfast it is." Then he picked up the bags and walked back the way they'd come.

Lexi watched him go, enjoying the sight of his long, easy stride, the way his muscles flexed under his snug jeans. He was so finely built that she still could hardly believe he was real, much less that he wanted anything to do with her.

"That's a mighty fine sight," whispered Helen.

"Amen," said Lexi.

Zach disappeared around the corner, and Lexi was finally free of his pull. She gave herself a good mental shake and said, "Okay, let's get you inside and see if we can undo whatever brainwashing these Sentinels have done to you."

Brainwashing?

Helen gave Lexi a long look as they went inside her suite. Clearly, Lexi had some issues that needed to be ironed out. At least she was here, safe and sound, and Helen was able to do the ironing.

"Nice place," said Lexi. "Is anyone else here?"

Helen looked around at the suite. It was actually pretty plain, but neat and tidy. She'd been living here for a few weeks, and kept meaning to decorate the place, maybe repaint a couple of rooms, but she just hadn't had the time. Whatever excess energy she had, she'd been pouring it into that freaking wall, imbuing the stones with the power to hold them together against whatever the Synestryn might throw at them next.

Who knew that magic could be so exhausting?

"No, it's just us. Drake is in a meeting with some of the men."

"Ah. The boys' club."

Helen rolled her eyes. "They can have it. I sat in once and my eyes glazed over in about thirty seconds. They can drone on for hours about maps and strategy and whatnot. All I need to know is where are the monsters they want me to set on fire."

Lexi gave a low whistle. "You? Set things on fire?"

Of course Lexi wouldn't believe it. When they'd first met, Helen had been terrified of cigarette lighters. Heaven forbid someone put a birthday candle on her cake. She'd freaked out more than once over the sight of a flame, but now things were different.

Now, fire was her weapon of choice.

She opened her palm and called a small flame to her, using the invisible river of power flowing into her from Drake. The orange puff of fire flickered in her hand, barely warm against her skin. "Things have changed," she told Lexi. "For the better."

Lexi's knees buckled and she sank to the couch in shock, her eyes wide. "Wow. Okay. Not at all what I expected."

"I imagine there's going to be a lot of that for you for a while. I'm still getting used to all this stuff. Some of it is really far out there. You should see this lady, Gilda, in a fight. It's like watching a freaking anime cartoon or something."

"How many women like you are there here?"

"A few. Me, Gilda, Andra and her sister, Nika, though she's not well. We're all hoping she pulls through."

"And Miss Mabel is here, too, right?"

"Sure," said Helen, letting the flame in her hand dissipate in a puff of smoke as she joined Lexi on the couch. "We can go visit her in a little while, but first, tell me what's happened to you. Why are you worried about me being brainwashed?"

"You probably don't think you have been, but that's okay. We can still fix you up."

"We?"

"I mean me. I can fix you up."

Helen wasn't buying it. Lexi was hiding something. "We who, Lexi?"

"Don't worry about it. Really. Just know that you and I aren't alone. We'll be able to get everyone out safely."

"Everyone who? Out of where? I don't know what you're talking about."

"Out of *here*."

"This is my home. I have no intention of leaving."

Lexi pulled in a long breath as if trying to gather her patience. "Okay. Fine. No problem."

Helen walked to the fridge, grabbed two cans of soda and handed one to her friend. "Listen, you need to understand a few things. First, I'm happy here."

"You were kidnapped. It's Stockholm syndrome."

"No, it's not. I'm happy. I love Drake. He loves me."

Helen could see Lexi wasn't believing a word she said, but eventually, she would. She just needed some time. "Second, you're safe here. No one is going to hurt you."

"That's what Zach keeps saying."

"He's telling the truth. You should listen."

Lexi's mouth flattened to a stubborn line.

Helen ignored it. "And three, Zach needs you. He may have been too full of pride to tell you, but he's dying."

A look of guilt crossed Lexi's face, but she covered it by taking a long drink from the can. "He mentioned something about that."

"Well, he's more up front than Drake was then. That's good."

"Not for him." She said it like she'd already decided to let Zach die.

"Tell me you're at least thinking about saving him." Helen had to get Lexi to save Zach. She'd grown fond of him since she'd moved here, and now that she was a part of this war, she knew just how important Lexi could be in aiding their fight to save the world from Synestryn invasion. She didn't think that starting out by telling Lexi she'd be fighting a war was a great strategy to get her cooperation, but hooking up with Zach . . . that was its own kind of enticement. Helen loved her husband, but that didn't mean she couldn't see what a fine-looking man Zach was.

Lexi turned her head and stared out the windows. "Honestly, I don't know what to think."

"I wouldn't lie to you. You know that, right?"

Lexi shrugged. "I know you'd never intentionally lie to me. What I'm worried about is that you may not even know what the truth is anymore."

"You think I'm brainwashed. That's what you said earlier."

"Yeah, the thought had crossed my mind."

"Why would you think that? Whatever gave you that idea?"

"My mom's journal. A group called the Defenders of Humanity."

Helen had heard a single mention of that group somewhere recently. "You're talking about the guys who tote shotguns and think the Sentinels are out to ruin their farmland?"

"It's more than that. They're tired of having a war waged right in their backyards. They're tired of having their land destroyed and their families afraid. They've been around for a long time. They know the Sentinels are up to no good. They also know how to stop them."

A cold shiver of dread ran through Helen. "What do you mean? How are they going to stop us?"

Lexi's mouth tightened and she said nothing.

"Those guys are a bunch of farmers, Lexi. They have no idea what's really going on. They're going to end up getting themselves hurt. Or killed."

"They told me you'd say that. And that if you did, there would be nothing I could do to save you."

This was getting out of hand fast. Helen leaned forward and took Lexi's hand. "I need you to listen to me, okay? Whatever they told you isn't true. They're not bad guys—they just don't know the whole story."

"And what if they do?" asked Lexi, thrusting out her pointed chin. "What if they're the ones who are right?"

"They're not."

"How can you be so sure?"

"Because I'm tied to Drake in such a way that I can see his mind. I would know if he was lying to me about something this big."

"How would you know?"

Helen pushed out a frustrated breath. "It's like trying to explain the concept of color to someone who was born blind. You're just going to have to take my word for it. Or go to Zach and put on his luceria yourself. Then you'll understand. I promise."

"What if that's how they get you? That could be the way they brainwash you permanently."

"I'm not brainwashed!" Helen had shouted it and she had to rein herself back in and control her temper. She was just too tired from all the extra work. She wasn't getting enough rest, and it was making her short tempered and cranky. Lexi deserved better—she deserved her patience. This stuff was a lot to absorb for anyone.

In a calmer voice, she said, "There are a lot of people here who aren't wearing a luceria. Talk to them if you don't believe me. Talk to the teens. If anyone is going to fight back against some mass brainwashing, it will be one of them. And of course, there's Miss Mabel, and you know how pigheaded she can be. Talk to any of them. No one will stop you."

"They might."

"No, they won't. You're free to do as you like here as long as you're not planning to hurt anyone."

Lexi shifted in her seat and her eyes darted away from Helen's.

"You're not planning to hurt anyone, are you, Lexi?"

In a small voice, she replied, "I don't want to."

"What does that mean? If you don't want to, you don't have to. No one can make you do anything you don't want."

Lexi pressed her thumbs against her temples like her head was hurting. "I just need some time to think. That's all."

Helen didn't believe that was all. Not for one second. Lexi had something up her sleeve, and as much as Helen loved her, she couldn't let her friend hurt anyone here. These people were her family, and she was sworn to protect them, just like Drake was.

But, instead of pushing the issue, Helen let it go. She'd let the men know Lexi might be a danger, and everyone would keep tabs on her. Once she was here for a couple of days and had a chance to see for herself that it wasn't what she suspected, she'd be more reasonable.

Helen only hoped that Zach had that long to wait for Lexi to believe the truth.

Lexi tested Helen's theory that she'd be free to roam around by doing so. After a tense lunch that she barely managed to choke down, Lexi left Helen's suite and ambled through the hallways until she found herself back in the big glass-ceilinged room.

By now, the lunch crowd had thinned out and the TV area was empty of kids. A few people sat at the tables, drinking coffee or finishing their lunches. Miss Mabel sat at the edge of the dining area, reading a giant, antique book. Every few seconds, she'd look up at the kids nearby, as if she had the need to keep tabs on them. After teaching public school for so long, Lexi guessed it was more a habit than anything.

She pulled out a chair and sat down across from the woman. Miss Mabel looked up and beamed at her. "Lexi! As I live and breathe. What are you doing here?"

She looked younger, as if some of the lines had been erased from her face. She still wore the same garish lipstick and the white bun on the top of her head was still held in place with a single yellow, number two pencil, but everything else about her seemed . . . different.

"You remember those rude men from the diner?" asked Lexi.

"Of course."

"One of them found me."

"Ah. Zach. That poor fellow has been pining for you since the day you ran off. I'm glad he finally caught up with you."

"Glad? They abducted you and Helen and dragged you here against your will. How can you take their side?"

Miss Mabel's eyes narrowed and she pointed a gnarled finger at Lexi. "Don't you get uppity with me. I may not condone their methods, but if it weren't for them, I'd be dead right now. So would Helen."

"So they say. You can't know that for sure."

"Yes, I can. I've talked with enough of the children here to know what happens to those the Theronai don't manage to find in time. So many of them have lost their parents, their families. The Synestryn do horrible things that don't even come close to the sin of forcing someone into safety against their will."

"How do you know the kids aren't lying?" asked Lexi.

Miss Mabel lifted a white brow. "Thirty years of experience. That's how."

"How do you know they're not brainwashed? How do you know their parents aren't out there, looking for their lost kids?"

The older woman shook her head, frowning. "You're a stubborn child and will probably only believe when you see with your own eyes, but when you're here long enough, you'll know what I know. You'll see some big, strapping man carry a bloody child through those doors—one that's crying and clinging to him like a lifeline. You'll read the paper and see photos of the parents brutally slain—torn to pieces by monsters. Only then will you know the truth, deep down, the way I do."

"How do you know it's not those same big, strapping men killing the parents? They do carry swords, you know."

"Are you really that blind?" asked Miss Mabel. "Can you really look around this place of refuge and see such evil? Because if you can, then I have to wonder what might be wrong with *you*."

And that was the crux of the problem. Since she'd been here, she hadn't seen a single sign of torture or mistreatment. Everyone seemed content, safe.

Miss Mabel stood, without the help of her walker, without even leaning on the table for support. Even though she was still not quite five feet tall, she was no longer stooped with age. She turned around in a circle, her movements smooth and fluid. "There's no brainwashing here, child. The Sentinels didn't have to take my pain away or free me from that blasted walker, but they did. And at great cost, too. I've never had a thing for vampires the way some of these youngsters do, but the one that healed me nearly made himself sick doing it. It took three Theronai willing to open up their veins and bleed for me to make it happen, too. These men may be big, rude brutes, but they're *good*, big, rude brutes. Without them, I'd hate to think of where the world would be. Maybe you should spend some time thinking about that for a while."

"I have been. Believe me. Nothing seems clear anymore."

"Then I'd say you need to go have a look around. See for yourself."

"That's what Helen said."

Miss Mabel sat back down and waved Lexi away. "Scoot. I've got work to do. There's an entire library of books here I haven't read and that just can't stand." She went back to her reading, dismissing Lexi.

With a sigh of weariness and confusion, Lexi left. All she could think of was that if the Sentinels wanted to keep Miss Mabel prisoner, the last thing they would have done was given her the ability to run away easier.

Like so many other things she'd witnessed, it made no sense.

The sunshine outside called to her. Maybe some fresh air would help her sort things out. And if not, at least she'd walk off some of the excess energy clawing around inside of her, making her anxious.

The outdoor exercise area was stuffed full of muscular men, all shirtless and glistening like they knew she was coming by and wanted to give her a fantastic show.

Most of them were Theronai—she could tell by their tree tattoos. A few humans mingled with them, sweating and pumping iron, though just not as much. Apparently, the Theronai were superstrong. Or maybe they'd just been lifting longer.

Lexi enjoyed the sight as she pushed through the

doors and walked right down the middle of the area as if she owned the place.

She was pretty sure they wouldn't let her pass, but other than a few interested stares—something she was used to—no one moved to intercept her.

So far, so good.

She followed a sidewalk to the right, and saw water shining in the distance, either a lake or a really big pond. The grass was thick and lush, and flowers were planted in pretty little clumps lining the walkway. As she cleared the corner of one wing, she saw a fenced-in area and heard the joyful squeal of small kids. Behind that iron fence and the low hedges along one side, she found about a dozen preschoolers playing. Some of them climbed on the sturdy plastic slide, or ran into the matching playhouse. Two boys were rolling a ball between them, their aim so bad they had to run after the ball, which was apparently part of the game, based on the way they laughed while doing it. Three girls were in a giant sandbox building a crooked sandcastle.

Lexi propped her arms up on the top railing and just watched them, ignoring the stares of the adults keeping track of the tykes. She hadn't expected to see kids here, and certainly not so many of them.

They seemed happy. Healthy. How could that be when they were being raised alongside monsters?

Unless, of course, Helen and Zach had been telling the truth all along, and it was Lexi's mother and the Defenders who had been wrong.

This was their home. There was no way she could destroy that, and certainly no way to get them all out to safety.

Which meant that not only could she not blow this place up, she couldn't let the Defenders do it, either. That much was crystal clear. She had to find a way to contact them and let them know there were kids here.

She turned away from the playground and went back the way she came. Only this time, when she tried to pass through the exercise area, four large Theronai stepped in her path.

"Let me by," she told them, craning her head back to look them all in the eye.

The one with a scarred face said, "Not until we touch you."

Lexi backed up and bumped into another man. He grabbed her upper arms and panic sliced through her for a split second before her body settled, and all the preparation she'd done kicked in.

This was what she'd been expecting all along and she knew just how to handle it.

Chapter 14

Nika was draped over Madoc like a blanket when he awoke. For a moment, he thought he was dreaming again, but in his dreams he didn't hurt, so he had to be awake.

The bedside clock said it was nearly two in the afternoon. He'd slept longer than usual, even considering how exhausted he'd been last night.

Nika's head was tucked under his chin and he could feel her breath sliding out of her lungs, tickling him as it swept through his chest hair. One of his hands was locked around her waist and the other cupped her ass. Her skinny legs had settled between his thighs, and his hard cock was throbbing against her stomach.

He had no idea how she'd gotten in his room, or what in the hell had possessed her to come, but all of that was inconsequential now. Nika was here, in his bed, and everything inside him screamed out that because of that, she was his for the taking.

Sweat beaded up on his skin and he started to shake against the need to flip her under him and fuck her—drive into her body until some of the pain bled off and he could think straight.

He hadn't asked her to come to him. She had to

be here because that was what she wanted him to do, right?

Something about that line of logic was flawed, and Madoc held still, fighting himself until he could figure out what was wrong. He tried to remember what he would have done before his soul started dying—before he'd turned from a noble man into this bloodthirsty killer he now was.

Nika was sick. Fragile. Completely crazy. The girl didn't know what she wanted. Maybe that was why he needed to keep himself in check.

Her fingers curled against his bare chest and she let out a sigh. Madoc's blood pounded through him fierce and hard.

Why the hell was she here?

To get fucked? Or had she needed him? Maybe she'd come here for help and been too tired to get back to her own room. It made more sense than anything else.

Slowly, so he wouldn't wake her, Madoc rolled her body over onto the mattress. He cradled her head in his hand, keeping it steady as her slight weight shifted. The girl was already too mixed up in the brain for him to do any more harm by jostling her noggin, but the part of him that used to be good remembered he was supposed to be careful with her. She might be able to save one of his brothers.

Her white hair spilled out over the sheets, blending in until only her dark lashes and pink lips were visible in the dim light of his bedroom. The pale nightgown she wore fell nearly to her ankles and hid the bony contours of her wasted body.

Madoc didn't like scrawny chicks. Nika shouldn't have done anything for him, but his dick thought otherwise. Not that he could listen to it for advice—the thing had a mind of its own.

Before he could stop himself, he looked at the ring on his finger, hoping for a sign that she could save him. As always, he saw nothing in the pale depths of the band—no pulse of color or glimmer of hope.

Madoc couldn't even find the strength to mourn what could have been. He was empty. Hollow. Void of everything but pain and anger.

But those faithful companions had served him well last night as he'd hunted. Sixteen more sgath had fallen by his blade. He didn't know if any of them had stolen pieces of Nika's mind, but if they had, she would be that much more restored when she woke today.

Killing was all he had to offer her, no matter how much he wished it were otherwise.

With a final glance at her, Madoc eased himself from his bed to dress for a few hours of pumping iron in the training yard. After that, he'd go find a whore or three to fuck, then head out to kill some more sgath at nightfall. Same ol', same ol'. At least now that they'd found out what was plaguing Nika, he had a reason to get out of bed each day.

"Madoc." Nika's faint voice drifted up from the bed.

He froze, knowing that if he turned around right now, he might change his mind about those whores and use her instead. She was here, and he hurt like hell. He could find some ease inside her body—scrawny or not—even if it was only for a while.

"I saw you last night," she said. "Hunting."

If she'd seen him, then a sliver of her mind had been in the beasts he'd killed. At least he was finding the right sgath. That was something.

"How was my technique?" he asked without turning around.

He heard a shift of fabric, the slight creak of the bed as it moved under her meager weight. She was getting closer to him. He could feel it in the tightening of his muscles, the awareness of the heat of her skin.

The soulless part of him dared her to touch him. Reach for him. It was all the excuse he needed to throw her down and use her. If she touched him, then she must want him to take her. He'd have no more reason to hold back. He could give into that baser part of him that wanted the release that only came from coming inside a woman. All she had to do was lay a single finger on his body and she'd be his.

Madoc stepped away, out of reach of the bed.

"You're afraid of me?" she asked.

She hadn't meant it to be a taunt, but Madoc's blood was running hot, and he heard it as one, anyway. He spun around, not even bothering to hide his thick erection from her sight like he might have before he'd lost his soul. His honor.

She looked almost ethereal, all pale and glowing in the darkness. She was kneeling on the bed, and her white gown pooled around her knees, hiding her body from his sight.

Madoc wanted to strip it from her and see her naked. Keep her that way. He didn't even care anymore if she was bony and weak. He'd find a way to fix her and make her healthy enough for the kind of treatment he had to offer.

When he spoke, his voice was rough with arousal. "No, but *you* should be afraid of *me*. What the hell were you thinking coming into my room? *Into my bed?*"

Nika frowned in confusion. "I've slept here every day and you haven't complained."

"Like hell you have," spat Madoc. "I think I would have remembered having a woman in my bed." Although, he'd slept like the dead for a few days now, so maybe he was wrong. Wouldn't that be just great to learn that he'd slipped so far he couldn't even keep himself safe anymore from whoever wanted to walk in?

She looked down, making her white hair slide out from behind her shoulder. "Oh. Right. I'm wearing my body today. That's what's different."

Madoc didn't have a fucking clue what that meant. "And you weren't before?"

"No. It was too weak to come with me. It must be better now." She closed her eyes and ran her hands over her body. She was obviously checking herself for something, and hadn't meant to give Madoc a sexy show by feeling herself up, but she had anyway.

The sight made him shake with need. He wanted those to be his hands, or at least for her to do that while she was naked. She was teasing him and he didn't like it one bit. He was going to show her what happened to women who teased.

His cock twitched against the confines of his boxers, and he barely caught himself in time to keep from reaching for her. It took every bit of his strength to lock his feet in place. If he touched her now, he knew how it would end. She would be naked, under him, and he wouldn't give a shit about whether or not she wanted it. Whether she liked it or not.

He closed his eyes, and it helped him regain enough will-power to speak. "Don't come here again," he ordered.

"But I need you, Madoc."

Her words hit him like a fist in his gut. They drove the air from his lungs and left him floundering for control. He'd spent centuries hoping to hear those words from a female Theronai, but it was too late. She couldn't save him.

Confusion fogged her blue eyes. She wasn't sane. She didn't understand what Madoc wanted to do to her— what she did to him—and he had to stop expecting her to be able to.

He gathered what little patience he could find and forced his voice to be gentle even though the pain raging inside him was anything but. "Nika, you need me to kill the sgath that hold your mind captive. That's all."

She moved across the bed, swifter than would have been possible for her in her weakened state. He didn't expect it, and wasn't fast enough to evade her grasp. She pressed her hand over his lifemark. Her palm on his bare skin was warm, but that was all. Madoc found himself hoping in vain to feel something—anything—even the slightest shift of the branches of his tree.

The single leaf frozen midway down his torso felt dead under her hand. And, of course, the other fake leaves he'd had tattooed on his chest remained still and lifeless.

She wasn't his. He knew it. He'd known it since that first night when they'd rescued her from the mental hospital. It was time to move on and stop letting her torture him.

"You're wrong," she told him. "I need *you*. Please don't send me away."

He wanted to agree. He wanted to give her everything she'd ever wanted, but he knew better. He wasn't capable of giving her anything but pain and regret. "I can't trust myself not to hurt you."

"*I* trust you."

He felt his lip curl in self-disgust. "Then you're a foolish little girl who deserves whatever she gets." He lifted her hand from his skin and let it drop, then turned away from her. "Don't come back again. If you do, I'll make sure you regret it."

Zach saw the commotion in the training yard and went to see what was up. He thought about ignoring it so he could get back to Lexi faster, but his sense of duty refused to let him walk away from his brothers. With

the wall still vulnerable, he wasn't taking any chances
that whatever was going on out there was more than a
testosterone-driven skirmish.

When he cleared the glass doors, he saw Nicholas,
Neal and Morgan backing away from someone. Their
big bodies shifted enough and he got a glimpse of who
that someone was.

Lexi.

She had a barbell in her hands, wielding it like a staff,
wearing that same feral expression she'd had on when
he'd first met her—the night she'd stabbed him. Lexi the
Avenger.

Samuel Larsten was on the ground, holding his
scarred hand against his head to slow the bleeding.
Nicholas held his hands up, as did Neal and Morgan, but
Morgan was grinning like a fool. "She's feisty," he said.
"I like that."

A primitive club of jealousy bashed Zach over the
head, and he was striding forward before he had a chance
to think twice about what he planned to do. With a powerful shove of his palms against the men's shoulders,
Morgan and Neal went flying in opposite directions.

Nicholas dodged his airborne buddies and stepped in
front of Lexi as if to protect her. From Zach.

"Out of the way," growled Zach.

"Not until you've cooled off, man," said Nicholas.

Possessive rage pounded against Zach, heating his
blood and making him see red. "She's mine."

"Maybe. Maybe not. All I'm saying is that you're not
getting near her until you calm the fuck down."

The clang of metal hitting concrete rang out from
behind Nicholas as the barbell fell from Lexi's hands.
A split second later, she sprinted away, her tennis shoes
slapping against the ground.

Zach wasn't about to let her get away. Not this time.

He bashed into Nicholas with the full force of his

weight, rocking the man back on his heels. It was all the room Zach needed to get past, and he broke into a dead run, following Lexi over the rich green grass.

The thrill of the hunt coursed through him, making his blood sing in his veins. Power flooded his limbs and a feral smile stretched his lips. He could run like this for hours and never get tired. Not when he was chasing prey with an ass as pretty as Lexi's.

He heard footsteps behind him, likely his brothers coming to save her from the big, bad wolf, but he didn't slow.

She headed for the line of trees shielding several cabins. Not all of the Sentinels liked communal living, and preferred having four walls all their own with no one on the other side. Currently, only two of the cabins were occupied.

He followed her through the trees, keeping the distance between them wide enough she could think she was actually getting away.

Nicholas ran up beside him, having finally caught up. "I can't let you hurt her," he said.

"I'm not going to."

"You need to back off."

"No. It's time to end this. I'm out of time, and I'm claiming her while I still have enough of myself left to be gentle about it," said Zach.

"Are you sure gentle is where your head is right now?"

Zach had been keeping a careful eye on Lexi, but he spared Nicholas a quick glance. The man's scarred face was puckered with concern. Zach felt a swell of gratitude, knowing his buddy would never let him do anything stupid that might hurt her. "I'm sure."

Nicholas nodded, keeping pace. "None of us there was compatible. Guess she's all yours. You'll understand if I can't stick around and watch, right?"

Watch Zach get what every man gathered there wanted more than anything—a woman who could save them and allow them to keep fighting the Synestryn. It had been hard watching Drake find Helen, seeing them happy together, holding hands and smiling. He loved Drake like a brother, but the jealousy raging through him had not been fun to suffer. He didn't wish to inflict that on anyone. "Yeah. Go back and tell the men she's safe. And to give us some time alone."

Nicholas disappeared back through the trees, and Zach picked up speed, closing the distance to Lexi. When she came into sight and veered to the left of Iain's cabin, Zach followed. His long legs ate up the ground as his body worked to get her back where she belonged— by his side, forever.

The next time she looked over her shoulder at him, he was within arm's reach. Her chocolate brown eyes widened, and she tripped over the root of a tree.

Zach grabbed the back of her shirt to stop her fall, then gathered her in his arms. He didn't stop moving. He swept her up and continued on to the nearest unoccupied cabin. It wasn't as posh as the suites in the main building were, but there would be a mattress on the bed to cushion Lexi's back and that was all that really mattered.

"I thought you were done running," he told her. His voice was rough and harder than he'd intended.

"Let me go." She was panting. Her cheeks were pink, and her chest rose and fell, pressing deliciously against his.

Zach booted the cabin door open and slammed it shut again once they'd cleared it. The doors bolted from the inside with thick, sturdy beams of wood over iron brackets. He bumped it with his elbow and the beam fell into the bracket, locking them in.

The place smelled a little musty, but the scent of pine

made it tolerable. It was dark in here, compared to outside, with only a dim ray of tree-filtered light sliding in through the dusty windows. The cabin was small, maybe two hundred square feet. A bed hugged one wall, and along the opposite wall was a fireplace and a table with two chairs. In the far corner, there was a bathroom with all the necessary equipment, though none of it fancy. Other than food, they had everything they needed right here.

"Put me down, Zach." Lexi's voice shook and she no longer sounded like a woman confident enough to go up against a group of large men armed only with a metal pole.

Zach did as he was told and laid her on the bare mattress. Before she could try anything, he crawled on top of her and caged her in with his body. He kept his weight on his hands and knees, keeping as much distance between their bodies as he could. He didn't trust himself enough to press his body fully to hers and keep control. As it was, his dick was hard and his blood was demanding he stake a physical claim on her body, and to hell with the luceria. He wanted her naked and wet and spread out for his pleasure. Just the thought of running his hands over her bare skin was enough to make him shake.

But he had to do this right. One step at a time, and that meant keeping his hands to himself and his dick in his jeans, much to his dismay.

"We need to talk," he told her.

"I just want to leave, okay?"

"It's too late for that. I don't have the time to find you again." He could feel his last leaf barely clinging to the branch. It was dry and withered, and he was sure he wouldn't last until morning. Not without Lexi giving him what he needed.

Zach traced a finger over her throat. He could feel her pulse skittering under his fingertip. Her skin was warm and so silky soft he had to close his eyes and soak up the feeling, completely losing himself in that single touch for a long moment.

"You're scaring me," she whispered.

Zach didn't want that. He wanted to make her happy. To make her feel good.

She'd told him that it felt good when he touched her, so Zach spread his hand over her throat, reveling in the striking contrast of his darker skin against hers, the roughness of his hands against the perfect silkiness of her neck. He willed a ribbon of energy through his arm, letting it spark between them, expanding into a million tiny fragments of sensation.

Lexi's eyes fluttered closed and she let out a soft sound of pleasure.

"Still scared?" he asked, forcing his tone to remain gentle even though the need to claim her raging through him was anything but gentle.

She grabbed his wrist, wrapping both hands around it. She didn't push him away, just held on, trembling in indecision.

Her bottom lip quivered, and he wanted to kiss it and drive away the worry he heard in her voice. "Helen says I'm wrong. Miss Mabel says I'm wrong. You say I'm wrong. You all say the Sentinels are the good guys. How can my whole life be a lie?"

Zach didn't want to talk. He wanted to demand she give him what he needed, both her body and her vow to stay by his side for eternity. He knew it was meant to be, that they'd both be happy together if she'd shed the lies of her human upbringing and let him show her the truth of their kind. Her kind, too.

She pinned him with a look of desperation—one so strong he knew he had to slow down. She needed him to talk to her and soothe her, and in the end, he could deny her nothing.

Zach fought back his pounding lust and willed himself to speak. "No one can force you to believe. All I can do is offer you a means to learn the truth for yourself."

Her gaze moved to his throat. To his luceria. "I . . . can't."

"Why not?" That question cost him another precious sliver of control, but he offered it nonetheless.

"If Mom was right, then once I put that on it will be too late. I'll be imprisoned."

"That's not the way it works. I can't force you to wear it, believe me. If I could, you'd already be my lady."

"Another lie?" she asked with a hint of defiance lifting her chin.

Zach smiled. He loved that about her. Here she was, trapped beneath him, locked in a cabin inside a compound she couldn't easily escape, and yet still, she didn't give up. His Lexi was a fighter to the core, and he was a lucky man to have found her.

"There's one way to find out," he taunted. "Unless you're afraid."

Sparks of rebellion lit her eyes. "Get over yourself. You're not scary enough to make me afraid. I've spent my life running from monsters scarier than you. Grow some claws or teeth or something and then we'll talk."

"So, what's stopping you?" He tilted his chin, baring his throat. "Take it. It's up to you how long you decide to wear it."

She reached up and Zach's body clenched in anticipation. Despite what she said, she *was* afraid. He could feel it in the way her arm trembled, the way her pupils had shrunk down to tiny dots of black. But even with that fear, she didn't back down. She ran her finger along the band and Zach felt that single touch slide through him like lightning, sizzling him to his toes. His dick strained for release and a hot hum of desire wrapped around his veins.

"I don't know what to do."

"Just take it." Zach was panting, sucking in enough air to hold himself in control.

She wrapped her slender fingers around the luceria and gave a slight tug. It split open and she gasped, dropping it, like it was a live snake, but the luceria didn't mind. It fell around her neck, locking into place as if it had been waiting its entire existence for this single moment in time.

Lexi's eyes went wide and she shoved hard against Zach. He moved back enough to let her sit up, but still straddled her legs, making sure she wasn't going anywhere. Not until this was done. Permanent.

Zach smiled at her. He couldn't help it. "I've never seen anything prettier in my life than you are right now."

She pulled on the luceria. "It won't come off."

Zach captured her hands before she could hurt herself. "You haven't given me your vow yet."

"I don't know what to say."

Zach wanted her forever. But to get what he wanted, he had to be smart, tread carefully. If she continued to see him as her enemy, she'd never learn to trust him, and if that happened, their bond would never work right. Trust was vital to the flow of power between them.

Even though he hated the idea, he knew what he had to do. If he wanted her trust, he had to offer his own. "Promise to wear it until you change your mind. That way, if you see something that isn't right and you no longer want to be with me, you'll be free to go."

"What will happen to you?"

"I've lived a long time. Don't worry about me."

"Whether or not I trust you, I don't want to be the one to kill you, Zach."

"You won't. Even if you decide to leave, my death won't be your fault. I'm headed that way fast anyway.

Any extra time you give me is a gift, extending my natural life." He just wasn't ready for it to end yet. Not if Lexi could be part of it.

With plenty of luck and patience, she'd see the truth and never take off his luceria. He would find a way to make that happen.

Zach rose from the bed and knelt beside it. He stripped his shirt off over his head, unsheathed his sword and made a small cut over his heart. "My life for yours, Lexi. Forever."

She shook her head, frowning. "I don't like that one. Give me a different vow."

The side of his mouth cocked up in a grin. "Sorry, honey. That's the one you're getting. It's your turn."

He pressed a drop of blood to the luceria, making it come to life. It shrank to fit her slender throat. She swallowed and the movement caused the luceria to glisten in a riot of green ribbons of color.

After taking a deep breath, she said, "I promise to wear this thing as long as I want. As soon as I don't want to wear it, then it comes off."

Her vow worked. He felt the subtle power of it weighing down on him. Light in the room expanded until it pressed against him like a blanket, sealing her vow inside of him.

She was his now. He was going to make sure it stayed that way.

His world tilted and fell away as the luceria revealed to him some treasured part of Lexi it wanted him to see. Zach held his breath and let the vision flow over him. Lights and colors sped past him and he came to a rocking stop outside the door of a mom-and-pop restaurant along a stretch of highway. Lexi was standing there, her hair in pigtails. She was five or six years old, but he recognized her dainty pointed chin and the defiant set of her shoulders even then. She was so cute, so tiny and vulnerable, it made his chest grow tight with the need to protect her.

Her mother, whom he recognized from the photos in Lexi's Honda, bent low so she could be heard over the intermittent roar of truckers as they sped by. "Do you remember your name?" she asked Lexi.

"Lucy James."

"Good. And where did we come from?"

She chewed on her lip a moment, then said, "Mini apples."

"Minneapolis. It's in Minnesota. It's cold there."

"I don't like the cold," complained Lexi.

"I know. You make sure to tell people that. It's a good reason for us to have left."

"But what about the monsters? I thought we left 'cause of the monsters."

"You can't tell anyone about the monsters. Remember?"

Lexi nodded her head. Her hair had been lighter then, but just as baby fine as it was now and it swayed around her sweet face. "If I tell someone, the monsters will eat them just like they want to eat us."

"That's right. It's our secret, okay?"

Lexi nodded again and colors around Zach started to blur once more as the vision changed. This time, Lexi was a few years older. She was in the car with her mother, looking out the window as they passed by a middle school. A pile of kids her age poured out of the doors, laughing and eager to get out of there. "Why can't I go to school?" she asked her mom.

"It's not safe. I teach you everything you need to know, Ali."

Lexi crossed her arms over her chest, slid down lower in the seat and pouted. "I don't like that name."

"Fine. You can pick your name for the next town."

"Alexandra Johnson."

"No. You can't use your real name. You know that."

"It's not fair. I'm tired of moving, Mom. I just want to be normal."

Her mother sighed as if preparing herself to repeat something for the thousandth time. "You're never going to be normal, Ali. The Sentinels want your blood. If we stay in one place too long, they'll find you and kill you. I'm not going to let that happen."

"We've never even seen one of the Sentinels, only their pets," complained Lexi.

"I've seen them. They look like men with trees growing on their chests, but inside, they're rotted meat and maggots."

"I don't believe you. You're just trying to scare me."

The car rocked to a skidding stop and people behind them honked their horns. Lexi's mom ignored them and turned in her seat, her blue eyes blazing with fury. "You should be scared. Only stupid people aren't scared. I want you to stop this nonsense or we're going to have to go see the Defenders again."

Fear bleached Lexi's face of color. "No, Mom. Please."

"So, you do remember the lessons they taught you?"

"Yes."

"And what did they teach you?"

Tears shimmered in Lexi's dark eyes. "Naughty girls die screaming."

Zach reached out to take her into his arms and comfort her, but before he could, the vision shifted again, melting the image of Lexi's tearful face into a wash of color.

This time, when the vision stopped, Lexi was driving. It was winter and snow was falling hard enough that there were only slight tracks on the road ahead of her. The Honda's windshield wipers were slapping back and forth on high speed, leaving filmy streaks of ice behind.

Lexi's body slumped with fatigue and her eyes were red as if she hadn't slept in days. Or maybe she'd been crying. Every few seconds, she'd check her rearview mirror and grip the steering wheel tighter in her gloved hands.

A snow-topped sign indicated a rest stop ahead and Lexi took the ramp. She parked her car as close to the bathroom as she could, but didn't get out. Instead, she climbed into the backseat, unrolled a sleeping bag and slid inside, shoes and all. She zipped it up to the top and pulled a stocking cap down over her ears. Already, snow had covered the car's windows, nearly blocking out the security light over her car.

She touched a photograph of her mother with the tip of a gloved finger. "Good night, Mom. Miss you." Her breath came out in a silver plume of frost. Even inside the car it was freezing.

Lexi snuggled down inside the sleeping bag as far as she could and covered her head. Even in the dim light, he could see the shiny fabric of the sleeping bag quake with her shivering.

Zach ached to go to her, warm her. But he couldn't. He wasn't really there—this was all in her past—and there was nothing he could do but observe and squirm in frustration.

How many nights had she slept in her car? How many nights had it been colder than this one? Even without the threat of Synestryn, she was still putting herself in danger sleeping at a rest stop. Any lunatic could have broken through the window and stolen her away, or killed her outright.

The fact that she'd survived despite the odds only made her that much more of a miracle. His miracle.

Finally, the vision faded, and even though only a brief few seconds had gone by, those seconds had changed

Zach. They'd given him a small part of Lexi and that somehow made him feel more whole.

As reality returned, placing him back inside the dusty cabin, Zach was finally able to touch her. He reached for her, realized he still held his sword and let it drop. He wiped the blood from his cut—which was already closing—on his shirt and moved onto the bed next to her.

Lexi stared out with unseeing eyes, witnessing whatever it was the luceria wanted her to see. He hoped that whatever she saw was something good—some brave, noble deed he'd done along the way. He didn't want her to see how much he'd suffered through his life. She deserved to only see the good parts, and not to be burdened by sympathy for him.

Lexi made a pained noise and swayed. Zach pulled her against him to steady her, reveling in the feeling of her so solid and warm in his arms. So alive and safe. She leaned her cheek against his shoulder and he could feel the rush of air from her lungs sweeping across his skin.

She was his. Even as his pulse steadied, the pain that had been with him for so long started to fade. In its place he felt a sense of contentment and purpose. Utter rightness.

"You okay?" he asked her.

She gave a shaky nod. "I hope so. That was. . . ."

"What did you see?"

"Battle. You and Drake and a hundred other men fighting back monsters. Century after century."

"Synestryn," he said, giving her the name for their enemy.

Her breathing had evened out, but her color was still not right. She was pale and trembling, but even so, she was strong enough to push him down so she could straddle his stomach and look into his eyes.

Lexi cupped his face in her hands and the feel of her

slender fingers on his skin rekindled some of that lust he thought the vision had quenched. Her expression was serious and her dark eyes slid over his features, studying them.

Was she already thinking about leaving? Storing up memories of him like she had photos of her mother?

"Why do you do it?" she asked.

"Do what?"

"Keep fighting? Keep living when all there is left is more battle and bloodshed?"

He didn't understand why she had all these questions, but he gave her the answers she needed—the truth. "Because we promised we would. Because there's no one else who can."

"You're not who I thought you were," she told him in a quiet voice. "You're not the villain my mother thought, either."

Relief swept through him like a cool breeze. "So you believe me now?"

She hesitated and he knew his relief had come too soon. "I want to."

"Then do."

"What if this is a trick? Part of the brainwashing process?"

Zach was torn between being insulted by her lack of trust and wanting to comfort her and drive away all the doubt that caused her fear. It had to be difficult for her to be so close to him when she was unsure of whether or not he was trying to turn her into some kind of mind-controlled zombie, or whatever other ridiculous ideas she had in that head of hers.

"How do I prove to you it's not? I mean, nothing I can say will convince you because you'll think it's all part of my diabolical plan to turn you into my brainwashed slave, right?"

She had the courtesy to blush, hearing her ideas laid out in such ridiculous terms.

"All I know to do is show you how to use my power. Maybe once you realize what it is you can do now, you'll realize that no sane person would ever allow a slave the kind of magic you now possess."

Lexi got off the bed and took a step back. "I'm not ready for anything else right now. This is already too much."

"That's just too bad. I'm not going to let you leave here believing I mean to harm you in some way."

"You can't make me do anything."

He rose from the bed and then grabbed her by the waist. She felt good under his hands, soft and slender. Her waist cradled his hands and he had to stop himself from holding her too tight. "Wanna bet?"

Her pointed chin shot up as she glared at him. "So this was all just a way to get me to do what you wanted?"

"No, it's a way for me to get you to do what *you* want. It's a way for me to teach you how to protect yourself just in case you decide to run away from me again. Not that I'd let you get far, but you're too precious to risk, even for a moment."

"What if what I want is to get away from you?"

Zach felt a smile of victory curve his mouth and tightened his hold on her body. "Try it. Go ahead. I dare you."

Lexi was pretty sure she was being served a heaping helping of bullshit. She wanted to believe he'd given her some kind of magical power, but that was the problem. She wanted to believe. "I don't buy it."

"Of course not. I know you won't believe anything I say until you see it for yourself. That's why I want you to do this—so you'll have proof."

"Fine. What do I do?"

"Can you feel the luceria?"

"Yes."

"How does it feel?"

"It's warm. Humming."

"Close your eyes," he urged. "You can feel it better if you close your eyes."

After a stubborn moment, Lexi did.

"The luceria connects you to me, to my power. You remember all those little sparks that kept jumping from me when we touched?"

Boy, did she. Lexi grudgingly nodded her head.

"It's like that, only more. Stronger."

Lexi could sense something there, but she couldn't quite reach it. There was some ethereal warmth pressing at her mind, but there was nothing to grab onto, nothing solid or real.

Whatever it was, she ached to possess it, like it belonged to her somehow—a favorite toy taken away before she'd really had the chance to play with it.

She tried harder, reaching out until her hands shook. In fact, all of her was shaking pretty bad.

Lexi pulled back before she no longer could, before this thing—whatever it was—pulled her in and never let go. Instantly, all that glowing warmth vanished, disappearing out of reach, leaving her reeling.

Her entire world had been turned upside down in the space of a few brief minutes and she was still spinning, looking for something to grasp onto to steady herself.

Apparently, that thing was Zach. She couldn't stop touching him. The solid mass of his body seemed to be the only real thing she could find right now and she held on to him like a lifeline.

His skin was smooth and firm under her fingers. The mass of power she had nearly touched gave her a rush that was only now beginning to fade. It left behind a vibrating core of energy that warmed her from the inside out. The luceria around her neck pulsed with more of that heady power, but Lexi didn't dare reach for it. She didn't want to find out that something so beautiful was a lie.

Her fingers slid up Zach's spine to the nape of his neck. He let out a deep purr of enjoyment and that sound shook her all the way to her Nikes.

She could make him feel good, which was another type of power rush entirely. Lexi'd had a few lovers in the past, but they never lasted long because she was never in one place for more than a few brief weeks. And not one of those men had ever wanted to pack up their lives and hit the road just to be with her.

Not that she blamed them. Life on the road was no fun, and Lexi wasn't going to dump that kind of hassle on anyone.

But with Zach, she didn't have to. Either he was telling the truth and she'd finally found a way to fight back against the things that wanted to hurt her so she no longer had to keep running, or he was lying and she was already trapped—too late for running.

Lexi knew which of those options she hoped was true, but she also knew better than to get those hopes up too high.

Her throat tightened around a lump of longing. She so wanted to believe Zach was the kind of man she'd seen in the visions the luceria gave her. That man was kind and selfless and dedicated. That man played with children and taught them how to fight so they could defend themselves. That man took those children in, providing for them, and making sure they'd never have to use the deadly skills he taught them.

And the women in his life had been the luckiest people on the face of this planet. Lexi had watched as he'd made love to them. She saw the way he had taken care to give them pleasure, rather than merely taking his own. She'd seen how he'd been gentle and sweet with each of them, ensuring their safety even after he'd left their beds.

Lexi had spent a lot of her life wishing she had the things others took for granted—a home, a family, a normal life, a sense of security—but never before had she felt the same kind of feral jealousy she'd experienced while watching Zach love the countless women that had drifted in and out of his life over the centuries.

She tried to tell herself that she didn't really want him, that it was just part of the whole brainwashing scheme, but she knew it was a lie. There was something deep inside her that rose up and shouted that he belonged to her, not those other women.

As her hands roamed over his beautiful back, drawing more sexy sounds from his thick chest, Lexi knew the truth. Enemy or not, she was going to find a way to have what all of those other women had had. For once, she was going to be reckless and take what she wanted from life, despite the danger.

Zach was hers and she was going to have him.

Lexi leaned down and pressed a soft kiss against his shoulder. His body clenched and his muscles stood out in hard ridges.

"Careful," he warned her. "Kissing me is a good way to get more than you're asking for."

Lexi ignored the warning, shoved him down onto the bed, straddled him, and kissed him again. This time, she moved to the side of his neck and slid the tip of her tongue over his salty skin.

"Lexi?"

She wasn't sure if he'd meant it to be a question, but she knew the answer. "Yes."

Zach looked at her. His green eyes gave off a primal glow of desire as they glided over her body, hovering over her throat and breasts long enough to make her squirm. "What do you want?" he asked.

"You."

He closed his eyes tight as if to block her out and said, "Be really clear, honey. I've got all kinds of delusions of grandeur going on here."

Lexi had never been shy about sex, and she wasn't about to start now. Not when she had so much to lose.

She stretched out beside him on the bed so her face was level with his. She grabbed the back of his neck and held him still while she closed the distance between them. The need to kiss him made her shake, but she held herself in check for just a moment longer, giving him the words he wanted. "I want you naked. I want you hard. I want you inside me. Clear enough?"

He opened his eyes and gave her a look so hot and full of potent male lust she broke out into a sweat. "Oh yeah. Crystal clear," he said.

She felt his muscles bunch and harden around her body, and the next thing she knew, she was beneath him, staring up at his full, tempting mouth. She still had a firm hold on his neck, and she tugged him down to her. His lips were gentle against hers and so eager she knew she wasn't alone in the craziness of her want for him. He wanted her, too. She could feel that want hard and thick against her mound, rocking in a slow, steady motion that made her body go liquid and pliant.

His tongue feathered against her upper lip, seeking entrance and Lexi let him in. The taste of him in her mouth drove her crazy. The slick glide of his tongue across the delicate skin just inside her lips made her want more. She could smell the spice of his skin and a subtler, earthier scent of aroused male swirling in the air around them. Her body was empty, aching and on fire. Her skin seemed to stretch, but was too small to contain all the need writhing inside her. She wasn't even sure what it was she needed, only that Zach was the one person who could give it to her.

A fine sweat covered her body, but did nothing to cool her down. Zach's mouth ate at hers, drinking in all the frantic noises she couldn't stop herself from making. Her hands clutched at his hard back, trying to pull him closer when there was no room left between them.

Zach slid his hand down her side and back up, easing his way beneath her shirt so his warm hands caressed bare skin. Lexi squirmed, trying to tell him she wanted more. She wanted to feel his hand cup her breast, his palm graze her nipple. Maybe that would ease the gnawing ache inside her.

But he didn't give her what she wanted. He just petted her as if soaking up the feel of her skin, in no hurry at all to move things faster.

Lexi was going to have to do it herself.

Her hands moved down his back, stroking hot, taut skin as she went. His jeans were snug, but not so tight she couldn't slide one hand down below the waistband, under the stretchy cotton of his boxers. The feel of his smooth, firm ass under her palm made her blood heat and pool hot and low in her belly.

Zach sucked in a startled breath and his hips ground against her in a single smooth circle. The pressure of the movement rubbed the seam of her jeans against her clitoris and sent a zing of sensation sizzling through her. Lexi let out a soft, desperate cry for more, but instead of giving her what she wanted, his body went still above hers.

She opened her legs, making room for his big body between her thighs. He fit against her perfectly, hovering over her, holding the rest of the world at bay. Nothing existed but the feel of his weight on top of her, the warmth of his breath as she sucked it into her own lungs, the stroke of his hand across her ribs and the taste of him on her tongue.

He surrounded her, and still it wasn't enough.

Lexi pressed hot kisses over his jaw and down the side of his corded neck. He growled, giving off a harsh, animal sound of pleasure and his weight shifted. A moment later, his long fingers slid up between her breasts and over her collarbone, his arm tugging at her shirt as he went. He stroked the luceria around her throat and sharp, hot spikes of energy raced through her.

"Open up for me," he murmured against her hair.

She had no idea what he wanted. Her legs were already spread as wide as they could go. In fact she was rubbing herself up against him, trying in vain to find that one sweet spot he'd hit earlier.

Another jolt of power spiked through her, making her gasp. The heat of it rolled along her skin, searing her until she was sure she would combust. It was almost painful, but not quite, and way too intense to be called pleasure.

"Come on, honey," he whispered in a coaxing voice. "Let me in."

"Gotta get my pants off," she told him. She was breathless, almost incoherent.

"We will. Definitely. But that's not what I mean. Let me in here." He traced his finger over one temple, across her forehead to the other temple.

Lexi didn't understand, but she was done trying to figure it out. Once they were both naked, it would all be fine. She was sure of it, so she went for the button on his jeans, trying to get him on the same page.

"Oh, no, you don't," he told her. "Not yet. We're going to do this right."

"Right. Right now. What's the difference? You're killing me."

An arrogant grin tilted his mouth. How could he smile when she was about to go up in flames? That gnawing need inside her was growing, like a hungry, living thing. If she didn't feed it soon, she was sure it would consume her.

She'd never felt anything like this before. The more she got, the more she needed.

Lexi tried to pop open that button again, but Zach gathered her hands and pressed them against his hot chest. His muscles were rigid and vibrating with tension.

He closed his eyes and another jolt of energy shot through her, arcing from where his ring touched the back of her hand, up her arm, to the luceria around her throat. She heard the energy pop and sizzle in the quiet cabin; then it ripped down her spine and all she heard was her own shocked cry.

The hungry thing inside her lunged for that power, consuming it and growing as it did. It pounded at her mind, demanding entrance, but Lexi resisted, keeping the doors on herself closed and locked like Mom had taught her.

Pressure built inside her head until it became painful. She couldn't breathe right.

Something was terribly wrong.

Zach pulled away from her, and Lexi let out a frantic scream, trying to pull him back. She needed him to fix this hunger inside her. To fill her up. But he didn't budge.

"Whoa, honey. Easy. Slow down."

Lexi couldn't. Slow wasn't going to fix this need clawing inside her, the pressure that threatened to split her skin open.

A concerned frown wrinkled Zach's dark face. "Lexi? What's wrong?"

"Need . . ." She didn't know what she needed, just that he had it. "Something."

His wide hand smoothed her hair back from her sweaty forehead. "*Shh.* Relax. It's okay."

"Doesn't feel okay."

"You're fighting it. Don't fight it."

She was fighting not to fly apart. "What the hell are you talking about?"

"It's the luceria trying to bond us together. Don't fight it. Just let go."

"If I knew how, I would."

"I can show you. Let me slide inside your mind, just a little, okay?"

Inside her mind? Like hell. She had too many secrets. She couldn't let him see them.

It took her a second to realize that was what he'd been talking about all along, telling her to let him in. He had been the one trying to breach her mental defenses, not some imaginary beast.

"You still don't trust me." It wasn't a question. His voice was flat with disappointment and resentment. "Fuck."

He rolled over and covered his eyes with his forearm. Now that he wasn't touching her, some of that desperation pounding at her started to ease.

She pulled in a full breath. Another. Slowly, the tightness in her skin abated.

Lexi risked a glance at him. His beautiful chest was rising and falling with his rapid breathing. A sheen of sweat shone over his hard muscles, and the bare branches of the tree quivered and bowed as if straining to get closer to her. His whole body was tight, resonating in time with her own feral sexual need, and his erection strained against the front of his jeans.

She stared at that thick bulge a moment too long and her mouth began to water. She wanted to take back up where they left off, without all the mind games. "Why would you do that?" she asked. "Why would you try to poke around in my head when I was more than happy to let you inside my body?"

"It's the way it's supposed to be. At least between people who trust each other."

"I didn't mean to lead you on," she told him. "I'm sorry."

His voice was deep and rough with unsated lust. "Not as sorry as I am."

She needed to put some space between them and think. Lying here, staring at his body, was doing nothing to clear her head. His presence left no room for rational thought. He was too big. He took up too much of her attention when she was near him.

"I'm going to take a walk," said Lexi. She sat up on the edge of the bed, letting her dizzy head settle.

He moved to sit beside her and though his jaw was tight, his tone was gentle. "I wish you'd stay."

"So I can frustrate us more?" So he could see that she'd been planning to kill him? "No, thanks."

"We were moving too fast, that's all. You just need some time to learn you can trust me."

She swallowed hard, trying to ease the tightness in her throat. "Zach, I need to be completely honest here. There is no way I'll ever trust anyone enough to let them rummage around inside my head."

"You're just not used to the idea. Give it time to grow on you."

"No. I mean it. We could be together for a dozen centuries and I'm still not going to give you that kind of power over me."

"What are you talking about? What power?"

"Are you serious? You don't think that being able to see inside my brain is like the ultimate power trip? Who knows what you could do once you're up there?"

"That's the point. If you trust someone enough to let them in, you trust them not to fuck you over."

"That kind of trust isn't in me," said Lexi.

Zach straightened his shoulders. "So, I'll go first. Go ahead. Take a peek inside and see whatever you like. I don't have anything to hide."

Lexi was tempted. The brief flash of images she'd gotten when she donned his luceria had intrigued her. She itched to see more, but it wasn't fair. She couldn't violate him like that.

"Sorry."

His hand covered hers and a flood of comforting warmth streamed up her arm. "You just need more time. I have to find the patience to give it to you."

She didn't think time was the solution to all this, but she kept her mouth shut. Maybe after she had some space to be alone and think, she'd figure out how to handle Zach's bizarre expectations. "I don't think I'll ever get used to all of this . . . stuff."

"Maybe you should talk to Helen about it. She's been through all this."

"Helen is a lot more trusting than I am."

Zach sighed. "Maybe. But don't worry. We'll figure this out, honey. We'll make it work."

Lexi gritted her teeth against the tears that stung her eyes. "And if we can't?"

"We will." Total confidence radiated out from him. "I won't let it happen any other way."

She wished she could believe him, but she knew better. Even if her fantasy was true, and Zach was everything he claimed to be, she'd already betrayed him. She'd planned to kill him and his people, and after seeing how he'd slaughtered the creatures who had tried to do that very thing, she wasn't sure he'd ever be able to forgive her. Sure, maybe he'd overlook it so he could keep on living, but that wasn't the kind of life Lexi wanted. She wanted a home. A place where she belonged. Not a place that tolerated her existence because Zach needed her to live.

Of course, what she wanted had never really mattered in the greater scheme of her life.

Lexi went to the door and lifted the heavy bar. "I'll be back later," she told him. She didn't dare turn around for fear of seeing the look of disappointment on his face. That wasn't something she could handle right now. Not on top of everything else.

Lexi shut the door behind her and felt a wave of desperate longing rush through her. She was ten yards away before she realized that what she felt hadn't come from her. It had come from Zach. She'd felt what he was feeling.

She pulled to a stop and slid her thumb under the slippery weight of the luceria. It was warm from her body—maybe even warmer than that. Frenetic vibrations of energy pulsed around it, as if begging to be used.

Lexi was convinced she'd made a terrible mistake putting the thing on, but it was too late now. She held Zach's life squarely in her hands, and she wasn't going to let him down.

At least not yet.

Maybe she wasn't the trusting sort, and maybe she'd never let him wade through her thoughts and invade her privacy, but she wasn't completely useless.

There was power inside the band around her neck, and she was damn well going to learn how to use it.

Chapter 15

Zach kept an eye on Lexi, holding back far enough that he didn't think she'd see him. He wanted to give her some space, but not so much she was in danger.

The sun hadn't yet set, so she was safe, but Zach wasn't taking any chances. He wasn't going to risk her leaving him again.

Now that she wore his luceria, his soul had stopped dying. He could sense that the decay of his lifemark had ceased, and although the pressure of the power housed inside him was still great, it was no longer painful. Lexi had saved him.

Zach wished like hell it was enough—that he didn't have to ask her for more. But he did. He needed all of her, not just the part she wanted to give. Not just her body, but her trust.

Maybe it would take years, but Zach vowed he would find a way to show her he was worthy of such a precious gift.

"What are you doing skulking around in the trees?" asked Drake from behind him.

Zach pretended he hadn't been startled, and turned around to look at his friend. "I'm not skulking. I'm keeping an eye on Lexi."

Drake's eyes slid down to Zach's throat, then grew

wide. A grin split his face and his eyes closed for a moment in relief. "She did it."

"Yeah," said Zach simply.

"Congratulations, man. That's fantastic news. Helen is going to be beside herself."

"You might want to hold off on telling her. I'm not sure how long it's going to last."

Drake's mouth tightened. "How long did she give you?"

Zach shrugged, feeling stiff and edgy. He looked back toward Lexi, watching her as she trailed her hand along the stone wall surrounding Dabyr. "Until she gets sick of me. Until I drive her away."

Drake's voice had an edge of steel in it when he spoke. "We won't let her leave. She'll come around."

"We'll see."

Zach moved through the trees, keeping pace with Lexi's progress. Drake was a shadow at his side.

"She doesn't want to forge any kind of mental connection with me," said Zach. He wasn't sure why he shared that information, but it was too late now.

"What do you mean?"

"I mean she's blocking me. Keeping me out."

"You should talk to Gilda."

"No, thanks. I'd really rather not go spreading our problems around. Especially if it turns out some of the other men are compatible with her."

"Right. Big secret. Got it."

Lexi looked their way and both men went still, hiding their position. After a few seconds, she went back to her walk, ignoring them.

Drake picked up a discarded soda can that had found its way into the woods. "You know," he said, "her resistance might have something to do with what Helen told me."

"What?"

"She said that Lexi came here planning to help Helen escape."

Zach's heart squeezed hard and the bitter taste of betrayal filled his mouth. "No wonder Lexi let me find her. She wanted me to bring her here."

"Sorry, man."

Zach watched her slow to a halt, then press her hand against her chest. She leaned forward, and suddenly he realized she was feeling him right now—feeling what he was suffering.

Part of him wanted to go to her and comfort her, but another part of him wanted to shout at her that she was getting exactly what she deserved. How dare she trick him like this? How dare she plot behind his back to steal his brother's wife away?

Zach clamped down hard on the scrawny connection that flowed between them. It was all one-sided anyway. What was the point in keeping it open?

"She was using me." Saying the words aloud made his fists harden into lethal balls. He wanted to strike out and pound on something until he drove away the pain and humiliation her treachery had caused.

"Maybe, but look where it's gotten you. She's wearing your luceria. You have a chance to make this thing work."

"Not without her cooperation," said Zach. His words came out like hard, cold chips of ice.

"Then get her to cooperate. Find a way inside her defenses. Trick her if you have to."

"She sure as hell didn't have any problems tricking me."

Drake's hand closed around Zach's arm. He hadn't realized until then, that he had started toward her in anger. "Easy, Zach. You need to stop and think before you act. Put yourself in her shoes, and if you can't do that, then go spend some quality time with the heavy bag before you go to her."

Zach swallowed down some of his rage and gave a tight nod. "She doesn't understand our world."

"Neither did Helen."

"Lexi's worse, because not only doesn't she understand it—she has all these wrong ideas her mom put in her head. She actually believed the Synestryn were our pets."

"Are you serious?"

Zach nodded. "I don't know if I'll ever get her to trust me."

"You certainly won't if you go after her with that lethal look on your face. You need a plan."

Zach wasn't sure anything as rational as planning was going to work for him right now. All he wanted to do was vent his anger, throw his weight around, and force Lexi to be what he needed her to be.

"Are there any cracks in her defenses?" asked Drake. "Anything you could show her or give her that would help gain her trust?"

"I've been trying to do that since I found her. Nothing has worked." Zach strained his memory, trying to figure out where Lexi's buttons were. There was the sexual chemistry between them, of course, but Zach wasn't completely sure that was the way to go. What if they slept together and she regretted it? It could be a huge step backward.

The only time he'd seen any real emotion coming from her was over her car.

Her home.

That was it. Zach knew what he needed to do. "Do you have a couple of hours you can give me to work on something?"

Drake gave him a puzzled frown. "Sure. Helen's taking a nap, getting rested for some more work on the wall tonight. What do you need?"

"Four more men, some heavy lifting, and a lot of luck."

*   *   *

Connal covered his body from the remaining rays of sunset with a heavy cloak and carried Zillah's box into the woods behind Dabyr.

Through the trees, he could see the new woman walking along the wall, trailing her fingers over the stone. He hadn't yet met her, which was a small blessing. It was easier unleashing Zillah's beast upon a woman he didn't know.

Whatever was in there had been pawing and hissing, scratching at the wooden box nonstop. It never slept, never rested. That alone was enough to alarm Connal, but even worse was the fact that a few moments ago, one of the creature's black claws had finally made it through the wooden cage.

Connal could feel it watching him. He could feel the compulsion Zillah had somehow infused the woman's blood with, forcing him to obey. He couldn't fight it any longer. He had to let the creature out.

It wasn't that Connal wished any of the Theronai harm—he simply could no longer take the torture of constant hunger. Zillah fed him. The Theronai refused. To Connal, that aligned his loyalties more clearly than honor ever could.

And now the Theronai were going to pay the price for their stinginess. Whatever was in the box would hunt the few women here down and incapacitate them. All he had to do was follow behind and drink his fill before taking their bodies to Zillah.

Lexi made her way all the way around the giant wall until she was back to the place where she'd started. The gaping hole in the stone was ten feet wide and she could see the subtle difference in the construction—the variation in the gaps between the rocks—where another ten feet of rock wall had been repaired.

Whatever had broken through here had packed one hell of a wallop.

And yet this place still stood.

A ridiculous smile tugged at her mouth. If the kind of power that could do this much damage didn't bring this place down, the few bricks of C-4 in her trunk weren't going to even make a dent.

Not that she'd ever use them. Not now that she'd seen all the human men, women and children here. There was no way she could blow this place up, even if she did think it was the right thing to do. Which she didn't. Not anymore. Dabyr was a place of safety and refuge. It was a home to hundreds of people. No way could she screw that up. A home was a sacred place. She could no more destroy that than she would spray paint over the *Mona Lisa*.

Lexi's hand ran over the rough stones where the repair had been done. She could sense a low vibration seeping out of the rock. It felt warm and clean, like sunlight in the middle of winter, and there was something else there—something powerful and elusive she could almost touch.

She closed her eyes and pressed both hands against the repaired section of wall. Fatigue. Weariness. The wall was tired.

Lexi pulled away, feeling her heart pounding against her ribs. How the hell could she feel that? And how the hell could a wall be tired? It made no sense.

Then again, not much of anything had made a lot of sense in this place. Especially Zach. He didn't want to have sex, but he wanted to read her mind? What kind of fucked-up logic was that?

She'd been asking herself that for hours and still had no answers. All she had was the beginnings of a headache and a rumbling tummy. She needed dinner.

Lexi turned to go back inside where she'd seen the

dining room, and for the first time noticed she wasn't alone.

Several large men stood guard around the opening in the wall. They hadn't been there before, but the sun was starting to set, and she'd bet money they were here to keep the monsters out.

One of them turned toward her, and she saw his shimmering luceria glisten around his thick neck. He had dark blue eyes and a tall, lean build. His face was narrow, but handsome, and he had a way of moving that was almost hypnotic.

When he saw her, he stepped toward her, making Lexi's body go tense. She didn't want another repeat of what had happened in the exercise area when all those men had closed in on her, making her choke on her panic. She was weaponless, and Zach was nowhere to be found.

The man must have seen her anxiety, because he stopped in his tracks and held up his long hands. His voice was as soft as the fading daylight. "I don't mean to frighten you, my lady. I only wanted to give you my vow."

Lexi didn't know what he meant, but it was one of those things that she was probably better off not knowing. "No, thanks. I'm good."

He frowned at her. "You prefer to wait for the ceremony?"

"Yeah, I'm not really into ceremonies much, but I'm sure you'll have a good time without me."

A half smile lifted one side of his mouth. "The ceremony is for you, my lady."

Why did he keep calling her "lady"? He must have been old like Zach, and not quite up on the way modern people talked. "No need to make a fuss."

He stepped closer without looking like he'd moved. His body just kind of slid over the ground.

The other men were watching now, and they, too, came closer, their intense expressions and looming body language showing way too much interest in her for her peace of mind.

A ripple of unease fluttered down her spine. "I need to get going. Catch you all later."

She backed away until she was well out of reach, then walked as fast as she could without looking like she was running away. She ducked into the trees and peeked over her shoulder to make sure none of them were following her.

She walked about thirty yards into the woods, back where the cabins stood nestled in the trees, isolated from the rest of the grounds.

The wind shifted, and suddenly Lexi felt like she was being watched. The past several weeks of outrunning Zach had taught her that feeling well. But this was different. It was more . . . malevolent, as if whatever watched her hated her.

She'd never experienced anything quite like it before, and it left her feeling edgy and nervous. Especially now that the sun had set and darkness came swiftly within the thick growth of trees.

She looked over her shoulder, peering through the trees, searching the deepening shadows for whoever might be there. She saw no one. Not even movement beyond the occasional swaying of leaves in the breeze.

As much as she wanted to tell herself she was being foolish, Lexi had learned to listen to those instincts. Someone or something was out there, and it was watching her. It was time to go back inside.

Lexi turned to go back to the main building when something streaked from the trees and lunged at her.

Instincts honed by years of dodging spilled food and avoiding near collisions with other waitresses allowed her to dodge the black streak.

She hit the ground hard, but a deep sense of panic exploded inside her, numbing her body and making her fast. She scrambled to her knees just as it scurried into the undergrowth.

A low growl vibrated the leaves, way too deep to have come from something about the size of a house cat. That feeling of being watched intensified until she was shaking with its malevolence.

That thing—whatever it was—wanted to kill her.

Lexi pushed herself up to her feet and backed away as fast as she could without stumbling. She didn't want to turn her back on it for a second. It was way too fast for her to outrun.

Right now, she would have given anything for Zach to be here with that lethal sword in hand, standing between her and the monster.

From somewhere far off, she heard a bellow of outrage. It resonated in her mind, strong and defiant.

A black streak of movement shot out from the thing's hiding place, right toward her face. Lexi flattened herself to the ground, but felt a tug on her sleeve. She looked down and saw the scalpel-precise cut in her shirt.

If it had hit her skin . . .

Lexi wasn't going to wait to see what would happen then. She grabbed a stick lying on the ground and pushed to her feet.

This time, she didn't waste time watching her back. She just ran.

A whistling hiss of air warned her a millisecond before the next attack came. She dove to the left, landing hard on her shoulder. The stick jerked back and hit her head, shocking her for a split second.

An angry growl sounded nearby. Too close. Her poor landing had jarred her, making it hard for her to tell where the thing had gone.

Before she could make it all the way to her feet, the

streak flew at her again. Instincts lifted the stick into its path and the wood cracked in half, sending the top part of her weapon flying.

Now all she had was a stubby foot of wood, and if that thing got close enough for her to hit it, she was in serious trouble.

Lexi hadn't even gotten to her hands and knees before the monster rushed her again, whistling toward her. She held up her feeble weapon, cringing against the blow she knew she couldn't evade.

The singing sound of metal on metal filled her ears, and before she could open her eyes to see what it was, Zach had jumped between her and the monster.

His sword was bare; his stance was violent in its intent.

Lexi hurried to stand, staying close to Zach. She didn't even bother to brush the dirt and grass from her clothes.

"Did you see where it went?" she asked.

"No." That single word was full of rage. His body vibrated with tension.

"What is it?"

"Dead. As soon as I see it."

Lexi scanned the surrounding area, trying to see through the building darkness enough to locate the thing.

That eerie growling hiss rose up from behind her. Lexi whirled around. Zach shoved her back behind his body with one hand.

A flurry of movement exploded from the underbrush, shooting bits of leaves out with the thing as it shot toward them.

Zach's blade sliced through the air and a scream of pain split her ears, too high and metallic to be human. A wet thump hit the ground to her right.

The creature had been sliced in two, and each half

had already begun to dissolve into a pile of writhing black maggots. They wriggled, burrowing into the earth.

Lexi's stomach heaved.

The heavy pounding of boots echoed nearby, growing louder. Lexi couldn't look away from the ugly sight. Whatever it was, it had wanted to kill her. If Zach hadn't shown up . . .

"Finish it off, Andra," ordered Zach in a tight voice.

"Cover your ears," she warned.

Lexi was still too shocked to move, but strong, warm hands cupped over her ears, protecting them from the boom of Andra's magic.

Dirt and squishy black bits flew up, splashing against the inside of an invisible bubble. That bubble full of ick rose up, leaving a perfect semicircular crater in the ground.

Lexi watched as Andra somehow moved all that weight over the wall several hundred yards before letting it fall.

"I think that'll do it," she said, dusting off her hands. "But I'll stick around, just in case."

"Thanks, Andra," said Zach, a little too loudly, as if the boom had messed up his hearing.

Lexi turned toward him, letting relief flood her. She clutched his shirt, burying her nose against his chest. He smelled of spice and warmth and safety. She breathed him in, letting his comforting scent calm her scattered nerves.

His wide hands slid around her body, moving up and down her back in a comforting rhythm.

"Are you okay?" he asked. His mouth moved against her hair. His warm breath soaked into her scalp, easing away the last remnants of fear left skittering inside her.

"Yeah," she responded. Because he'd saved her. "Are you?"

He was tense, rigid. "I should never have left you alone."

"Don't ruin all this goodwill I'm feeling toward you by turning caveman on me."

He hugged her tighter. Voices faded as the men left to scour the grounds for more monsters.

Lexi didn't want to have any part of that hunt. She was still shaking and needed to relax. "Can we go inside now? I'm feeling a little vulnerable out here in the dark."

"Anything you want, honey."

He pulled away enough that he could look down at her. His pale green eyes were lit with concern, giving her a much needed distraction. He was such a beautiful man with such a beautiful mouth. The muscles under her palms called out to her, making her want to touch his body until she knew it better than her own. She wanted to soak him up, absorbing all that strength and confidence.

He said something, but she didn't hear the words. She was too busy fighting the urge to kiss him and take back up where they left off in that cabin. Everything about him called to her on a deeply feminine level. If she ever did get those jeans of his off, she knew they would be good together, totally explosive.

A warm grin curved his mouth and Lexi reached up to run her finger over his bottom lip. He took her hand and pressed a soft, hot kiss into her palm. "When you look at me like that, I don't care whether or not you're listening."

"Listening to what?" she asked, hearing the dazed drone in her voice.

"I said I have a surprise for you. Wanna see?"

Against her will, her eyes slid down his body to his crotch.

Zach let out a bark of laughter, and lifted her chin with his hand. "You're killing me, woman. Come on."

He threaded his fingers through hers and led her on a winding path through the trees. They came out into a clearing, and from here, she could see the back wall of the main building and a bustle of activity in the exercise area.

She tensed up and Zach squeezed her hand. "No one here is going to hurt you. They're just all anxious to meet the new girl, that's all."

She took a deep breath and forced it out. She wasn't used to being around so many people, especially not ones as massive and powerful as the shirtless men pumping iron only a few yards away.

Zach led her through the group without mishap, but she could feel the intense stares of too many eyes on her. She felt like prey when they watched her like that, and she couldn't help but suffer through a little spurt of fear that urged her to run and hide. She'd been doing that all her life, and standing her ground now was harder than she'd ever imagined.

Strong, comforting fingers slid up and down her forearm. Zach's low, soothing voice slid into her ear. "Just a little farther."

Even once they were through the glass doors, she was sure they were still watching her. She didn't need to look back to check.

"You hungry?" he asked her.

She had been before the attack, but not as much now. Her stomach had tightened up, making hunger flee. "I can't sit here and let them watch me eat."

"I was thinking something a little more private. Dinner for two."

Lexi nodded. Anything to get away from all those eyes. "Okay."

"Good. It's part of your surprise."

Zach led her into a hallway, and the noise of the people in the dining area faded behind them. Lexi pulled in a breath, then another. Finally, she was able to fill her lungs and exhale some of the tension inside her.

She focused on the doors sliding by them, counting them as she went. She probably should have been paying more attention to the twists and turns along the way, but her nerves were too raw for anything so complicated.

Zach pulled her to a stop outside of a doorway and pointed to his right. "Helen and Drake's suite is two doors down. I thought you might want to be near her." He took her hand and put a plastic card key in her palm. "This is for you."

Lexi looked at the key. There were no markings on it, just white plastic with a wide magnetic strip running along one side.

"Go ahead," he told her, grinning. "Open it."

Lexi slid the key in, and the light switched from red to green. She pushed the door open and stepped inside.

The first thing that hit her was the smell of freshly baked bread. She sucked the scent into her lungs, groaning as her hunger came back in full force.

Zach was right behind her, so close she could feel the heat of his body. She handed him his key and went to find that bread. Before she could move away, he grabbed her wrist and put the key back into her hand. "It's yours, Lexi. This whole suite is yours."

Lexi blinked up at him, waiting for the too-good-to-be-true daydream to fade. "What?"

"This is your new home." Zach curled her limp fingers around the card and gave her a smile so sweet she found herself tearing up.

"Home?" She repeated the word, trying to wrap her mind around the concept. She'd never had a home without wheels before.

His arm swept out, motioning to what lay behind her. "What do you think?"

Numb from shock, and with a layer of thick suspicion to protect her, Lexi turned around. She took three steps down the short entry hall until she could see the whole place. The living area was huge, with high ceilings and towering windows overlooking a swath of trees lining the lake's glistening edge. The walls were painted a soothing green that blended perfectly with the comfortable-looking leather furniture. A giant TV hung on the wall and empty shelves stood by, waiting to be filled with books and trinkets.

None of which Lexi owned.

A miniature kitchen was tucked into one corner, already stocked with a coffeepot and a table for two. Candles burned between two covered plates of food, and a deep, red wine glowed inside delicate crystal glasses.

On weak legs, she moved forward to where the bedrooms were. Two of them. Each with a private bathroom and closets big enough for her to park her car inside.

"Two?" she asked in disbelief.

"In case you want to invite a guest to stay," said Zach. "Or you could use it for an office or computer room or something. Whatever you like. It's yours to do with as you please."

Hers. She still couldn't grasp the concept.

The bedrooms were both completely furnished with king-sized beds, piled high with thick down comforters and mounds of superfluous pillows, glowing in silken fabrics she had no names for. One was decorated in a rich, deep blue and the other was done in pale, buttery yellow.

They were both more beautiful and luxurious than anything she'd ever seen in real life.

"You can pick whichever one you like, or you can sleep in them both. It's up to you."

Lexi rushed inside, scoping out the bathrooms. One of them had a giant tub big enough for two, and the other boasted a large walk-in shower with body jets and enough nozzles to make her feel like she was in a car wash.

"Wow." She couldn't form words. She couldn't even think straight.

She stood there, in the yellow bedroom, shaking. Zach came to her, a warm smile on his face. He took her shoulders into his hands and asked, "Do you like it?"

Lexi opened her mouth, realized she was beyond speech, and shut it again.

His thick thumb wiped tears from under her eyes. She hadn't realized she was crying until now, but she couldn't seem to stop the flow.

She swallowed and pulled in air. She knew how to speak; she just had to gather the strength to do so. "It's . . . amazing."

Zach's grin widened.

"But I can't accept it."

His smile faltered and he pulled her a little closer to his warmth. Her thighs brushed his and his hands were gentle against her face. "Why not, honey?"

"It's too much, Zach. Way too much."

"It's just a suite," he said with a shrug.

No. It was so much more than that. It was a home—a place of refuge, of hopes and dreams. It was a mythical concept that, until now, Lexi had never even dared hope to obtain. And Zach was just *handing* it to her.

The urge to accept his gift was nearly overwhelming. This was the one thing she wanted more than anything else. Walking away from it was going to rip her apart. "I'm sorry."

"But why? Everyone here is given their own home. Why shouldn't you have one, too?"

"I can't pay for it."

"We don't need money. We need *you. I* need you. Believe me, you'll earn your keep and then some once I teach you how to use your magic. Just ask Helen."

"Helen doesn't have her own place. She lives with Drake."

"Because she wants to, not because she has to. Besides, we have all these vacant suites just sitting around. You don't want them to go to waste, do you?"

"Sitting around? Fully furnished and decorated?" she asked in disbelief.

Zach gave her a sheepish look. "Well, no. We took the best stuff from several different suites and put it here for you, but that's not the point."

"The point is that, as much as I wish I could accept your generous gift, I can't. We don't even know if this thing between us is going to work out."

His jaw bunched with a pulse of anger, but then disappeared as if he'd forced it away. "I have to believe it will, Lexi."

He needed her to survive. Deep down, Lexi knew she'd never let him die. Regardless of whether or not she stayed with him, she'd wear the luceria and keep him alive until it was her turn to go, or until he found another woman to take her place.

Another woman. A deep, ferocious surge of jealousy rose up inside her, striking her blind for a brief moment. She didn't want him to find another woman. As selfish as that was, she wanted to be the only one in his life—the only one who could save him.

It linked them together, made him almost like family. She wouldn't give that up without a fight. But neither could she mislead him into thinking she could ever be the kind of woman he wanted. That level of trust he asked of her just wasn't part of her makeup. Lexi didn't think she'd even trusted her mother enough to let her roam around in her mind.

She took Zach's rough hand in both of hers, reveling in the strength and power radiating out of his body. "I want things to work out, too, but still, this is too big a gift for me to accept."

She could see a shadow cross his features and tighten his dark brow. She'd hurt his feelings, but that couldn't be helped. She'd lied to him for so long, she owed him as much honesty as she was capable of giving.

"Fine. Don't accept it yet, but don't turn it down, either. Just stay here for now. If you want to keep it, it's yours. If not, no pressure. Okay?"

Lexi looked around at the luxury and comfort this place had to offer. Living here was going to be easy. Not falling in love with this place was going to be hard.

"Okay. I'll stay, but just for now. We still have a lot of things we need to work out between us."

He stroked her face, his fingers achingly gentle as they glided over her skin, like she was made of paper-thin blown glass. "I know. But we've got time. For now, let's just share a quiet meal. You need some time to adjust, and I'm starved."

Lexi needed more than just time. She needed courage. She knew she had to tell him about the Defenders and her conspiring with them to blow this place up. Eventually, he would find out, and it was going to be easier on both of them if she did the grown-up thing and spilled her guts.

She wasn't sure how he'd react, but she knew he wouldn't hurt her. She trusted him at least that much, even if it was only because he needed her to survive.

The other men here—the ones who stared at her with hungry eyes—she was pretty sure they weren't going to be quite so understanding.

Zach stuffed Lexi full of food, hoping that would help relax her. She'd been right about them having a lot of things to work through, and most of those were better handled on a full stomach.

He lit some candles he'd found earlier, and they cast a warm glow over Lexi's living room. Zach was no interior designer, but he thought she liked the soft, comfortable things they'd put in her home. The way her eyes lit up every time she glanced past him and looked around had convinced him of that.

He'd given her a home. He'd made her cry, but in a good way. Now all he had to do was get her to stay here. Maybe let him move in with her. After two nights with her in his arms, he didn't think he'd be able to handle an empty bed.

He'd made sure that both beds in her suite were big enough to hold the two of them, just in case. He promised himself he wouldn't push, but the idea of getting her naked and making her feel good was swiftly becoming an obsession.

She slid the last bite of chocolate cake off her fork and sat back with a contented sigh.

"That was fabulous, Zach. Thank you."

"I'm not much of a cook, but I did order it from the kitchen myself."

Her eyes glowed with the smile he'd put there, making his chest grow warm with satisfaction.

"I left all the important numbers on the fridge for you in case you need someone, or don't feel like eating in the dining hall."

"Yeah, I'm not so sure about that yet. All those men staring at me is a little freaky."

Zach stood and held out his hand to her. "They'll get used to you, just like they're used to Helen now. Just give them a few days."

Lexi put her small hand in his, and it looked so perfect there, surrounded by him, protected.

"What about the dishes?" she asked.

"I'll set the trays in the hall later. No rush."

"But"—she looked from the dishes to her sink and back again—"I don't want to leave a mess."

In her new home. She hadn't said that part, but he could feel it in the air, hovering on her lips.

"You want to wash them?"

She grinned and nodded, like a child asked if they wanted to go into the toy store.

Zach shrugged. "Whatever makes you happy, honey."

He had to have someone bring them some soap and dishcloths—he'd forgotten to stock those things for her—but a little while later, they'd finished the domestic chore and Lexi was beaming.

Who would have thought that something as simple as washing a sink full of dishes could make her happy? He found himself looking around, seeking out something else that might make her smile.

"So, what now?" she asked. "It's dark. Do you go monster hunting?"

"Usually. Joseph has given me a few days off to help you settle in. I'll have to check the schedule, but I think I'm supposed to be on guard duty next week. We've got extra men on the job here since the repairs on the wall still aren't finished."

Zach led her to the comfy leather sofa, and they sank into its pillowy depths. Lexi bounced up and down a couple times, grinning, then settled down beside him. She hadn't pulled her hand away from his. In fact, she'd threaded her fingers through his, locking them together.

"Will I have a job, too? If I stay, I mean."

He wasn't letting her leave, but he decided it was best to keep things light and not go all caveman on her. If she tried to go, then he'd make things clear.

"You and I will be a team," he said. "Joseph Rayd—our leader—will assign us our duties as soon as you're able to channel my power consistently."

"Yeah, I've been thinking about that, and I want to practice some more."

"Great. We'll go out in the training yard and try some things, see what works for you."

"What kind of things?"

"Fire is good. Kills lots of snarlies. Helen kicks ass throwing fire around."

Lexi shook her head, making her fine hair sway. "I never would have believed it if I hadn't seen it for myself."

"There's probably going to be a lot of seeing-is-believing for you at first. I promise you'll get used to it."

"I'm tough. I'll manage," she said. "What else?"

"Learning to protect yourself is vital. That's my job, but I'm only one man, and I want you to be extra safe, just in case. Andra's pretty good at creating shields, so she may be able to give you some pointers. She's also really good at blowing things up."

The color slid from Lexi's face and her hand started to sweat. "I think I'll take a pass on that one. Just for now."

Zach made a mental note that the idea had freaked her out. It might be a sign what her specialty would be, if Helen's initial fear of fire was any indication. He'd convince her to try something later, but now wasn't the time. He wanted her relaxed and comfortable so she wouldn't notice when he sneaked inside those mental walls of hers. Once he was there, once she knew he posed no threat, then they'd deal with the rest.

"Sure. It's up to you. We won't go into the field until you're comfortable."

She gave him a playful grin. "Can I fly?"

"Maybe. Everyone is different. Gilda—another woman here like you—she can jump so far it's almost like flying, but she's been doing this for centuries, so she's had some time to work up to it."

"I think I'll save that one, too. I don't want to learn the hard way I can't fly."

Her fingers had relaxed again, and her shoulders were no longer up by her ears. Zach tugged on her hand, urging her to come closer.

She kicked off her shoes, curled her legs under her and fit her body against his. Her shoulder was under his arm and her head rested against his chest.

A sense of complete rightness filled him up, making him glow inside. He draped his arm around her, his hand resting on her luscious hip. The ring on his finger hummed happily. In fact, all of him was happy and content.

All his plans to gain her trust and crack her defenses turned to dust and blew away. They were inconsequential compared to the monumental satisfaction he felt right now.

Zach may have offered her some walls and a roof over her head, but she was the one who'd given him a home. *Lexi* was his home. He just hadn't realized he'd been missing it all his life.

Her slender fingers slid up his chest until they reached the bare skin of his throat. The band that had been there so long, covering his skin, was gone, making his flesh ultrasensitive to the touch. Lexi stroked him, as if knowing that was the case, and Zach's body started to heat up with a predictable dose of lust. The woman went straight to his head.

"Your skin's so much lighter here," she said.

"Starved of sunlight since I was born." Zach shivered and his muscles clenched. Hot blood raced to his groin, making him so hard so fast it was painful.

"Did I hurt you?"

"Not my neck," he told her between clenched teeth.

She shifted so she could see his face. Her bittersweet

chocolate eyes glided over him, searching for the source of his discomfort. Inevitably, she saw his erection and her lashes lowered, covering a flare of feminine greed. A sultry smile warmed her mouth, making it almost irresistible. "Want me to kiss it and make it better?" she asked.

A punch of raw desire hit him in the gut, making him grunt against the force of it. "You're trying to kill me, aren't you?"

Lexi shook her head. "No. I want you, Zach. But I want you without the mind games. Think you can do that?"

He wasn't sure, but he knew he'd try like hell. He'd do damn near anything to give her what she wanted, wanting only her in return.

He nodded.

"Just sex," she told him, licking her lips.

It wasn't what he wanted, it wasn't the way things were meant to be between them, but he knew he'd take what he could get. Especially if it involved getting Lexi naked just for him.

Zach tried to agree, but his vocal cords were clamped tight inside his throat. He settled for action instead of words, taking her mouth in a soft kiss.

Lexi let out a groan of satisfaction and deepened the kiss, sliding her sweet tongue against his. She grabbed his head and speared her fingers through his hair, holding him while she drank her fill.

Zach tried to let her set the pace, but he couldn't keep his hands to himself. He wasn't that strong. He clasped her hips in his palms and pressed her down against his straining erection. The contact, even through all those layers of clothes, shot sparks along his spine and ripped an animal sound of lust from his throat.

All his good intentions to woo her, make her trust him, slipped through his fingers, lost and forgotten. They paled in comparison to the glowing fire of need burning up his insides.

Lexi's fingers slid down his body and tugged the hem of his T-shirt over his head, baring his chest. Breaking their kiss pissed him off, and he flung her down on the couch where he could keep her right were he wanted her.

Her lips were red and wet and puffy and her eyes glowed with anticipation. She splayed her hands over his chest and Zach felt his lifemark swaying, the bare branches arcing toward her touch.

Before he forgot himself and wound up hurting one of them, Zach unbuckled his sword belt and laid it within arm's reach. It flickered to visibility, the silver leaf pattern that adorned the hilt and scabbard glowing in the yellow light of the candles still burning in the kitchen.

He wanted to see Lexi's skin by that warm light. All of it.

"Take off your shirt," he told her, unwilling to trust himself to do the job without ripping it from her body. His voice came out heavy and dark, almost sinister, but there was nothing he could do about that. Not now, while his need for her pounded at him.

Lexi hadn't heard him. Her eyes were closed as her hands slid over his chest. Sweat tried valiantly to cool his overheated skin but couldn't keep up with the task, not while Lexi was touching him.

The look of total absorption, total enjoyment, on her face was humbling. The idea he could please her with something as simple as his bare chest made him feel powerful, gave him more hope for their future than he'd thought possible.

If he could please her, she'd stay, and Zach was more than willing to put his enormous force of will to the task of giving her pleasure.

The luceria shimmered around her throat, glowing in pale, luminous plumes of jade and emerald greens.

A burst of possessiveness exploded inside of him. He wasn't going to let her go. He wasn't going to let her hide from him. He wanted every part of her. Her body, her mind, her soul. All of it. Forever.

Lexi sucked in a gasping breath and her eyes flew wide. She trembled beneath him and her fingers dug into his shoulders.

"What was that?" she asked in a desperate voice.

Zach didn't know what she meant, and he wasn't going to waste what little rational thought he had left figuring it out. He needed that to remember how to get them both naked. Now.

He slid his hands under her shirt, rubbing his knuckles across the satin skin of her belly. Sparks of power poured out of him, sinking into her wherever he touched. Her muscles quivered under his fingers and he felt her breathing speed, saw her nipples tighten under her clothes.

The urge to feel those stiff points against his tongue took over, and he shoved her shirt up onto her arms. He couldn't remember how to get her bra off, but he pulled the lacy bit of fabric down and what he wanted was right there, tight and eager and begging for him.

Zach cupped her soft breast in his hand and covered her with his mouth. She rose up off the couch in a powerful arc. The movement ground her thigh against his dick, and he nearly came right then. It took several sucking breaths through his nose to calm down, but he couldn't bring himself to move his mouth. Her nipple was hard against his tongue and the woman taste of her skin filled him up and made him hungry for more all at the same time.

Lexi took his hair in her fists and held him tight, making sexy noises of encouragement. Her hips rocked beneath him, rubbing him just right. Too right. He didn't want to come yet and end the pleasurable torment.

Hanging on the edge of insanity felt too good and he wanted her right there with him when he fell.

Somehow, he managed to open her jeans and his fingers slid down beneath her panties until he felt her slick heat. She was wet and ready for him so fast he wanted to fall to his knees in thanks. He wasn't sure he was thinking clearly enough to do this right, and he really wanted it to be right for her.

She pulled his head up and covered his mouth in a scorching kiss. Eager, needy sounds filled his lungs and he drank them down, dying to hear more.

"Need you," she told him.

Words weren't possible for him anymore.

She pulled away from him, shedding her shirt and stripping out of her bra in record time. Somehow, she got out from under him and knelt in front of him on the couch, working to shimmy out of her jeans.

Zach's world ground to a halt. The flickering of the candles' flames over her naked, flushed skin slowed to a lazy caress of heat and light. Her nipples were shiny and distended from the suckling wetness of his mouth. Her pale breasts cast loving shadows over her ribs. The gentle curve of her stomach glistened with perspiration. Slowly, so slowly he thought he'd go mad, Lexi pushed her jeans and panties down, baring herself to him until she knelt there, naked and glorious, offering herself to him.

A gift he could not refuse.

She leaned forward until her mouth was level with his chest and pressed a kiss against his lifemark. Buzzing filled his head and his tree quivered under her mouth.

Her breath swept out over his chest and she looked up at him from beneath long lashes. It was the kind of look a man dreams of seeing just once in his life—full of desire and lust and enough heat to scorch his soul. Even without being able to see inside her mind, he knew without a doubt that what was happening between them was exactly what she wanted.

Her fingers went to his jeans and this time, he didn't stop her from popping the button. She wanted just sex, so that was what he'd give her. Enough to make her scream with pleasure. Enough to leave her aching for more, because he was sure he was never going to get enough. If this was the only part of her she'd let him have, he was going to use it to his full advantage.

He helped her rid him of his clothes and shoes, then fisted his hands at his sides while her dark eyes roamed his naked body in stark appreciation.

"You are one fine-looking man, Zach."

"Lay down." The words came out short and sharp, but at least they came out. It was more than he expected.

Lexi shook her head and scrambled away in a flurry of supple arms and legs. She said something as she left, but Zach didn't hear it. His blood was pounding in his ears, his pulse a roaring drumbeat of need.

She'd left him. Again.

Zach watched her beautiful ass sway as she walked. The leopard tattoo on her shoulder stared back at him, taunting him with its green stare. She had two of the sexiest dimples he'd ever seen at the base of her spine. Somehow, that didn't make the sight of her leaving him any easier to bear. All of those nights of hopeless desperation—the nights he'd spent hunting for her while he suffered through horrible, painful spasms—came back to him.

She wasn't going to leave him. Not now. Not ever again.

Animal instincts—the need to claim his mate—took over and he pounced. He wasn't sure how he'd gotten across the room, but he had, and Lexi was pinned under him on the carpet, her eyes wide with apprehension.

Zach didn't care. She'd tried to leave him again, like he was so much garbage tossed into the street. He wasn't going to let her do that to him. Not this time.

He pushed her thighs open, shoving his knee between them. His dick slid along her slick folds, throbbing and thick and hot. Her breathing sped and her fingers clenched against his chest. He had her arms pinned so she couldn't move, but that was fucking tough. She'd tried to run away. She needed to know he wasn't going to let it happen.

"Zach." His name was a ragged plea for something he couldn't decipher.

She was so wet, so ready for him. He pushed forward, sliding into her body easily, nudging the head of his erection just inside her. She was snug and hot and the urge to shove his dick into her until he came was nearly overwhelming.

He held back, though he wasn't sure why.

Her eyes fluttered shut and a dark pink flush spread out over her cheeks. Hot ribbons of power flowed out of him, easing some of the pressure inside him, helping clear his head.

Her mouth was open, her warm breath filling the space between them. Her breasts were soft against his damp chest, her hard nipples stabbing up at him.

He pushed his hips forward, needing to be inside her all the way, filling her up, claiming her.

Lexi went tense and he felt her body clamp down hard on his dick.

"Let me in," he ordered.

She didn't respond. She didn't relax. He didn't want to hurt her, but he couldn't stop, either. Not now that he was so close to being part of her.

Zach didn't know what else to do, so he covered her throat with his hand, locking the two parts of the luceria together. Power rose up in him, churning and bubbling.

He channeled that power through their link and forced it to slide right inside her.

She gasped and arched off the floor, lodging him deeper inside her tight body. Bright blue sparks of energy spilled from her skin, sinking into the soft carpet. She shook, her muscles clenched and her eyes squeezed tight.

He was hurting her.

Zach panicked and lay there frozen, pinning her body in place. He'd hurt her, but he couldn't pull back, couldn't stop. He couldn't let her go.

He found enough strength to say, "I'm sorry." He was sorry for hurting her. Sorry that he wasn't going to stop.

Chapter 16

Lexi's body was not her own. It was an alien thing, needy and desperate, filled with so much sparkling energy she could hardly find the space to breathe.

Zach's weight held her down, giving her nowhere to run. His thick erection was poised inside her entrance, stretching her so tight it almost hurt. She hadn't been ready for that. She hadn't been ready for the heat of those tingling ribbons of energy sinking into her from the inside, too.

Bare skin on bare skin.

And he was most definitely bare. Smooth and hard and slick inside her. The thought nagged her, gave her a flicker of worry, but she couldn't focus on it enough to figure out why. All she could do was shudder under the force of his presence, the intensity of those pale green eyes staring into her.

"I won't let you leave," he growled at her, his voice vibrating his heavy chest and the tips of her nipples pressed against it.

Everything had been fine right up to the point where she walked away to go into a bedroom. That was when he'd flipped out and come after her like some kind of wild animal. That feral look was still there. His jaw was bunched. Sweat lined his brow. She could feel the tight cords of muscles as he strained to control himself, the strong beat of his racing heart. She wasn't sure how long he'd hold out.

The need to soothe him rose up inside her. She wasn't sure if it was because she was afraid of what he'd do to her, or if she was afraid of what she might let him do.

"I wasn't leaving you. I just wanted to break in one of the beds."

"Beds?" He said it like he didn't recognize the word.

Lexi wriggled her arms free and Zach pressed more of his weight down on top of her, giving her a warning rumble from his throat. She'd never heard a man make a sound like that, and she had to fight back the sliver of fear that threatened to worm its way inside her.

There wasn't room for fear. She was already bursting at the seams with more sensation than she could handle.

She made her muscles go lax under him, telling him with her body she wasn't trying to run.

Some of the tension in his jaw eased and she realized in that moment he was acting out of fear, not anger. He was afraid she was going to run away again. And why wouldn't he be? She'd done it before.

"I'm not going anywhere," she told him. She stroked his face with gentle sweeps of her fingertips over his forehead, his cheeks, his mouth. "I'm right where I want to be."

And it was true. There was nowhere else she wanted to be more than with this man, reveling in the pleasure he gave her with his mere presence.

She pulled his head down so she could kiss him, telling him with her lips and tongue that she surrendered. She was his.

Her body softened, relaxing around his erection, easing the way for him to push deeper inside her. He was big, and it had been a long time since she'd had a man—none of whom could have prepared her for this, anyway.

Zach stretched her to the limit, making nerve endings she didn't know she had zing to life. She was trembling, vibrating under the pressure of so much sensation. With slow, aching progress, he merged their bodies until there was no more room left for him to fill.

He pressed his forehead to hers, his body going still. His breath came out in hot bursts, mingling with her own. His erection moved inside her, throbbing with heat.

Lexi whimpered, shocking herself with the sound of her need ringing so clearly in her voice.

"Hurt?" He uttered the single word in a gritty voice.

"No."

A flare of satisfaction lit his eyes; then he slid his arms around her, gathered her body against his own and started to move. The slick, gliding sensation of him leaving her body hollowed her out, making her ache. She clutched at his shoulders and arched her hips toward him as he slid back into her in one smooth stroke.

Potent heat raced along her spine and filled her head. A noise of raw pleasure filled the space between them, but she couldn't tell who'd made it. Maybe both of them. His thick arms cradled her, holding her steady as he set a slow, deep rhythm. Sparkling globes of light danced in her eyes, and when they cleared, all she saw was shimmering ribbons of power flowing into her. They connected them, joining them securely with no means of escape.

Not that she wanted any. Everything she wanted was right here, within arm's reach, and all of it was a gift from Zach.

His mouth covered her nipple, sucking it into moist heat. Arcs of pleasure leapt to her womb, making her clench around his thrusting erection.

Zach growled against her flesh, the vibration causing a new riot of pleasure to swirl deep inside her.

The power of his body amazed her. The fluid clench and release of his muscles pushed her higher with every beat of her heart. Heat poured off of them, causing the air around them to pop and sizzle. Zach folded her knee up against her body, making room for his hand to snake between them.

The shift in position had him hitting a new, more sensitive spot. He slid his fingers through curls covering her mound until she felt his work-roughened fingertips glide along her slippery folds. With unerring accuracy, he cradled her clitoris between two thick fingers. The rocking of his body moved his hand just enough to make her insides tighten like a coiled spring. The exquisite pressure of his hand was perfectly calculated to force her to go where he wanted.

Lexi had no choice but to give in. She was so tired of fighting, so tired of nothing in her life being easy. Until this very moment.

Zach covered her mouth with his just as her climax crashed over her. All the tension inside her exploded out in a burst of light and sensation. It drained away only for a split second before slamming out of her again.

It was too much all at once. He overwhelmed her, destroyed her, made her whole.

Her muffled cries of release filled her ears and she felt Zach's arm tighten around her. Another trembling wave of pleasure shimmered from her just as his erection swelled and pulsed inside her. The last gentle echo of her orgasm rippled out of her, making her tighten around Zach as he growled from the depths of his own completion.

Their breathing slowed as sweat cooled their bodies. Zach's mouth was at her throat, giving her nibbling, sucking kisses she was sure would leave marks.

A satisfied smile stretched her mouth. Let him mark her. She didn't care. She felt too good to care about anything other than the comforting weight of his body on hers and the protective circle of his arm, still clutching her hips, keeping them joined.

Zach shifted, giving her room to breathe, but not much. He held himself up on his elbows and stroked her hair away from her sweaty forehead. An odd, almost vulnerable look lined his dark face.

She wanted to comfort him, to give him whatever words he needed. But deep down, she knew that what he needed from her wasn't words. It was actions. He wanted her to open herself up and let him in. Not just her body, but her mind.

How could she do that? How could she put that kind of trust in the hands of a man she had believed to be her enemy for so long?

Then again, after what they'd shared, how could she not?

It hadn't been just sex. That was what she'd wanted it to be, but it was more than that. She'd seen how much he needed her—how vulnerable he really was to her whims. She had the power to crush him, to destroy his world with little more than a thought—will the luceria to fall from her neck and it would kill him—and yet, somehow, he trusted her enough not to.

That kind of trust was humbling. Life changing.

"You're thinking too much," he told her. "I must not have done a good enough job if you're still able to think straight."

Lexi gave him a smile and kissed the tip of his nose. "If you'd done any better, it would have killed me."

An arrogant grin stretched his mouth, making his white teeth gleam in the dim light. "Care to give that theory a try?"

She couldn't take any more intensity right now. She felt too brittle. Too fragile. "Rain check?"

"As many as you want, honey. Just say the word."

His generosity made her shields crack more with every kind act. She wasn't sure how he knew just which weapons to wield against her to make her crumble at his feet, but he seemed to have an instinct for it.

He pulled from her body, still as thick and hard as if he hadn't come. But she knew he had. She could feel his semen seeping from her body, see it shining on the dark head of his penis.

They hadn't used a condom. That was what she'd forgotten earlier.

The ramifications of that slip slammed into her, one on top of another until she could do nothing more than look at him.

Lexi had never even considered having a child. She'd never drag a kid across the country, living out of the back of her Honda, putting it in constant risk of being attacked and killed by monsters. Or, worse, taken like so many of the stories she'd heard over the years.

But things were different now. She had a home, and although she hadn't yet fully accepted it in her head, in her heart, this place was hers. It was safe. She could raise a child here without worry, knowing there would be others here just like him or her. Her child would feel normal. Her child would go to school and play with other kids and have a real life.

A family.

She started to shake as the foundations for her entire life, her plans for her future shifted beneath her.

"What's wrong?" asked Zach, panic tightening his words.

"I'm not on birth control."

His hand slid over her hair in a comforting caress. "It's okay. You don't have to worry. I can't make you pregnant."

"You can't?" Shimmering dreams withered and went dim before they'd even finished forming.

"No. Our men are sterile. Something the Synestryn did to us." Despite the gentleness of his hand, his words were short and curt. Bitter.

"I'm sorry." And she was, but not only for him.

"Yeah. Me, too, but it's ancient history." He stood and reached a hand down to her. "How about we check out that new shower of yours?"

Lexi nodded. A shower sounded good. Distracting. She had too many things moving through her head right now. Too many questions. Too much confusion. Washing some of them away sounded like a great idea.

Angus found Gilda in the Hall of the Fallen. A low fire burned in the hearth, warming the room, making the polished swords of the dead warriors glow.

Gilda sat in a leather chair with a sword in her lap. The gray silk of her gown shimmered in the firelight, hugging her body and making him ache to slide his hands over her lush curves. It had been too long since he'd last held her in his arms and made love to her—nearly a week. She'd been distant lately, and no matter how hard he tried, he couldn't seem to bring a smile back to her lips.

His failure grated over his nerves, stealing from him his usual steady patience and iron control. If she wouldn't tell him what he could do to ease her, he was going to find his own way to help her—one he was fairly sure she wouldn't approve of.

The large leather chair seemed to swallow her small body, making her look weak and vulnerable. Protective instincts honed over hundreds of years rose easily to the surface, quickening Angus's step.

Her slender fingers ran lovingly over the blade. Their son's sword—Angus recognized it now that he was closer. He knew every knick and scratch on the blade, every smooth spot worn down by his son's strong grip.

Gilda's dark eyes fluttered shut as she pulled a memory from the mirrored depths of the steel, reliving a moment of their son's brave past. A single tear slipped down her cheek and she pulled in a sobbing breath.

"Gilda," he said quietly so he wouldn't startle her.

She lifted her head and the force of her beauty drove through him like a hammer's blow. Every line of her face was perfectly formed, every curve exquisite. Even the fathomless depths of her black eyes drew him in and made him tremble against the need to touch her, comfort her.

Time had not altered her appearance much over the centuries. There was a maturity about her, though she had no wrinkles. Wisdom shone in her every move, though not one of her hairs had gone gray as his had. She was timeless beauty and unfailing loyalty.

Angus loved her so much, sometimes he was sure his heart would burst open under the strain.

"You shouldn't be here," he told her. "It's not healthy for you to wallow in these memories."

"They're all I have left of him. A record of my mistakes."

He took the sword from her hands and hung it back in its rightful place of honor. "Not all the mistakes made by our people are yours."

"Our children have died, and there is no one to blame but myself," she said.

"Sibyl still lives. And Maura."

Gilda's jaw hardened. "No. Maura is dead. Only her body lives on."

Angus disagreed, but now wasn't the time for that old argument. They both knew it too well. "What of Sibyl? She is back home with us. Safe."

"For how long?" asked Gilda, staring into the fire.

"The wall is going back up as fast as we can manage."

Anger tightened her full mouth, and Angus couldn't

remember the last time he'd seen her smile. "The wall did not protect her before. It will not now, any more than you or I can. Her abduction proved that beyond doubt."

"Hope is not lost. Don't you see that?"

She stood and spun around, her gray skirts swirling in an angry arc. "You think just because a few female Theronai have come through our gates that all is well? Are you really that foolish?"

The barb stung, but he accepted the pain without complaint, forgiving her for it even as it left her mouth. He knew how much strain she was under. She was not herself—not the same woman he'd grown to love over the years, though he could love her no less, even if he tried.

"I think," he said carefully, "that things are changing for the better. I prefer to live in hope than dwell in despair." He pulled in a deep breath, steeling himself for the reaction he knew she would have at his next words. "Which is why I'm going to agree to allow Tynan to try to restore my fertility. He thinks he has a cure."

Her body stilled and only her eyes moved. They narrowed to dangerous slits, seething with emotion too strong to name. Angus reached out for the connection of the luceria that bound them together, seeking to feel what was going on behind those eyes, but he met a hard wall.

She was locking him out. Refusing him.

Angus reeled in shock. She'd never once denied him like that. Not even when she was angry. Sure, he'd felt her pull back on her emotions and filter out the things she didn't want him to feel, but never had she refused him so completely—never once slammed the door in his face like that.

Anger and loneliness choked him, but he refused to

back down. "I knew my decision would bother you, but I had no idea how much."

"Bother me?" she asked in a deceptively quiet voice. "You make a decision like this without even asking my opinion, and you think I'm merely *bothered*?"

"Angry, then. If you'd let me in your thoughts, I'd be able to tell, wouldn't I?"

She ignored his taunt and her fists clenched in her skirt, ruining the smooth silk. "I will not bear another child. Not even for you."

"Nor have I asked you to. I know your feelings on the matter."

"And yet you would allow Tynan to repair you?"

"Yes, so that he may learn how to repair the other men. You may not want children, but what about the other women who have come to us?"

"I assume none of them would like to see their babies slaughtered as I have mine. You'd be doing them a favor refusing Tynan," said Gilda.

Angus sucked in a deep breath, reaching for patience. The depth of Gilda's grief for their dead children knew no bounds. She hadn't healed as was natural, as he had healed. Her grief had not lightened over the decades. Somehow, all the fear and anger and loss had festered inside Gilda, growing bigger and darker with the passage of time.

He should have seen it before. He should have sought to help her sooner, but he hadn't, and now he was afraid that the affliction she suffered was too large and deep to be healed.

Except, possibly, by the birth of another child. One they would protect and keep from harm. One who would save its mother from her grief.

Angus's soul ached to hold a babe in his arms, to hear the sound of its laughter and feel the pride of watching it grow up strong and brave and kind. He cherished all of his children, even those who had made poor choices. He missed them, and there would always be a hollow place in his heart that he couldn't still hold them and speak to them, but that hollowness had not destroyed him. It had not ripped away his will to live or his ability to see the joy surrounding them. It had not tarnished the pride he had in working to keep so many humans safe.

"I won't turn my back on my responsibilities," said Angus, meaning more than just his responsibilities to his men. Gilda also needed him, though he doubted she would agree.

"No, instead you'll turn your back on me."

He reached for her, but she flinched, and he let his hand fall away. "Never that, love. You are now and have always been the center of my world. I would do anything for you."

"Anything except deny Tynan?" Her hands unclenched and her face smoothed to impassivity. "Do as you will. I won't try to stop you, but know this: as long as there is even the slightest chance you are fertile, I will not allow you to bed me."

Angus almost laughed at her ludicrous statement until he saw the glint of lethal hostility shining in her eyes. The laugh bubbling inside him died, and he clamped his lips shut over the rotten sound.

"You meant it. We've made love more days than not for centuries, allowing nothing to come between us. How can you mean that?"

"I will not bring another child into this world."

"Not even if it's what I want?"

She gave him a level stare. "I love you. I've tried to give you whatever you wanted, but in this I cannot bend. I don't love you enough to watch another child of mine die."

"We won't be able to resist each other," said Angus with complete confidence.

"To prevent another child's death, I will. Believe me."

Angus did not doubt her sincerity, but neither could he back down. He had to help find a way to heal all of them, to bring children back into their lives. "I have to do this, Gilda. The men need me. But if you insist, we can use human forms of contraception."

"No." The word was flat, final and ugly. "If you do this, you will not touch me."

A heavy sense of defeat fell on Angus, making him feel old and weary. He and Gilda had been through so much and always come out the other side stronger and closer than before. This time, for the first time, Angus questioned that possibility.

She'd shut him out of her thoughts. She'd never done that before. She'd never turned her back on him.

Angus couldn't stand here and face her like this, unable to find a way to help her, and unwilling to give her what she thought she wanted. He had to act with his conscience, and pray that eventually, Gilda would see it was the right thing to do. The only thing to do.

He turned away, leaving the Hall of the Fallen and Gilda behind.

As the thud of his boots echoed in the long hallway, Angus suffered in silent frustration. He had to do this. He had to give his people hope for some kind of future. If Tynan's calculations were off and this possible cure did harm instead of good, Angus would be the only one to suffer.

And if it succeeded, these walls would once again ring with the sound of happy children. Theronai children.

Angus was filled up with a renewed sense of purpose. He was going to help his men. Whether or not he ever had another child, he vowed that he would do whatever was necessary to see that his men did. They would rebuild their ranks and hope would be restored. Angus would not allow any lesser outcome.

Gilda was hurting right now. Weak from her efforts to restore the wall. Of course she would react badly to such a sensitive subject. It was hardly her fault that she suffered so, and he would forgive her. Hell, he already had. But that didn't mean he was going to let her continue to destroy herself.

They weren't done yet. Not by a long shot. She'd shut him out, but Angus refused to let it stand. She was hurting too much for him to do so. Whether or not she realized it, she needed him, and if that meant he had to trick her, then that was what he'd do. His woman was a stubborn one, and sometimes, the only way to get through her thick skull was by sheer force of will—the kind of force a man like Angus was more than equipped to exert.

He'd seduce her. She wouldn't be able to resist him. She never had.

And once his child was growing inside of her, she'd find joy again. She'd soften and see he only wanted what was best for her—what was best for all of them.

Gilda watched Angus leave, keeping her knees locked until he was safely out of sight. As the carved wooden door clicked shut, she crumpled to the floor. Her body was weak and useless, but she made sure the barrier she'd put between them was still safely in place.

Tears wet her cheeks, but she ignored them. She was too weak to hold them in, too tired to care whether or not anyone saw.

Physically, the strain of using so much magic day after day was taking its toll. Her body trembled, barely able to stand up to the effort of moving around as if nothing was wrong. Mentally, she was in tatters. Blocking Angus out had taken the last of her reserves, and she could only hope that the barrier stayed safely in place until the wall was restored and she had a chance to rest.

But she'd had no choice. That barrier had been necessary.

Gilda couldn't let Angus find out the truth. It wasn't the Synestryn who had robbed Angus of his ability to have children. It had been Gilda. She'd sterilized all the Theronai men in a fit of anger and grief the night their youngest son died.

Standing over the bloody patch of grass that had been the only thing left of her son, she knew she could never again watch another child die. And the only way to ensure that was to never have another child.

She hadn't meant for her magic to go beyond Angus. She hadn't meant to put so much power into her spell, causing it to seek out and sterilize all the men, ensuring she could not conceive by any of them. She hadn't meant to allow her grief to bind with that power, giving it enough strength to make it irreversible. At least to her.

Maybe Tynan had found a way where she hadn't.

But she'd robbed the men of something so fundamental that what she had or hadn't meant to do mattered little.

If Angus ever found out what she'd done—if any of the men did—she was sure they would hate her, shun her. Or worse, banish her. Send her to the Slayers like a man whose lifemark had died, letting those beasts do with her as they would.

Death would come, but not swiftly. Gilda had heard the stories of what the Slayers did to female prisoners.

She couldn't let that happen to her. More important, she couldn't let that happen to Angus.

Their fates were bound together. If she died, he would

die with her, and Gilda loved him too much to let him
witness her rape and murder. She'd be kinder to end her
own life, or even kill him first, rather than have him live
through that, helpless to stop it.

Gilda tried to push herself up, but her arms were too
weak. Normally, Angus would have sensed her weakness and been by her side, lifting her into his thick arms
and caring for her until the weakness abated.

But this was not normal. Angus couldn't feel her
weakness. He couldn't feel anything. Not even the shame
that burned so bright inside her she was sure it would set
her skin aflame.

Gilda covered her face with her hands, wishing she'd
done things differently.

Wishing changed nothing. Of course, neither had decades of pouring all of her strength into finding a way
to reverse the magic she'd wrought. Nothing she'd done
had helped. The longer the men remained sterile, the
stronger the magic seemed to grow. She'd tried everything she knew, short of telling anyone what she'd done.

Maybe it was time to confess, or at least tell Tynan
what she'd done. As much as she protected her secret,
she was constantly worried that one of the Sanguinar
would find out. She refused to let anyone but Logan feed
from her, and then only when it was vital. Angus was
more likely to give of his own blood than allow hers to
be shed, and Gilda had accepted his protection, knowing
that he inadvertently hid her secret with his kindness.

Angus was too good a man for her. Gilda knew it, but
it changed nothing. She wasn't going to let him go, even
if there were a hundred compatible women waiting in
line.

And she wasn't going to let him lie with her. The
chance that Tynan could find a way to reverse her magic
was too much of a risk.

Losing Maura had nearly killed her. Sibyl's refusal to

speak to her was like dying over again each day. Time did nothing to ease the pain her last living child's rejection caused her.

But Gilda deserved what she got. All of it. It was her fault none of the men could have children, just as it was her fault her baby girl would never grow into a woman.

Gilda stared into the fire while she waited for the tears to stop falling, while she waited for the shaking in her limbs to ease enough to allow her to stand.

She was alone now. Her mistakes had killed those she loved and driven the rest away. All that was left for her was grief and regret, and neither of them were going to help her stand. She was on her own. It was time to get tough.

Chapter 17

Lexi left the giant shower before Zach could distract her with his luscious body. One look at his erection bobbing against his muscled abs and all she wanted to do was go to her knees and suck him into her mouth, feel him explode against her tongue.

Unfortunately, that wasn't going to get her any closer to 'fessing up about the bomb in her trunk, so she kept her eyes on his chin, got clean and got out as fast as she could.

She'd just finished dressing when he came into the room, wearing only a damp towel around his lean hips. His erection had abated and she found herself wondering if he'd gotten himself off in the shower without her.

The odd feeling of resentment straightened her spine and left her feeling robbed. If he was going to come, she wanted to be the one making it happen.

"If you don't stop staring, I'm never going to fit into my jeans," he told her.

Lexi clamped her eyes shut and hurried back into the bathroom to brush her hair. When she came out, Zach was dressed, sitting on the edge of the bed, pulling his heavy boots onto his feet.

"I thought we could go out and try a few things, see how you handle my power," he said.

"There's something I need to tell you first." Her voice shook with apprehension and Zach's eyes shot to her face, narrowing in concern.

"You can tell me anything you want, honey. No need to be afraid." He patted the bed next to him, but Lexi knew if she got that close, she'd lose her nerve.

She started to pace, keeping out of arm's reach. "You already know I was raised not to trust you, right?"

"Yeah."

"And that I truly believed you were the bad guys."

"Which is why you kept running away."

"Right," she said.

"I understand, honey. I'm not holding it against you. You can relax."

Maybe he wasn't holding her upbringing against her, but how was he going to feel about her plan to blow him up? "I'm not alone, Zach. A lot of people out there think you all are the bad guys."

"You mean the Defenders."

She nodded. "My mom was in pretty tight with them."

Zach shrugged, drawing her eyes to the impressive width of his shoulders. The urge to run her fingers over his smooth skin and the muscles lying beneath made her mouth water, but that was just tough. She had to get through this.

"I wouldn't exactly say I was tight with them, too. I thought they were mean and kind of corny, but near the end, right before you found me ..."

Zach stood and took a step toward her. Lexi held up her hands, telling him to stay back.

His green eyes narrowed. "Toward the end, what, Lexi?"

Lexi, not honey. That didn't bode well.

"I was desperate. I had no money. I couldn't find work. Getting fake social security numbers has gotten so much harder recently, and I didn't have the kind of cash to fork over for a new identity."

"You should have called me," said Zach. "I hate the idea you suffered like that."

She gave him a sheepish grin. "Yeah, well, you were kinda the reason I felt the need for that new identity in the first place. I was pretty sure you'd be able to track me down."

"I tried. You weren't easy to find."

They were getting off track. "Anyway, I was desperate, so I went looking for these guys that my mom used to stay with when things got bad."

"The Defenders," guessed Zach.

"Yeah. They took me in like I was one of their own. Their leader, Hector Morrow, even remembered me from when I was a kid." And she remembered him, too.

"I'm glad you had a place to go."

"You're not going to be glad when you hear the rest."

Zach took another step toward her, this time ignoring her desire for him to keep his distance. He covered her shoulders with his palms, and ran his hands down her arms. The touch of his skin on hers made her head spin, and wrapped her in a cocoon of comfort.

Man, she was going to miss that. No way was he going to be touching her like that when he heard the truth.

"As long as you're safe, I'll be fine. Finish your story."

"It's not a story. It's an explanation. I want you to understand why I did what I did."

"Did what?"

"Not yet. Let me finish."

Zach nodded and Lexi pulled in a fortifying breath. "The Defenders gave me a job at that bar. They gave me a place to sleep. They fed me. They promised me they wouldn't let you find me."

His jaw bunched then, and an angry glow brightened his eyes. "None of them would have stopped me. You know that, right?"

Lexi swallowed a sudden burst of nervousness. "I'm glad it didn't come down to that, to be honest. These men aren't bad guys."

"It wouldn't have mattered if they were saints if they'd tried to stop me from finding you."

"Well, they didn't get the chance. Instead, we ... came up with a plan."

Zach's fingers tightened around her arms slightly and his voice hardened. "What kind of plan?"

Lexi couldn't look him in the eye. She was too ashamed of what she'd done. "It's ugly, Zach."

"Just. Tell. Me."

Time to suck it up.

Lexi thrust her chin out, straightened her shoulders and looked him right in the eye. "The Defenders have been trying to find your home for a long time. When they knew you were looking for me, they said I'd make great bait. I agreed."

"So you did want me to find you. I knew it," said Zach.

"Yes. That's why I called Helen. I was sure she was brainwashed. I knew she'd tell you where I was."

"So, that night you called and sounded so scared?"

"It was a trick. I knew you'd come if you thought I was in trouble, though, at the time, I thought it was because you wanted the pleasure of killing me yourself."

His jaw bulged with anger; his throat worked as if he was trying to choke down her words. A vein in his temple throbbed.

Lexi was running out of time to finish her confession. She had to get it all out so he could be good and angry all at once. She wasn't sure she'd have the guts to face him like this again. "So, I called. You came, just like we planned. I was supposed to get you in my car and lead them here, but then my car stalled out."

A look of deadly suspicion crossed his face. She was sure this was the look the Synestryn saw right before he cut them down. "Why your car?"

"Because that's where the explosives are. I have a trunkful of C-4 and the Defenders taught me how to use it." She refused to flinch. "I was sent here to blow this place up, along with everyone in it."

Lexi had been planning on killing him.

Shock didn't even begin to cover what he was feeling right now. Betrayal came closer, but not nearly close enough. His body shook with anger and a hurt so deep he didn't know he had any nerve endings there until now. Years of suffering had not prepared him for a blow like this.

Lexi, the woman he was meant to spend his life with, to love and defend, had planned to kill him.

And everyone else here—all those innocent souls he was sworn to protect.

Zach couldn't wrap his head around it. Maybe he never would be able to, but there'd be time to try later; right now, he had to deal with this crisis and make sure no one got hurt. Including Lexi.

The Theronai were not going to take her treachery lightly.

"Is there any risk of that shit going off?" he demanded.

"No. It's safe. I have to hook everything up to the C-4 before there's a threat."

"Are you sure?"

"I wouldn't be standing around here if I wasn't. There are kids around. I'd never risk harming them. You believe that, don't you?"

He had no choice but to believe her for now—until he had time to check for himself.

"You used me," he choked out, barely able to form the words. The pain of her betrayal ran deep—deeper than he would have thought possible considering their short time together.

"I did use you. I don't expect you to forgive me, but I didn't know what I was doing."

"And now that you do? Now that you know how fucked up this plan of yours was?"

Her dark eyes held steady, begging him to believe her. To trust her. "I'm sorry. Really, Zach, I would never hurt the people here. You know that, right?"

He wanted to believe her, but the lives of too many people were at stake. "There's only one way I can know for sure, Lexi."

"How? I want to fix this. I really do. That's why I'm spilling my guts here." She looked sincere. She held his gaze and didn't squirm when he glared back at her. It looked like she wasn't trying to lie.

Anymore.

Still, the fact that she had lied made her suspect. Zach knew only one way to prove her innocence. "You're going to let me in your head. You're going to let me see your thoughts."

"No, Zach. That's too creepy. Too intrusive."

"Too fucking bad. You've made this mess by lying, and that's the only way to clear it up. I'm going to have to tell Joseph what you've done. I can't possibly vouch for you if you aren't willing to let me do this."

"There's got to be another way."

"There isn't."

Lexi backed away, hitting the wall behind her. "I'm a private person."

Zach followed her, watching her for any signs she

might try to flee. "Not anymore. We're doing this, Lexi. One way or another. I have a vow to these people to uphold."

"What about your vow to me?"

"I'd give my life to protect you, even as angry as I am, but what I'm going to do to you in no way violates that." And he was going to do it. Even if he had to force her. It wouldn't be pleasant, but it would be a hell of a lot gentler than what Joseph might be forced into doing to get the truth out of her. He might call in one of the Sanguinar, and Zach wasn't going to let one of them tromp through her mind.

"I don't want it."

"I don't care. This is serious."

"So am I," she said, lifting her chin.

Fuck. He knew damn well that if she fought him on this, he might end up hurting her. Still, it had to be done. He had to be sure, without a doubt, that there was nothing else she was hiding from him. Too many lives were at stake if he was wrong.

"This is the only way I can protect you, Lexi. If we don't do this, someone else will, and they won't be as careful with you as I will."

She stared at him for a long moment. Her pupils had tightened down to frightened dots of black. All the color had faded from her cheeks, leaving behind the gray pallor of fear.

Zach couldn't stand to see her like this. He had a job to do, and he'd do it, but that didn't mean he couldn't make this as easy on her as possible. No one else knew yet. He still had the time to take it slow. Go easy.

He smoothed her baby-fine hair away from her forehead. It was still damp from their shower and clung to his fingers, tying them together. "I need you to let me do this. If you make me use force, it's going to hurt."

Her head fell back against the wall and he saw her

throat work nervously. "Yeah. Okay. I got myself into this. I'll take my punishment like a big girl."

"It's not a punishment." Though that might well still be headed her way.

"Sure feels like one."

"Just close your eyes and relax. I'll do the rest."

Lexi did as Zach told her and tried not to get sick on his feet.

She couldn't believe she was going to let someone muck about inside her head. If she'd known that would be the cost of dealing with the Defenders, she would have decided to starve first.

Zach's hand splayed over her throat, and she felt her necklace lift until it came in contact with his ring. The two bands locked together like magnets, and a slow trickle of warm energy sank into her skin, radiating out from the necklace.

The hair on her body lifted, and a potent shiver raced through her, lighting up nerve endings as it went.

Lexi let out a low groan of pleasure. She couldn't help it. Whatever he was doing felt too good, almost like a narcotic streaking through her system.

Her bones softened, and her body slid down the wall. Zach's strong arm eased her down slowly, keeping her from falling hard. She ended up in a loose heap on the floor with her shirt dragged up her back, leaving it bare against the cool, hard wall.

"That's right," he whispered. "Just relax."

She didn't really have an option, not that she was complaining. If she'd known being mind-fucked was going to feel this nice, she might have let him do it before.

Her eyes were barely open, just cracked enough that she could see Zach's dark face hovering above her. He was so beautiful, so manly. That mouth of his was full and soft, unlike the rest of his hard, lean body, and he knew how to use it to make her feel so good. Just kissing him was better than full-blown sex with other men. She wasn't sure how that worked, but she was pretty sure that if she spent some time studying it, she'd figure it out.

Lexi reached for him, her arms going around his neck in a sloppy stack of limp fingers. She couldn't find the strength to hold on, and her hands slipped back into her lap. She tried again, but Zach gathered her wrists in his free hand and held them in place.

"Just relax," he told her.

If she got any more relaxed, she was going to sink into the carpet, making a wet puddle. Maybe that was what he wanted. She thought she could do it if it was.

"You're doing great, honey."

Honey. He wouldn't call her that if he hated her, right?

Lexi latched onto that idea and held it close. She didn't want him to hate her. She wanted him to love her.

Love. The thought shocked her to stillness. Why would she want him to love her? That would only complicate things. She hadn't even decided if the life he led was going to work out for her or not. Sure, he'd gone a long way toward convincing her to stay. He'd given her a home, made her feel like a queen. Made her feel important. Needed.

What girl wouldn't want to get used to something like that? It just showed she was sane.

But love was a big deal. It changed things. Made them harder. Messier.

Better.

A blunt pressure behind her eyes made her wince, distracting her from her train of thought.

"Don't fight it," said Zach.

Lexi wasn't fighting anything, but her mouth wasn't working well enough to tell him that.

The pressure increased until it was pain. A whimper fell from her lips and the pain eased off somewhat, but didn't disappear.

"You're fighting me, honey. You've got to let down those guards of yours."

"Don't know how," she heard herself whisper.

He was silent for a moment, and she felt a subtle tension running through his hand. A single pulse of fear slid into her and she could tell instantly that it wasn't her own. It had a different feel to it. A different shape, more jagged and rough than her own.

It was Zach's fear. He was afraid. For her.

Something was wrong, but Lexi couldn't figure it out.

"It's okay. We'll try it again. This time, I want you to picture a thick brick wall in your head. Can you do that?"

She gave a small nod as the wall popped into existence inside her mind.

"Good. Now take that wall down, brick by brick. You don't need it anymore. You're safe with me."

Safe. That was nice.

Lexi did what he said, tearing down the wall, only she never reached the bottom. There were always more bricks, like they were growing up from whatever passed as earth inside the fluid constructs of her head.

Refusing to give up, she kept doing what he'd said while the pressure behind her eyes once again started to build. Heat grew inside her head, making her shake. The wall kept growing, keeping up with every attempt she made at shrinking it.

Pain radiated out, filling her skull to bursting. A noise sounded somewhere distant: a shrill cry of pain and the dry rattle of panting breaths. Hard bands tightened on her wrists and a brittle heat bit into her neck.

This was wrong. Even without any sort of experience

at these kinds of things, she knew in her soul this was all terribly wrong.

The brick wall shot up, thickening as it grew. Taller than Jack's beanstalk and wider than she could see, the thing kept growing and swelling, fighting against the pressure that filled her head.

A buzzing sound clogged her ears. Her blood burned as it sped through her veins, searing them from the inside out. There was nowhere to run to make it stop. Nothing she could do.

Dimly, she felt a popping inside her head, like little bursts of static electricity igniting oxygen. As each spark burst, she felt less of the world around her. Hearing faded. The cool press of the wall against her lower back became a memory. The feel of Zach's hands around her wrists disappeared, along with feeling in the wrists themselves. Awareness of her body dissipated like fog under the sun until there was nothing left but the brick wall and an incessant pounding against it.

Then suddenly the pounding stopped. Or maybe it hadn't stopped, but she could no longer sense it in any way. Everything but the wall slipped away and Lexi let it all go. She didn't need any of it. All she needed was to let go.

Chapter 18

Lexi was limp in Zach's arms. Sweat trickled down his temple, mocking his pounding headache. He was shaking like he'd just finished a three-day battle with no water, and it took all his strength to keep himself sitting upright. Which was sad, considering the wall did most of the work for him.

He'd failed. Nothing he'd tried seemed to work. Lexi was too strong, her defenses impenetrable.

She didn't trust him. Deep down inside, where it mattered most, she didn't trust him. He knew that was why he'd failed.

Zach waited for the weakness to fade enough he could move; then he shifted Lexi so her head was resting at a more comfortable-looking angle on his shoulder. The luceria shimmered under the bright bedroom lights, showing off an angry swirl of greens and maybe some blue.

The blue hadn't been there earlier, and with a sick sense of dread, Zach realized that whatever had just happened had actually reversed the process of bonding them closer together.

Shit.

Rabid frustration gnawed at his insides. He wanted to lash out and vent some of his anger, but there was no one around who deserved that kind of treatment. The source of Lexi's mistrust was her mother's teachings, and he was sure the woman had only done what she thought she had to do to protect her child.

Zach refused to hold that against her. She'd kept Lexi safe all those years when he couldn't and he owed her respect, not resentment.

He gave Lexi a little shake. "You okay?" he asked.

She didn't answer. Her breathing had evened out and her pulse was steady and strong, but she wasn't awake.

What if he'd damaged her?

A sick sense of panic trickled through him and he pulled out his cell phone. He wasn't sure if Logan was at Dabyr or not, but he was the only one of the Sanguinar Zach trusted enough to let him touch her.

"Are you at home?" he asked as soon as Logan answered.

"I was just about to leave. Why?"

"I need you. It's Lexi."

"I'll be right there."

Now for the hard part. Zach dialed Joseph Rayd, the leader of the Theronai. As much as he hated it, Zach had to tell Joseph about the explosives.

Joseph answered on the sixth ring; his voice sounded strained. Tired. "Yeah."

"I need you to come to Lexi's room," said Zach.

"Whatever it is, it can wait. Kinda busy." He sounded more than just busy. His voice was strained, like his throat was so tight he was having trouble shoving the words out. A hint of anger and something else shaded his words, chilling them. "Now's not a good time."

Zach looked down at Lexi's limp form. "It's gonna have to be. We have a . . . situation."

A muffled curse came over the line, and he knew Joseph was on his way. "What's one more, right?"

Zach had no idea what he meant, but he could guess. Something was going down, and it wasn't good.

"Give me a sec," said Joseph. "I'll be there."

Zach shoved away his weakness and got Lexi settled comfortably in bed. He left her just long enough to open her door for Joseph, then went back to her side. By the time he was back, she was starting to wake, pushing herself up on the bed.

Her arms trembled, so he helped lift her up and shoved a couple of fluffy pillows behind her back.

Lexi rubbed her temples and blinked her eyes. She saw him, and although he had no idea what the look on his face was, it must have been bad, based on the way her eyes widened and she reached for him like he was about to fall over a cliff.

"Are you okay?" she asked.

His eyes strayed to the luceria around her throat. There was definitely a lot of blue in there now. He'd lost ground with her.

"Fine." The word came out hard and clipped.

"You look like you're going to puke. Did something happen while I was passed out?"

"You were only out for a few seconds."

"Then what's going on?" she asked.

"That's what I'd like to know," said Joseph from the bedroom doorway. His hulking body filled the space and his face was set in rigid angles. "This had better be damn important."

"It is," said Zach. "We have a problem."

"Great. Just what this place needs. Another problem." Joseph let out a weary sigh and crossed his arms over his thick chest. "Get on with it. I don't have all day."

Zach felt Lexi grow tense more than he saw it happen. The air around her seemed to get colder and was scented with the tang of panic.

"It's going to be okay," Zach told her. "Joseph won't hurt you."

A disgusted sneer crossed Joseph's face. "Of course I'm not going to hurt her. What the hell is going on?"

Zach found Lexi's hand and gave it a comforting squeeze. He opened his mouth to speak, but she beat him to the punch. "It's my mess. I'll tell him," she said.

Zach nodded, and a sense of pride curled around him. She might be afraid, but she wasn't going to let it stop her from doing the right thing.

He loved that about her.

Lexi pushed herself upright and swung her legs over the side of the bed. "I suppose I shouldn't beat around the bush," she said.

"That would be nice," agreed Joseph. "I'm a busy man."

"I originally came here to blow this place up. The C-4 is in my trunk."

Joseph was still for a moment; then he slowly pushed himself away from the doorframe, his face getting darker and darker with every passing second.

Zach moved his body so he was between Joseph and Lexi, and he put his hand on his sword. "Stay where you are," he warned Joseph.

That furious stare swiveled around until it was squarely on Zach. "You brought her here."

"I did."

"He didn't know," said Lexi. She was at his side, trying to get past Zach, but he didn't budge. "None of this is Zach's fault."

Joseph's words came out like slabs of ice—cold and heavy. "You've committed an act of war."

"No, she planned one. She didn't actually commit it."

"Bullshit," growled Joseph. "She brought explosives onto our property—into our homes. There are humans here. *Children*."

"I know," said Lexi. "That's why I didn't follow through. I'd never hurt kids. I thought you were all monsters. I see now I was wrong. I'm so sorry."

"Sorry doesn't mean shit, little girl. Your action is punishable by death."

"Over my fucking corpse," said Zach. He pulled his sword and held the naked blade with the tip pointing at Joseph's heart.

A movement from the doorway caught Zach's eye, but he didn't turn. "Apparently, I've come just in time," drawled Logan from the doorway. "Someone care to fill me in?"

"Zach was just sealing his fate by siding with the enemy," said Joseph.

Lexi slipped out from behind him and wrapped her hand around the razor-sharp steel. If Zach so much as breathed hard, it would slice right through her delicate skin.

"Stop it with the macho shit," she ordered him. "You're making it worse."

Anger and a sickening sense of dread rolled around inside him, making him queasy. He couldn't let Joseph hurt her, no matter how much she'd messed up.

Lexi turned to Logan, keeping her hand on the sword's sharp edge. "I made a mistake. A big one. Joseph flipped, which is totally understandable, and now these two are leaking testosterone all over my new place."

"Perhaps we should start by putting the weapon away," suggested Logan.

Joseph's jaw bulged, but he lifted his hands, palms out, and took a long step back. "I'm not going to hurt her. Yet. She deserves a chance to speak."

Zach gathered every strand of control he could find and pulled hard. Lexi looked up at him, her eyes pleading with him, though for what, he wasn't sure. Put the weapon away? Get her out of this mess? Go back in time so they'd never met?

"Shit," he spat. "Get your hand off my sword, and I'll back down."

Lexi did and Zach sheathed the sword.

His protective instincts were still running hot, pounding through him like a jackhammer. He wasn't sure he was going to be able to control himself enough to think rationally, but he had to try. For Lexi.

"Good," said Logan. "That's a good start. Now, my lady, if you please, can you give me a little more detail?"

"I brought a trunkful of explosives here to blow you all to hell. Needless to say, I've changed my mind. I'm not really a big fan of killing, so it works for me."

"Why did you want to kill us?" asked Logan with only the faintest interest coloring his cultured voice.

"Because I thought you were the bad guys."

Logan nodded. "Given the way these two were acting just now, I can hardly blame you."

"She's committed an act of war," grated out Joseph. "She was going to kill the children."

Logan's voice poured out like cool water over scorched earth. "I understand how upset that must make you, Joseph, but I think we can make an exception, considering the circumstances. We need her, and she did confess."

"That doesn't make it okay. Not by a long shot. We don't even know if she's lying," said Joseph.

"Zach will know. They're connected. He'd be able to see if she's lying." Logan turned to Zach. "Isn't that right?"

"No," said Zach, feeling like a traitor to the one woman who could save his sorry ass. "I tried to get into her head, but it didn't go so well."

Logan's gaze narrowed with suspicion and he swiveled his head around toward Lexi. "Is this true?" he asked her.

Lexi shoved her pointed chin up and looked Logan right in the eye. "I'm too thick-skulled, I guess."

"You had to have been blocking him. Keeping him out," said Joseph.

"I didn't mean to."

"She tried to let me in, but it didn't work," said Zach. "She's built up too many mental defenses or something."

"Whatever defenses she has, they won't work on me," said Logan as he glided closer. His lips lifted just a fraction of an inch—enough for Zach to see the pearly gleam of his fangs.

Instincts swarmed up inside Zach, filling him with a potent, feral rage. Lexi was his. He'd vowed to protect her and he meant to do just that. No matter who he had to slice down to do it.

"No fucking way," growled Zach as he shoved Logan back. "You're not getting her blood."

"It's the only way to be sure," said Logan.

"Then you're just going to have to keep wondering, 'cause no one is making her bleed."

"What is he talking about, Zach?" asked Lexi, her voice thinned by a hint of fear. She was at his side and took a half step closer.

"Logan here wants to suck your blood and take a walk inside your head."

"Let him," ordered Joseph. "It's the only way you're going to get out of this alive."

Lexi's hand wrapped around his biceps. Her fingers were cold and trembling. "There's got to be another way."

Joseph came forward, looming over her, making him look bigger and meaner than Zach had ever seen. He was typically a reasonable, gentle man, but all that had fled as he faced down Lexi. "There isn't, and I won't take a chance you're going to hurt my people. You do this or I'll kill you myself."

"You'll have to kill me, too," said Zach. "You've been out of the field so long, it'll probably be the last thing you do."

"Enough!" shouted Logan. "No one is dying here tonight. There is a simple way to settle this."

"One that involves you sucking her blood, leech?" said Zach.

Logan's pale eyes flared brighter for a second, giving off an eerie glow. "I believed us to be friends, Zach. I'd hoped that you'd trust me not to injure your woman."

He didn't. He didn't trust anyone enough to let Lexi bleed.

Zach's body tightened and his hand strayed once again to his sword. He was going to have to cut his way out of here.

He was going to have to kill his friends.

As he moved to do just that, Lexi put a staying hand on his arm. "Don't," she said softly. "I know what you're thinking, and you can't. I'll let him have my blood."

"No."

Lexi stepped in front of him. Her eyes roamed over his face and she offered him a brave smile. "It'll be fine. I was the one who made the decision to come here under false pretenses. I was the one who agreed to kill people before I had all the facts. I'll be the one to deal with the consequences."

"You'll be perfectly safe," said Logan. He put his hand on her shoulder and she flinched slightly before allowing the touch.

Zach hated this, but what choice did he have? She'd agreed. She'd sealed her fate.

Zach gave Logan a hard stare, full of the promise of vengeance. "She'd better be."

Logan decided that his smartest course of action was going to be to make this as quick as possible.

Zach was seething with barely controlled rage. Joseph had maneuvered so that he could restrain Zach if necessary, and Lexi—brave child that she was—had squared her shoulders and was staring Logan right in the eyes.

"This won't hurt," he assured her as he lifted her wrist to his mouth. No sense in tempting fate by putting his lips to her throat. Logan wasn't entirely sure that Joseph was strong enough to hold Zach back if things turned difficult.

"Just do it," she growled at him.

Such a cute little thing. Her dainty chin was high, and her dark eyes were set on kill. It was entirely possible that she was still planning to destroy them, but given that she'd agreed to this treatment, Logan doubted it.

He took a firm hold on her wrist and stepped so close she had no choice but to keep looking into his eyes. Logan gathered what meager power he had left and let it bloom in his eyes, sucking her in. Capturing her.

Her glare faded and a sleepy weight lowered her lids. It took only a brief second to ensnare her, but he could feel her starting to fight against him as she realized what had happened.

Before she could react, he bit into the delicate skin of her wrist, piercing her vein. Sweet, hot blood poured over his tongue like the purest rain. She'd never been bled before. Logan was her first, and the power filling him was a heady mixture of innocence and strength.

The starving monster within him roared to life, taking over his body. He drew from her wrist, sucking down her power in huge gulps. He didn't waste time breathing. Every second counted, and somewhere in the back of his mind, he knew that Zach wasn't going to stand by and allow him to feed for long.

Her heartbeat thrummed across his tongue as she became part of him. Wherever she went, for as long as she lived, he'd be able to find her again so he could feed on her.

He felt her weaken, and his arm wrapped around her waist, holding her upright. She struggled, but he didn't relent. He needed more. So much more.

"Enough," he heard in the distance, but ignored the command in that voice.

All that mattered was the warmth of her blood pouring into him, filling up all the empty holes in his belly.

Logan's head spun as his power returned. His body warmed and his skin prickled as he was restored to his true self, not this frail, gaunt body starvation had wrought.

Muscles swelled and his bones hardened. The constant, nagging hunger that plagued him dissipated more with each gulp.

The weight of the woman in his arms increased as she weakened, but it didn't matter. Logan was strong now, easily able to support her meager weight.

Her heartbeat fluttered and Logan's head started to spin.

He still hadn't started breathing and his lungs were burning for oxygen.

"Stop!" The imperious shout shocked him back to himself. He was supposed to be doing something— something important.

Treachery. He was supposed to be searching inside the woman for signs of treachery.

Before he lost his chance, Logan shoved himself into her mind, slamming through the formidable shields she'd built up. They were thick and strong, but Logan was much stronger now, thanks to her blood. He had no trouble breaking down what had taken years to erect.

She was terrified. Weak.

Logan was killing her and he hadn't even realized what he'd been doing.

Immediately, he sealed the wound on her arm, licking away the remnant of blood left behind. He scoured her mind, searching through it swiftly, before it was too late.

He saw flickers of her life—brief flashes of people and places she'd seen. He felt moments of triumph and panic, sorrow and joy. Her life was like many others, full of a bright mix of feelings and memories and hopes.

Logan found the ones he wanted and rifled through them. She was fading fast, sinking into unconsciousness.

He took some of the soaring power she'd given him and let it seep back into her through his hold on her arm. If she collapsed, he was sure Zach would cut him down.

A faint memory nagged him. He'd tasted blood like hers before; he just couldn't remember where or when.

Focus. He needed to concentrate on the part of her holding her plans to destroy his home.

Logan honed in on those thoughts, saw a collage of male faces he didn't recognize, then singled out what he needed.

Lexi was telling the truth. She had no intention of killing them. Not since learning they were not the monsters she'd believed.

Logan struggled to find his voice, and when he did, it came out rough and scratchy. "It is as she says," he told Joseph.

Both men deflated visibly in relief, and Zach rushed forward to take Lexi's limp body from Logan's arms. He settled her on the bed with exquisite care, as if her body were made of blown glass.

"She needs fluids," said Logan.

Zach gave Logan a feral stare. "You took too much."

"Her defenses are formidable. It was necessary." It was a lie, but one he sensed Zach would accept. The last thing he needed was to anger Zach enough that he cut

Logan down and wasted all the precious power flowing in his veins.

That power was needed elsewhere. Project Lullaby was reaching a critical stage, and all his kin sleeping below the earth needed to be fed.

"Give her a couple of hours and she'll be fine," said Logan.

"You'd better pray that's the case, leech."

Joseph gave Logan a small formal bow. "Thank you for your services." It was a dismissal and Logan knew it.

Fine. He had better things to do, anyway, and the rich blood filling him up was going to make them all possible.

Alexander was one of the few people who truly loved hospitals. He saw hope where others saw only sickness and despair. It was within the walls of hospitals like this that he found the opportunity to save his race from extinction.

The sterile smell, combined with that of weak human bodies, filled his nose as he glided along the tiled hallways. It was late, well past visiting hours, but no one questioned his presence. In fact, few even noticed him passing by. He was no more than a blur of movement, a whoosh of cool air sliding over their skin.

His senses on high alert, Alexander moved with unerring accuracy toward his target. He pushed the wooden door open and slipped inside, unnoticed by the nursing staff at the desk nearby.

The room was dark. Quiet. No TV filled the silence, only the faint sigh of breath moving in and out of a woman's body, the dry rattle of a man's labored breathing much faster than her own. She reeked of grief and despair, but Alexander would shortly fix that. He'd long ago learned that the hope for his race—the Sanguinar—was tied closely to the fragile hopes of certain, special humans—those with strong blood surging in their veins, the blood of the Solarc himself.

Alexander drew in a long breath through his nose, detecting the spicy richness of that blood. Hunger rolled in his belly, but he'd lived with it long enough to set the urge to feed aside for as long as he needed. His task was more important than his hunger, for if it went well, one day his people would no longer feel the gnawing emptiness of starvation again.

He moved slowly so he wouldn't startle her, clearing the fabric curtain that blocked the sight of the bed from the doorway. A man lay there, still and gaunt. He looked to be in his sixties, though Alexander guessed him a decade younger. His skin was tinted yellow with sickness and hung loose on his frame. A thin clear tube at his nose fed him oxygen and a thick drainage tube snaking from his side gave away a recent surgery.

Alexander checked the chart. Cancer. It was almost always cancer.

That suited him fine. He'd honed his skills well, and battling those voracious cells was almost second nature to him now.

The woman was seated in a rigid chair, slumped over the bed in sleep. Her short blond hair was a mess, as if she hadn't combed it in days, and a bright flush reddened her cheeks.

Alexander pressed his hand against her forehead, feeling the heat of her fever streak up his arm. She'd spent enough time at the man's side to catch some illness, likely because she hadn't been taking care of herself.

Briefly, Alexander questioned whether she was a good candidate, but dismissed the notion in moments. Anyone who dedicated herself to one she loved to the point of self-sacrifice was going to be a valuable asset to their plans.

The woman stirred at his touch, jerking awake. She

looked up at him with wide brown eyes and eased away from his hand.

"You're sick," he said in a low voice.

She blinked a couple of times and ran her hands through her hair as if to straighten it.

Alexander suppressed a knowing smile. His kind were beautiful and always seemed to have that effect on humans. Too bad it had been decades since Alexander had felt the urge to have sex. He was too hungry to think of much else, and too weak to act on it even if the thought had crossed his mind.

"I'm fine," she said. "How's Dad?"

Ah, so this was her father. And she thought he was a doctor.

Alexander supported that false assumption and looked at her father's chart. He knew enough about human medicine to see the pattern of death hanging all over this man. "He's weak. Dying."

The scent of grief rose up stronger, nearly choking Alexander. It had a cloying smell, like old flower petals on the verge of decay.

"Isn't there anything you can do?"

This was his opening, given so easily he nearly balked at taking it. "What is your name?" he asked.

"Meghan Clark." Tears made the words tremble with despair.

"Meghan," he repeated, using the power of her name to gather her attention to him. "There is one thing I know that might help, but you won't want to do it."

They never did. At first.

"Something experimental? If he's dying, how dangerous could it be for him?"

"It's not dangerous for him," said Alexander, lacing his words with a hint of what he was—dark, desperate. Hungry.

Meghan leaned back in her chair, putting more space

between them. Her eyes flicked to the nurse's call button, but it was on the far side of the bed, well out of reach. "Who are you?"

"All you need to know is what I can offer: hope."

Her throat moved as she swallowed nervously, and Alexander's eyes clung to the slender column of flesh and bone and blood. He could see her pulse pounding, hear the swoosh of blood pumping through her veins.

His stomach clenched painfully, and he had to grit his teeth to stay his ground and not lunge for her. Feed from her until only a husk of the pretty female remained.

That would get him nowhere in the long run. Down that road lay starvation.

"What kind of hope?"

"I offer you an exchange. I can save your father, and in return, I want something from you."

"You're not a doctor, are you?"

"Not as you think, no."

She stood slowly, straightening her spine and shifting so that he could no longer see her father's face.

Little Meghan Clark—who stood only to his shoulder, who he could kill with a mere thought—was protecting her father.

The humor of the situation made him smile, though he tried not to uncover his fangs. He didn't want her raising a ruckus.

"I'm not going to let you touch him," she said.

"How am I to cure him if I can't touch him?"

"I don't believe you can. I don't know what sick joke you're playing, but I want you to leave." She swayed a little on her feet. Maybe the fever and her weariness were taking more of a toll on her than he'd thought.

"Relax," he said, imbuing the word with the dwindling remnants of his power.

Meghan Clark sagged and Alexander grabbed her before she could fall. The heat of her skin sank into him, making him shiver. He was cold all the time now, even when he fed. He'd gotten so used to it he'd forgotten what it was like to be warm.

"I'm not going to hurt you or your father. I merely seek to offer you a trade."

"What kind of trade?"

"I will save his life in return for another."

Her eyes widened and she struggled against his hold. Alexander tightened his grip, being careful not to injure her.

"Stop fighting me," he ordered.

"I would never kill someone, not even to save my father." Fury made her words hard, and as she flung them at him, he felt every single one.

He was so tired of being mistrusted. So tired of fighting for every little scrap of strength he needed to survive.

He was tired, period. Maybe it was time to go to sleep in the chambers beneath Dabyr, let another take his place, just for a few years. Not that there were any of his kind left who had the same level of ability he did.

If he went to sleep, he was sure he'd never wake again. The fact that he had to decide whether or not that was his best option frightened him.

"I'm not asking you to kill anyone. All I want is for you to take a trip. Go to Minnesota."

Her struggles ceased and she looked at him like he was crazy. "Minnesota? I don't understand."

"There's a man there. If I cure your father, then I want you to go there. Meet him."

Her eyes narrowed in suspicion. "Why?"

Because he was the man whose blood would best meld with hers. He was the man who Alexander wanted to father her children. Of course, telling her that would only scare her away. He'd learned that the hard way.

Tynan preferred a more direct approach, but Alexander preferred subtlety. He liked letting the humans think they weren't being manipulated. He believed it made the bonds between them stronger, more pure—the blood of their children richer.

"Does it matter why?" he asked. "All I want from you is this one small boon. Is it too much to request in exchange for your father's life?"

Meghan shook her head. "I don't know about all this. It's probably some kind of fever dream."

"Then what's the harm of agreeing? If your father doesn't recover, you owe me nothing."

She pulled from his grip and he let her go, keeping a hand at her elbow in case she started to go down again. She turned her head and stared at her father's gaunt form. "That's all? I just take a trip if . . . when he gets better?"

"That's all."

Meghan looked up at Alexander again and gave him a single nod. "Fine. It's a deal."

The power of her promise wound around him, giving him hope that almost felt like warmth, but not quite. "There's one more thing," he said.

"What?"

Alexander gathered her in his arms and turned on his magic, seeing the faint glow of blue light wash across her face—a glow that came from his eyes. Ensnaring her was easy enough; it barely took any energy at all, which was good, considering he had so little to spare. "I'm going to need some of your blood."

"Blood?" she asked in a faint whisper. She was beyond fear now, floating in a light trance where normal inhibitions meant nothing.

"Just a little," he said, lowering his mouth to her fragile neck. "Just enough to drive away your illness. I need you to be nice and healthy for your trip."

Chapter 19

Nika roamed the halls of Dabyr, following the faint trail of power left in Madoc's wake.

He was avoiding her, but she didn't care. She needed him. He was the only thing that kept the sgath from taking her away, out of her body. Surely he wouldn't leave without at least saying good-bye.

Then again, maybe she hadn't told him with her voice how much she needed him. Sometimes she mixed up the things she said with those she thought, so she couldn't be sure.

Where was he? She needed to find him before it was too late and he left her alone.

Nika didn't want to be with the sgath tonight; she didn't want them to rip her from her body and fling her out into the darkness. Every time she was with them it made her sick, and she didn't want to throw up the food she'd managed to choke down earlier. She wanted to be stronger, healthy, like her sister Andra was.

It was the only way she was ever going to find her sister, Tori. The real Tori, not those stranger's bones Andra had buried.

But healthy and strong were a long way off. Her body was fragile, her bones brittle. It was going to take time to rebuild her strength, and the only time it was even possible was when Madoc was there to drive the dark things away long enough for her to eat.

A wave of weakness hit her and she sagged against the wall. The sgath out hunting pulled on her mind, clawing at it, threatening to tear it apart into little bloody chunks. They wanted her to come hunt with them, to feed on the flesh and blood of the humans they found.

They used her to communicate with each other. She was sure of it.

There were fewer of them now, thanks to Madoc and the other Theronai who had made hunting them their top priority. But the sgath that remained were stronger. Smarter. Louder. She had trouble resisting their call.

Nika couldn't stand the thought of going with them tonight. She needed Madoc, so she pushed herself up and followed the humming stream of power he had left behind as she drifted through the silent halls of Dabyr.

The trail ended at a door like all the rest of the doors in this hall. Nika turned the knob, found it unlocked, and pushed it open.

The suite was dark, but a flickering rectangle of light glowed on the carpet, falling from the open doorway of one of the bedrooms.

Madoc's trail led there, so she followed it into the light.

A large bed filled the room, and on it was a giant of a man. He was handsome in a rough sort of way, and several days of stubble shadowed his jaw. A bandage covered his left temple and several bruises marked his face with sickly greens and yellows. His hands were huge, lying at his sides, and next to the bed sat Sibyl with her tiny child-sized hand wrapped around two of the man's thick fingers.

In her other arm, she cradled a porcelain doll that looked just like her, wearing a pretty blue ribbon in her hair.

The doll's glassy black eyes opened and looked at Nika. Malevolence flowed out of the thing, making Nika take a hesitant step back.

A second later, Sibyl looked up slowly. Her blond ringlets drooped limply over her shoulders and a haunted shadow darkened her bright blue eyes. She was afraid.

The girl showed no surprise at Nika's arrival, as if she'd been expecting her all along.

"Come and sit with me," said Sibyl.

Nika hesitated. Madoc wasn't here. She could feel the emptiness of this place without him, and the need to seek him out grew stronger with every breath she took.

Still, he had come here. Maybe this man was important to him. Maybe they were friends. "Who is he?" asked Nika.

Sibyl's voice cracked as if she hadn't used it in days. "Cain. My bodyguard."

"Is he sick?" she asked.

"He was wounded the night I was taken. The Sanguinar have done all they can."

"Andra told me you can see the future. Don't you know what will happen?"

Grief hung on her words, making them fade as they went on. "Not to Cain. That's why I allowed him in my life. He was . . . quiet."

Nika's weak legs began to shake with weakness now that she was no longer walking. She stepped forward and eased herself down on the bed, being careful not to touch the man lying there. She couldn't bear the touch of any man but Madoc.

"He was here earlier, checking on Cain," said Sibyl as if reading her mind. "He just left to go hunting."

"Did he say when he'd be back?"

"No."

Briefly, Nika considered asking the seer when he'd

come home, but she pushed the notion away. Sibyl was clearly suffering, aching for the man lying on the bed.

Nika was going to have to answer the call of the sgath and go find Madoc for herself.

"How long has he been like this?" she asked the child.

"Nearly two weeks. He grows weaker every day. I cannot stop it."

"Do you think you should be able to stop it?"

Sibyl shrugged, shifting the doll in her arms. The thing was still staring at Nika, and her stomach gave a twist. "If he were anyone else, I'd know what to do, even if that was knowing it was time to let go."

"Do you think that's what he'd want? For you to let go?"

"Cain was a fighter at heart. He couldn't bear to see me suffer. He's a good man." Tears wavered in Sibyl's eyes for a brief second before they disappeared.

"Do you want me to ask him?"

Sibyl's head snapped up and for a second, Nika thought she saw the doll's eyes narrow. Another trick of her mind, no doubt.

"How would you do that?" asked Sibyl.

Nika looked down at the prone man, seeing the power he had once wielded in his thick limbs and barrel chest. Even unconscious, he had an air of strength about him that dwarfed Nika's waking energy.

There were so many scary things out there, and they needed every warrior they could find to fight them. If there was a chance Nika could help, she had to try. "I'd just shed my body and go into his."

"You can do that?"

Nika nodded. "I think so. Would you like me to try?"

"Is it safe?"

For Cain, yes. For Nika . . . there was no way to be sure. Every time she left her body there was a chance she wouldn't make it back, but it was one she was willing to take. If her husk died, she'd seek out Madoc and become part of him. She'd never have to be away from him again, even if he didn't know she was there.

"It's safe," said Nika.

Sibyl's grip on the doll tightened and she gave a single nod.

"What would you like me to tell him?"

The little girl bit her lip as if she were going over a huge list, sorting out what was most important. "Tell him I need him." She swallowed and met Nika's gaze. Fear loomed in her bright eyes, making them shimmer with it. "Tell him I don't want to be alone."

In that moment, Nika realized that she had more in common with this child than she had with anyone else here, including her sister. It was a sad commentary on Nika's twisted life, perhaps, but all the same, she was going to do whatever she could to ease Sibyl's fears.

Nika lay down beside Cain, lining her body along his. She felt insubstantial next to him, like she could sink into the covers and no one would notice the loss.

Gritting her teeth, Nika threaded her fingers through Cain's. Her stomach rebelled at the touch, but she swallowed until she was sure her food would stay where it belonged. If she was to get better, she had to learn to control herself. This was as good a place to start as any.

Nika closed her eyes and willed herself to slide through her arm and into Cain. It was frighteningly easy how readily her spirit left its shell, as if it ached for the chance to be rid of the weak sack of skin that imprisoned it.

She streaked through powerful muscle and solid bone until she could slide her spirit inside Cain's mind.

He was trapped inside a nightmare. Nika forgot why she was here in the face of so much blood and pain. She saw Cain fall under the blows of three different kinds of demons. His huge body flew across a room as if he was a rag doll. Blood coated the walls, dripping like gallons of paint. There was no way he could have lived through that, but apparently, he had. Or maybe that wasn't what had happened to him, but something his mind had made up to replay over and over inside his dreams.

The screams of a child echoed in his head, growing fainter with each passing second.

Sibyl!

The word resonated, shaking Nika's spirit with its ferocity.

He imagined what was happening to her. He saw her being torn to shreds by oily black claws. He saw the bloody muzzles of sgath as they fed on her entrails. He saw their powerful jaws rip her limbs from her body as they trotted off to clean the meat from her bones like dogs.

None of that had happened to Sibyl, but Cain didn't know it.

"She's safe," said Nika, hoping to calm the churning mass of images flashing through his head.

A powerful awareness sped toward her and she could hear his thoughts pounding against her fragile essence, threatening to shatter her. "Who are you?"

"Nika. Sibyl sent me."

"Sibyl is dead."

"No. She's with you now. Holding your hand. Can't you feel her?"

Images of Sibyl's broken body and lifeless blue eyes welled up, pummeling Nika until they nearly drove her from his mind.

"Stop it!" she ordered him, throwing as much force of will as she could into the command.

The images stopped, and Cain's mind quieted. A flicker of hope bloomed inside him, the color of spring leaves. The scent of rich, freshly tilled soil wafted around her, though she had no idea how she could see with no eyes or smell with no nose.

"She's alive?" he asked.

"She asked me to give you a message. She needs you. She doesn't want to be alone."

"Alone." The word shimmered with emotion. Guilt, most of all. "I've left her alone."

"Go back to her," said Nika. "Don't leave her to suffer."

The landscape changed, and suddenly Cain was standing before her. Nika hadn't realized until then that she'd constructed a physical shape for her consciousness. She looked like herself, or at least like she thought she should look. Her hair was dark here, and her body was strong and lithe, not thin and wasted.

"Who are you?" he asked.

"Nika."

He stepped forward and the ground beneath her feet filled with soft grass, blooming with flowers. The air warmed and swayed around her ankles.

He'd done that for her—changed the setting so that she'd be more comfortable. Nika could feel his inborn need to see to her comfort, though she had no idea why he would care.

"Nika," he repeated. "Can you help me?"

"Help you do what?"

"Get back to Sibyl. I don't know how to find her."

Nika nodded. "Take my hand."

She braced herself for the touch, steeling herself against the grating sensation on her skin. But it didn't come. He took hold of her hand and it didn't hurt.

"Follow me," she told him. She wasn't exactly sure what she was doing, but her instincts were strong, so she listened to them. "Close your eyes."

Cain did, and Nika leapt up, pulling him with her. She led him out of the deeper parts of his mind, toward the surface. The farther they went, the harder it got, but Nika kept pulling.

In the distance, she could see the shimmering surface of his consciousness, like she was looking up out of a swimming pool. She saw Sibyl seated beside Cain, and her own skeletal form lying next to him. Sibyl's doll was still watching her, as if it could see her spirit gliding through Cain's body.

Maybe it could.

Weariness dragged at her, like claws around her ankles, pulling her down. Nika gave a swift kick, and finally, Cain's head broke the surface.

She heard his gasp of breath, felt his powerful body shudder as he sucked in air. But there was none for her. Nika still had to find her way back into her own body, and it was a long trip.

As tired as she was, as fast as her strength was fading, she wasn't sure she was going to be able to make the whole journey.

At least she'd wakened Cain and given him back to Sibyl.

Madoc couldn't rid himself of the nagging need to go back to Cain. He'd been there only a few minutes ago, but everything inside him was screaming for him to go back.

Maybe his buddy had taken a turn for the worse.

Grief grabbed Madoc by the throat and he fought to breathe as his heavy boot steps pounded through the halls. He remembered his love for his brother, even if he could no longer feel it coursing through him, strengthening him. All he felt now was fear that they'd lose a great warrior.

He pushed open the door to Cain's new suite and went back through the dark living room to the bedroom. He wasn't a big fan of Sibyl's, but he'd suffer through the creepy girl's cold stare long enough to check on his friend.

The first thing he saw was that Cain was awake. He was sitting up in bed and Sibyl's tiny arms were wrapped around his neck in a tight hug. The man hugged her back for only a second, before he gently pried her hands away.

The second thing he saw was the sick look of fear coating Cain's rough features. Since Madoc couldn't remember the last time he'd seen Cain afraid, it freaked him out.

For good reason.

Nika was in his bed. Lying next to the fucker. She was icy white and unnaturally still, her left hand red and blistered.

Rage crashed around inside Madoc, slamming into his ribs until he was sure they'd crack. He couldn't lose her. He'd fought so hard to free her from every sgath he could lay his hands on, and he sure as hell hadn't done it so she could die on him now.

"What did you do to her?" His voice came out sharp and cold.

Cain's green eyes met Madoc's and went wide. He tried to speak, but nothing came out. The man had been unconscious for days and his throat was likely a tube of sandpaper.

"He didn't do anything," said Sibyl. "Nika offered to help." She scrambled from the bed and fetched him a cup of water.

"Help? How? She's barely strong enough to stand up on her own."

Madoc went to Nika's side and pressed his fingers against her slender neck. A faint pulse beat below the paper-thin surface of her skin.

She was alive.

He wanted to feel relief, but all he felt was the need to pound his fists into Cain until she woke up.

Like that would help.

Madoc was afraid to touch her more than necessary. She was so frail. Breakable. But the urge to feel the warmth of her skin under his fingers was too much to resist. He smoothed her white hair away from her face, displaying the thin blue lines of the veins running along her temples.

"She brought me back," whispered Cain. His voice was shredded tatters of sound, but he got his point across. "I felt her getting weaker. She pushed me up to the surface and sank back down. I tried to grab her, but she was already gone."

Gone.

The word echoed in Madoc's head like a gunshot blast.

Gone.

No fucking way.

"Get out," he barked.

Cain gave him an odd look, but slid from the bed, putting his body between Madoc and Sibyl as he led her from the room. He was weaving on his feet, barely able to stay standing but that was just too fucking bad. He deserved whatever he got for doing this to Nika.

The door shut behind them with a click, leaving him alone in the room with Nika.

Madoc wanted to gather her up in his arms, but he didn't dare. He was shaking so hard he'd break her for sure.

"Nika. Wake up."

She pulled in a breath, but that was it.

"Damn it, Nika." His voice was too loud in the quiet room. Too hard. Still, he couldn't control it. He was too desperate to fix this. Make her better. Pack her away and keep her safe for eternity. "Wake the fuck up!"

Her eyelids fluttered and Madoc held his breath. Slowly, her eyes opened, revealing the blue of clear winter skies. So fucking pretty it broke his heart.

"You came back," she said on a weak puff of air.

"Never left." Though he'd been on his way out. The less he was around her, the better. He wanted her too much to keep resisting her, especially when he woke up with her draped over him, his own living, warm blanket.

"Is Cain okay?"

"Fucker's fine. What the hell were you thinking, pulling a stunt like that? Getting in another man's bed?"

"Sibyl needed him."

Such a simple statement, but it said way too much about her for Madoc's peace of mind. Nika hadn't stopped to think what it would cost her to do whatever the fuck she'd done. Sibyl needed Cain, so Nika woke him up.

Who else was going to need something that might get her killed?

Her bony fingers wrapped around his wrist and she pulled his arm to her chest. Her breasts were small, almost nonexistent, but he felt them all the same—soft and warm against his forearm.

Blood pooled in his cock, making it swell and throb. He should not have been turned on by this stick figure of a girl, but he was. No matter how hard he tried, he couldn't get her out of his head.

Maybe if he just took what she unknowingly offered and gave her one nice, hard ride, he'd get her out of his system.

Yeah, and maybe he'd kill her in the process, too. He wasn't a gentle man. If he fucked her, she'd feel it. And then some.

She was so damn fragile. He had no business getting so close—letting her touch him.

"I don't want you to ever do that again, understand?"

Nika didn't answer. She'd fallen asleep, her breathing deep and even. It was a natural sleep. Poor girl had exhausted herself saving Cain.

Madoc owed her one for that. All the Theronai did. They needed every warrior they had, and Cain was one of the best.

And because Madoc owed her for her sacrifice, he worked his wrist out of her grip, turned and walked out of the room without looking back.

The farther away from her he stayed, the safer she'd be. All she needed from him was the blood of a sgath on his blade, as much and as often as possible.

It was time to go hunting.

Chapter 20

"So, what now?" asked Lexi. She was propped up in bed with a glass of juice. Both Zach and Joseph were staring at her as if they expected her to perform some kind of circus trick.

"Now you tell us everything you know about these Defenders," said Joseph. She could tell by the rigid set of his shoulders and the cold glint in his hazel eyes that he still didn't trust her, no matter how much Logan vouched for her.

Fine. She didn't need his trust. As long as Zach believed her, that would have to be good enough.

Lexi let out a gusty sigh. "I don't know a lot other than the fact that they want to get rid of all the Sentinels."

"They're dorjan," stated Joseph with a twisted sneer of loathing.

"What are dorjan?"

Zach's mouth was tight as he said, "They're humans who work for the Synestryn in exchange for something they want. Money, power, that kind of thing."

Lexi shook her head. "That doesn't sound like these guys. They know about the Synestryn, but they sure as hell don't work for them."

Joseph let out a snort of disbelief. "Why would they want to kill us unless they were working for the Synestryn?"

"Because you screw up their land with your battles. Nothing will ever grow again on land that has been bloodied by your war. They know they're not strong enough to fight your pets, so they figure that if you Sentinels go away, then the Synestryn will go, too and their land will be safe."

Both men looked at her like she needed to be fit for a straitjacket.

Zach recovered first. "You're telling me that these Defenders actually believe the Synestryn will just leave if none of us are here to keep them in check?"

"Yeah." She looked from one man to the other, getting more and more uncomfortable by their silence. "Why? Are they wrong?"

"Dead wrong," said Joseph. "They're not our pets. We can't control them. If we die off, there'll be nothing to stop the Synestryn from taking over this planet. They'll turn the whole thing into one giant set of cattle pens and bleed out every human for food."

"Oh." That didn't sound good. "We really need to let the Defenders know how wrong they are."

Zach shook his head. "Men like that won't listen. We've tried in the past with other groups. Usually, over time, they fall apart until someone comes across the ravings of a lunatic in his journal."

A journal like her mother's. Lexi winced as the stinging truth hit her. Her mother had been one of those lunatics and had raised Lexi to follow in her footsteps. Had she not seen it with her own eyes, she'd still be sure these men were walking evil.

"What else do you know about them?" asked Joseph.

"They're led by a man named Hector Morrow. He lives north of Dallas. His daughter was killed years ago and he blames it on you."

"How did you meet him?" asked Zach.

"My mom stayed with him sometimes when I was growing up. When we ran low on cash or she thought the monsters were on our trail. He'd put us up and give Mom a job, and we'd stick around for a couple of weeks— just long enough to get back on the road." She omitted the part about the lessons Hector taught the kids in his sphere of influence. That man had caused her more nightmares with stories of his daughter's death than any real monster ever had. The one thing she'd learned from him was that if she wasn't good, the monsters would find her and eat her. If she was bad, she'd die screaming in pain, just like his daughter had.

"Has he asked you to do anything else?" asked Joseph.

"You mean besides blowing your compound to hell? No. Not that I remember." She looked from one man to the other. Joseph was across the room, lounging with one massive shoulder propped on the wall. Zach was sitting on the bed with her, his body between them. Lexi was pretty sure that wasn't an accident.

Zach clearly still didn't trust Joseph around her.

An odd sense of peace unfurled inside her. Zach was protecting her. No one had cared enough about her to protect her since her mother had died. It was nice to feel that again. Comforting.

Lexi wasn't going to make him sorry for giving her that gift. She was going to step up and do whatever needed to be done to fix this. "I need to go take care of the C-4, get it out of here so nothing bad can happen by accident."

Joseph's jaw hardened. "You're not getting anywhere near those explosives, girl. I've got a man taking care of it."

"One who knows how to handle explosives?"

He lifted a dark, mocking brow. "We've lived centuries. I think we've got it covered."

"It's relatively safe stuff so long as the detonators aren't connected. Which they aren't."

"How were you going to trigger the device?" asked Zach.

"Timer. I had ten minutes to get clear," said Lexi, feeling more and more guilty as she laid out their plans.

"And if it wasn't enough?" asked Joseph.

Lexi shrugged, but her joints felt rusty and stiff. Whatever Logan had done to her wasn't wearing off fast. "I guess I would have gone down with the rest of you."

Zach cursed, spitting out a violent word. Joseph merely stared at her. "You would have died? Willingly?"

"It wasn't my first choice, no, but I was tired of running. Tired of being afraid all the time."

Zach took her hand and wrapped his around it, warming her chilled fingers. "You don't have to run anymore."

Lexi eyed Joseph. "I'm not so sure about that, Zach. Looks like your fearless leader here would prefer if I hit the road."

"Like hell," said Zach.

"You're not going anywhere," ordered Joseph. "I want you right here where I can keep an eye on you."

"So, now I'm a prisoner?" she asked.

Zach's dark face hardened to a stony scowl as he turned to Joseph. "She's not, is she?"

"I don't want her leaving the compound. I don't want her making any calls. Is that clear?"

"I've got to call the Defenders and let them know you guys are the good guys."

Joseph pushed away from the wall with a deceptively lazy shove. "Not going to happen. Let them think we found you out and killed you."

"They'll only try again. Someone needs to convince them you guys aren't the monsters they think you are."

Joseph shook his head. "There's no reasoning with men like them. Let them try again. We'll be ready."

"What are you going to do?" asked Zach.

Joseph's shoulders seemed to bow slightly as if a weight had settled atop them. "The only thing I can. Erase the threat."

Zach leapt from the bed so fast it looked like he'd been launched from a catapult. "You don't mean to kill them, do you?" he asked in disbelief.

"When they were merely a nuisance, getting in our way? No. But now?" He shook his head in sorrow, but his eyes were rock hard. "They meant to kill us all. They meant to kill the children. And they'll try it again. I can't let that crime go unanswered."

"You can't retaliate, Joseph. They're human."

"I can't let that matter. Not anymore. This was an act of war. I'm going to make sure it doesn't happen again." Joseph's eyes went to Lexi and she felt a chill glide over her spine. There was no mercy inside that man. No compassion. "I want a list of names. Every person you ever met who was connected to the Defenders."

"I won't give it to you," she told him. "I won't help you kill them. They're wrong, but that doesn't mean we can't straighten this out. Bring them here, let them see what I have, and they'll understand."

"It's too late for that. You will give me that list."

"No, I won't."

"Then I'll order Logan to take it from you," said Joseph as he turned to leave the room. "It won't be as comfortable for you, but it will be just as effective."

Lexi heard the door to her suite slam shut, making her jump.

"I've never seen him like that," said Zach.

"Does he mean it?"

"Every single word."

"Where does that leave us?" she asked.

Zach shook his head. "Something's wrong. This isn't like him. Give me a few minutes to check something and I'll be back, okay?"

Lexi nodded. "Sure. Whatever you need to do."

He cupped the side of her face in his big hand and Lexi leaned into the touch. "You'll be here when I get back, right?"

"I promise." She felt the weight of that promise slam down on her, pinning her to the bed.

"Get some rest. I'll be quick. Call my cell if you need me."

With that, he left. Lexi wasn't sure what he was going to go do, but she was fairly sure she didn't want any part of it.

When Zach found Drake, he was outside, helping Helen repair the broken section of wall. Helen knelt on the ground, both her slender hands on a stone the size of her head. Drake's fingers wrapped around her nape, clearly visible beneath the twin braids restraining her dark hair—hair the same soft brown color as Lexi's now that it was no longer dyed.

Zach ached to go back to Lexi's side and comfort her, make sure she knew that her mistake was not an unforgivable one, but he couldn't do that yet. Not until he knew for certain that their leader was in his right mind.

A subtle hum of power vibrated in the air around Drake and Helen as she poured a stream of protective magic inside the stone, strengthening it against attack. Sweat beaded on her skin, and the back of her red shirt was dark and clinging to her spine.

Zach stopped in his tracks a few feet away and stared. He had his lady, his Lexi, but he didn't have what Drake did—their unity, their connection.

Lexi said she trusted him, but she had yet to trust him enough to allow them to become close enough to fulfill their purpose. She hadn't even trusted him enough to let him see her thoughts or know her feelings. Even after Logan had broken through, when Zach reached out for Lexi, all he felt was a cold, hard wall. There was no living warmth, no welcome.

Maybe her upbringing had scarred her, and they'd never have what Drake and Helen did.

As a spike of grief rose up in him, Zach shoved it away. He refused to let it stand like that. They would have a full life. They both deserved it, especially Lexi, after all she'd suffered. She deserved a home, a family and Zach wanted to be that for her. Always.

He loved her too much not to fight for what he knew they could have together. She was everything he'd ever wanted, and he was going to do whatever it took to make her happy.

All he had to do was give her the time to come to trust him, to show her each day that he was worthy of that gift. Eventually, he'd break through that stubborn skull of hers and see what he saw. They belonged together.

But before he could go back to her and get to work on those plans, he had a job to do. He kicked his ass in gear and went to Drake. "Got a sec?"

Drake must have seen something in Zach's expression because the look of pride and adoration he wore when watching Helen dropped, and all that was left was his serious game face. "I'll be right back," he told Helen. "Just stay here and rest a minute."

She nodded and curled up on her side in the grass, heedless of dirt and bugs. Apparently, rebuilding this wall was taking its toll. Even Gilda was nowhere to be seen, and she was the strongest Theronai in the compound.

Angus worked alone on the far side of the construction zone, hauling rock with brute strength. The only thing that would have kept Gilda from his side was sheer exhaustion.

Good. That meant Angus could lend a hand, too. They were going to need all the help they could get.

Zach led Drake in that direction. When Angus saw them approach, he set the rock down, brushed off his hands and came to meet the pair.

"Is something amiss?" Angus asked in a rough voice.

Zach did a quick scan to make sure no one else was nearby and said, "Yeah. I think we have a problem."

He did a quick recap of what went down with Lexi and Joseph, making sure they both knew about her treachery. The story would get out soon enough, and it was better if it came from him than the rumor mill.

"He actually said he was going to kill the Defenders?" asked Drake in stark disbelief.

"Yeah," said Zach. "I'm afraid Joseph may have run out of time."

"His lifemark," guessed Angus, rubbing a hand over his craggy face. "You think it's bare."

"It would explain the way he was acting with Lexi."

Drake sighed, his eyes dark with grief. "We have to find out. And I need to tell Helen what's going on with Lexi. Give me two minutes to explain things to her and I'll be back."

Drake walked away calmly, like he had all the time in the world. Anyone watching would never guess what was going on.

"We could ask Nicholas to check with his electronic eyes," Zach told Angus, "or we could do the job ourselves. Right now."

Angus suddenly looked older, more worn down. The passage of centuries had been good to him, leaving behind a few lines and even more gray hair, but from one second to the next, Angus began to look like an old man. "We'll do it now. Keep it quiet. If we have to send him to the Slayers, then I want it done tonight, before anyone knows."

Send him to the Slayers. The old laws demanded that they put down any Theronai who had lost his soul. They could be evil, dangerous. Since the Slayers were the oldest Sentinel race, they were the ones who carried out the law they'd created. With brutal expediency.

It didn't matter that their races were enmeshed in a stagnant war. It didn't matter that the Slayers had bred with humans to the point that they were no longer the fearsome creatures they had once been. All that mattered was that they'd carry out the law.

If Joseph's tree was leafless, the Slayers would execute him.

Helen's legs shook as she raced down the halls toward Lexi's new suite, and not just because she was physically exhausted.

Lexi had been planning to kill them. Her family. Her husband.

Helen still had trouble believing it. How could she have been so wrong about the woman she'd thought of as her friend?

She knocked on Lexi's door and when it opened, Lexi stood there with her nose red and her eyes bright. She'd been crying, and not sweet little girly tears, either. From the size of the wad of soggy tissue in her hand, they'd been big fat sloppy tears of remorse.

All Helen's thoughts that she'd been wrong about Lexi dissipated. Whatever choices Lexi had made since they parted ways, she was regretting them now. There wasn't a single question in Helen's mind.

The need to comfort her rose up inside Helen and she wrapped her arms around the smaller woman, holding her tight.

Lexi sniffed, her voice muffled against Helen's shoulder. "They told you, didn't they?"

Helen nodded against Lexi's head. Her hair was

darker now, softer. No more blinding blond spikes, but it was a good look for her, even if it did make her appear more vulnerable, more human.

"Everything is going to be fine," said Helen.

Lexi pulled out of the hug and Helen grudgingly let her go. She shut the front door. "I'm not so sure about that. The way Zach left here in such a rush, I'm sure everything is not fine. Something's going on, isn't it?"

"Let's sit down. Have some tea. We shouldn't have to face all of this without a few basic comforts, right?" It was a stall tactic and Helen knew it; she just wasn't ready to get to the hard stuff yet. As sad as it was, even though they'd only known each other a few months, Lexi was Helen's closest friend, not counting Drake. She couldn't believe that she was such a poor judge of character that she'd befriend someone who was willing to kill innocents.

Lexi moved quietly in her kitchen, fumbling around to locate things in the new space. Her movements were jerky, and her fingers trembled as she pitched the tissues and washed her hands.

"I was going to rescue you," said Lexi. "I was sure you'd been brainwashed into believing these were the good guys. Guess I was the one with the sudsy brain all along, huh?"

"I can't blame you for acting in line with what you thought was right."

"Even if I wasn't?" Regret made Lexi's words come out faint and hard to hear.

"I was wrong about Drake, too, at first. This whole world is pretty surreal, and it takes some getting used to."

"Do you hate me?" Lexi asked in a small voice.

"No. Of course not."

Lexi put two mugs of water in the microwave, giving Helen a somber glance over her shoulder. "I was going to kill Drake. You know that, right?"

Helen nodded, her throat too tight to speak. She couldn't even think about losing Drake. He was part of her. If anything happened to him, she was sure it would end her.

"And you still don't hate me?"

"No. You never would have gone through with it," said Helen.

"I would have. If it hadn't been for Zach and the way he treated me, I would have."

"You're wearing his luceria. That's a long step away from hating someone enough to kill them."

Lexi shrugged. "I didn't want him to die. If wearing this thing keeps him alive, then I'll wear it. It's the least I can do."

"And the magic part is pretty cool, too, huh?"

"I wouldn't know. It doesn't work for me."

Lexi had kept her back to Helen this whole time, so Helen took her arm and urged her to turn around. A bright flush of embarrassment made Lexi's face as red as her nose.

In a gentle voice, Helen asked, "What do you mean it doesn't work for you?"

"I mean I'm broken." She tugged at the luceria, which pulsated in vivid greens and blues. "This thing doesn't work on me the way it's supposed to."

"Give it time. It took me a while to get the hang of using fire."

"Yeah, Zach told me you're a regular Firestarter. Hard to believe."

"For me, too. I guess I never thought I'd love someone more than I feared fire, but I was wrong."

"So, you love him?" asked Lexi. Her dark eyes dropped to the floor like she couldn't stand to look at Helen.

"I do. So much."

After a brief silence, Lexi said, "I'm happy for you, Helen. I really am."

The microwave pinged, giving Lexi an excuse to turn her attention elsewhere.

Helen wasn't letting her off the hook quite so easily.

"It seems to me that if my fear of fire prevented me from using it, maybe you've got some fears of your own to deal with."

Lexi snorted and dropped tea bags into the mugs. "Too many to count. Guess that's the problem."

"You'll get over it."

"How can you sound so calm? So confident? We don't even know each other. Not really. And you just found out I was trying to kill the man you love."

"I know it wasn't your idea. You're not the violent type."

Lexi carried the steaming mugs into the living room. "Have you forgotten that whole episode at Gertie's Diner? I stabbed Zach. That's pretty violent."

"He was being too forceful. He deserved a reminder that he can't manhandle women that way."

Lexi shook her head, giving Helen a small smile. "I'm not sure he'd agree."

"He didn't hold a grudge, did he?"

"No. The man is relentless. I have no idea why he keeps forgiving me for every shitty thing I do."

"He needs you, Lexi. We all do. If we have to overlook a few mistakes, then that's what we'll do."

"I wouldn't call what I've done a mistake. It's bigger than that."

"You're feeling guilty. Good. You should, but we have to move on. We're . . . desperate."

"How desperate?"

Helen wasn't sure how much she should tell Lexi. It was obvious she was still getting used to this new life, and Helen knew from experience how difficult and enjoyable the transition could be. But if Lexi wasn't ready to commit herself to the fight yet, she didn't want to scare her away. They needed her too much.

Helen settled for, "Desperate enough that Zach and the rest of the Theronai will be willing to give you the benefit of the doubt. You aren't the only one here who had the wrong impression about the Sentinels and what they do. Besides, we need all the help we can get." That last part came out in an almost breathless string of exhaustion, despite Helen's best efforts to stay strong.

Lexi's expression hardened and angry sparks lit her eyes. "They've been working you too hard, haven't they?"

"*I've* been working me too hard. It's my choice. We've got to get that wall up. It's important."

"Important enough that you're killing yourself to make it happen?"

Helen waved a dismissive hand, but her arm was too heavy to pull off the kind of nonchalance she'd been going for. "Stop being melodramatic. I'm not killing myself." But it was a close thing. She couldn't get enough sleep to drive away the weariness that pulled at her. Every day, she woke up more tired than the one before. If something didn't happen soon, she was going to make herself sick, maybe burn out.

"Can't you take a break?" asked Lexi.

"Not really. The days are getting shorter, the nights longer, which means there's a better chance of attack every day. The wall is the only thing keeping the Synestryn out. We've already had to fight back two attempts to break through just in the last week. It's just going to get worse as winter approaches."

"And you think I can help?"

"I hope so. We need all we can get right now. There

are a lot of people here that depend on us, a lot of kids that have nowhere else to go. If this place falls . . ."

Lexi held up her hands to ward off anything else Helen had to say. "I get it. This place can't fall." She sucked in a long breath and let it out slowly. "Okay, just tell me what I need to do."

"First, we need to get rid of whatever's in the way— whatever's keeping you from using Zach's power."

"Do you think the problem is on my end?"

Having been where Lexi was, she was certain of it, but instead, she said, "We'll figure it out. It's as good a place to start as any."

"Fine. I'm game. I've got a lot to make up for. I'll do whatever it takes."

Helen was no expert, but she had a few ideas of what might be wrong and even more ideas how they could fix it. Lexi was going to enjoy at least a handful of them, and Zach was going to enjoy even more.

Chapter 21

Zach approached Joseph's office with a heavy heart. He prayed he was wrong, that Joseph's soul was still healthy, but he couldn't think of any other reason why his brother would turn away from his chosen path so far he'd be willing to kill the Defenders.

With Angus on one side, and Drake on the other, they made a formidable trio as they went into Joseph's office without knocking. If this confrontation got ugly, they were going to need at least this much manpower to subdue the man they'd chosen to lead them.

Joseph looked up from his desk with bleary eyes. His hair was messy and the growing number of grays at his temples sparkled under the bright lamp. Papers cluttered the place and maps were pinned up on three walls. Centered in front of him was a stack of photos. Zach couldn't make them out because of the glare across their glossy surfaces, but he had more important things to worry about.

"What's this?" asked Joseph. "You don't look like you're here for a social call."

Best to just get on with it. "Show us your chest," said Zach.

Joseph stiffened and stood to his full, towering height. "Excuse me?" he asked in a low, cold voice.

"I think your lifemark is bare. I think that's why you've turned your back on the humans."

Joseph's jaw bunched three times before he was able to get the words out. "I haven't turned my back on any-one. Who the fuck do you think I'm trying to protect?"

"You said you were willing to kill the Defenders."

"I am. But only because I know it will save lives in the long run." Joseph looked at Drake, then Angus. "Did he tell you everything? Did he tell you that Lexi was planning to massacre us? That she was working for these Defenders?"

"Lexi is not the point," said Zach.

"He told us," said Angus, his voice as calm and even as a still pond. "The girl was mixed up. My bet is these Defenders are, too. We can't go out and slaughter every group who has it in for us. Not that much time in the day."

"Have I suggested that? No. I haven't. And before you go asking for a strip search, take a look at these." He picked up the photos and tossed them across the desk.

Rubble. Tons of it. Broken walls, shattered floors, splintered roofing. Concrete was crushed like someone had dropped an asteroid on whatever building this had once been.

"What is this?" asked Zach.

"Our African stronghold. Or at least what's left of it," said Joseph.

Zach flipped through the photos until he saw the rows of bloody, broken bodies laid out. Dozens of them. Dozens of children, their dark eyes frozen in death.

Angus looked up, but Zach couldn't pull his eyes away from the photos. "Who did this?"

"Defenders—or their African equivalent—managed to sneak a man inside. He used explosives like Lexi had planned to do. He tore the place apart in the middle of the day."

"Were there Sanguinar there?" asked Zach, feeling a sick sense of dread roll through his gut. The Sanguinar were cursed by the Solarc to always dwell in darkness. If any of them dared let the sun touch their skin, it would have summoned the Solarc's warriors into this world, and if that happened, those warriors—the Wardens—would kill anyone in their path.

Joseph nodded, confirming Zach's fears. "The Wardens came and killed anyone who hadn't died in the explosion."

"How many?" asked Drake.

"Forty-three Sentinels. Three hundred seventeen humans, most of them children. Twelve people survived. *Twelve fucking people.* And they made it only because they weren't there. They were on their way here to see if Nika is compatible with them."

Unbelievable. Even seeing the photos, Zach had a hard time accepting it as truth.

"So, when I say I'm willing to take out these Defenders—men who are planning to do that to the people under my roof, under *my protection*—I'm not doing it because I have no soul. I'm doing it because I have no choice." And to prove it, Joseph ripped his shirt open, sending buttons flying off to hit the walls. He stood there, baring his muscular chest, displaying a small, but healthy set of leaves still clinging to his lifemark. "Satisfied?" he asked, but it came out as more of a challenge.

Zach wasn't. Not by a long shot. Things had taken a turn for the worse, and nothing about it satisfied him.

"What do you plan to do?" asked Angus, still as calm as if they were talking about the best way to clean their swords.

"I'm going to use Lexi to lure them out of hiding, and I'm going to make sure they never have a chance to do something like this to one of *my* people."

"She won't help you kill them." Zach knew in his

heart it was true. She'd grown up with these people, and no matter how wrong they were, Lexi wasn't going to help Joseph take them down.

"Yes. She will." His voice rang with absolute authority.

"How can you be so sure?" asked Drake, voicing the question Zach couldn't.

"Because I'm not going to give her a choice. I suggest you start trying to convince her now. It will save Logan the trouble of sucking the information out of her later."

A dangerous, lethal anger rose up inside Zach. He was already launching himself at Joseph when Drake and Angus grabbed his arms to restrain him. "I won't let you hurt her," growled Zach, barely recognizing his own voice.

"Logan won't hurt her. He'll make her feel good."

And he would, too. Logan could make her come just staring into her eyes if he wanted.

A red haze flowed over Zach's vision and his muscles tensed, aching to slam his fists into Joseph's jaw. Joseph couldn't order Logan to so much as touch her if he couldn't talk.

He lunged at Joseph again, but the men at his side held him back.

"Time to go," said Drake.

Angus gave a grunt of acknowledgment, and they lifted him and carried Zach back out of the room. Zach fought against their hold, but they were fast and strong as hell, and they got him out the door in two seconds.

He landed a solid blow to Drake's ribs and found himself slammed up against the hallway wall, pinned there by four hard hands. His feet barely touched the ground, giving him no leverage.

Zach's breath sawed in and out of his lungs, making them burn with fury. He should have come here on his own. He would have taken Joseph down and no one could have stopped him.

"Stop it!" barked Drake, getting right into Zach's face. His buddy's tone cut through the fog and helped him regain enough sanity to stop trying to bash his ribs in.

Zach shoved hard at his anger, trying to push it away, but all he could think about was Logan's mouth on his woman's neck, taking her lifeblood from her, draining her, making her come. "I'm not letting Logan near her."

"Of course not," soothed Angus. "You're going to march your ass back to her suite and you're going to convince her to play nice so Logan won't have to."

Disbelief shocked the air from Zach's chest. "You agree with Joseph? You think we should kill these men?"

Angus was quiet for a moment as if collecting his words. "I won't let Gilda or Sibyl end up like one of the bodies in those pictures, lying in the mud. As soon as those Defenders started making plans to kill my family, they gave up their right to keep breathing."

"And what about Lexi?" demanded Zach. "She helped them make plans, too."

"The difference is she's no longer a threat," said Angus. "Those men out there are. I won't let that stand. One way or another."

None of this sat right with Zach. He preferred the black and white world where he knew exactly what to do. All these shades of gray pissed him off. "So what you're saying is that if they're no longer a threat, you'll let them live?"

Angus's blue eyes pinned Zach in place. They burned with a kind of wisdom only centuries of pain and heartache could ignite. Zach had nothing but respect for this man who had trained him to be the warrior he had become. All that training kicked in, waking up the reflex where Angus talked and Zach listened.

In a tone so full of calm reason Zach had no choice but to agree, Angus said, "What I'm saying is that the only person who can save their sorry asses is Lexi. Get her to cooperate. Maybe we'll get lucky and find a way to keep the rednecks breathing."

"It's worth a shot," agreed Drake.

Of course he was right. Angus always was.

All that anger Zach had built up deflated, making him feel tired. "Great. Now all I have to do is figure out how to get her to spill her guts when she thinks we're going to use that information to kill the people that sheltered her and her mother when they hit hard times. No sweat."

Lexi wasn't entirely convinced that Helen knew what she was talking about—how to break down the barrier between her and Zach—but her suggestions were more than a little intriguing. They all involved a lot of touching and bare skin, and just the thought was enough to make Lexi's heart beat a little harder in anticipation.

Helen had left a few minutes ago, and now that the place was quiet, Lexi was left alone with her thoughts. Her fears.

What if she couldn't do what these people needed her to do? What if she couldn't be like Helen?

It wasn't even a question of whether or not it was what she wanted. Not anymore. She owed these people for her treachery, and she would find a way to make it up to them. But more important, she owed the Defenders for all the times they'd sheltered her and her mother. She couldn't just walk away from them without at least trying to fix this mess.

There had to be a way to get those good ol' boys to see things the way she did now. And maybe, if she could access all that power inside of Zach, she could find it. All she had to do was let them see what she'd seen, like some kind of mental slide show. She was convinced that if she did that, they'd come around and everyone could live happily ever after.

Yeah, right. Even she was smart enough to know the chances of that were slim. Still, that didn't mean she shouldn't try.

But first, she had to get through her own damn stubbornness and tap into all of Zach's strength so she had a fighting chance. From what Helen had said, it was like swimming in sunlight, all warm and happy.

Lexi needed a good dose of happy right now.

She curled up on the couch, tucking her legs under her, and watched the door. It wasn't locked. She wasn't sure if Zach had a key, and wanted him to be able to get in if she fell asleep. Which was a real possibility.

Logan had taken enough blood to leave her feeling light-headed if she stood too fast. She hoped that chugging down liquids would help her recover faster, but what she needed was about twelve hours of hard sleep. Maybe later, after the lives of so many people weren't resting on her shoulders, she'd get it.

While she waited, Lexi tried to reach out to Zach through the luceria like Helen had taught her. There was supposed to be a connection between them that held them together even when they weren't near each other.

She closed her eyes and focused on the ring of skin where the band touched her, searching for that connection.

It was warm, as if it had its own living heat, and she could feel the slightest humming coming from the thing every once in a while. She imagined a silvery wire joining her and Zach. All she had to do now was get a signal to travel through it.

Lexi tried pushing a thought through the connection, telling Zach to hurry back to her. Nothing happened. It was like trying to push a rope uphill.

So, maybe she should try pulling.

With her eyes shut, and the silver wire firmly in her mind, Lexi pulled. At first, she didn't think it had worked, but then she felt an odd tingle encircle her neck and slide down her spine. She sucked in a breath and held it.

She pulled harder, and in her mind, she made the wire grow thicker.

Rage slammed into her, driving a bellow from her lungs.

Zach was pissed. She could feel it as clearly as if it had been her own fury pounding through her. In fact, it took her a few seconds to separate the two feelings so she didn't start trashing her new place to vent out some of the feral emotion.

Even though she'd separated it in her mind, she was still shaking with the force of it, aching to go to him and beat the hell out of whatever had pissed him off.

She found herself pacing, stalking across the carpet in an effort to burn off some of the rage. Sure, she could have pulled back so she didn't feel it anymore, but she wanted to feel it. It meant she'd succeeded. Like an infant that craved new sensations, she couldn't stop herself from pulling harder, seeking out more.

Slowly, the anger faded and in its place was bleak acceptance. Resignation.

Whatever was going on, it was over now. The tingle of his bloodmark on her back told her he was getting closer. Coming back to her.

The need to comfort him was strong, growing stronger with every step he took. There was a deep sadness weeping inside him, shedding tears he'd never let fall. And surrounding all that vulnerability was a fierce need to keep her safe.

From what, she had no idea, but she was glad she'd managed to make this small connection to him, glad she knew without a doubt that he would do everything in his power to see to her safety.

It was humbling to feel the force of his need to protect her. Humbling and empowering. She felt like she could walk off a cliff and not worry. Zach would catch her.

He opened the door and locked it behind him. His body was tense, the muscles of his arms and shoulders bunched up with tightly held control.

Lexi stared at him, soaking him up. He was such a potent man, filling up the entryway with his power. His feet were braced apart, and he had the oddest look on his face. His smooth brown skin was stretched in a grimace, as if he was really dreading what he had to do now. But his pale eyes glowed with confidence, reassuring her that all would be well. He wouldn't let her fall.

Lexi went to him, needing to soothe him, wanting to touch him. Dying to try some of the things Helen had told her about.

She ran her hands over his muscled chest and locked her fingers around the back of his neck.

Zach's eyes fell shut and he pulled in a deep breath. It pressed the two of them closer, flattening her breasts against his ribs. Lexi felt her nipples bead up under the thin lace of her bra.

So did Zach.

He let out a nearly inaudible growl of need and grasped her hips in his big hands. "We need to talk," he told her.

"We will. After."

Helen said that making the connection with Zach would be easier during sex. Intimacy and trust helped loosen up the flow of power or something. Lexi didn't really understand it, but she was ready to put Helen's lesson to good use.

She went up on tiptoe, and pulled Zach down so she

could kiss him. The first brush of his lips against hers pulled a moan of pleasure from her body, but it wasn't nearly enough. She needed to taste him, to feel the slide of his tongue against hers.

Zach didn't make her wait. He bent his head lower and deepened the kiss, parting her lips so she could taste his heat, his need for her. Like a starving man, he fed from her mouth, holding her tight so she could feel the restrained strength vibrating in his arms.

When she was breathless, he pulled back just enough to look down at her. Desire lit his eyes, making them a luminous green. She hadn't let go of that silver wire and through it, a single pulse of physical need throbbed between them. She hadn't even needed to concentrate. It just happened.

It was working.

She licked her lips and gave him a victorious smile.

Zach's eyes zeroed in on her mouth and she saw his pupils widen, felt his grip on her body tighten. "Bed," he said, "before I forget to use one."

Lexi nodded and Zach lifted her up until she was straddling his hips. She felt the thick heat of his erection against her, rubbing her through her jeans. As he carried her back to the bedroom, every step sent a jolt of sensation streaking through her, making her body tighten.

Zach laid her down and unbuckled his sword belt. The sword flickered into visibility, glowing in the light from the hall. He hadn't bothered to switch on the light in the bedroom, and she briefly considered turning the lamp on, until he stripped his shirt off over his head.

Then Lexi wasn't thinking about anything at all other than the beauty of his chest, the breadth of his shoulders, the shadowed ridges of his stomach. The tree on his chest swayed slightly and Lexi climbed to her knees on the bed. She pressed her hands against his hot flesh, loving the smooth, hard contours of his body. She couldn't get enough. She could spend a year touching him and it still wouldn't quench her need to feel his skin under her palms.

Zach stood there, rigid and still, while she touched him, running her finger over the intricate branches, down the thick trunk until his jeans barred her path.

She looked up at him while her fingers made quick work of the button and zipper. His ribs expanded and contracted as if he'd just finished a long run. A gleam of perspiration shone along his forehead, and his jaw was clenched tight.

Lexi pressed a kiss over his navel, swirling her tongue against his skin. His stomach muscles bunched and a dark smile of feminine satisfaction stretched her mouth.

He was all man, and he was all hers.

Working the snug jeans down over his lean hips was harder than it would have been without his heavy erection taking up so much room, but she didn't mind the extra effort. It was more than worth the trouble. She didn't stop to help him out of his boots. She couldn't wait that long to get what she wanted.

Lexi wrapped her fingers around his penis, reveling in the smooth hardness of his body, the contrast of her paler skin against the light brown of his. Even in the dimness, it was easy to see her hand sliding over him. And even if she'd been blind, as soon as she heard his low groan of enjoyment, she would have known she'd done it just right.

Concentration was difficult, but Lexi was determined to make this work. She found that silver wire that lay there, forgotten in her mind, and gave it a hard tug.

A wave of raw lust filled her up, making her suck in a harsh breath. His lust, pure and potent, so ferocious she had no idea how he could stand it. Lexi's head fell to his abdomen and she shut her eyes, trying to find enough sanity to remember what she'd been doing. It was important. She'd had some kind of plan; she just wasn't sure what it was.

She smelled the male heat of his skin, the muskiness of his need for her. Inside her tight grip, Zach's erection throbbed, making her go liquid. The silver wire between them shimmered.

Power. She was trying to reach Zach's power. Sex helped. Intimacy helped even more.

Right. Lexi remembered now. She could do this. In fact, she'd never wanted to do anything more in her life as much as she wanted this.

"Lie down," he told her.

Not part of her plan. Lexi shook her head, letting her hair brush over his hip. "Not yet."

She felt his aggression swell and knew she was about to lose control over her carefully choreographed plan. Before he could take over, Lexi took his erection into her mouth, letting him sink deep.

Zach hissed in pleasure, and his whole body clenched tight. His palms cradled her head, his fingers sliding convulsively over her scalp.

She eased back, letting him slide almost free. Her mouth watered as she swirled her tongue over him, drawing a gasp from his powerful body. He tasted good. Hot, male—an intoxicating combination of need and hunger only she could fulfill.

Her own body ached, but what she wanted was more important than pleasure. She wanted hope, the promise of being what Zach needed most. A partner.

The luceria vibrated around her throat, heating more with every stroke of her lips and tongue over his hard flesh. She could feel something beautiful hovering just beyond reach, only a hairbreadth away. That something shimmered and pulsed, flooding her vision with color and light. Beautiful jade green, like Zach's eyes, so full of promise she could almost taste it.

Lexi reached for it, struggling to stay focused.

Her head spun, and the rich taste of Zach's body disappeared. She heard a tearing sound. Cool air assaulted her skin and when she opened her eyes to figure out what had gone wrong, she found herself on her back, her shirt ripped open down the front, Zach's frantic fingers undoing her jeans.

This wasn't at all what she had planned.

"Zach, wait," she said.

He stilled and looked at her, his face tight with unsated lust. She saw his mouth work as if he were trying to find words, but none came out. Instead, she felt the luceria tremble; then she was filled with a rush of desire so jagged and hard it ripped through her, making her cry out against the force of it.

Her body shuddered, and her eyes rolled back in her head. Pure, raw pleasure streaked through her body, pooling in her womb, pushing her to the edge of orgasm. She wasn't big enough to hold so much sensation. It didn't give her any room to breathe.

And she didn't care.

Before she had time to adjust to so much feeling, Zach gave her more. She felt it stretch their connection, making the luceria heat under the strain. And then all thoughts of plans and connections were driven from her mind as a bubble of pleasure burst inside her, making her come.

She rode the waves of sensation, letting them drag her along, taking them where they pleased. She thought the power might tear her apart, but instead, it cradled her and eased her back down to reality when it was through buffeting her about.

Her eyelids were heavy, but she forced them open. Zach was poised above her, supporting his weight so that his arms bulged with muscles. She felt the head of his erection press against her core and she was so slick and soft he slid in easily. Her body stretched to accept him without complaint. In fact, every inch of ground he gained made her loose limbs coil with a new stirring of desire.

Lexi's breath still hadn't evened out from her orgasm, and already, he was driving her toward another. If she didn't act fast, she was going to lose her opportunity to strengthen their bond.

Zach moved inside her, seating himself deep. She could feel his heartbeat throbbing in his erection, see it pounding in the vein along his neck. His eyes were open, a sexy, slumberous green, watching her. She saw his throat work as if he were trying to speak; then in the midst of all his churning lust, she felt a subtle flutter of concern slide into her.

He was worried about her.

She offered him what she hoped was an encouraging smile and said, "I'm fine. Better than fine."

He gave a satisfied nod and closed his eyes in relief. Without further hesitation, his powerful muscles bunched and flexed as he set a steady rhythm.

Lexi ground her teeth, trying to stay focused on her task, but it was nearly impossible. His need for her was flowing into her like water, his body filling her up, driving her higher. She couldn't concentrate or remember what Helen had told her to do. Not anymore. There was too much feeling inside her to leave her any room to think.

Defeated, but in the sweetest way imaginable, Lexi gave in and let go. She drove her fingers through Zach's silky hair and pulled his head to her. She kissed his mouth, his jaw, down his neck. Every touch of her lips to his skin was rewarded with a deep sound of pleasure. Every flick of her tongue filled her up with his intoxicating taste.

Her man. All hers.

Zach cupped her breast, pinching her nipple between two fingers. Erotic currents streaked through her body, making her arch her hips into his thrusts.

Her body trembled, weak from stress and blood loss, but Lexi ignored the tremors. Zach's body tightened and he sped the pace, shifting so every stroke hit just the right spots. Her world spiraled down to the minute space between their straining bodies and the sizzling jolts of electricity that arced between them.

A deep rumble shook Zach's chest, resonating inside Lexi. He wrapped his arm around her hips, held her still and thrust deep and hard inside her. She felt his erection swell and pulse, felt the heat of his release fill her as tiny sparks danced along her limbs.

It was too much. She couldn't take any more sensation. All that coiled tension sprung free and ricocheted inside her body as the climax tore through her.

Light danced in her vision and she felt the warmth of sunlight engulf her, sweeping her away.

Minutes later, though she had no idea how many, she found enough strength to open her eyes. Zach was draped over her, his breathing slowing. Sweat cooled her body where currents of air touched her. Everywhere else she was warm and utterly content.

Zach seemed to be in no hurry to move, and she liked him there. He was careful with his weight so he didn't crush her, but solid enough she felt protected beneath him. Her hip joints had been pushed to their limits, making room for his big body between her thighs, but even that ache was a pleasant one.

Her head still spun, but it had cleared enough for her to remember the goal of her seduction, such as it was. Zach hadn't exactly made it a challenge.

The notion that he was so easy, that he wanted her so much, made her smile.

In the dim quiet of the room, their bodies sated and

happy, Lexi reached out, struggling to access Zach's power. So far, she'd figured out how to pull feelings from him, but she hadn't been able to send them back, nor had she been able to find that ribbon of energy Helen described. It was as if the connection between them was broken.

Or maybe it was just different.

A thin film, like the skin of a bubble, hovered between them. Lexi poked at it, expecting it to pop, but it held firm. She pushed harder and still nothing happened.

Zach levered his body up on one elbow. His face was bright with excitement. "I felt that . . . pressure. Try it again."

Lexi did. She shoved at the barrier until it made her dizzy, but didn't break through.

Exhausted, she let out a frustrated sigh. "Sorry."

Zach smoothed her hair back from her damp forehead and gave her an encouraging smile. "Don't be. It'll come. You just need some rest. And maybe some more practice."

He was still semihard inside her, the "semi" part quickly becoming a memory. But, rather than take advantage, Zach pulled out of her and stretched out along her flank. He pulled the sheet up over her damp body and ran his finger along the luceria. His eyes darkened as he watched the play of his finger as if the sight turned him on. Maybe it did.

"I hope that's enough," she said.

"It will be." His voice rang with complete confidence. "But for now, you need to rebuild your strength. Make some new blood. Fucking bloodsucking bastard." A scowl wrinkled his dark brow.

Lexi soothed it away with her thumb. "I'm fine. Really."

"Roll over and let me pet you." His voice was gruff, but Lexi didn't mind. She sensed that he simply didn't want her watching emotions play over his face. Whether he felt vulnerable, or whether he just didn't want her to worry, she wasn't sure, but she humored him and rolled onto her stomach.

Zach's wide, warm hand slid along her spine, pushing the sheet away as he went. The chill of cool air didn't touch her, though. Not with Zach at her back, throwing off heat like a furnace.

Lexi closed her eyes and enjoyed the feeling of him stroking her. Tiny sparks jumped into her skin, but she was getting used to that now, and they were almost like a mini massage.

He traced his finger over her leopard tattoo, following the sinuous curves of vines surrounding the animal.

"Why did you do this?" he asked.

"To keep you from finding me. Mom was convinced my birthmark would draw the monsters to me, so she used to cover it with makeup. When I was older, I got inked."

His hand moved down to the base of her spine where the filigree swirls she'd fallen in love with at fifteen lay embedded in her skin. She felt him shift, moving his body down, felt his warm breath sweep out over her bottom as he moved in for a close inspection.

"There," he said, touching a spot just to the right of her spine. "I see it. The ring that marks you as a Theronai."

"Yep. That's it. Mom said it was dangerous, so we got it covered. When I saw that mark you left on me at Gertie's Diner, I knew it was bad news. I figured if I covered it up, it might keep you from tracking me."

"It did. Funny how none of us knew it would work like that. How on earth did your mom know?"

Lexi shrugged her tattooed shoulder, drawing Zach back up her body to the image of his eyes in a leopard's body. "I'm not sure. The guy who fathered me gave her all kinds of instructions on how to keep me safe, and a bunch of dire warnings about how important it was for her to keep me hidden until I was grown. Guess Mom took them to heart."

"I wish I could thank her for taking care of you so well."

A deep, old heartache, worn down to smooth edges by time, bloomed up inside Lexi. She missed Mom every day, wished she could share her life with her now that things were better. Safer.

Mom would have liked Zach. After she'd finished trying to kill him, of course.

"Why a leopard?" asked Zach.

"It was the way you moved. Like a predator. The way you looked at me like you were hungry, made me feel hunted."

"I was hunting you. And as for the idea of eating you all up . . . that promise."

A languid heat curled inside her belly. "Anytime you want."

Zach growled low in his throat, but moved away. "You need your rest. If I get started now, you won't sleep for hours."

Fatigue weighed down on her, tugging her toward dreamland. As much as she wanted Zach, she knew she'd give in to his effortless seduction if he stuck around. The man was irresistible, even when he wasn't trying. "Not sure I can last that long."

He gave her shoulder a quick kiss and levered himself out of bed. "Which is why I'm going out for a while. Naked Lexi is too tempting to resist, and I'm determined to be a good boy and let you sleep. If you think you can."

"I think I'd like to try. There's a lot going on in my head right now."

Zach nodded. "Yeah. A lot of that going around."

"Wanna talk about it?"

"Not now. Tomorrow is soon enough. Get some rest.

I'm going to go out and see if I can lend a hand at the wall. Unless you'd rather I stay."

Lexi needed some time to think, and she sure as hell wasn't going to sleep if his manly body was right there, distracting her with its yumminess. "No, you go on. They need your help. Helen said it's not going well."

"It's not, but we'll get through. We always do."

Lexi watched as he covered his firm butt with his discarded jeans, blocking her from the lovely sight. "Spoilsport," she teased.

Zach let out a laugh, shaking his head. "Stop trying to make me blush, woman. I might have to retaliate."

"Sounds like fun."

He buckled his sword belt around his hips and the thing shimmered before it faded from sight. "You're in no shape for more fun." He bent down and kissed the tip of her nose. "Sleep. Then we'll see if we can't find something to amuse you."

He was just closing the bedroom door when Lexi stopped him. "Zach? What if I can't do it? What if I can't ever tap into your power?"

He stilled with his hand on the knob and gave her a smile so full of confidence it almost made her believe in miracles. "You can."

"But what if I can't?"

He looked her right in the eyes and said, "I'll love you anyway."

Chapter 22

Zach was regretting his confession of love by the time he hit the training yard. He kept feeling around, trying to connect to Lexi, seeking out some kind of reaction to his declaration. But all he felt was a yawning void of nothing stretching out between them.

Shit.

He knew she was trying. He couldn't fault her for that, but it still bothered him that things weren't working between them like they should.

Because she still didn't trust him. That had to be the problem.

Frustration rode him hard as he neared the crumbled ruins of the wall. He checked his cell phone to make sure it was working and Lexi could reach him; then he threw himself into some good, hard labor. Lifting rocks was that, and then some.

An hour after Zach left, Lexi had convinced herself that he didn't really mean that he loved her. It was just a manner of speech. A saying his people used or something.

I'll love you anyway.

She wanted it to be true so much it made her heart ache. No one had loved her since her mom, and she found herself dying for more, craving it like she did oxygen.

Which was completely unfair of her. Here she was wanting his love when she wasn't yet able to give it back in return. It wasn't that Zach wasn't lovable. Hell, she'd never met a man who sang to her soul the way he did. She was sure she could love him.

If she allowed herself to truly believe all of this was real, and that he was what he seemed.

There was still a sliver of doubt lodged deep inside of her that maybe everything she'd seen and felt since the night Zach had found her in Gus's bar had all been some kind of trick. A hallucination brought about by the monumental powers the Sentinels wielded.

And no matter how many times she told herself that this had to be real, that sliver of doubt still stung and nagged her, drawing her mind back to it over and over. She wanted all of this to be true so badly that she was sure it would be swept away from her. Someone would lift a curtain and show her reality, and all her hopes and dreams would dissolve like a sugar cube tossed into hot water.

Deep down, Lexi sensed that it was this last bit of doubt that was holding her back, but she didn't know how to shake it. It was the only thing protecting her, and no matter how safe she felt in Zach's arms, she knew that, too, could be part of the illusion. Her only true safety lay in holding on to that doubt, keeping it close to her heart so at least that part of her was invulnerable.

If this was all a lie, and that curtain was opened, then at least Lexi would know that she'd held back the most important part of herself. She might be stripped of her pride and humiliated, they might laugh at the foolish woman who fell under their spell so easily, they might even kill her, but at least she wouldn't die heartbroken.

It was cold comfort.

Lexi threw back the covers, found some new clothes that weren't ripped in half, showered, and got dressed.

Her first instinct was to seek out Helen and talk to her, but she was busy on the wall, or if she wasn't, she was probably sleeping. Since Lexi was useless when it came to lending a magical hand, the least she could do was stay out of the way and not slow everyone else down.

There was only one thing Lexi could do to help: get the Defenders to see reality and side with the Sentinels. There were hundreds of them—maybe even a few thousand—scattered across the country. If they joined forces with the Sentinels and helped fight the Synestryn, maybe it would help even the playing field.

Sure, they were just humans without any magical powers, but they were heavily armed and completely dedicated humans. Even if they only agreed to provide eyes and ears, it might help tip the scales in the Sentinels' favor.

It was worth a shot.

Plus, if she managed to convince the Defenders that everything she hoped was true, then that would go a long way toward pulling out that last splinter of doubt.

And if she couldn't convince them? Well, she wasn't sure what she'd do then, but she had to try.

Lexi wasn't stupid enough to meet with them face-to-face, but a phone call couldn't hurt. They already knew where she was, and since the bomb hadn't gone off, they also probably knew she'd been compromised.

She figured out how to get an outside line, and dialed Jake Morrow, Hector's son. It was breaking the chain of command, but Jake was a much more reasonable man than his father. If anyone was going to listen to her side of the story, it would be him.

Zach stared out over the broken wall, realizing for the first time just how vulnerable they really were. And how long it was going to stay that way.

They'd worked all night and had only added two feet

to the structure. All the rocks were piled up, ready to be used, but they could only be put in place after one of the women had woven defensive magic through the molecules of the stone. Otherwise, the only thing it was going to keep out was humans and animals.

Dawn was drawing near, and all but a few Theronai had gone inside to seek their rest. There was nothing more they could do now that Helen and Gilda had gone inside to sleep, neither one strong enough to stand without help.

Drake had had to carry Helen, and though Gilda had accepted Angus's support, she hadn't allowed him to do the same. There was an odd kind of distance between them that Zach didn't understand, but he hoped like hell it went away soon. This place needed them strong, functioning as a team.

It needed him and Lexi to do the same.

Zach's back ached, but he ignored it, preferring the mindless monotony of labor over the worries eating away at him.

What if Lexi's fears were right and she never managed to access his power? He was sure the failure would crush her, not to mention the fact that he had no clue what that would mean for him. His lifemark was no longer dying, but it wasn't renewing itself, either. There were no new leaves forming, no buds.

Patience. He needed to stop worrying and have some faith. It had only been a couple of days. He needed to give Lexi some time to figure things out. Heaven knew she was trying.

A warm smile pulled at his mouth. He could hardly wait for her to try again.

A small whimper of sound rose up to his ears, barely audible. Zach stilled and held his breath, listening. It came again, a little louder this time, from the thick brush on the far side of the wall. It sounded like a wounded animal.

Or a child.

Fear kicked hard, making Zach's body move into action. Had one of the human children wandered out through the opening and gotten hurt? There was so much chaos around the wall's break, it could have happened.

The sound came again, a little sobbing noise of pain and terror. Definitely not an animal.

Zach shouted to the closest man, "Neal, come here. Back me up."

The sky had lightened enough that the floodlights shining on the work area had been turned off. The humans who had needed the illumination had all gone inside for food, anyway.

Deep shadows left dark pockets over the landscape, but Zach had served perimeter duty enough times that he knew the area well and had no trouble negotiating the dips and ruts in the dim light.

Neal was bare-chested. He pulled a T-shirt from his waistband and wiped the dust and sweat from his face. "What's up?" asked Neal. His voice was deceptively lazy as he came up beside Zach, moving so smoothly, it was hard not to watch.

"Thought I heard something. Like a kid."

"Doubt it," drawled Neal as he dropped the shirt and drew his sword.

Zach had been teamed up with Neal often enough to know that despite his casual manner, the man could go from zero to killer in about three seconds.

"Yeah, me, too. Guess we'll see." Zach checked the sky. "Whatever it is, can't be that bad for long. Sun's almost up."

The pitiful sound came from the bottom of a shallow ravine about fifty feet away.

"It sure as hell sounds human," said Neal, but he didn't put away his sword.

They reached the edge, and Zach saw a movement in the brush below. Something wearing pale blue. "Help me," said the kid, and it was definitely a kid. "I'm stuck."

Both men slid down the side of the ravine, which was maybe seven feet deep and twenty feet wide. During the rainy season, the crevice would be running with water, but right now, it was filled with scrub brush, mud and weeds.

Neal sheathed his sword as Zach pushed through the brush toward the kid. It was a little boy, maybe ten. He was wearing faded blue jeans and near him was a fishing pole and tackle box. His feet were sunk into the mud up to his calves and he'd fallen back, lodging his arms and his butt in the thick mud as well.

Zach didn't recognize the boy, but there were a lot of kids at Dabyr, more all the time.

"What's your name, son?" Zach asked as he looked for a way to reach the boy without getting stuck himself.

"Clay."

"Are you hurt, Clay?"

"I twisted my ankle." He sniffed and looked like he wished he could wipe the tears from his face before Zach got close enough to see them. His night vision was good enough that he had no trouble making out the shiny streaks over the kid's face.

"Don't worry. We'll get you out of here."

His voice wavered with genuine fear. "Are you gonna tell my mom?"

Absolutely, but no sense in freaking the kid out. He had to learn how dangerous it was to go outside the walls—learn it well enough that he never did it again. "Don't worry about that right now. Let's just focus on getting you out of here."

From behind him, Zach heard the metallic click of a gun being cocked. He turned to see what was going on, already knowing it was bad.

A burly man in denim overalls stood on the sloping land behind and above Neal with a matte black gun pointed at the Theronai's head. "Move and I'll blow his brains out," said the stranger.

Zach stepped in front of the kid to protect him from stray bullets.

Neal's hand moved to his sword.

"I wouldn't do that," said another man behind Zach.

Zach whirled around and saw a skinny human with a scraggly beard on the far side of the ravine. In his hands was a shotgun, and it was pointed at the boy.

Outrage surged through Zach. This whole thing had been a trap with the kid serving as bait.

"You won't kill him," said Zach. "That child is one of your own."

"He's not my kid," said Skinny, his voice chilly with indifference. "Go ahead. See if I'm bluffing."

The boy's eyes overflowed with tears and his nose started running. "You said we were going fishing."

"Shut up," barked Skinny.

"What do you want?" asked Zach.

"You and your buddy here are coming with us."

"Like hell," drawled Neal. And then he went into a blur of motion that severed the man's weapon hand at the wrist, sending it spinning through the air.

The man screamed, holding his bleeding wrist against his body.

Zach didn't wait to see what Neal did next. Instead, he lunged for the kid and ripped him from the mud. He spun, putting his back to the shotgun, holding his breath in anticipation of the blast.

None came. Zach tossed the child into some nearby brush to cushion his fall and drew his sword.

"Run!" he ordered the boy.

A second later, white-hot pain bloomed across his back as power poured into him, stretching his insides until he thought he'd explode.

He roared in anger and spun around in a clumsy arc, slamming his fist into the man behind him. The man stumbled back, revealing two more men crouched in the brush.

Zach drew his sword and charged.

One man lifted some kind of gun and fired. A staticky crackling sound split the air, and an instant later, another sledgehammer of pain slammed into Zach's chest.

The second man aimed and fired.

Zach's muscles clenched down, completely out of his control. The branches of his lifemark shivered in pain, and a thin, high squeal trickled from his throat against his will.

He crumpled to the ground, landing on his side, gasping for air, trying to blink the spots from his vision. When it cleared, he was staring at a pair of worn work boots. He tried to move, but couldn't. One of those boots pulled back and slammed into his head, flipping him onto his back. He looked up and saw an old man whose face was shadowed by a cowboy hat holding some kind of stun gun in his hand.

Wires trailed out of the thing, leading straight to Zach.

That was what had taken him down? Stun guns?

"Worked like a charm," said the man. "Just like that creepy fella promised."

Zach had trouble making sense of what the man had said, but he didn't waste time figuring it out. In the distance he saw Neal slumped on the ground, his head bleeding heavily, a pair of wires streaming from his bare chest. As Zach watched, several leaves on his lifemark fell as he lay there, twitching.

The addition of so much energy into Neal's body so fast with no way for him to release it was going to kill him. Zach had the benefit of being connected to Lexi, but Neal wasn't so lucky.

Skinny lifted another stun gun from his belt and aimed it at Neal. Zach didn't think his friend would survive another shot.

Zach tried to reach for his sword to cut that bastard down before he could kill Neal, but he couldn't move. He couldn't even seem to find enough air to call for help.

If he didn't do something, they were both dead. Maybe the boy along with them.

That was the thought that burned through the paralysis and got his body moving again. He found the hilt of his sword and pulled it free of the sheath.

"Oh no, you don't," said a gruff voice.

Shock made Zach's body go numb, and a second later, he realized he'd been kicked in the head again. Funny how it didn't hurt.

He tried to react, but nothing seemed to be working right. He lost the grip on his sword as his limp fingers fell away uselessly. Even his neck didn't work. He couldn't turn his head to look at his attackers and defend himself.

Another blow rocked his body. He was blacking out. He reached for Lexi's mind, trying to call out a warning: Dabyr was under attack. He wasn't sure if he got through or not, but as his vision faded, he knew it was too late for him and Neal. There was nothing she could do in time to save them.

Jake Morrow answered Lexi's call on the first ring, even though it wasn't quite six a.m. yet. He didn't sound sleepy, either, which made her wonder if he had spent a sleepless night, too.

"Hello?" he asked.

"It's Lexi."

"Thank God," he breathed out in relief. "We'd thought they'd killed you."

"I'm fine. In fact, better than fine. We were wrong about the Sentinels, Jake. And that's not some kind of brainwashing talking, either."

She hoped.

Silence flowed over the line for a moment. "Are you alone?" he asked.

"Yeah, why?"

"I just wanted to make sure you could talk freely."

"I can. I am, Jake. I'm not sure where my mom got all the ideas she drilled into my head, but they're all wrong. These men are good. They're giving up their lives to protect humans from the Synestryn."

Another long pause made her nervous. "I want to know what you've learned. Can you meet me so we can talk about it?"

Meet him. Only one reason he'd want to do that rather than talk on the phone. "You don't believe me. You think I'm brainwashed, don't you?"

"I just want to be sure, Alex. The only way to do that is to get you out of there. Away from any hold they might have on you."

"It's Lexi, not Alex. I'm not in hiding anymore."

"Maybe you should be. Just meet me for a few minutes, and let me judge for myself that it's really you talking."

It wasn't smart. She knew how they operated. If they thought she was brainwashed, they'd no longer trust her, or worse, they'd see her as the enemy. "I can't. I'm sorry, Jake, but I don't trust you not to do something rash."

"They know about the C-4, don't they?"

Lexi closed her eyes in frustration. She wanted so badly to help Jake see what she had, but didn't know how to make him open his eyes. "Yeah. I told them."

She heard a hiss of sound that could have been Jake uttering a curse, but she wasn't sure. "That wasn't a good idea. They'll make us pay."

"They're reasonable people, Jake. All we need to do is sit down together and talk things over. Let them show you around here, see all the kids they've saved, and you'll know they're not the monsters my mother and your father thought."

"There are kids there?"

"Lots."

"Holy fuck. No wonder you didn't trigger the detonator."

"Yeah, even if they'd been the bad guys, I couldn't have done it." Another long stretch of silence had Lexi gripping the phone hard. "Jake? Are you there?"

Jake lowered his voice as if he was trying to hide their conversation. "Listen, Lexi. I only have a few seconds. You've got to get out of there. Get all the kids out of there. Right now."

A feeling of doom weighed down on her, sliding down her throat until it sat heavy in her stomach. "Why?"

"Do you really need to ask? Just do it."

The Defenders were attacking. Lexi hadn't done what she'd come here to do, so they were taking matters into their own hands.

There was a loud thud and a grunt of pain. She had no idea what that noise was, but panic welled up inside Lexi, making her stomach heave.

Desperate, she said, "Call it off, Jake. Make your dad call it off."

But it wasn't Jake's voice that came back over the line. It was Hector's. The deep grating sound of his anger was unmistakable. "It's too late for that now, little girl. We've got your man."

Just as he said the words, Lexi's head was filled with the sound of Zach's frantic cry. *Lexi! We're under attack!*

Oh, God. It was too late. They had Zach.

She made a choking sound and nearly dropped the phone. Her whole body was numb with disbelief as she reached out for Zach, needing to be near him. As always, the only thing that greeted her was silence. She couldn't feel him.

Hector went on as if her world hadn't just spun out of control. "You've got a couple of choices. You can raise the alarm, and we'll kill him and his buddy right now, or you can walk calmly out through that break in the wall, and we'll let him live. It's up to you. What are you going to do?"

"Don't hurt him," she told him to stall for precious seconds to think. Her mind flew through her options as she spoke. A sketchy plan formed in her head, giving her an idea of how she could protect the people of Dabyr. "Let me talk to Zach."

"No can do. The man's out like a light, bleeding all over the goddamn place."

Oh God. Zach.

Lexi closed her eyes and swallowed hard, trying to clear her head of the image of his broken body lying helpless at Hector's whim.

She wasn't going to let Zach die. His people needed him too much.

She needed him too much.

Lexi couldn't let them kill Zach and whoever was with him, but she knew if she just walked out without warning anyone that there was a good chance even more people would die.

"Why do you want me to come out? Why not just kill me along with everyone else?" she asked, proud of the fact that she could actually form words in the midst of the chaotic jumble of panic and fear rolling around inside her.

"I promised your mother I'd look out for you. I'm a man of my word."

There was more to it than that—she could hear it in his voice—but Lexi didn't waste any time trying to figure it out.

"What'll it be, girl? You coming out, or do I gut him now and let you hear him gurgle out his last breath?"

"I'm coming," she whispered.

"Good girl. I figured you'd see things our way."

"What are you going to do to me?" she asked.

"Are you worried we'll hurt you? You're one of us. What they did to you isn't your fault." Understanding sounded odd coming from Hector's lips. He was not the understanding type. "We'll clear up your confusion, and then you can tell us everything you've learned about that place. You're going to be a valuable asset."

That was it? They wanted information?

Something about that didn't seem right, but she was running out of time and not coming up with any new options. "And you promise you won't hurt Zach?"

"No, we'll let you have the honors of killing him and his buddy yourself once you're in your right mind again. I have to admit I'll enjoy the show. I've seen how ferocious you can be when you're angry. And once he no longer controls your thoughts, you're definitely going to be angry."

"How will I find you?" she asked.

"Don't worry. We'll find you. Just walk out, and we'll do the rest."

Lexi would never hurt Zach. Never. But Hector didn't need to know that. She'd play along and make sure that she did everything she could to keep the people here safe, and then she'd save Zach.

Sure, she had no idea how she was going to do all that, but she was good at thinking on her feet. She'd come up with something in the ten or fifteen minutes it would take her to get out through the broken wall.

Yeah, right.

Before she lost her nerve, Lexi dialed Helen's cell phone.

Drake answered, sounding surly. "What?"

"It's Lexi. Can I talk to Helen?"

"She's sleeping."

Great. Now she had to deal with a man she barely knew, one she didn't trust, at least not like she trusted Zach. "We have a problem. The Defenders are planning to attack Dabyr."

"When?" he asked, the word a sharp chip of ice in her ear.

"Now. I need you to evacuate everyone, but do it quietly. They may have a way of watching us. If they know what you're up to, they may move in sooner."

"You knew about this all along, didn't you?" he demanded.

"No. I swear." There wasn't time to convince him, so she didn't bother to try. "Is there any secret exit out of this place? A safe room where people can hide or something?"

"I'm not telling you that. You think I'm some kind of fool?"

"Just do it, Drake. Get everyone to safety."

"Is there another bomb?" he asked.

"I don't know what they're planning, but I'm sure they've got something up their sleeve. And I think they're close." Lexi pulled in a deep breath and let it out in a confession. "They have Zach and someone else. I don't know who."

A feral rumble of anger vibrated over the line. "Where are they, Lexi?"

"I don't know, but I'm going to find out. They're coming for me now."

"You can't go alone."

"If anyone comes with me, Zach is a dead man."

"Fuck," he spat, and in the background, Lexi heard the faint sound of Helen's questioning voice. "What are you going to do?"

"I'll have to figure it out on the fly."

"Not good enough. There's too much risk."

Lexi's heart was pounding hard. She'd already started to shake thanks to a nice big dose of adrenaline. Standing here talking with Drake was getting her nowhere. "I don't have any more time to argue with you. Get the kids out, damn it!"

She hung up the phone, grabbed a sharp knife from the kitchen—the only weapon she could find—and headed out the door.

Though she heard no sirens, lights in the building started to switch on as she raced over the dew-soaked grass. Drake had raised the alarm.

She just prayed he'd done it in time.

Chapter 23

Grace raced through the halls to Torr's suite, her heart pounding hard with fear. Less than a minute ago, her phone had rung, waking her from a dead sleep. Joseph's recorded message said there was danger of an impending attack and to go immediately to safety, down into the halls below the humans' wing of Dabyr.

She'd sent her stepbrother down with another family, but she couldn't yet go herself. She had to find Torr and get him to safety. The Theronai were too busy taking care of the children, and she couldn't risk that he'd be forgotten in the chaos.

She hugged the wall, avoiding the crush of people flowing past her. After a few turns, she was past the crowd. She sprinted down Torr's hall and came to a skidding stop outside his door. It was unlocked as usual, and when she went inside, Torr was in his bed, which was raised so he could look out across the grounds as he liked to do.

The sun was just beginning to lighten the landscape in a pretty pink glow. Everything looked normal, though she knew that wasn't the case. The only other time the alarm had been raised like this was the night the wall came down.

"We have to go," she told him, her voice breathless as she hurried to his bed.

"What's happening?"

"There's some kind of attack. I don't know any details."

His jaw tightened and a look of fury crossed his features. "You shouldn't have come for me. You need to get below with the other humans."

She attached the straps to the hoist she used to lift him. "I'm not leaving without you."

"This is foolish. There's nothing they can do to me."

"They could kill you."

"I'm already dead, and we both know it."

"Not yet, you're not, and I'm not going to let it happen tonight, either."

"I'm not worth the risk, Grace. Please, go below so I know you're safe. Now."

She ignored his order and continued laying the bed flat so she could lift him into his chair. His body was limp as the machine hoisted it from the bed into his wheelchair. His eyes were blazing with anger, and she could practically hear his teeth grinding.

"Do you have any idea what it would do to me if you died trying to save me?" he demanded.

"We're not going to find out."

"You don't even know what the threat is. Synestryn could be marching through the halls as we speak."

The thought made her shudder, but she didn't stop moving. She would not leave him. "All the more reason for me to take you with me. We'll have time to get to safety. Both of us."

She hesitated only a moment before she took the time to fasten the straps that held his body in place. Time was short, but if he slid from his chair, she'd never be able to lift him back into it without help.

She clicked the last buckle shut, and she looked in his eyes. She was close enough she could feel his breath sweep past her cheek. She wanted to kiss him so badly her body trembled in the effort to hold back.

Besides, there wasn't time for that now. Later, there would be time. She promised herself she'd be brave enough to kiss him. Soon.

His voice was thick with longing. "You're killing me, Grace."

"No, I'm saving you."

"If I lost you . . ." He trailed off, his throat bobbing.

She touched his cheek, feeling the warmth of his skin under her chilled fingers. "That's exactly how I feel. I can't lose you, either."

His eyes drifted shut. "Please. We can't do this. You can't do this to yourself."

She knew he was talking about their relationship, but she chose to purposefully misunderstand him. "I'm not doing anything I don't want to do. I need you to be safe."

Before she wasted any more time, she wheeled him out the door, toward the tunnel entrance.

If anything happened to Torr, she wasn't sure she'd survive. She'd already lost so much in the Synestryn attack on her family. She couldn't lose him, too.

When Zach came to, he was lying on his side, trussed up tight with ropes digging into his skin hard enough to cut off his circulation. He looked around, trying to figure out where he was, but the cramped confines of the dark space gave him no clue. All the windows were covered, and his prison was on the move. He could feel the vibrations beneath him, hear the hum of tires on the road.

Beside him, Neal was bound, his bloody head leaving a dark wet spot beneath him. His chest moved as he breathed, but not much. Not nearly enough for a man his size.

Little light filtered into the small space, but it was enough to tell Zach that it was daylight outside. At least all the blood they'd spilled wouldn't be drawing Synestryn out to play.

His head pounded and his muscles were stiff from all the convulsing, but other than that, he could hardly feel a thing. His arms and legs were asleep from loss of circulation. As he shifted, he realized he was on a soft surface, like a mattress. He pushed himself up and looked around enough to figure out he was in the back of a motor home, lying on a bed. The door to the main cabin was cracked open about a foot, and through it, he could see several blurry forms moving about.

Blurry? Great. He must have been hit harder than he thought.

The motor home slowed to a stop. He heard steps, felt the thing shift as new weight was added. Several people got in, closed the door behind them. They started moving again, heading down the road.

"Where's Zach?" It was Lexi's voice, clear and demanding.

Zach's heart leapt, reveling in the sweet sound of her voice. Then his foggy brain realized what her being here meant.

Lexi had been taken by these assholes, too.

The air in Zach's lungs froze solid, keeping him from breathing. He reached for his sword, but not only did his hand not move; he was sure they'd stripped the weapon from him before bringing him here.

Still every protective instinct he possessed rose up on its hind legs and howled. Zach tried to scream a warning, but all that came out was a muffled sound of defeat. They'd taped his mouth shut, gagging him and his groggy noggin hadn't even realized it until now. Not a good sign all was well upstairs.

Zach struggled to move, forcing his numb body to comply. He needed to get to her. Protect her. Save her.

"He's in the back," said a man.

"I'm going to see him." Her voice was firm, but wavered with fear.

"Fine," said the man. "But be quick. We've got a show to put on. Folks are waiting."

A second later, Lexi's face came into sight, close enough that she was no longer a blur. Her chocolate brown eyes glowed with tears of concern she didn't let fall. Her fingers trembled as they feathered over his face. When she drew them back, they were smeared with his blood.

"You could have killed him," accused Lexi, turning to the man standing behind her. He was tall, thick with both fat and muscle. He had an air of authority about him so heavy that the other men in the motor home stood several feet back so they didn't have to stand under that weight.

Maybe they were afraid of him.

"Them boys are tough," said the man. "Gotta hit 'em good and hard to take 'em down. Those stun guns worked like a charm. We'll definitely be adding those to our arsenal."

Lexi peeled the edge of the tape away from Zach's mouth. It stung, but he welcomed the pain. It meant he was still alive. There was still a fighting chance.

"You okay?" she asked him in a strained voice, like she was barely holding herself together.

As soon as his mouth was free, he said, "Get out of here."

She gave him a sad, watery smile. "Not without you."

"Enough of a reunion," said the big man behind her. "We've got things to discuss."

Lexi turned, exasperation vibrating along her slender back. "I'm not brainwashed, Hector. You've got it all wrong."

"Just let her go," said Zach. "You've got me and Neal. You don't need her, too."

Hector pushed Lexi aside and leaned down over Zach. Hatred glowed in his eyes, making them bulge. "That's where you're wrong, boy. Lexi's part of the bigger plan. And you . . . Well, the girl's taken a liking to you, which makes you downright useful."

Useful. Oh shit. He was leverage.

He had to get out of these ropes, but he couldn't feel his fingers to work the knots loose. "Just go, Lexi," pleaded Zach.

Hector gave him a cold smile. "She will. Don't worry. We just need to get her rigged up first."

A sick sense of dread pooled in Zach's stomach. Rigged up. That didn't sound good at all.

When Hector reached across the small space into the minuscule closet and pulled out a vest covered in wires and blocks of military-grade explosives, Zach knew just how bad it was.

That vest was way too small for any of the men present to wear. It was Lexi's size.

Lexi stared at the vest, and fear fell down on her like an avalanche, leaving her freezing and suffocating. She locked her knees to stay standing, but the edges of her vision faded out to gray.

"That's for me, isn't it?" she asked Hector.

"Custom-made by my own hands," he said. "Boys."

Two men behind her grabbed her arms. She'd been too shocked to even think about fighting until now. But now that they had her locked in their hard grips, her survival instincts kicked in and she fought back, lashing out with her feet and fists. She landed several blows, but the men holding her were strong, corn-fed men who were used to a few hard knocks.

They worked for Hector, after all.

"Stop your fussin' and strap in," said Hector as he started sliding her arms through the holes with quite a bit of help from the men holding her. "We got a schedule to keep."

Zach let out a bellow of pure rage and thrashed around until he hit the floor. His body was trussed up tight, coiled with thin, strong rope. There was no way he was getting out of that without help.

Lexi was frantic, dying to do anything to stop this from happening. She knew the power to do so was there, right at her throat, hovering in the luceria, and she reached for it, straining against the barrier that separated them.

Zach's eyes fell shut and his body stilled, like he'd felt her trying. His eyes locked onto hers, and he gave her a single nod.

Had it worked? Lexi didn't feel any power, no flow of energy like Helen had described. She pushed again, but the barrier was still in place, locking her out.

Defeat deadened her body, making her go slack inside the two men's grips. She still couldn't reach him. He was there, willing and ready to share with her everything she needed to save him, Neal and herself, but she couldn't touch it.

"It's time," said Hector. "Before the Sentinels figure out you're all missing." He grabbed a Windbreaker and put it on her as if she were two years old. And like a two-year-old, she wanted to fight him every step of the way. Only the fact that she was wearing a weapon kept her from doing so.

"I won't do it," whispered Lexi. "Whatever it is you want, I won't do it."

"Yes, you will. You're going to march your ass right

back into that compound and stand in the middle like a good girl until I trigger the detonator."

"Like hell I will," said Lexi.

"You will, or we're going to start removing pieces of lover boy here, one at a time. It's your life or his."

"Go, Lexi," said Zach. "You can take that fucking thing off once you're out of here."

Hector grinned. "You don't think I already thought of that?" He pointed a pudgy finger at a series of metal disks running down the front of the vest attached to wires that wrapped all the way around. "Magnetic connectors. Break the circuit and the thing goes boom. The only way our girl is coming out of this vest is in little pieces."

Oh God. Her stomach heaved and she had to swallow to keep from puking all over the wires. Who knew if that would set the thing off?

Hector must have seen her skin go green, because he zipped up the Windbreaker, protecting the device from sight and gastrointestinal mishap.

Zach growled in defeat and wriggled toward Hector. Hector kicked him in the ribs hard with the tip of his boot, making Zach suck in a pained breath.

Lexi flinched and a cry of anguish escaped her lips, betraying her feelings for Zach to Hector.

Your life or his.

No. They were both going to die, and Lexi knew it. They were tied together. If she died, so did he. And even if that weren't true, there was no way Hector would spare Zach once Lexi had done what he wanted. His hatred was too strong. His need to avenge a daughter dead more than twenty years had burned all mercy from him.

"This won't bring Mindy back," said Lexi. "There are human girls in there just like her. You want me to kill them, too?"

Hector's face darkened to a deep, livid purple. "Don't you dare talk about her," he warned. "You're not good enough to even speak her name. You're one of *them* now."

"There is no us and them. We're all the same. We all want the same thing—to destroy the Synestryn so they can never hurt anyone again."

"We're not the same. We're better than you are. This is our planet. Ours!"

Hector's men started to back away, their faces going white with fear. Lexi knew as well as they did what would happen next. Hector would start lashing out at whoever and whatever was nearby.

Lexi stood her ground, keeping her chin high.

"Don't do this, Lexi." Zach's voice was strained, and she could feel his fear for her beating at that barrier between them. He was screaming at her to run, but if she did, Hector would be left behind to try again.

Her only chance to stop him was to take him down right here, right now. He'd given her the weapon—strapped it to her body—all she had to do now was find the courage to use it.

Lexi looked at Zach. His hair was matted with blood. More blood had leaked into his eyes—those beautiful leopard green eyes that had always intrigued her so much, even when they frightened her. Eyes that pleaded with her now to run. Save herself.

In that moment, she knew the truth. There was no more question of brainwashing, no more slivers of doubt to get in her way. He hadn't tricked her or coerced her as Hector was doing now.

Zach had been nothing but honest with her from the start. He'd hidden nothing, not even his need for her, not even the power she held over him.

One single thought and the luceria would fall from her neck. She'd be free, but he would die. He'd placed his life in her hands. His trust.

There was only one way she could repay him, and it was going to kill them both.

Lexi wished she'd figured out the truth sooner. She wished she'd known him years ago, that they'd had more time together before now.

She wished she could have loved him longer.

"Are you willing to die for your people?" she asked him.

"Yes," he said without hesitation.

"So am I. It's the only way."

Zach's eyes widened slightly in understanding, then closed in grief. Final. Absolute. He gave her a nearly imperceptible nod—permission to follow through with her plan.

Someone new came into the motor home, but Lexi didn't turn away from Zach to see who it was.

"They're ready," she heard Jake say behind her.

"Enough of this," roared Hector. "Get your ass outside. People are waiting."

Lexi ripped her gaze away from Zach and stared up at Hector. "You're going to give me time to say goodbye," she told him.

"No, I'm not."

"What can it hurt, Pa?" said Jake. "There's nothing she can do to stop this. Give her a minute with the man she's dying to save."

Lexi looked at him then, startled by the unexpected support. Jake's left eye was swelling shut, and a dark bruise was forming on his cheek. So *that* was the sound she'd heard over the phone. Hector had hit him when he'd found Jake telling her to evacuate the buildings.

Hector crossed his arms over his heavy chest. "One minute. And I'm not leaving. Say what you've got to say with an audience or not at all."

Lexi nodded and rushed forward, kneeling on the ground next to Zach. While she was down there, she pulled the kitchen knife from her shoe, her movement hidden by the voluminous folds of the Windbreaker.

She reached around him, hugging him hard, and slid the knife between the ropes. She didn't have time to be careful, and she worried that she might have cut him, but that was all she could do. It wasn't much of a chance, but it was something.

Zach's eyes glowed with emotion as he looked at her. Warmth flowed into her through their link, comforting her. "I love you," he said. "Death isn't going to change that."

The tears she'd been holding back since the men had grabbed her outside the walls of Dabyr broke free and slid down her cheek, hitting the navy Windbreaker with a soft patter. "I love you, too," she told him, meaning it more than she was able to express in the few brief seconds they had left together.

More than anything, Lexi wished that barrier between them wasn't there, so he could feel her love for him the way she could his. She wanted to bathe him in it, make sure he knew her words were genuine.

"I can take off the luceria. If it will be easier on you that way." She wasn't sure how long he'd live after she'd taken it off, but it might give him a few more days, hours even. She didn't want to rob him of any of them.

"No. I don't want you to be alone. I'll be there with you to the very end."

When she died. He hadn't said it, but they both knew that was what he'd meant.

Even though he couldn't feel her through the thing, she could feel him. She could feel his love, his comfort. "I don't want to be alone, either."

"We're meant to be together," he whispered, his tone fervent. "I still believe that. I'll find you. Somehow, I'll find you."

Lexi believed him. He was too powerful a man to let

something as paltry as death stand in his way. "I'll be waiting," she said; then she kissed him.

His mouth was warm and soft, so gentle against hers that she wondered how she could have ever thought he'd meant her harm. She squeezed every bit of her love for him into that kiss, telling him what words couldn't.

"That's enough," said Hector. "It's time to go."

Chapter 24

Hector led Lexi to the center of a caravan, mostly of pickup trucks with Texas plates. The size of the gathering of Defenders left her stunned. She'd never seen so many of them together in one place.

"They're all here for the show," said Hector as he led her by the arm to the group of waiting people. "We'll be able to see the fireworks from that hilltop over there. Gonna be quite a spectacle."

"You're wrong about these people, Hector. They mean you no harm." Though Lexi sure did. She was going to blow his ass to hell. "You're going to be sorry you were too thick-skulled to listen to reason."

"That's the brainwashing talking. Don't worry. You won't have to suffer much longer."

No. She wouldn't. Still, she had a few more moments to help him see the truth. Unless a bunch of white knights rode in, that was the only thing that had even a chance of saving her. "There are human children in there. Did Jake tell you that?"

"He did. It doesn't matter. They're all under the Sentinels' spell. Nothing I can do for them but put them out of their misery."

"I thought you tried to help people escape their pull. That's what you were going to do with Helen."

Hector shrugged. "I told you what you wanted to hear to get you to do the right thing. Do you think that if I'd told you your friend was a lost cause you would have cooperated?"

"So, you were using me from the start."

He let out an ugly bark of laughter. "Hell, girl. I started using you before you were born. Your mom was the suggestible sort. She believed everything I told her. Even wrote it down."

So that was where all Mom's journal entries had come from. No wonder they sounded so crazy. Hector *was* crazy. Whatever noble goal he'd had, assuming there had ever been one, it had been lost along the way.

"Mom trusted you," said Lexi. Anger and resentment burned bright inside her, but she kept it hidden.

"They always do. Too bad Jake doesn't have the knack for making people trust him the way I do. Isn't that right, Jake?"

Beside her, Jake said nothing. He kept his battered face down, staring at the ground. His body was tense and she could feel his anger seething just below the surface.

"At least Jake listens," said Lexi.

"He's just easily swayed, like his mama. My boy is a pure disappointment," Hector told Lexi as if his son wasn't standing right there.

Jake flinched; then he stopped walking altogether and fell back.

Hector didn't even spare him a glance. What kind of father hurt his son like that and didn't care?

Lexi realized then she was wasting her breath trying to make him see the truth. Even if she lived to be a hundred, there wasn't enough time left to make Hector Morrow change his mind.

He was going to die ignorant, and there was nothing Lexi could do to change that.

So, rather than waste the last seconds of her life

trying, Lexi shut her mouth and focused on Zach. She could feel his presence, hovering inside her, holding her close even though he was yards away. She could also feel his determination to free himself. She wasn't sure if he'd found the knife she'd left behind, or even if he'd been able to use it, but he hadn't given up yet.

Maybe if he got free in time. . . . No. There were too many of them, all armed. Even Zach wasn't capable of taking down over a hundred armed Texans.

The weight of the explosives strapped to her chest seemed to close in on her. Reality had left her numb, accepting. She wasn't fighting her fate the way Zach was. The only way to stop Hector and his men from trying to hurt the people of Dabyr was to kill them.

Lexi snaked one arm inside the huge Windbreaker. All she had to do was flip open one of those magnets and it would all be over. No more threat. No more Defenders.

At least Helen would be safe. Dabyr would be safe.

Lexi figured it was the least she could do after her willingness to blow the place up.

Hector pulled her to a halt inside a ring of vehicles parked in a clearing. He raised his voice so it carried out over the crowd. Lexi didn't listen to his words. She was too busy counting, tallying up the number of lives she was going to end today. One hundred twelve.

She wondered if these men were as ruthless as Hector. If they lived, would they take up where he'd left off? Would they be scared away and go back to their families to live nice, quiet lives? And what about the Defenders who weren't present today? How would they react to what she was going to do? Would their zeal to defeat the Sentinels increase because they'd suffered so many losses? Or would there even be enough of them left to pick up the pieces and carry on in Hector's stead?

Suddenly Lexi felt the burden of her decision weigh down on her. It was one thing to think about blowing these men up. It was another to look into their eyes and then do it. These men had wives, children. People loved them. How could she end their lives without knowing anything about them other than that they fell under Hector's spell the same way her mom had?

I'm here. It was Zach, comforting her. Had he felt her indecision? Her guilt?

Lexi reached out for him, wanting to hold him in her mind the way he did her. Comfort him. The barrier rippled against her touch, but didn't break. She pushed harder, but the thing seemed to strengthen more the harder she pushed.

I won't leave you, honey. There was love in his words. So much it made her eyes sting with tears.

Lexi closed her eyes and let his love swell up inside her, filling her up with warmth and light. Zach was with her and she was no longer afraid. She knew exactly what she had to do.

I love you, she told him, and this time, she felt her message go through. She'd done it! She felt Zach's surprise, his elation that she'd been able to reach him.

The men surrounding her cheered as if they knew what had happened. Hector lifted his fist in victory. "Today, our enemy falls!" he shouted. More cheers erupted.

"It's time," Hector told Lexi. "One of the men will drive you back to the wall and get you hooked up with a camera so I know when to push the button. And so I know you're not trying any funny stuff. Go on in like a good girl and I'll let your man live."

It was a lie, but Lexi let it go. She had bigger concerns than Hector Morrow's last few lies.

I'm coming, honey. Hang on.

No! she tried to tell him, but she wasn't sure her message had gone through. It was too dangerous. These men would shoot him down.

Hector pulled a device out of his pocket. A remote trigger to detonate the bomb. The black plastic gleamed under the bright morning sun. A green LED blinked cheerfully, indicating everything was working fine.

For a moment, she was trapped by that flashing light, wishing her job was already done. Her whole body trembled with anxiety, especially her fingers, firmly grasping a pair of magnetic disks.

"May I speak?" she asked him. "If I'm going to die, I'm allowed some last words, right?"

Hector narrowed his eyes; then a calculating grin curled his fleshy lips. "Go ahead. Say what you like. These men all know that you're the Sentinels' pawn. You're only going to prove my case."

He held up his fist and the men surrounding her quieted. "The girl here has something to say."

The men laughed as if he'd just told a joke. Then again, maybe her speaking out at this point was funny. Ridiculous.

"I know you all think I'm brainwashed, but I'm not." They laughed louder, but Lexi ignored them. "I've been inside those walls and I know what kind of people the Sentinels are. They're the kind of people who shelter orphaned children. The kind of people who lay their lives on the line every night so that you can all sleep safer in your beds." The men's laughter died. "And even though every one of you here would rather kill them than speak to them and learn the truth, if it was one of your kids at risk, one of your kids who had been orphaned, they'd take them in and keep them safe. No hard feelings. No grudges."

The men started looking at one another uncomfortably, shifting from one foot to the other. She lowered her voice and watched as these men moved toward her, straining to hear what she had to say in her last moments. "We do have enemies. We do need to fight, but you're fighting the wrong war. The Synestryn are our real enemy. They're the ones who want our blood. Our children's blood."

They were close enough now.

Her fingers gripped the cold metal disks lining the front of the vest. She shoved her fingernail between two of them, feeling the magnetic tug that held them locked together tight. All she had to do was twist her fingernail and pull and it would all be over. She'd take all these men down with her, freeing the Sentinels and those they protected from the threat the Defenders posed.

I love you, Zach. She had to tell him once more. Make sure he knew.

Her words pushed through the barrier easily this time, melting it away. Power roared into her body like a tidal wave, making her rock on her feet. Her body seemed ready for it, craving it. Her cells soaked it up, making her feel stronger with every passing heartbeat.

There was no more room inside her for fear or indecision. She knew exactly what she needed to do, and thanks to her love for Zach, she had the power to do it.

She felt Zach's love wrap around her, warming her, sliding over her skin like a caress. The tingling heat soaked into her and she was sure, if she looked, she'd be glowing.

Her voice rose up, loud and strong, resonating with the energy that pulsed inside her. She pulled in a deep breath, praying she could channel that power and control it. "Every one of the Sentinels would sacrifice his or her life to save one of you." She scanned the crowd, looking each man in the eyes. "And I am one of them. Remember that when you tell your kids what you've seen here today. Remember that a Sentinel once held the power of life and death over you. And let you live."

With that, she used her newfound power to create a wall strong enough to hold in the force of the explosion, to channel it up into the sky. Then she ripped apart the magnets, triggering the bomb strapped to her chest.

Giant hammers slammed into her from every side, crushing her body, but there was no pain. An instant later, a searing wave of heat swept over her, burning everything away. In her last brief, flashing moment of life, all she felt was Zach's love holding her close, surrounding her, cradling her, staying with her to the very end. Just as he'd promised.

Zach had finally managed to free himself from the ropes, grab his sword from the main cabin of the motor home, and go racing after Lexi when he felt the barrier between them melt away.

Power surged out of him, driving him to his knees in shock. Rocks cut into his flesh, dug into his joints, but he hardly felt it. His body was still numb and tingling from being bound for so long, and although he'd nearly scraped the skin from his forearms escaping the ropes, there was no pain.

Instead, he was surrounded by a soothing warmth as if Lexi held him in her arms.

I love you, Zach, she whispered to his mind. The words were tinted with acceptance of her decision. Courageous resignation.

Zach felt her emotions trickle through and knew what they meant. She was going to detonate the device early. Take as many of the Defenders down with her as she could. He'd seen her plan glowing in her eyes—heard it in her voice as she asked Hector if he'd be willing to die for his people.

So would I.

Zach tried to shout a warning that he'd escaped and was coming for her, but it was too late. Light flashed, brightening the morning sky and thunder rolled out over the land.

"No!" shouted Zach as he raced toward her—toward the last place he'd felt all that love flowing from.

A column of smoke and fire spewed up as if all the energy of the explosion had been shoved into an invisible tunnel.

He reached out with his mind as his feet flew over the dew-soaked ground. The echo of her love flowing through the luceria had not yet died off, but that was all that was left: a hollow echo dying to morbid silence as he ran.

Chapter 25

Zach scrambled up the ridge until he could see the gathering of men below.

Anger and grief warred within him, leaving no room to breathe. She was gone. His sweet Lexi was gone.

His limbs were heavy and clumsy as he climbed, his frantic rage pounding hard in his veins until it vibrated his bones. Blood seeped from his torn skin, making the rocks slippery.

The only consolation he had was that he'd be joining her soon. Whatever life held for them after they left this world, they were going to go through it together.

But first, Zach was going to kill every one of those fuckers for taking Lexi from him. He wasn't sure how long he'd have before his time was up, but he was pretty sure it would be long enough to get the job done.

With his sword in his bloody hand, Zach stalked down the ridge, the metallic taste of vengeance on his tongue. The Defenders were packed around her, staring at the starburst of scorched earth and the crater that cradled her body.

Her body? Surely after an explosion like that there wouldn't be one.

The urge to gather what was left of her in his arms burned strong inside him, but not nearly as strong as his need for blood. He wanted to feel the blood of these men splatter over his face, still hot with the life he was cutting from them. He wanted to feel it drench his arms until it dripped from him. He wanted to watch as it pooled on the ground, wetting the earth with his rage and grief.

The Defenders hadn't noticed his approach. A satisfied smile stretched his lips and bared his teeth.

"Zach, no!" For a second, Zach thought it was Lexi calling him, and his steps faltered as he turned to find her.

But it wasn't Lexi. It was Helen. She was clinging to Drake's arm, weaving on her feet with fatigue.

She and Drake walked toward the Defenders, who were now looking from them to Zach with wide, frightened eyes.

Zach readied his blade and braced himself for the bullets that would no doubt be biting into his skin any moment. But rather than fire their weapons, the Defenders started to scatter like roaches cast into sunlight.

"No!" shouted Zach. He wasn't going to be able to reach them all.

Helen lifted her hand and a ring of fire spewed from the earth, locking them inside a hot, crackling embrace. Even with the barrier preventing their flight, they all managed to stay well out of Zach's reach.

He stalked toward them, hungry for their blood, and ran into an invisible wall.

Rage surged inside him and he sliced at the obstacle, making it waver and shimmer like heated air.

"You're not getting through it," said Andra. Her feet were braced apart, her long, lean body housed in leather and denim.

Paul stood at her side, weapon bare, his eyes on Lexi's body. "You might as well not waste your strength."

Where had Andra come from? Zach hadn't seen her approach. Or Paul's.

"Let me through," he ordered between clenched teeth.

"Nope," she said. "Not gonna happen."

Paul strode forward toward Lexi, and Zach felt a searing possessiveness scald his insides. He ran for her, unwilling to let another man touch her. Paul knelt at her side, reached out a hand.

"No!" shouted Zach as he reached Paul's side, shoving the other man away from her. "Don't touch."

Paul held up his hands. "I was just checking for a pulse."

Pulse? Why would there be a pulse?

There was a grating metallic sound that Zach knew meant danger, but he ignored it. Lexi absorbed all of him. His attention, his emotion, his hopes and dreams.

She was everything to him, and she was gone.

He should have found a way to save her. His job was to keep her safe, protect her. *He* should have been the one lying there in a blackened crater. *He* should have been the one whose hair was singed and flesh scorched.

"Drop the guns or lose a testicle," said Andra in a warning tone.

Zach didn't care if they shot him or not. Even his need for vengeance was fading away, losing importance as Lexi's body grew cold.

The urge to keep her warm for as long as he could swept through him, taking over. He gathered her limp body in his arms and cradled her on his lap. Her head landed against his shoulder, smearing his clothes with soot and ash. Her eyebrows were mostly burned away, her eyelashes short stubs. Her pointed chin was no longer thrust up in defiance, but tucked against her chest.

Zach's fingers traced her face, memorizing the soft curves and gentle lines. Soot blackened his hand, making the swirling jade green of his ring stand out in contrast.

Movement? If she was gone, there would be no movement in the color. They'd be fixed at the time of death. Immovable.

A faint breath of hope washed over his skin. Zach pressed his fingers to her neck. Her skin was warm, a bit too warm, even. And beneath the silky softness the faintest pulse of life thrummed through her veins.

Lexi was alive!

Joy tore through him in a vibrant surge of light and color. His head spun with shock and a jubilant cry rose from his soul, echoing the morning air. He kissed her lips, and although she didn't respond, her breath filled his lungs. He sucked it into himself, cherishing the proof of life that expanded inside him, warm and sweet and perfect.

There was some kind of commotion around him, but Zach ignored it. His total focus was on Lexi, on the minute vibration of her stubby eyelashes as she tried to lift her eyelids, on the subtle tightening of her mouth as if she'd felt his kiss, on the pale streaks of skin where his tears had washed away the soot covering her beautiful face.

God, he loved her. So much, he thought the ferocity of it might tear him apart, and yet it didn't. Somehow, it made him whole.

"Wake up, honey," he coaxed her. His voice was tight with emotion, strangled by tears.

He smoothed her hair from her face, feeling the coarse bits of burned strands breaking off under his palm, leaving only softness behind.

Gilda knelt beside him, heedless of the ash blackening her gray gown. She reached toward Lexi, but Zach shifted away, shielding her with his body. No one else could touch her. Only him.

"I mean her no harm," said the Gray Lady, her voice steady and calm. "I simply wanted to offer my aid as the Sanguinar cannot help her here, under the sun."

"Mine," was all Zach could manage to squeeze out past the tightness in his throat.

"Of course she is," soothed Gilda. "May I touch her?"

A small pale hand reached toward Lexi. No threat. Just Gilda.

Zach relaxed his hold and gave Gilda a slight nod.

Angus stepped up beside her, a sword in his hands. Zach's protective instincts rose up and a deep, warning growl filled his chest.

"Stay back, Angus," said Gilda.

"You're weak," he replied, his tone sharp.

"I have no need of you now," she said.

Angus's body tensed as if he'd taken a physical blow, but he moved away, allowing Zach to pull in a full breath.

Gilda laid her hand on Lexi's head, and a pale, watery light spilled out from under her palm. Lexi's eyes snapped open and she reached up as if to brush Gilda's hand away.

"That's enough," said Zach. "Stop!" His command was harsh and completely out of place. He heard the noises around him die down as if his outburst had drawn their attention.

Gilda moved her hand and shrank back into the dim hum of activity around Zach and Lexi. Zach didn't bother to see what they were doing. He didn't care. Nothing outside of the treasure he held in his arms had any meaning to him. The rest of the world could fall away and Zach wouldn't miss it.

He had Lexi and he needed nothing else.

Chapter 26

It took Lexi a couple of days to regain her strength. She floated in and out of awareness, fighting the gray morass that tugged at her, sucking her away from reality into a world of chaotic dreams and hallucinations. During that time, there was one constant, one thing she knew was real and solid.

Zach.

He'd never once left her. Not even when the searing heat of the explosion had crowded around her, sucking the oxygen from her lungs. He was there, solid and strong, holding her inside the safety of his vast power, protecting her body.

He was still beside her, his strong body stretched out beside her, his arm looped across her chest with his palm splayed over her heart as if he were tracking her pulse.

Lexi levered herself up on the bed, knocking his thick arm into her lap. He woke instantly, his bloodshot eyes scanning her body, taking her in as he had the other times she'd resurfaced during the past few days. His chest was bare, and hundreds of pale, shiny leaves had sprung from the branches of his lifemark.

"You okay?" he asked, his voice a raw shred of sound.

She nodded, not trusting herself to speak past the arid tightness in her throat.

Zach reached over to the bedside table and grabbed a cup of water. He held the straw to her lips and she drank, feeling the cold of the water go all the way down. It felt good, but not nearly as good as it did to see Zach whole and safe beside her.

"Are you hungry?" he asked. "Need to use the bathroom?"

"No," she said. "I just want to look at you."

She scanned his face, so beautiful to her. Especially his eyes. They glowed with love. For her.

"I love you, Zach."

His big body shuddered in pleasure and he wrapped his arms around her, surrounding her with his heat.

Lexi sighed in contentment, remembering the feel of his protective embrace as it shielded her from that explosion. "Thank you," she said against his shoulder.

"For what?" he asked.

"For saving me."

Zach pulled away, looking at her with an anguished expression of self-loathing. "I didn't save you, honey, though I wished like hell I had. You did that all yourself."

"No," she said. "I felt you wrap your arms around me, shield me."

He cupped her cheek and she leaned into the touch. "I wasn't there. I'd just gotten free of the ropes, and I ran to you when that bomb went off." He swallowed hard, then in an anguished tone said, "I *wasn't there for you.*"

"You were there. Or your power was. It slid over my skin and held off the crushing weight, the heat."

"You're the only one who can use my power."

She shook her head. "You're wrong about that. I had no idea how to use it. And even if I did, you're the one who supplied the power, the one who showed me what to do. I saw you in my head, holding me close and I was safe. As far as I'm concerned, that makes you my hero."

"I'm not sure I agree, but you're too weak for a good argument right now."

He was right. She was weak, but she felt her strength returning more by the minute. "What happened to the man who was with you?"

"Neal is recovering, though the attack cost him dearly. He needs to find his lady fast or he'll be out of time. The energy in that stun gun added to the power growing inside him in a way we had never considered."

"I'm sorry, Zach. I'm sorry I brought all of this down on you."

"He doesn't blame you any more than I do. Neither do the others. You can't control the actions of the Defenders."

"What happened to them?" she asked, not sure she wanted to know.

"Several of our men had a nice, long talk with them. I don't think they'll bother us anymore. I *know* Hector won't. Joseph took him into custody to answer for the crimes of those he led."

"What will they do to him?"

"One of the Sanginar will put a peace binding on him. Then they'll let him go." Zach didn't sound happy about that last part.

"What's a peace binding?"

"It's a way of keeping someone from choosing to harm us. Anytime he tries to hurt us, it will make *him* hurt instead. It's usually nonlethal, effective, and much better than he deserves. He should be executed for what he did to you."

Lexi shrugged. "Let it go. He's not worth our time. Except, maybe just enough to see how he reacts to that peace binding thing. I'd like to see that."

Zach's grin was feral. "I'll make sure you get to, honey."

She stifled a yawn. "With Hector out of the picture,

the Defenders will need a new leader—someone who's willing to help us fight the Synestryn. Maybe we can convince Jake to take the job."

"Why him?"

"He's nothing like his father. He's reasonable and kind. I'd like to talk to him, bring him here, let him see what I have."

Zach's mouth tightened. "I'm not sure that's a good idea."

"We might be able to make him and the rest of the Defenders an ally. They're already out there. They know about the monsters. We might as well use their eyes and ears. Besides, most of them are proud men. Allowing them to help us may be the only chance we have to protect them."

"We'll talk to Joseph about it when you're better to see if he'll allow it."

"I've been on my own a long time. I'm not going to start asking permission to talk to people. I'll damn well talk to who I want, when I want."

Zach gave her a lopsided grin. "Your chin's back up."

"What?" she asked.

He tapped her chin with his forefinger. "Whenever you get stubborn about something, really dig in your heels, your chin goes up."

She thrust it higher, making him laugh. The joyful sound floated over her, easing her body's aches, mending the bruises on her spirit caused by suffering through all that fear. It was going to take her a while to get over a scare like that, but she knew Zach would be with her, helping her through.

Lucien gritted his teeth against the pain of traveling to Earth. Steam rose from his skin and held his concentration until the shimmering gate closed behind him.

The Sentinel Stone was cool and solid under his fingers, its detailed carvings biting into his side as his weight slumped against it.

As the last light of the portal faded, Lucien let go and slid to the soft grass at his feet.

It was night here, of course. They could only come here at night. Sunlight bowed to the Solarc's command, and would give away the trespass of an errant son like him as surely as if they were standing in the same room. Only careful calculation and planning would ensure that none of the men who traveled here as Lucien did would fall under the Solarc's gaze.

As Lucien's senses began working again, he drew in the scent of dust and freshly trimmed grass. He heard voices in the distance, though whether they were human or Sentinel he couldn't say. The sky was dark, the stars hidden by the nearby glow of human lighting.

Lucien squinted to sharpen his focus and recognized the strong lines of Dabyr looming only a few yards away.

His calculations had been right. He'd ported through the right Sentinel Stone. Now all he had to do was find out exactly *when* he'd arrived.

Those voices rose higher, the guttural English words stabbing at his sore ears. Lucien pushed himself to his feet in time to see a throng of armed Theronai headed right for him.

Knowing this could end badly for all involved, Lucien held up his hands, showing them naked of weapons.

The men gathered around, their swords shining bright under the light of the single moon. "Who are you?" demanded the man in front. He had a weathered face and bright blue eyes shadowed with sorrow.

"I am Prince Lucien, son of the Solarc," he said, his mouth clumsy around the sharp edges of their language.

An overabundance of suspicious eyes narrowed at him.

"How did you get in?" asked the man.

"I ported in through the Sentinel Stone."

The bodies of the men parted, allowing a woman to pass. She had long black hair and wore a gray gown. Though she was small, her presence filled the open space as her black eyes fell upon him. The luceria around her throat shimmered, marking her as one of his father's creation.

Lucien bowed his head. "My lady," he said, imbuing his tone with respect.

The man who had been speaking to Lucien took a protective step nearer the woman, obviously her mate.

"Why are you here?" she demanded.

Too many reasons to name, so Lucien focused on the one foremost in his mind. "I sensed my daughters were here. I had hoped to set eyes on them."

The woman's lips parted in shock. "Daughters?"

"Yes. Are they here?" Lucien asked.

"I am Gilda, the Gray Lady," said the woman. "If your daughters are here, you may see them. What are their names?"

The strange, human names fell easily from his lips though he'd never spoken them aloud in his own home for fear of his father hearing. "Jackie, Helen and Alexandra."

A feminine gasp rose up from the back of the group, and a woman stepped forward. Her hair lay in twin plaits over her shoulders and the gentle curve of her cheek, so much like her mother's, made his fingers itch to reach out and touch her to see if she was real. The luceria at her throat was a rich, fiery red.

Lucien had never set eyes on her before, but he knew in an instant that she was of his blood. His daughter.

"I'm Helen," she said, her soft voice wavering with emotion.

Lucien lurched forward, his body clumsy from the physical toll his travel had taken.

A dark man at Helen's side lifted his blade and shifted his body so that it shielded Helen's. "Stay back," he warned, his mouth tight with anger.

"Forgive my lack of grace," he begged. "I have no intent to frighten any of you."

"Let me by, Drake," said Helen. "He's not going to hurt me."

The crowd around them began to grow, and hushed voices repeated for the newcomers what had passed.

Helen reached out her hand and Lucien saw that it trembled. "Where did you come from?" she asked.

"Athanasia."

Gilda hissed and pulled Helen's hand back. "Liar. The gate is closed."

"Not to me. Nor to a few of my brothers who also pass through to this world."

Gilda didn't believe him. He could see her mistrust shining on her face. "Why do you come now?" she asked.

"You're losing the war against the Synestryn. My father's anger barred the gate shut, but a few of us know the folly in that. We know that if you Sentinels fall, there will be nothing left to stand between us and the Synestryn. We have grown weak in our decadence. They would destroy us."

Gilda's voice trembled with rage. "So, you came here to beg us for help? To build our morale so we'd fight harder? Do you really think that we care whether or not your people are wiped from the universe? Do you think we're willing to sacrifice more for you who shun us?"

Lucien's heart ached hearing the bitterness spewing

from this woman. Only the deepest loss created anger such as hers. A loss Lucien knew all too well. "How many of your children have died?" he asked in a tender voice.

Gilda's jaw hardened, but he saw the sheen of tears brighten her black eyes for a mere second before anger burned them away. "Go back to where you came from. We have no need of you here."

"But you do," said Lucien, looking out to the desperate men gathered around him. "Your men are dying, and my brothers and I have been working for a long time to save them."

The man bonded to Gilda caught on first. "You've come here and bedded human women, haven't you?"

Lucien nodded. "We've sired daughters. It's hard to know how many since we can't travel here often, and time passes much more swiftly here on Earth."

"My mother," whispered Helen. "You were her one-night stand?"

Lucien frowned at the term, not understanding. "I lay with your mother, if that's what you mean. And seeing you here, a grown woman. . . . I met her only months ago. Had you been born in my world, you'd yet be a babe."

Helen looked at her husband, then back at Lucien. "I thought you'd abandoned us."

"Never. If I'd been able, I would have been with you every day. But it is . . . impossible."

Helen stepped forward and took Lucien into her arms. He stood there, stiff in her embrace, unsure of what to do. He didn't know her, hadn't seen her grow, and yet he loved her still. How could that be? How could so much love pour out of him and he still remain intact?

Lucien didn't know, but now, in this moment, he didn't care. Helen was here and safe. She'd found her place among these people.

She pulled away, sniffing back tears. "You said there were others. I have sisters?"

Lucien nodded. "Two. Jackie and Alexandra. Are they here?"

Gilda shook her head. "No. But we must find them. Assuming they are still alive."

"Wait," said Helen's husband. "Alexandra might be Lexi."

Helen's eyes widened and she scrambled for something in her pocket. She toyed with it a moment. "Lexi. What's your real name?"

Lucien's daughter smiled and it was the most beautiful thing he'd ever seen in his long, long life.

"You should come outside," she said. "We've got a surprise for you."

Chapter 27

Lexi and Zach rushed outside toward the commotion in the training yard. Lexi's body was still a little weak and Zach was right at her side, his strong arm at her elbow, supporting her.

A throng of people had gathered around the engraved boulder on the training field, and at the center of that commotion was a man Lexi had never seen before.

He had odd liquid gold eyes and rich, dark hair. He was beautiful in the same perfect way the Sanguinar were—as if he'd been sculpted to sit on a shelf and be admired—but he didn't have their pale, gaunt features. He looked healthy. Robust, like the Theronai.

Helen stood at the edge of the crowd, anxiously shifting her weight from foot to foot as she waited for Lexi to come near. She looked younger, and was glowing with a childlike glee.

Just seeing her friend look so happy made Lexi's heart warm.

"What is it?" she asked.

"You're never going to believe it," said Helen. She clamped her lips shut like she was holding in a secret, then blurted out, "Our father is here. He came from this other world where the Sentinels all came from. He wants to meet us."

Meet us? Us?

The import of Helen's words finally sank in and Lexi had to grab Zach's arm to keep from sinking to the ground. "We're sisters?"

Helen nodded, making her braids sway; then she hugged Lexi tight around the neck. "No wonder I spilled my guts to you when I barely knew you. I guess we had a connection even then."

Lexi was too stunned to speak. It was too much to believe. Her father was some kind of alien from another world. And he was here.

"Easy," whispered Zach. His grip on her arm tightened and he slid his arm around her body to steady her. She hadn't realized until then that she'd nearly fallen on her ass.

"I want to see him," said Lexi.

Helen led her forward to the man with the odd swirling gold eyes. Lexi looked up at him, really looked. He stood there silently, letting her study him, not even blinking, but his eyes were liquid with emotion.

"So, you're the guy?" she asked.

He frowned slightly for a second, then nodded. "I wish I could have found you sooner," he said.

"Me, too."

He flinched and Lexi wanted to take the words back.

"He couldn't be here, Lexi," said Helen. "On our planet."

"I'm twenty-six. I think he could have found the time in there somewhere to make the trip. At least send a postcard."

"Time is different there. Plus, he has to be careful. If his father finds out he's here, he'll be executed."

Lexi's father reached out his hand. "No, she's right. I should have found a way. I'm sorry, Alexandra."

"Lexi," she said. "I go by Lexi now."

He nodded and she saw his mouth form the word silently as if memorizing it. "I am Lucien."

Zach's fingers slid over her arm, soothing her. Lexi wasn't sure how to feel about all this, but she knew one thing for sure: life was too short to hold grudges. Whatever his reasons for not being in her life, he was here now. She didn't want to lose whatever time she'd have with him by being angry.

Lexi ignored his outstretched hand and hugged him. He wrapped his arms around her, and although he didn't look old enough to be her father, she knew in that instant that he was. She felt his love surging through her, filling in all the empty holes her past had left behind.

"Mom's gone," she whispered.

"I'm sorry."

"She was a good woman." And Lexi knew then it was true. Sure, her mom had been wrong about a lot of things, but she'd gotten the big things right. She'd taught Lexi to be strong, to stand up for herself and to take care of the people around her. She'd given her love and taught her the important things, like treasuring every day and never giving up. She'd taught Lexi how to love unconditionally.

And now, standing in front of this man she didn't know, Lexi let that lesson live on. She was going to love this man, her father, regardless of his failings. He hadn't been there for her all her life, but he was here now. And he'd given her Helen. He'd given her a family.

"How long can you stay?" she asked him.

"Not long. Just until sunrise."

Lexi's hopes sank. "That's only a few hours."

He gave her a sad smile. "I know, but it's the way it must be. If the Solarc learns I've come here, your life and the lives of your sisters will be in jeopardy."

"Sisters? As in plural?"

"Jackie is not here," he said. "You must find her." He

lifted his head and addressed the men. "She may be able to save one of you. And there are others. Daughters of my brothers and cousins."

"How many?" asked Joseph.

"More than twoscore, though we know not if they all live."

"And are you having more children?" asked one of the Sanguinar Lexi had not yet met.

Lucien's eyes dimmed with sadness. "Not I. I cannot come back. Too many trips through the gate weakens us. It's hard to shield our passage, and we must prevent detection above all else."

"But there are others who are coming?" the Sanguinar asked.

"Yes. More join our cause every day. We know you are all struggling. Suffering. We seek to help you in any way we can."

"We're starving," said the Sanguinar. "We need more blood."

"I know. We do what we can, but we will not risk getting caught. Before I leave, you may have some of my blood. It will sustain you for a while."

The Sanguinar's eyes glowed an eerie silver, and Lexi felt a shiver of revulsion run through her father's body.

Lucien reached inside his shirt and pulled out a photo. "Here are three more women you should find. Daughters of my brother, Eron."

Beside Lexi, Helen gasped. "That's Andra and Nika when they were young."

Andra moved forward and took the photo out of Lexi's hand. "It is. This was taken right before Tori was killed."

"Tori?" asked Lucien.

Andra's mouth tightened. "Our baby sister."

Lucien held his hand out for the photo. "I would ask you let me take this token of remembrance back to your father. I would gladly issue him a message should you wish me to do so."

Andra gave a tight nod. "Tell him I am fine, as you can see. Nika is alive, and Tori is dead."

Lucien's eyes shut and she heard a string of fluid, graceful words leave his lips. "I am sorry for your loss."

"At least we had each other growing up," said Andra. "You can thank him for that."

"May I see Nika? Speak to her?"

"No," said Andra. "She's too . . . weak for that."

"Is there anything I can do for her?"

"Are you a healer?"

"Sadly, no."

"Send one," demanded Andra. "If there is one of you who can heal her mind, then you can send him here."

"I will try," said Lucien. "I vow it."

Andra's knees buckled and Paul grabbed her arm.

"Time to go," said Angus in a booming voice. "Let's give Helen and Lexi some time alone with their father."

The crowd cleared out, but didn't go far. Not that Lexi blamed them. It wasn't every day that an alien came to visit.

"Tell me of your lives," asked Lucien. "I would like to have bits and pieces of you to take back with me to warm my thoughts."

Though it was hard at first, Lexi found shining slivers of her life to share with the father she'd never known. As Helen and she shared stories, they flowed out more easily, and Lexi realized that her life hadn't been nearly as grim as she'd imagined. There were lots of good times, and this one, sitting around under the stars with her new-found family, was now going to be tucked among them.

Slowly, the sun crept toward the horizon, signaling their time was at an end. Helen and Lexi bid Lucien good-bye with sloppy, teary hugs all around. Zach found a digital camera and took pictures of them together, printing one out for their father to take with him.

Lucien held his to his heart and wept. Those tears were still falling as he raised his hand and summoned a ring of shimmering light.

Lexi held Helen's hand as he stepped into that light and vanished.

"Do you think we'll ever see him again?" asked Helen.

"He said he couldn't come back."

"Maybe things will change. Maybe this Solarc asshole will stop being a dick."

"You should have asked Lucien if that was possible," said Lexi.

Helen blushed. "I'd never talk that way in front of my dad. Are you kidding?"

Lexi looked at Helen and burst out in giggles.

They clung to each other, laughing and crying as the sun came up.

Chapter 28

Lexi couldn't stand the idea of going back inside right now. The morning air felt good on her skin—cool and clear and scented with dewy grass. And Zach. He was at her side, her silent shadow, allowing her the time she needed to absorb everything that had happened to her in a short few days.

She had a father. A sister. A home.

It was more than she'd ever hoped for, and making it even sweeter was the fact that she had Zach to share in her joy.

"You should go back in and rest," he said.

"In a few minutes. I just want to feel the sun on my face for a while."

He nodded and slipped his fingers through hers. His ring gave off a happy buzz, and she felt a current of energy slide up her arm, warming her.

Lexi ran her hand along the stone wall surrounding Dabyr, tracing it with her finger as she neared the broken section. There were a few Theronai posted to guard the opening, but most of the activity had dwindled. Without Helen and Gilda, there was little they could do. Apparently, each stone could only be put in place after the women had done their magic.

Lexi could feel that magic running through the rock at her fingertips. It was old and had once been powerful, but that power had grown weary over time, allowing small cracks in the armor to form. Those cracks called out to her, begging to be filled. She could almost hear their creaking voices rasping at her.

A churning ribbon of power wove through her, and for the first time, Lexi knew what Helen meant. That power was there, flowing easily into Lexi's fingertips, obeying her will.

She wanted Dabyr to be a safe place for all who lived here. She wanted the children to go to sleep at night without wondering if this would be the one the monsters found them. She wanted them to play and laugh and know in their hearts that for as long as they stayed within these walls, nothing could harm them.

All that want—all that need—came sliding out of Lexi, traveling through her fingers into the chunks of stone beneath them.

Subtle cracks along the surface fused together and deeper ones, ones she could only see inside her mind, closed shut. A deep grating vibration spread down the wall, away from the opening. Lexi watched as it moved into the trees, casting resting birds into the air. She saw ripples form on the surface of the lake, heard the frightened cry of people near the main building.

"Lexi?" said Zach in a low, questioning tone. "What are you doing?"

"Fixing the wall."

She kept pouring power into the task, feeling it flow through her like water, liquid and easy. Molecules of rock shifted, locking tighter together until the surface of the stone gleamed like a hard shell.

Armed men came running their way and the few guards posted here turned to gawk at her.

"Am I doing something wrong?" she asked Zach.

"No, it's just . . . amazing. That's all. You're doing in seconds what others have been trying to do for days."

"Should I stop? I don't want to hurt any feelings."

He grinned down at her, his green eyes glowing with love and pride. "Don't stop. This is a good thing, Lexi. Very good."

After a brief explanation by Zach, men started hauling rock into the jagged opening. Lexi touched each stone as it was laid, lacing it with a living power that would survive long after she was dead and gone. It got harder as she went along, but she never once broke her stride or felt the need to stop.

She and Zach were covered in dust and sweat when Helen found them. "Wow, Lexi! You rock."

Lexi groaned at the bad pun.

Helen surveyed the work, which was nearly complete. "How did you do this?"

Lexi shrugged. "Don't know."

"It's her gift," said Zach. "Protection is Lexi's gift the way fire is yours, Helen. It's how she survived that bomb. I just didn't figure it out until I saw this."

"Cool," said Helen. "I wonder what our other sister's gift will be."

Zach grinned. "I don't know, but if she's out there, our men will find her and bring her back. You won't have to wait long."

"And then we can be a family," said Lexi as she grabbed Zach's arm to gain his undivided attention. "All of us."

Zach's grin widened and he looped his arms around her waist. "You think I want to be a part of a crazy family like yours?"

"I know you do."

"How do you know?" he taunted.

Lexi let him have it. She opened up the floodgates

that had stood between them for far too long, letting him experience everything she felt for him. She played it through her mind in fast motion, from her initial fear, through the mistrust, to hesitant hope, to the very end. A bright, shiny love she was sure would never fade or tarnish.

Zach's fingers clenched against her waist and his eyes fell shut. A deep groan of pleasure rose from his chest and became a soft sigh of joy.

When he opened his eyes they were shining with happiness. "God, I love you, Lexi."

"You're just saying that because my dad's a prince."

He let out a booming laugh and tipped her chin up with his finger. "Tell me you love me, too. Here. In front of witnesses."

"Why?" she asked, sensing how important this was to him.

"Because I want them all to know how lucky I am."

Lexi went up on her tiptoes and kissed him, not caring that they had an audience who had now begun to cheer. Helen's shouts of joy were the loudest.

Sisters. Sheesh.

"I love you," she told him, grinning. "And you'd better not make me regret it."

Zach grinned right back. "No promises."

Read on for a sneak preview of the next novel
in the Sentinel Wars series

LIVING NIGHTMARE

Available from Signet Select in November 2010

Nika wasn't crazy, and the only way to prove it was to dig up the bones lying inside her sister's frozen grave.

The shovel bit into her palms, rubbing them raw. A cold gust of wind threatened to rip down the hood of her heavy coat and suck the precious heat from her skin. She turned her back to the wind and kept digging. There wasn't time to crawl into the car she'd stolen and warm up. She had to finish this before the Sentinels found her and took her back to Dabyr.

Nika was now much stronger than she had been a few months ago when she'd barely been clinging to life, but with each pitiful, half-full shovel of dirt, she realized she wasn't yet strong enough to be doing this. Not alone, and certainly not in the dead of night—the only time no one would be around to see her desecrating a grave.

It was dangerous to be here in the dark. She knew that, but she had no choice. No one would listen to the crazy girl without proof, and the bones lying six feet down were the only tangible proof she could find that Tori was still alive.

Tori was out there. Nika could feel her baby sister's presence inside her splintered mind, amidst all the other sinister, alien beings who shared the space. Tori wasn't like she used to be—she wasn't the sweet, innocent child the Synestryn had taken—but she was still Nika's sister. She was still loved. She deserved the chance for freedom no matter the cost to Nika.

Besides, if Nika could bring her home and stop the torture Tori endured, both their lives would be better. They were connected—though not as strongly as they'd once been—and Nika wondered sometimes how her sister had survived this long.

The night the Synestryn stole Tori, Nika had promised her she'd never leave her alone. Now, almost nine years later, she'd kept that promise despite the fact that it had nearly killed her more than once.

Tori was slipping away, and Nika had the feeling that her sister was doing it by choice, that she was pushing them apart for a reason Nika couldn't understand.

Nika refused to give up on her. With or without help, she was going to find Tori and free her from her captors. Or die trying. That was definitely another alternative—perhaps the more likely one given the way her muscles were already burning with fatigue.

If she couldn't finish the simple job of digging a hole, how could she possibly execute a rescue mission?

After an hour of digging, she'd barely made a dent in the frozen soil. At this rate, she'd still be here come daybreak when the authorities could see her and drag her to the closest hospital's mental ward. She couldn't go back there. Eight years being restrained and questioned and tortured by doctors with their fake smiles and dead eyes was more than she could stand. If she had to go back to that life, she really *would* be crazy.

And even if that was not where she ended up—if she went back to Dabyr—the chances of escaping their watchful eyes again were slim. She was only going to have one shot at this—one shot to prove that Tori was still alive and needed to be rescued.

Time to dig faster.

The shovel slipped in her weak grip, scraping off a layer of skin. She should have brought gloves, but hadn't thought that far ahead. Remembering a shovel had been foremost in her mind, consuming the small space she had left for rational thought.

She'd also forgotten money and food. She had no idea how she'd get back home—the gas tank was nearly empty. She had left her cell phone at home so they couldn't use it to track her and find her before she was done. Anything that happened after she'd collected the stranger's bones seemed distant and unimportant.

A tugging kind of pressure pulled at her mind. Nika froze instantly, fighting it. The shovel fell from her frozen fingers. She clutched her head, knowing it would do no good.

She didn't want to go there tonight. She didn't want to be pulled into the mind of a monster to hunt and kill and feed. She had too much work to do.

An eerie howl vibrated the base of her skull, and it was all she could do to not lift her chin and howl along with the creature. Her own vision winked out and was replaced by another's.

Tall, frozen grass parted along her muzzle as she hunted for her prey. The warmth of food glowed bright in the darkness ahead. Hunger roared inside Nika's mind. The remembered taste of blood made her mouth water.

She struggled to pull from the sgath's mind before witnessing its kill, but this one was strong. It liked having her with it. It liked knowing she didn't want to be here, that she suffered.

Nika gritted her teeth and stopped trying to fight its

pull. Instead, she focused on the feel of its limbs, the cold earth against the pads of its paws. Wind ruffled its fur, but it was warm, even in the cold.

Not for long.

She took the chill of her own body, the weakness of her own limbs, and forced those feelings into the sgath. The beast stopped moving and a low growl reverberated through it as it fought her. It didn't like what she was doing to it. It didn't like the cold.

A throbbing filled her skull as she fought the sgath. She whispered to it that it was too tired to hunt. Too cold. It needed to sleep.

The sgath roared into the darkness and thrust Nika from its mind, shutting her out.

She landed on her butt, hitting the pitiful mound of frozen dirt she'd managed to scratch from Tori's false grave. Fatigue kept her glued to the spot as she tried to catch her breath. Her chest burned as the cold air filled her lungs over and over again, coming out in silvery plumes. Her body trembled with cold and weariness.

How could she keep going? How was she going to dig all the way down and open the casket lying below? Why had she thought she could do this alone?

Why had Madoc abandoned her? She hadn't seen him in seven months.

Her older sister Andra said the distance was for the best—that he was too angry and dangerous for her to be around him. Everyone seemed to be blind to the truth: he was in pain and he needed her to make it stop. It was so glaringly obvious to her, but no one else seemed to see it.

And that, in a nutshell, was the story of her life. She saw things no one else did, and no one believed her.

All that was going to change as soon as she had the bones. The Sanguinar would be able to tell they weren't Tori's, and if they couldn't, DNA tests would. One way or another, she was going to make the people around her listen.

If she lived through the night.

Already she could feel more sgath clawing for her attention, trying to suck her into their minds. They sensed her weakness. Even though there were fewer of them than there had ever been before—thanks to Madoc's quest to make them extinct—those that were left were stronger and smarter than the rest. They'd evaded Madoc's blade, hidden from him, learned from the mistakes of the others.

Most nights Nika could resist their pull, but she was weaker tonight, outside the magically enhanced walls of Dabyr, which had apparently helped protect her. Her escape from Dabyr had been nerve-racking. The drive here—the first driving she'd ever done—had been terrifying. All that combined with the effort of physical labor was too much for her.

She wanted to be stronger than this. She wanted to be healthy. She wanted to be *normal*.

Wishing wasn't going to get her or Tori anywhere, so she pushed herself to her feet, brushed the dirt from her hands, and picked up the shovel. It was time to get back to work.

Nika let the cold have her. She let the wind drag her hood from her head, stripped out of her puffy coat, and put the thought of her chilled fingers and aching legs in the front of her thoughts. Any sgath who wanted to have her along for the ride tonight was going to end up freezing its furry butt off.

"What the fuck do you mean Nika's gone?" Madoc growled into the cell phone.

Rage was always close to the surface, spurred on by his constant pain, bubbling, waiting to be let loose. His soul was nearly dead, and hiding that fact was getting a lot harder as each day passed. He needed to finish killing all the fuckers that had taken Nika's blood before it was too late and he no longer cared whether or not they ate the crazy chick's mind.

Joseph sounded tired. "She stole one of the cars in the garage and left."

Something suspiciously close to fear wriggled inside of him, making the pounding pain in his chest swell. He needed some relief. Now. All those fucking hours of meditation he'd just finished hadn't done jack shit.

"Where the hell was her sister?" he demanded.

"Andra and Paul are up north searching for a lost kid. I tried to call her, but couldn't get through. They're probably deep in the bowels of some cave, out of cell phone range."

"If she was gone, then who was supposed to be watching Nika?" He was going to have to find the person responsible and beat the hell out of them. No help for it.

"No one. I keep trying to tell you that she's better now. Stronger. She's an adult and doesn't need a keeper."

"Obviously you were wrong," snarled Madoc. "You should have had someone babysitting her."

"You can have the job anytime you like," said Joseph.

"Not interested." If he got near her he'd hurt her. He knew he would. He didn't normally go for scrawny chicks, but there was something about her that turned him on and made him feel violent all at the same time. Not a healthy combination—especially not for Nika.

"So you've said. Too bad you're the closest to her—or at least to where her car stopped. Nicholas tracked the car to Omaha, and since you're nearby, you're volunteering to go check it and see if she's still in it."

"Send someone else. I shouldn't be anywhere near her."

"Why? 'Cause she seems to have a thing for you? Wish I had such problems."

"She doesn't have a *thing* for me. She's crazy. That's why she refuses to stay away. Chick's got issues."

"Don't we all. Listen, just go find her, okay? Nicholas will text you the info so you can find the car. If she's not in it, you'll have to track her down. And hurry the hell up. I don't like having her out there alone at night. Who knows what could happen."

Joseph hung up, leaving Madoc writhing in frustration and fear. For her. The last place on the planet he wanted to be was near Nika, and yet the thought of her alone in the dark, weak and helpless, was more than he could stand.

"Fuck." He flung the curse out into the night, sheathed his sword, and stomped back to his truck. The nest he had been ready to cut into would have to wait. Nika couldn't.

Nika's plan had worked. The sgath hated the cold, and every time they brushed up against her mind, they flinched back in anger.

Of course, the flip side of her brilliant plan was that she was freezing to death. Her body shivered, and she could no longer feel her fingers or toes. The shovel kept slipping, but at least she couldn't feel the blisters forming on her palms anymore.

She worked for another hour without interruption and was smugly pleased with herself. Until she heard the first hungry cry of a sgath hunting nearby. This time, the sound wasn't inside her mind—it was in her ears. It was real, and it was close.

They'd found her.

Panic gripped her by the neck and choked the air from her lungs.

How had they found her? She'd been so careful to drive only during the day when they were all asleep and couldn't read her thoughts. And tonight none of them had tried to pry from her where she'd gone when she left the safety of Dabyr. They couldn't know where she was.

Tentatively, Nika sent her mind out, searching for any nearby Synestryn. Their alien thoughts and uncontrolled hunger would be easy to find among the humans nearby. Their thoughts were bleak, festering spots of darkness among the bright, clear human thought patterns.

If there was only one Synestryn and it wasn't too strong, she could probably control its mind long enough to kill it with the shovel. If she was lucky.

Her body fell away as she went seeking into the night, searching for the source of that eerie cry of hunger. She found one Synestryn slinking through the dark less than a quarter mile away. It was small—the size of a dog— and it was weak with hunger. That hunger gave her the edge.

She could take it.

Nika had just begun to whisper into its mind to come her way when she felt another Synestryn nearby. Then another. There were three, then four, then seven. They were closing in. They smelled blood. Her blood.

Before they could trap her within them, Nika pulled back into her own mind and scanned her body for signs of blood. There was a smear on the leg of her jeans, muddy, but definitely blood.

She looked at her hands. Sure enough, the shovel had scraped off several layers of skin until she bled. The Synestryn smelled it and were moving in to feast.

The car was parked outside the metal fence several hundred yards away. As cold and weak as her legs were, she wasn't sure she was going to make it to the car before they made it to her, but she had to try. She couldn't let them get her blood. Thanks to Madoc's recent killing spree, she was just now regaining the pieces of herself that had been taken the night her family was attacked. She'd spent almost nine years living inside a nightmare, unable to tell what was real and what wasn't, and she refused to go back to that hell.

She'd rather die than let them have her mind again.

Nika grabbed the shovel, knowing it was the only weapon she had to hold them at bay, and sprinted for the fence.

Behind her a loud chorus of rasping howls rose up into the night as the Synestryn closed in.

Madoc found the stolen Volkswagen Bug outside a cemetery, but Nika was not inside the car as he'd hoped. Intense pressure rolled through him in a painful wave, growing until he was sure it would tear him apart. He sucked in huge gulps of frigid air, but it did little good.

He needed to be killing or fucking—bleeding away some of the pressure—not chasing after a girl who was too crazy not to go running off alone in the dark.

Clearly, what he wanted had no bearing on reality.

Madoc fought the pain back with a snarl, slammed his truck to a stop, rammed the gearshift into park, and left the engine running.

One way or another, this wasn't going to take long. If she wasn't nearby, then he'd call Joseph and tell him to send someone else to search for her. If she was, he was going to shove her back in the Bug and follow her ass all the way back to Dabyr, where she belonged. No more joyrides. No more scaring the shit out of him. She was grounded.

But first he had to find her.

He leapt the fence and landed with a thud as his heavy boots hit the frozen ground. The wind had picked up, tugging the front of his leather jacket open.

If Nika was out here in this wind, she was going to be

freezing her bony ass off. Not that he cared. Served her right for leaving home, where she was safe and warm.

They want to touch me. I don't like it, Madoc. It hurts when other men touch me.

She'd begged him to take her with him last time he was home, to get her away from the male Theronai who came from the four corners of the world to see if she could channel their power and save their lives. That had been seven months ago, when he'd gone home in a moment of weakness, needing to see her again. Unfortunately, watching her flinch away from those men—seeing pain pinch her features—was more than Madoc could stand. He'd hit the road and hadn't been back since.

Best decision he'd ever made. Being on his own was safest for everyone. Besides, he had plenty of hookers to keep him company. That and a pile of nasties to kill was all he needed.

A high-pitched, feminine cry ripped through the cold night air. Fear shimmered inside the noise, and with it came instant recognition. That was Nika's voice. He'd heard her cry out in fear too many times not to recognize it.

Madoc spun around toward the sound, releasing his sword from its sheath with an almost inaudible hiss of steel on steel. He raced over the ground, letting the rage that was bubbling barely below the surface free.

Whatever or whoever had made her afraid was going to die.

He cleared the top of a rise, saw Nika, and nearly came to a dead stop. Half a dozen sgath surrounded her. Her back was against a thick tree. Moonlight shone off her stark white hair, and she wielded a shovel like some kind of war club, batting at the Synestryn that dared to inch closer. Her blue eyes were wide with fear—a familiar sight—but the snarl of rage twisting her mouth was new and completely startling.

She swung the shovel, hitting one of the sgath in the head. There wasn't enough force behind the blow to do any good, and it bounced off, shaking her entire body. She looked unhurt, but that wasn't going to last for long if he didn't step up and take over.

Madoc closed the distance, lifted his blade and let out a battle cry.

Immediately, six pair of glowing green eyes turned toward him. A slow smile stretched his mouth. Playtime had finally come.

ALSO AVAILABLE

FROM

Shannon K. Butcher

BURNING ALIVE
The Sentinel Wars

Three races descended from ancient guardians of mankind, each possessing unique abilities in their battle to protect humanity against their eternal foes—
the Synestryn. Now, one warrior must fight his own desire if he is to discover the power that lies within his one true love...

Helen Day is haunted by visions of herself surrounded by flames, as a dark-haired man watches her burn. So when she sees the man of her nightmares staring at her from across a diner, she attempts to flee—but instead ends up in the man's arms. There, she awakens a force more powerful and enticing than she could ever imagine. For the man is actually Theronai warrior Drake, whose own pain is driven away by Helen's presence.

Together, they may become more than lovers—they may become a weapon of light that could tip the balance of the war and save Drake's people...

Available wherever books are sold or at
penguin.com

THE DRESDEN FILES

The *New York Times* bestselling series

by Jim Butcher

"Think *Buffy the Vampire Slayer* starring Philip Marlowe." —*Entertainment Weekly*

STORM FRONT

FOOL MOON

GRAVE PERIL

SUMMER KNIGHT

DEATH MASKS

BLOOD RITES

DEAD BEAT

PROVEN GUILTY

WHITE NIGHT

SMALL FAVOR

Available wherever books are sold or at penguin.com